'Taut, strongly plotted ...
provides a rush of blood
to the head and stings your
page-turning fingertips'

INDEPENDENT

'This is
Bonfire of the Vanities
with attitude'

THE TIMES

PENGUIN BOOKS

THE MARKETMAKER

Michael Ridpath spent eight years working as a bond trader at an international bank in the City of London. He is the author of two other novels, *Free to Trade* and *Trading Reality*. He grew up in Yorkshire, and now lives in north London with his wife and three children.

THE MARKETMAKER

Michael Ridpath

PENGUIN BOOKS

PENGUIN BOOKS

Published by the Penguin Group
Penguin Books Ltd, 27 Wrights Lane, London w8 5tz, England
Penguin Putnam Inc., 375 Hudson Street, New York, New York 10014, USA
Penguin Books Australia Ltd, Ringwood, Victoria, Australia
Penguin Books Canada Ltd, 10 Alcorn Avenue, Toronto, Ontario, Canada m4v 3b2
Penguin Books (NZ) Ltd, Private Bag 102902, NSMC, Auckland, New Zealand

Penguin Books Ltd, Registered Offices: Harmondsworth, Middlesex, England

First published by Michael Joseph 1998
Published in Penguin Books 1998
3 5 7 9 10 8 6 4 2

Copyright © Michael Ridpath, 1998
All rights reserved

The moral right of the author has been asserted

Phototypeset in 10.25/12.5pt Linotype Sabon
Phototypeset by Intype London Ltd
Printed in England by Clays Ltd, St Ives plc

for Julia and Laura

Acknowledgements

Thanks are due to the many Brazilians in London and Brazil who took the time to tell me about their country and themselves. In particular I should like to thank Jaime Bernardes of Editorial Nordica, who was an excellent host and guide; Maria Silvia Marques, formerly Treasury Secretary of the City of Rio de Janeiro; Luiz Cezar Fernandes, Chairman of Banco Pactual; Jorge Mamão, People's Administrator of the Rocinha *favela*; Heckel Raposo, security consultant; Pedro Paulo de Campos, Managing Director of Oppenheimer in São Paulo; and Allan and Stephanie Walker.

I should also like to thank Aidan Freyne and his colleagues at Salomon Brothers Emerging Markets Desk in London for their time and patience, and Phil Cavendish for all his help.

1

The man sitting opposite, coolly watching me through a haze of cigarette smoke, controlled the financial future of a continent. More importantly, he controlled mine.

'Thank you for coming in to see us, Nick,' he said. 'Jamie has told me a lot about you. A lot of good things.' His voice was deep, his enunciation careful, his accent public-school English with a tinge of South American.

'He's told me a lot about you too.'

In fact, for the last week Jamie had briefed me thoroughly on Ricardo Ross. His father was Anglo-Argentine, his mother Venezuelan, and he had been educated at a private school in England. He had been with Dekker Ward for ten years, and over that time had transformed it from a sleepy third-tier London stockbroker into the leading force in the Latin American bond markets. Ricardo's élite Emerging Markets Group was now the envy of traders and salesmen in London and New York, and Jamie believed Ricardo would soon become one of the foremost figures in world finance.

And here he was, interviewing me for a job.

He looked good. Monogrammed striped shirt, delicate gold cuff-links, thick dark hair immaculately shaped. In a nod towards informality, his French silk tie hung a quarter of an inch below his undone top button, and his shirt sleeves were rolled up just enough to reveal a paper-thin Swiss watch.

'Would you like a cup of coffee?' he asked.

'Thank you.'

We were in a cramped, workmanlike meeting room in a glassed-in corner of the trading floor. He reached for the phone on the small round table between us and hit a button. 'Alberto? Two cups of coffee, please.'

In less than a minute a tiny old man neatly dressed in a black suit and tie brought us two small cups of coffee.

'What I miss most about living in London is the coffee,' said Ricardo. 'It's improving, but it still has a long way to go. Try this. It's Colombian. I can promise you, you will not find a better cup anywhere in London.' He sat back in his chair, one elegantly trousered leg resting on the other. He allowed the slightest of smiles to play across his narrow, handsome face. I noticed that every few moments the fingers of his left hand twitched, deftly playing with his wedding ring.

The coffee was smooth and rich, an entirely different drink from the Nescafé instant I was used to.

Ricardo sipped his, took a moment to savour it, and carefully replaced the cup in its saucer. 'How many of the guys have you seen so far?' he asked.

'You're the seventh.'

Ricardo smiled. 'A long morning. So, you know all about Dekker Ward by now?'

'I've heard a lot. But it's your firm. You tell me.'

'Well, I only run the Emerging Markets Group here,' he said, nodding towards the dealing room behind him. 'The rest of the firm is back in the City, where they've been for a hundred and fifty years. I can leave them to Lord Kerton, the chairman. We like to keep our distance.'

They certainly did. We were sitting forty-odd floors up above Canary Wharf, three miles to the east of the City of London.

'But your group makes ninety per cent of Dekker Ward's profits?'

'Ninety-five.' Ricardo smiled.

'How do you do it?'

'We're the best at what we do,' he replied. 'By a long way. We dominate the market for Latin American debt. We lead-manage more bond issues for Latin American borrowers than our next three competitors combined. We trade more aggressively than anyone else on the street. We know everyone. If you want to borrow money, you have to talk to us. If you want to invest money, you have to talk to us. We made this market. It's ours, and there are big profits in it.'

'I can imagine there are. But how did you get to that position?'

'We're always a step ahead of the rest of the market. We spotted the opportunity before anyone else did. When Andrew Kerton brought me in, ten years ago, I think he just wanted to build up a profitable little sideline to the rest of the firm. I'm sure he had no idea how big we'd become. Back in the eighties, when the rest of the world had written off Latin America, we were persuading people to invest again. Mostly Latin Americans who had money invested offshore. We teamed up with Chalmet, a private Swiss bank. They had plenty of clients who were eager to put money back into the area.'

He paused to take a drag of his cigarette. His eyes flicked at me to check if I was following him. I was.

'Then the big commercial banks, who had lent billions to the region in the seventies, began to sell their

3

loans at a big discount. We helped them, stood in the middle. In the early nineties, many of these loans were converted into bonds, known as Bradys. We traded them, passed them on from the commercial banks to new investors. And in the last few years people have been willing to invest new money into Latin America. So we've been organizing bond issues for everyone from Brazilian glass-manufacturers to the Republic of Argentina.'

'Don't you have any competition?'

Ricardo chuckled. 'Certainly we do. Everyone is involved in this game. But we were there first, we have all the contacts, we have the best people. If any other firm wants to lead a bond issue for a Latin American borrower, they know they have to invite us as a co-lead. Those are the rules.'

'And if they're broken?'

'Then the issue fails. Nothing happens without our support.'

'A nice position to be in,' I said.

Ricardo nodded. 'But we have to be on our toes. That's why I want to make sure we always have the best people in the market. Without that, we're nothing.'

I glanced out of the window of the little meeting room, into the trading room behind, with its jumble of desks and equipment, and the men and women talking, dialling, staring at screens, milling around. The muffled murmur of all this action seeped in through the glass walls. I wondered what these people were doing, who they were talking to, what they were talking about. Numbers flickered on countless computer screens. What did they all mean?

Beyond this mysterious activity stretched the clear blue sky, the empty space above London's Docklands.

Ricardo followed my gaze. 'They're young. Smart. Hard-working. They all have different backgrounds, from the Argentine aristocracy to a Romford comprehensive. There aren't many of us, but we're an élite. There's no room for passengers. Every one of us makes a contribution.'

I nodded. Ricardo was silent, waiting for my next question. What I really wanted to ask was, 'In that case why the hell am I here?' Instead I settled on something a bit more intelligent. 'What about the emerging markets outside Latin America?'

'Good question. There's not much we can do in Asia. There are plenty of banks out there, and the market for debt is pretty boring. Eastern Europe is more interesting, although even that is becoming more respectable. Did you know Slovenia is rated single A? That's almost as good as Italy.'

I shook my head.

'But Russia. That's the real prize. In many ways it's similar to the South American countries, and the profit potential is just as big. Maybe bigger.'

'So that's why you might want me?'

'That's the idea. I need someone who speaks Russian and understands economics and who's smart. Someone I can train up in the way we do things round here. Someone who's hungry and who has loyalty to the Group. We had some trouble with our Eastern European team recently. I don't know if Jamie told you?'

'They walked out, didn't they? To Bloomfield Weiss?'

'That's right,' said Ricardo. His voice was steady, but now his wedding ring was dancing across his fingers, never resting in place for more than a second at a time. 'I made a mistake there. I took them on as hired guns, and they left me for a master who'd pay them more. I trusted them. I left them alone to build their own business. In future I'm going to rely on my own people. People whose loyalty I can count on.

'I trust those people back there. We're all a team, we all work together, and we all make money together. A lot of money. You see that guy there, the oriental-looking one?'

I followed Ricardo's glance, and could just see a squat man of about forty laughing down a telephone. 'Yes. I met him earlier. His name's Pedro something, isn't it?'

'That's right. Pedro Hattori. He's a Japanese-Brazilian. He's my chief trader. Last year his total compensation was in eight figures.'

I thought for a moment, counting up the zeros in my head. Eight figures! Jesus! That was more than ten million pounds. Or dollars, or something. That was more money than I could possibly conceive of any individual actually earning.

My astonishment must have shown. Ricardo laughed. 'How much do you make?'

'Fourteen thousand, seven hundred and fifty pounds a year,' I said. 'Plus London weighting.'

'Well, if we take you on we'd pay you thirty thousand pounds a year, with no waiting. If you produce income for us, then you get a bonus above that. How much depends entirely on you. How does that sound?'

'Er . . . Fine.'

'Good. Now tell me a bit about you. Why do you want to join us?'

I launched into my spiel. 'I've always found the financial markets fascinating—'

He held up his hand to stop me. 'Hold on, Nick. You've spent the last six years studying Russian. If you'd really found finance so interesting you'd be working in a bank somewhere, wouldn't you? And we wouldn't be having this conversation.'

His blue eyes rested on mine, waiting patiently for the truth. I remembered what Jamie had told me. 'Whatever you do, don't bullshit Ricardo. All he wants to know is who you are and what you want. Then he'll decide for himself.'

Well, Jamie had got me this interview in the first place. I would do it his way.

'When I left Oxford, the last thing in the world I wanted to do was go into banking,' I said. 'The suits, the mobile phones, the silly salaries, the greed.'

Ricardo raised his eyebrows. 'So what's changed?'

'I need the money.'

'Why?'

'Doesn't everyone need money?'

'Some need it more than others.'

I paused. How much should I tell this man? Then I remembered Jamie's advice.

'I need it more than most,' I said. 'I have a large mortgage, which I can't meet, and my temporary job finishes at the end of this term.'

'And when's that?'

'Friday.'

'Ah, I see. Can't you get another one?'

'It will be hard. The number of positions for Russian lecturers is decreasing, and there are more of us about. Most are better qualified than me. There isn't much I can do about that.'

Ricardo nodded. 'So you're hungry. I like that. But how hungry are you?'

'What do you mean?'

'I mean, if you were to have a nice job and a nice

7

salary so you could service your nice mortgage, would you be happy?'

'No,' I said. 'If I'm going to do this I want to earn a lot of money.'

Ricardo raised his eyebrows. 'And what will you do with it when you've got it?'

'Quit. Read.'

The eyebrows shot up again. 'Isn't that what you do at the moment?'

I sighed. 'No. What I do now is churn out research papers, teach, prepare for teaching, and admin. Lots of admin. And I don't earn enough from all that to pay for the flat I'm living in. I'm trapped. This gives me a way out.'

Ricardo was listening closely to all this, focusing his whole being on me, making me feel as though I was the most important person in the world. I was flattered; I couldn't help it.

'I see,' he said. 'But what makes you think you'll be any good? I mean, you've done well academically. A first in politics, philosophy and economics from Oxford. Then a master's in development economics. A glowing reference from the head of your department at the School of Russian Studies. But how do we know you can apply all this to the real world?'

'I'm sure I can do it,' I said. I thought for a moment, trying to put into words something I had trouble admitting to myself, let alone anyone else. But I knew if I was to get this job, Ricardo needed to understand. 'I love Russian literature. I love reading it, I love teaching it. But since my contemporaries left university, I've seen them make a fortune in the City. They're no more intelligent than I am. It's not as if they have any innate business skills that I don't. I suppose I just want to prove to myself that I can do it. I work hard and I learn quickly. I'll figure out how it's done.'

'Are you a workaholic?' he asked.

I smiled. 'I binge.'

Ricardo relaxed and returned my smile. 'Well, Jamie said you're the most intelligent person he's ever met. And I trust Jamie's judgement.' He watched me for a reaction. He didn't get one. My instinct was to protest at this, but I had the sense to keep my mouth shut. Good for Jamie, I thought. He was always prone to exaggeration, and for once I was glad of it.

'There's one other thing I'm curious about,' Ricardo continued. 'What about the morality of joining the City? Somehow I imagine that when you studied development economics they didn't teach you that international capitalism was the saviour of the Third World?'

'That's true,' I said. 'In fact, at that time you could fairly describe my economic ideas as socialist. But then I lived in Russia for two years and saw the Soviet system disintegrate around me. I've seen what a mess state planning can make of an economy.'

'So you believe in the free market?'

I shook my head. 'No, I'm afraid I don't believe in any one economic system. There's a lot of suffering in the world. I've read too many Russian novels to believe that there's very much we can do about that. It's always been there and it always will be there.'

'Well, I think you're wrong,' said Ricardo. He leaned forward, his eyes grabbing mine. 'Take South America for example. The nineteen eighties was a decade of poverty and hopelessness. The whole continent took a giant step backwards. And why? Because it was starved of international capital. OK, that was itself a result of the foolishness of the bankers who had lent too much money in the seventies, and the corrupt politicians who had borrowed it. I admit that. But now the outlook is much better. Thanks to us as much as anyone else, foreign capital is pouring into the region once again. And this time it's being spent on things that will provide a real return. Factories, roads, education. It'll make a big difference to the lives of millions of people. I'm proud to have been a part of that.'

'I hope that's true,' I said, unable to keep the doubt from my voice.

'I can see you're not convinced.' Ricardo leaned back and smiled. 'Still, a touch of realism isn't bad in our business.' He paused and drew from his cigarette, never taking his eyes off mine. They were deep blue, and contrasted sharply with his thick black hair, and tanned skin. They showed power and a piercing intelligence, but somehow they were welcoming, not threatening. 'Come here,' they said, 'you're safe with me.' Although I had only known him for quarter of an hour, I felt drawn towards Ricardo Ross. I could see why Jamie thought so highly of him.

I just sat there, letting him assess me, waiting for him to decide.

It didn't take long. 'Good,' he said. 'Now, just stay here a moment. I want to have a word with the guys.'

He left me in the conference room, while he walked back to his desk. I watched as he called over the people I had seen earlier in the day. There was Pedro Hattori, then I recognized the tall Argentine aristocrat, the American woman who was head of Research, the Cockney trader, a Mexican salesman, a Frenchman whose job I had forgotten, and finally I saw the fair hair and broad shoulders of Jamie, with his back to me.

Well, he had certainly done a good job for me so far.

The next three minutes seemed to take for ever, but finally the group broke up, and Ricardo returned. He held out his hand. 'Welcome,' he said, with a broad smile.

I hesitated for just a moment. Shouldn't I think about this? Did I really want to change my life now, to sell out to the City?

Thirty thousand a year, with maybe much more to follow? Or nothing?

I recalled the letter I had received the week before from Mr K.R. Norris at my building society. If I didn't meet the arrears on my mortgage payments within thirty days, then they would repossess my flat.

It was a simple decision. I shook his hand. 'Thank you.'

'I'll see you at seven on Monday morning,' said Ricardo.

'I'll be there,' I said, and made for the door.

'Oh, just one more thing.'

I turned. Ricardo glanced at my suit. Polish. One hundred per cent polyester. I tried not to wear it unless I absolutely had to.

'How many suits do you have?'

'Er. One.'

Ricardo pulled out a cheque book, and wrote in it with a slim fountain pen. He tore off the cheque, folded it and gave it to me. 'Use this to buy some clothes. Pay me back whenever you can.'

I put the cheque in my pocket, and Ricardo showed me out of the little meeting room to the lifts. I caught Jamie's eye as I left, and he gave me a broad grin.

As the lift sped the forty floors down to earth, I opened the cheque and studied it. It was large with an intricate pattern in green, and it was drawn on Ricardo's personal account at a bank I had never heard of. The words were elegantly penned in black ink. Pay Nicholas Elliot five thousand pounds only.

'Congratulations, Nick!'

Kate looked up at me with her big hazel eyes, and took a gulp of champagne. She and Jamie had come round to my flat to celebrate.

'Don't congratulate me, congratulate your husband. You wouldn't believe what lies he told Ricardo.'

'Just doing what comes naturally.' Jamie smiled his broad white smile. 'No, I knew what I was doing. Ricardo's looking for someone just like you. And I know you won't let him down.' He laughed. 'You'd better not. Or it won't be just you looking for a job.'

'Well, thanks anyway, Jamie.'

'It'll be good to work together. Just like those Hemmings tutorials, do you remember?'

'I hope for Dekker's sake you know more about the markets than you knew about Plato.'

'It's just the same. Shadows on the wall of a cave. You'll soon discover that.'

Jamie and I had been good friends ever since we had found ourselves tutorial partners in our first term at Oxford. We were different. Jamie approached university more energetically than me, throwing himself into a series of different indulgences: playing rugby, drinking, smart parties, scruffy parties, affected *ennui*. The one thing he did consistently was chase women. This he was good at, with his twinkling blue eyes, and his broad infectious grin, which he used to reward anyone who paid him attention. I followed him at an amused distance through most of these activities. I was less successful with women than he, being tall, dark-haired, unremarkable and a little shy. But we had fun together. And after university the friendship had broadened and deepened.

'I can't believe you're going to become a banker!' exclaimed Kate. 'Especially after all the grief you've given Jamie.'

'I know. Shocking, isn't it?'

'So when are you getting the BMW? And you'll need a mobile phone. And some braces.'

'Hold on, Kate, one step at a time,' said Jamie. 'Do you have any pinstripe underwear, Nick?'

'Does Ricardo wear pinstripe underwear?' Kate asked him.

'How the hell would I know?'

'Oh, I don't know, it's just all you people at Dekker are so close . . .'

'I shall wear my M & S Y-fronts with pride,' I said.

We drank our champagne. I was in good spirits, excited. I was feeling more and more sure I had made the right decision.

'So, what did you think of the Marketmaker?' asked Jamie.

'The Marketmaker? Who's that? Ricardo?'

'Yeah. That's his nickname. It comes from when he was about the only person in the world who made markets in Latin American debt. Now everyone trades the stuff, but he gets the credit for developing the market into what it is today.'

'Well, I was impressed. But I suppose I expected that. What surprised me was how approachable he is. I mean, it would be wrong to say he was just an ordinary guy, because he clearly isn't, but he seemed to treat me like a real person.'

'That's not so strange,' said Kate.

'I don't know. I suppose you think that someone that powerful would treat someone like me like dirt. He's used to dealing with presidents of countries, not unemployed academics.'

'That's part of his secret,' said Jamie. 'He makes you feel special whoever you are. Whether you're the finance minister of Mexico or the coffee boy.'

'Well, at least you can keep the flat now,' said Kate, glancing round the small living room. It was pleasant enough, and looked out through some french windows on to a little garden. But it was tiny. My whole flat was tiny. There was scarcely enough room for all my books, let alone human beings as well. I didn't know how Joanna and I had managed to spend so much on such little space. Sure, the location was good, just a few minutes' walk from Primrose Hill in North London, but even so. Six years later the market had still not climbed back to the level it had been when we'd bought the property. Sometimes I doubted whether it ever would.

'Yes, I'm glad,' I said. 'I've grown quite attached to the place. I would have hated to lose it to the building society.' I was looking forward to writing to Mr Norris to inform him of my change of fortune.

'Joanna might not have had much of a financial brain, but she had good taste,' said Jamie.

'She was awful!' said Kate. 'She was never good enough for you, Nick. And the way she left you with this place!'

I smiled at Kate. The subject of Joanna never failed to get her going. And I probably had been taken advantage of. Our relationship had survived my two years in Russia, and when I'd returned we'd decided to buy a house together. It would be a good investment. Joanna, with her two years' experience in a merchant bank, was the financial brains behind the purchase, and she had found the flat. When, three years later, we'd split up and she had gone off to New York with an American investment banker, she had let me have her half and all the furniture in return for giving me the mortgage obligation as well. It had seemed like a good deal at the time, especially since she had put up all of the original equity, but my salary had never proved up to the task.

Or at least not until now.

Kate shivered. 'It's freezing in here. Can't you put the heating on?'

'Er, no,' I said. 'It's OK. The old woman upstairs keeps her flat at eighty degrees. Some of that seeps down.'

'Heat rises,' said Jamie drily.

Kate paused a moment, looking embarrassed. I found there were often moments like this with my more affluent friends. Paying bills, to them, was an administrative inconvenience rather than a financial problem that never quite got solved, only postponed. Then she brightened. 'Oh, come on. You can afford it now. You can make this a tropical paradise all summer, if you want.'

'That's true,' I said. The real problem was that the boiler had broken in February. I could still get hot water, but no heating. It would cost eight hundred pounds to fix it. It had been a cold winter, and was still a chilly spring. But Kate was right, I could get a new boiler now. And sort out the damp patch in the kitchen. And maybe buy some new shoes.

I was fed up with my life of near-poverty. Being a poor undergraduate was fine. Being a poor postgraduate was OK. But I was approaching thirty and I still couldn't afford to go on a decent holiday, buy a car, or even fix the bloody boiler. Hell, one of my students who had scraped a poor second last year, had landed himself a job for eighteen thousand a year as a consultant, five thousand more than I earned. And he was only twenty-two!

Jamie was obviously following my thoughts. 'Life's going to change, you know,' he said.

'That was the general idea.'

'It's hard work at Dekker. I wouldn't say that Ricardo wants you twenty-four hours a day. He just settles for that part of the day when you're awake.'

'Huh!' Kate snorted.

I glanced at her, just long enough to acknowledge what she had said. At least I was single. There would be no one to miss me. 'I can work hard, you know that.'

'Mmm. But we'll see what you're like at seven in the morning.'

I laughed. 'I've often wondered what the world looks like that early. Now I suppose I'll find out.'

'And you'll have to give up rugby,' said Jamie.

'Do you think so? Surely I'll be able to manage something. I might miss a few training sessions, but the team needs me.' I was the star number eight of the School of Russian Studies rugby team. They'd be in big trouble without me.

'No way,' said Jamie. 'I used to play a bit when I was at Gurney Kroheim, but when I went to Dekker I had to give it all up. It's the travelling that kills it. You have to leave at weekends with next to no notice. No team will put up with that for long.'

I caught Kate's eye. It wasn't just rugby teams that suffered. 'That's a pity,' I said. 'I'll miss it.'

'I do,' said Jamie. 'I still manage to keep fit, but it's

not the same. I suppose I just have to get rid of my aggression in other ways.'

Jamie had been a very good player, better than me. He had played behind me in the Magdalen College team as scrum half. He was short and stocky with broad shoulders, and strong legs, and he would shrug off tackles from men twice his size. He was a fearless tackler, too. I'll never forget the time I saw him up-end the All Blacks' number eight as he came charging round the side of the scrum. He had played some games for the university team, and if he hadn't been so distracted by the other temptations of university life, he could have earned his blue. Now, as he said, all that aggression was harnessed in the service of Dekker Ward.

He drained his glass, and picked up the champagne bottle. 'Empty. Shall I nip out and get another? There's an off-licence just round the corner, isn't there? The table's booked for eight thirty, so we've got another half-hour.'

'I'll get it,' I said.

'No. It's on me. I'll be back in a minute.' With that he put on his coat and let himself out.

Kate and I sat in silence for a moment. She smiled at me. She's definitely getting more attractive as she gets older, I thought. She had always been pretty, rather than beautiful, with short brown hair, a bright smile, and those big eyes. But as she had grown from a girl into a woman and a mother, she had changed. There was a softness and roundness to her and, since her son had been born, an inner serenity that I could not help but find appealing.

I had liked Kate from when I had first met her, jammed half-way up a staircase at a crowded party in the Cowley Road. We had bumped into each other occasionally after that, and I had introduced her to Jamie in our last term at Oxford. He had moved swiftly and decisively, and unusually for him the relationship had stuck. Three years later they had married, and a year after that Kate had had a son, my godchild. She had given up her job in a big City firm of solicitors to look after him.

'How's Oliver?' I asked.

'Oh, he's great. He keeps on asking when you're going to come and play Captain Avenger again with him.'

I smiled. 'I was rather hoping the Captain would be out of fashion by now.'

'Not yet, I'm afraid.'

Kate took another sip of her champagne.

'Are you sure you're doing the right thing, Nick?' she asked quietly.

There was genuine concern in her voice. It alarmed me. Kate had common sense, lots of it. And she knew me well.

'Yes,' I said, with more confidence than I felt. 'After all, Jamie's having a great time at Dekker, isn't he?'

'Yes,' she said flatly. 'He is.'

2

The air bit fresh and cold into my face as I coasted down the streets of Islington. It was so much better pedalling through London at six thirty in the morning than at midday, although I was surprised at the number of cars on the streets even this early.

The sun hung low to the east, a pale fuzzy orb behind the remnants of the early-morning mist. Young trees thrust bravely up out of the cracked pavements, brandishing their budding branches at the tall lines of buildings frowning down upon them. Daffodils added splashes of colour to the scraps of green which occasionally fought their way into the urban landscape. Sometimes, during a rare lull in traffic noise, I could even hear a bird shrilly proclaiming his ownership of a scruffy bush or tree.

I tried not to go too fast, although it was difficult when faced with the unaccustomed sight of a hundred yards of clear road. My bike, although it looked as if it had fallen one too many times off the back of a lorry, could reach a healthy speed. I had bought it at a police auction a couple of years before, and had selected it for its combination of appearance and performance: it would be the last bicycle in any rack to be stolen. But this morning I wanted to take it easy, to avoid getting up too much of a sweat.

I was wearing one of the three new suits I had bought with Ricardo's money. I had found it impossible to conceive of spending more than three hundred pounds on each one, and even that had been difficult. Two pairs of smart black shoes had cost sixty quid each, but I still had most of the five thousand pounds left, and I looked smarter than I had ever looked before in my life. I had even had my hair cut.

I swung through the City, and on to Commercial Road. To the right and above me, I caught glimpses of the tall white tower of Canary Wharf. It rose up above the textile outlets and curry-houses of Limehouse, a solid white block reaching into the mist. A single light seemed to be suspended several feet above it, blinking through the haze from the invisible roof. I would be up there soon, looking down on the rest of London. I wondered if I would be able to see the School of Russian Studies.

I winced as I remembered my final meeting with Russell Church, the head of my department. He had been furious when I'd told him my plans to stop teaching. But until I had finished my Ph.D., still at least six months away, he couldn't promise me a permanent job, and even then it would be difficult. I worried that I'd let him down, but I'd had no choice. Things had to change.

I felt better now, cycling down Westferry Road, the debris of the East End behind me. On either side was water, the Thames on one side in full flood, and the West India Dock on the other. In front was the gleaming Canary Wharf complex, with its giant tower protected by a thick wall of smaller, but still substantial, office buildings. Suddenly everything was in pristine condition, from the close-cut lawns and flower-beds of

Westferry Circus to the newly painted blue cranes, which stood like heavy artillery pieces guarding the approaches to the wharf. To the left a driverless train whispered along the raised rail of the Docklands Light Railway into a station elevated fifty feet above the water.

I rode past the security check, and down into the underground car park, a corner of which was leased by Dekker Ward. I asked the attendant where I could put my bike, and he pointed to a cluster of motorcycles: a Harley-Davidson and three BMWs. The car park was weird. It was shared with a big investment bank, and it was already half full of investment bankers' cars. They were nearly all German – Mercedes, Porsche and BMW. When pushed together like this, they displayed a stunning lack of imagination, alleviated only by a black, low-slung Corvette, and a bright red Ferrari Testarossa. I left my bike unlocked; somehow I thought it would be safe from theft, a shard of broken glass among these opulent jewels.

I climbed the stairs into the square at the foot of the tower. It, too, was pristine: lines of small trees fresh out of the nursery, a fountain playing tidily in the centre, neat low walls, benches of expensive wood. The tower stretched eight hundred feet up into the air in front of me, its roof still obscured by the mist and by steam billowing out of pipes near the top. Even at this hour there were quite a few people about. They trickled out of the railway-station entrance, out of underground car parks, and out of a procession of taxis, and headed to the squat bulky buildings at the corners of the square or, like me, into the central complex of Canary Wharf itself.

Nervously, I made my way through the ultra-modern atrium with its 1980s shops – Blazer, the City Organiser,

Birleys, a sushi bar – and into the brown marble lobby of One Canada Square. I entered a lift alone and shot upwards forty storeys until I reached Dekker's floor.

I waited in the reception area for Jamie, perching on the edge of a deep black leather sofa, under the occasional stare of a well-groomed blonde receptionist. He was out in a minute, striding over, hand outstretched, grinning broadly. White rabbits cavorted on his tie. 'You made it. I didn't think you would. Did you pedal all the way?'

'I certainly did.'

He looked me up and down. 'Nice suit. I hope you've got rid of the old one. Mind you, you'd have to be careful how you dispose of it. Toxic waste and so on.'

'I'm keeping it. Sentimental value. Besides, it's probably the only genuine emerging-market suit here.'

Jamie laughed. His clothes weren't showy, but I knew he spent large amounts on them in Jermyn Street and its immediate neighbourhood. I couldn't tell this by looking at them, but Jamie had assured me that the kind of people he dealt with could. According to him, it was a necessary expenditure.

'Well, if you do insist on cycling in, I'll show you the health club later on. You'll be able to take a shower there.'

'No, I'll be OK.'

'Nick. Trust me. You're a hotshot banker now. Take a shower. Now, come through. Let me show you your desk.'

He led me through some double doors. After the dimly lit quiet of the reception area, the trading room hit me in a burst of sound, light and movement.

'I'm afraid your desk is on the outside,' said Jamie,

as my eyes tried to make sense of the activity in front of me.

'The outside?'

'Yes. Sorry, I'll explain. You see those desks there?' He pointed to a group of about twenty dealing desks in the middle of the room arranged in a square, each facing outwards. I saw Ricardo standing by one of them, talking on the phone, and most of the others were manned. 'That's the inside. It's where all the salesmen and traders sit. It's a good set-up. We can all communicate with each other across the space in the centre. These desks here,' he pointed to three lines of desks facing each edge of the square, 'these are the outside. People sit here who don't need to be in the thick of things, Capital Markets people, Research, Admin, you.'

I looked suitably dismayed.

'Don't worry. You can sit with me this week. You'll find out what's going on soon enough.'

Just then there was the sound of hands clapping twice. It was Ricardo. 'OK, *compañeros*, gather round. It's seven fifteen.'

Ricardo leaned against the back of his chair, and faced into the square of desks. Everyone moved into the central space. I glanced at them. They were all looking at him expectantly, outwardly relaxed, but I could feel the tension as they prepared for the week's action. As Ricardo had promised, they came in all shapes and sizes, although the majority had a well-groomed Latin look to them. Many of them were smoking. I recognized most of the people who had interviewed me, including Pedro who was sitting, perhaps symbolically, immediately to the right of Ricardo. Like a number of other men in the room, he was wearing a cardigan. Apart from me, they were all jacketless. I tried to take my own off with as little movement as possible.

'Morning, everyone,' Ricardo began. He stood up straight in his crisply ironed blue-striped shirt. I could just make out the initials RMR embroidered in red on his chest. 'I trust you all had a good weekend. I'd like to start by welcoming a new member to our team. Nick Elliot.'

Everyone turned towards me. Fortunately, I had just wriggled out of my jacket. I smiled nervously. 'Hallo,' I said.

There were smiles back, and murmurs of 'Good to have you on board.' It was friendly. I appreciated it.

'Nick speaks Russian and understands economics, and I know he's going to be a valuable member of our group,' Ricardo continued. 'He's never worked for a financial firm before, so he hasn't had a chance to pick up any bad habits. I want you all to show him how Dekker do things. Now, what's happening out there? Pedro?'

Pedro Hattori spoke some gobbledygook about Bradys, euros, squeezes, Argy discos and Flirbs. I tried to follow, but floundered. Then an American called Harvey talked about the US Federal Reserve policy on interest rates. This was more familiar territory, but then I lost it again when he started on WIs and five years on special. Charlotte Baxter, head of Research, was next. She was a tall American woman with long mousy-brown hair in her late thirties. I had been impressed by her when I had first met her at my interview. She talked about the likelihood of discussions between the Venezuelan government and the International Monetary Fund breaking down again, and the implications this would have. Though I knew little about the subject, I could see it was good stuff. Jamie took careful notes.

Then Ricardo went round each individual in the group. They were exchanging gossip, information, impressions, hunches. Everyone was clear and concise. And well informed. People didn't seem to me to be making political points or grabbing glory, presumably because Ricardo discouraged it. But they all watched closely for his reaction, and his occasional words of encouragement were lapped up.

He came to the last of the group. 'Isabel? How's the *favela* deal coming on?'

Isabel was a slight, dark-haired woman of about thirty. She was half sitting on a desk, sipping a cup of coffee. 'Jesus, I don't know. My guy in the housing authority really wants to do it. And I think his boss wants to do it too. But his boss's boss?' Her voice was low and husky, and she spoke with a slow, relaxed drawl. Her English was good, with a slightly nasal accent, which I would recognize later as Brazilian.

'Can you fix it?'

'I'm a *carioca*. Rio's my home town. Of course I can fix it.' The corners of her mouth twitched. 'I just don't know if I can fix it this century, that's all.'

Ricardo smiled. 'I'm sure you can, Isabel. But I'm happy to go down there with you if you need me. I could talk to Oswaldo Bocci. Get him to run a few favourable stories. Maybe a piece about how this is the best chance Rio has to begin to do something about the *favelas*. He owes us after that deal we did for him last year.'

'The local press are positive already,' said Isabel, flicking a strand of dark hair out of her eyes. 'And I'd like to leave Oswaldo out of it unless we're really desperate. I'm flying down there on Wednesday night.

I hope I can sort things out then. If that doesn't work, maybe you should call him.'

'Well, good luck,' said Ricardo. 'Presumably, we can apply this model to other cities?'

'Oh, yes. We should be able to use it everywhere. Certainly in Brazil. As soon as we've closed the Rio deal, I'm going to talk to São Paulo and Salvador. But this structure should work anywhere in Latin America where there are people living in shanty-towns, which is everywhere. We need World Development Fund support for each deal, but they seem to think it's a good use of their funds.'

'Would it work in Romford?' It was Miguel, the tall Argentine aristocrat.

'Oi, you leave Romford alone!' protested a burly young man with a loud tie and very short hair. His name was Dave, I remembered.

'Perhaps you're right. It's a lost cause.'

'Thank you for that suggestion, Miguel,' said Ricardo. 'In fact you'd be a good choice to open our Essex rep office. But, seriously, this is a flagship deal. Once we've closed it, I want the rest of you on the road looking for more. Now, Carlos?'

Carlos's rumblings about a possible deal for the United Mexican States passed me by. My eyes were still on Isabel. She wasn't exactly good-looking. Her nose was a bit too long, her mouth a bit too wide. Her clothes were nothing special, blue shortish skirt, cream blouse, black shoes, and her hair hung, untamed, around her face. But there was something about her that was very feminine, sexy. Maybe it was her voice, or the way she held herself. Or it could have been her eyes, large, deep brown, almost liquid, half hidden under long lashes. Just then they darted towards me, and caught my stare.

The corners of her mouth twitched again, and I hastily switched my gaze to Carlos.

'Did you understand all that?' asked Jamie, when it was over.

'Some of it. I have a lot of questions. There's a lot to learn.'

'Like how to stare at Isabel and stop your mouth from dropping open at the same time,' said Jamie.

'Was it that obvious?'

'Don't worry, we've all done it. You get used to her after a while.'

'There's something about her. I don't know what it is.'

'She's as sexy as hell, that's what it is. But I wouldn't make it too obvious. She bites.'

'Really? She looks friendly enough to me.'

'Well, don't touch. Don't even look. Trust me.'

I shrugged, and sat at Jamie's desk. I had never seen a fully equipped dealing desk before, and Dekker's were state-of-the-art. Jamie explained it all to me. There were five screens, which provided news, prices and analysis in a range of different colours. Jamie seemed to have an unpleasant predilection for pink. To add to the clutter was a phone board with thirty lines, a fan, a Spanish–English dictionary, two volumes of the *Bankers' Almanac*, and a small silver rugby ball commemorating an Argentine sevens tournament. The whole was framed in a collage of yellow Post-it stickers and topped with a haphazard scattering of paper.

'OK, let me tell you the basics,' said Jamie, after he had shown me how to get the rugby commentary up on the Bloomberg information service. 'All the guys on this half of the square,' he gestured with his arm, 'are sales people. Our job is to talk to customers, give them information, find out what they want to do, and then buy and sell bonds from them. These people,' he pointed to the other half of the square of dealing desks, 'are the traders. They make markets in hundreds of different bonds. So when one of our customers wants to buy or sell something, we ask one of the traders for a price. He gives us a bid and offer. We reflect that to the customer, who will either sell at the bid price or buy at the offer price. In theory, the bid/offer spread should be profit for us.'

I nodded. So far, so clear.

'The other way we make money is through new issues. See those people there?' He pointed to some of the desks outside the square. I noticed that Isabel was at one of them reading through a sheaf of documents. Jamie followed my eyes and coughed. 'Of course you do. They're known as Capital Markets. Their job is to talk to potential borrowers and put together a bond issue that raises money for them at the lowest rate. Which, by the way, is usually pretty high. Investors aren't going to take on the risk that one of these countries defaults again without demanding a decent return.'

Jamie spent the next couple of hours explaining how Dekker functioned. I listened closely, turning over each new piece of information in my mind, seeing how it fitted in with what I had heard before, using it to try to anticipate what he had yet to tell me.

I listened in to his calls through a second phone plugged into his desk, as he spoke to his customers. These turned out to be a wide range of different types of institution: a small French bank, a British merchant bank, a Dutch insurance company, an American hedge fund.

He talked about Venezuela and the IMF negotiations.

He exchanged rumours on a future Mexican deal. He talked about football and what was on television the night before. He bought and sold millions of dollars of bonds, always selling at a price slightly higher than he was buying. Many of these trades were recorded as 'DT' and then a number. Jamie explained that these were numbered accounts at the firm's Dekker Trust affiliate in the Cayman Islands.

Lunch was an exotic goat's cheese and salad sandwich, and a Coke brought round by a kid in overalls carrying a big tray. There was no need to leave the desk. No time, either.

Conversations moved with the time zones, picking up Brazil late morning, the rest of the continent and New York in the afternoon, California in the evening. In fact, the pace quickened as the day wore on: many of the other players in the market operated out of New York or Miami. Our day lengthened to incorporate theirs. Much of all this was in Spanish, and I couldn't understand it. I would have to learn Spanish.

At about six o'clock I went to see Charlotte and her team in Research, and returned to my desk with an armful of reports. The political and economic analysis was excellent. I was particularly impressed with the quick and dirty notes marked 'For Internal Distribution Only'. These made heavy use of informal sources: local bankers, government officials, traders in New York. I read deeper and deeper, fascinated.

Isabel's desk was next to mine. She seemed to be constantly busy, reading through the piles of papers next to her, tapping out notes on her computer, or going over documents on the phone in what I assumed was Portuguese. I tried not to stare, but I couldn't help my eyes drifting over towards her every now and then. Her face was partly obscured by strands of dark hair as she worked. Occasionally she would pause, bite her lower lip and stare ahead into space. She was delectable. Even when I wasn't looking at her, I could just catch the scent of her perfume in the air, or hear her voice on the phone. Concentrate!

Once, as my eyes flicked up towards her, I saw her looking back at me.

'You're enthusiastic,' she said, smiling.

'I've got a lot to learn.'

'It gets easier once you start actually doing it. Where did you come from? Before here?'

'Until last week, I taught Russian.'

She raised her eyebrows. 'Really. And what brings you to Dekker?'

'I needed the job. And Jamie was good enough to introduce me. Why they took me on, I'm not quite sure.'

'Are you a good friend of Jamie's?'

'Yes. Very good friends. I've known him for ten years.'

There the conversation ended. She turned back to her phone and picked it up. I wasn't sure whether I had said something wrong.

And then my own phone rang.

It was the two consecutive rings of an external call. That was funny. I didn't think I had given anyone my number yet.

I picked it up. 'Dekker,' I said, in my best imitation of the clipped tones I had heard around me all day.

'Can I speak with Martin Beldecos?' said a female American voice over an international line.

I hadn't heard of him. I looked around. Nearly everyone had gone home, with the exception of Ricardo, Pedro and Isabel. She was deeply involved in a telephone conversation of her own, and Ricardo and Pedro were too far away to ask.

'Er, he's not here at the moment,' I said. 'Can I give him a message tomorrow?'

'Yes, it's Donald Winters' assistant here, from United Bank of Canada in Nassau. I have a fax I need to send Mr Beldecos. Can you give me his fax number?'

'Hold on a sec,' I said. There was a fax machine a few steps away. I nipped over to it, checked the number, and gave it to the woman. She thanked me and hung up.

I dug out the internal telephone list, and looked up BELDECOS, MARTIN 6417. That was my extension! No wonder the phone call has come through to me. He must have been the previous occupant of my desk.

The fax machine behind me spluttered into life.

I walked over to the machine, and took the single sheet back to my desk. It was addressed to Martin Beldecos at Dekker Ward on United Bank of Canada Nassau Branch fax paper. The message was short and simple.

Following your inquiry, we have been unable to identify the beneficial owner of International Trading and Transport (Panama). We transferred funds from their account with us to Dekker Trust's account at Chalmet et Cie's Cayman Islands branch under the instructions of Mr Tony Hempel, a Miami-based lawyer who is the Company Secretary of International Trading and Transport.

The fax was signed by Donald Winters, Vice President.

'Isabel?'

She had just put down the phone. 'Yes?'

'I've just got this fax for Martin Beldecos. Where does he sit?'

Isabel didn't answer me straight away. She tensed, and drew in her breath.

'He used to sit right where you are,' she replied eventually, in a monotone.

'He left, did he?' I could tell something was wrong with Martin Beldecos's departure. 'Was he fired?'

She shook her head. 'No. No, he wasn't. He was killed.'

I exhaled. 'How?'

'He was murdered. In Caracas. Thieves broke into his hotel room while he was asleep. He must have woken and surprised them. They knifed him.'

'Jesus! When was this?'

'About three weeks ago.'

'Oh.' I shivered. It was an eerie feeling to know that the last occupant of this desk, this chair, was now dead.

I wanted to ask her more, but she seemed reluctant to talk, and I didn't want to risk saying the wrong thing.

'OK, um, so what shall I do with this?'

'I'll take it,' she said.

I handed her the sheet of paper. She glanced at it, paused, frowning for a few seconds, scribbled something on it, and put it in an out-tray on a nearby desk. Then she shuffled the papers in front of her, stuffed some of them into a briefcase, and put on her jacket.

'Good night,' she said.

'Good night. See you tomorrow.'

She left me alone, sitting in a dead man's chair behind a dead man's desk.

3

I was in the office by seven the next morning. I was glad of the bike ride. If I was going to be stuck inside all day, I would need the fresh air. Ricardo was there when I arrived. If he hadn't been wearing a different shirt I would have sworn he had spent the night at his desk.

I smiled at Isabel as she came in. She gave me a quick smile and a 'Hi'.

I dumped my jacket at my desk, grabbed a cup of coffee, and walked over to Jamie's. He was chatting to Dave, the big trader from Romford.

'Morning,' said Dave. 'So we didn't wipe you out on your first day?'

'I'm still here.'

'What time did you leave last night?' asked Jamie.

'About eleven.'

'A good first day's work. Let me guess, Ricardo was still here when you left?'

I nodded. There was a pause as we took in our early-morning dose of caffeine.

'I heard about Martin Beldecos,' I said. 'Isabel told me last night.'

'Bad news, that,' said Dave. 'Very bad news.'

'Isabel said he was murdered.'

'That's right,' said Jamie. 'I heard the police in Caracas have caught the men who did it.'

'That's not all I heard,' said Dave, lowering his voice. Jamie and I looked at him expectantly.

'Yeah, there's a rumour that it wasn't just a hotel burglary gone wrong. Miguel was down there last week. The word is it was a contract killing. One of the drug gangs.'

'A contract killing?' said Jamie in astonishment. 'On Martin Beldecos? Martin Beldecos, the compliance officer with the glasses and the receding hairline? What, was he trying to grab the paper-clip franchise for South America?'

'That's what Mig said!' Dave protested defiantly. 'You know he knows people down there – '

We were interrupted by the sharp clapping of hands. 'It's seven fifteen, *compañeros*!' called Ricardo. The room was silent as we all clustered round him.

The morning meeting made a bit more sense than it had the day before. The market was spooked on the Venezuelan news: prices were off five points. But people down there in the know held the view that the break-down of talks with the IMF was just posturing by their aged president. This information we decided to keep to ourselves until we had taken advantage of the lower prices to quietly pick up a few Venezuelan bonds for our own books. Then we would tell the world.

The meeting ended and Jamie and I walked back to his desk.

Dave's words were still on my mind. 'Do you think this guy Beldecos was murdered by a contract killer?' I asked him.

Jamie snorted. 'Of course not. Dave has a vivid imagination. And despite the slicked-back hair and the

34

Italian suits, Miguel is just an old gossip. The poor guy was killed by hotel burglars.' He shuddered. 'It could happen to any one of us, that's the really scary thing. Now, let's get on with it.'

I wanted to ask Jamie more about Martin Beldecos but, like Isabel, he seemed reluctant to talk. And I didn't want to seem too morbid; after all, I hadn't even known the guy. So I let it drop.

The trading day began.

I listened. There was a lot of activity that morning. Activity translated into noise. Not necessarily volume of noise, more diversity. There was the murmur of a dozen different conversations, some in English, some in Spanish, the sharp cries of people telling their colleagues to pick up the phone, the regular crackle of prices from the brokers' loudspeakers on the trading desk and, of course, the staccato conversation of customers on the phone. But it wasn't just the humans who made a noise, the machines did. A range of whirs, hums and occasional grinding clanks emanated from the different computers and screens. And underneath it all was the low, almost imperceptible murmur of the great building itself. It took concentration and practice to separate all these sounds, and to tune in and out of the frequencies as you skipped from conversation to conversation.

Except they weren't conversations. They were information transactions. As brief as they could be while still being unambiguous.

'Hey, Pedro! Where'd you do Argy pars to discos?'

'Fifty-six and a half on the pars and sixty-seven and three-eighths on the discos.'

'He says he can get a quarter away on the discos.'

'Shit. OK, I'll give him them at a quarter.'

'You'd do ten by eleven?'

'Yep.'

'You're done!'

And so the bonds flew around the little square of desks, and from there to different corners of the globe: Tokyo, Zurich, Bahrain, Edinburgh, New York, Bermuda, Buenos Aires. We even did a trade with the investment bank ten floors below us. Hundreds of millions of dollars flowed in and out of Dekker Ward's accounts throughout that day. But when it was all totted up it would show that a few hundred thousand more flowed in than flowed out.

I was beginning to understand what was going on. The skill in investing in these markets lay in assessing and comparing risk. Was Brazil riskier than Mexico? If so, how much riskier? If Mexico yielded 10.25 per cent, should Brazil yield 11.25 per cent? Or 11.50 per cent? Or more? How would this relationship change in the future?

But it was more complicated than just a country by country comparison. Each borrower had a whole range of bond issues outstanding: Brady bonds that had been born out of old rescheduled bank debt; eurobonds; bonds issued by the state governments, by state banks, by private banks. All these traded in a certain relationship depending on a mixture of rational analysis and the whims of different investors throughout the world, all with their own views and prejudices.

It would take a while to sort all this out, but I was sure I would get there, and I was excited by the prospect. And Dekker was the right place to be to do it. It was a well-oiled information-gathering machine. Ricardo was right: Dekker knew everybody. When something happened, Dekker always either knew or guessed it first.

No wonder it made so much money. I couldn't wait until I was really part of it, player rather than a spectator.

My attention was caught by a large man in a light grey double-breasted suit who was standing by Ricardo's desk, going through some figures with him. I hadn't seen him before.

'Who's that?' I asked Jamie.

'Can't you guess?'

I looked at him more closely. He could be the same age as Ricardo, perhaps a bit younger. But he was bulkier, with a heavier face.

'It's not his brother, is it?'

'Yep. Eduardo Ross.'

'Does he work at Dekker?'

'He certainly does.'

'What does he do?'

'Nobody knows exactly. Except Ricardo. Odd jobs, special projects, stuff Ricardo wouldn't trust with anyone else. He's responsible for Dekker Trust in the Caymans, for example.'

'What is this Dekker Trust?' I asked.

'It's our sister company in the Cayman Islands. It's where we put stuff that we don't want the authorities here to see.'

'That sounds a bit dodgy.'

Jamie laughed. 'It's not, really. We have many clients who are quite shy. They're not criminals or anything, Ricardo's very careful not to deal with anyone who smells of organized crime or corruption. But they might be involved in legitimate offshore trading, tax avoidance, foreign-currency activities and so on. They expect us to maintain absolute confidence in their activities, and Dekker Trust allows us to do that.'

'I see,' I said doubtfully. 'And is this operation owned by Dekker Ward?'

'No,' said Jamie. 'Or at least not a hundred per cent. Chalmet, the Swiss bank, owns a big chunk, I think Dekker Ward does own some, and the rest is owned by the employee trusts.'

'Employee trusts?'

'Didn't Ricardo tell you about them?'

I shook my head. Jamie paused for a second and then lowered his voice. 'That's how you get to make real money here. Ricardo lets some of the employees invest part of their bonus in these trusts. They're run out of the Cayman Islands, or at least that's where they're booked. The management decisions are actually taken by Ricardo. Their returns are spectacular. I mean, a hundred per cent a year isn't uncommon.'

'Whew! How does he do that?'

'With what he knows? It's easy. He uses every trick in the book. Leverage, options, warrants, you name it.'

'Is it legal?'

'Of course it is. But it's better if it's done offshore. Discreetly. We wouldn't like the regulators looking for holes, even though there aren't any.'

'And how big are these funds?'

'That, my friend, is the biggest secret of them all.' Jamie lowered his voice to a whisper. 'But I reckon they have to be more than five hundred million dollars.'

It took a moment to sink in. 'And that's all owned by people in this room.'

Jamie smiled. 'Most of it. Obviously our guys in Miami and the Cayman Islands have some of it. But I would guess at least half of it is Ricardo's.'

I suddenly realized that I was surrounded by one of the richest groups of men and women in the world.

God. If I stuck around, I would get some of that too.

'Eduardo administers this?' I asked.

'Ricardo needs someone he trusts to do that kind of thing. And he trusts Eduardo more than any of us. Oh, yes, and he's also responsible for checking out new employees.'

'What do you mean checking out new employees?'

'Oh, you know, looking for drugs, bad debts, gambling habits, homosexuality, socialist leanings, mental instability, criminal record.'

'You're joking!'

'No. It's true.'

I was shocked. 'So he checked me out?'

'Must have. Or, at least, he will have got a firm of investigators to do it.'

'But why didn't you tell me?'

Jamie winced, and then gave me one of his broadest, most winning smiles. 'Because I knew if I told you you wouldn't apply for the job. Besides, I've told you now.'

'You jerk,' I said. Jamie laughed, but I didn't think it was funny. I felt as though my privacy had been invaded, as though someone had stolen part of my life, or at least borrowed it for a bit. Someone I didn't know.

'Oh, come on, Nick,' Jamie said, realizing he had misjudged my reaction. 'We've all been through it. And you're probably the cleanest guy in the room.'

'Apart from the mortgage,' I muttered.

'Which you were sensible enough to tell Ricardo about at your interview. What are you worried about? He's not going to tell anyone else.'

I still wasn't happy.

'Look out, here he comes,' Jamie hissed.

Eduardo strolled over to Jamie's desk. The other

salesmen acknowledged him with smiles and greetings. Even I could tell their friendliness was false.

He held out his hand to me, a smile on his full lips. 'Nick Elliot? I'm Eduardo Ross. Good to have you on the team.' His voice was as deep as Ricardo's, but his accent was a mixture of North and South American, with the emphasis on the South.

I stood up and shook his hand awkwardly. 'Thank you.'

'Jamie, do you mind if I borrow him for a moment?'

'Not at all,' Jamie replied, flashing his smile at Eduardo. Eduardo flashed one just as wide back.

'Good. Come to my office.'

With a panicky glance towards Jamie, I followed Eduardo into an office in one corner of the trading room. The windows were smoky from the outside, which was why I hadn't noticed him before. On the inside, there was a clear view of the trading floor. I could easily see Jamie picking up the phone to coax his customers to buy a few more bonds.

It was a large office, and opulent. There were a couple of cream leather sofas, the walls were panelled in a polished blonde wood, and on one of them hung a photograph of the red Ferrari I had spotted in the underground garage, adorned by its tanned and muscled owner and two raven-haired beauties. Eduardo seated himself behind a huge desk that seemed untroubled by the usual clutter of day-to-day work. Over his shoulder I caught a breathtaking view to the west of the City of London. I realized that I hadn't checked yet to see whether I could see the School of Russian Studies. Too absorbed in what was going on, I supposed.

Eduardo followed my eyes, and grinned. 'Not a bad

view, eh? You know, you can see Windsor Castle on a good day.'

'Spectacular,' I agreed.

'Take a seat.' Eduardo opened a humidor in front of him, and offered me a cigar. I shook my head, and he picked out a large one, and carefully placed it in his thick, sensual lips. He rolled the cigar around for several seconds before lighting it. The effect verged on the obscene. He watched me watching him with amusement.

There was a knock at the door, and a very young, very pretty girl with fine blonde hair came in. She looked as though she belonged in a school classroom rather than Eduardo's office. 'The position report, Mr Ross,' she said, and dashed over to his desk to put it on one corner.

'Ah, thank you, Penny,' he replied, taking the report himself. And as she was leaving, 'You English produce such exquisite virgins, don't you think, Nick? It's a shame they become spoiled as they get older.'

Involuntarily I glanced at the girl, who blushed bright red and made for the door at as fast a walk as she could manage.

Eduardo chuckled. 'Excuse me. I just think she looks so delicious when she blushes.' He tossed the report in the bin.

I didn't answer. I couldn't think of anything to say.

'Ricardo has told me a lot about you, Nick,' he went on, in a friendly tone. 'He's excited to have you here. You're already making a good impression. We like to train up our own people, and he thinks you are exactly the right raw material.'

'Thank you.' Praise is always welcome when you've just started a new job.

'We're very sensitive to our new employees' needs,' he continued. 'We like to make them feel at home early on. And we don't like them distracted. Now, I understand from Ricardo that you have quite a large mortgage obligation. Well, we would like to ease that burden for you.'

My pulse quickened. This was one financial issue I had long been interested in.

'We thought we could perhaps take over the mortgage from your building society, and charge a lower rate of interest, say three per cent? Until, of course, you can afford to pay it down. Which shouldn't be more than a couple of years if you do as well here as we expect you will.' He smiled at me, and took a puff of the cigar. The heavy tobacco rolled towards me. Like Ricardo, he too had charisma, but it was of a different sort. His large face, heavily creased brow, and thick black hair brushed neatly back, gave him a kind of powerful handsomeness, that held me in awe. This was not the sort of man you met on an average day at the School of Russian Studies.

For an instant, I felt a surge of relief. Those mortgage payments had been the bane of my life for so long. And now the problem would go away, just like that.

But it was only an instant. Although I was coming to terms with Dekker and its ways, some instinct told me to be careful. I had come willingly to work for Ricardo. Somehow I felt Eduardo was trying to buy me.

Without thinking it through, I said, 'No, thank you. It's kind of you to offer, but I should be able to support my mortgage quite easily now on my own.'

Eduardo's gaze darkened for a moment. He puffed at his cigar. Finally he smiled again.

'There are no strings attached,' he said. 'Plenty of

City firms give their employees subsidized mortgages. Take it. There's no harm.'

He had a point. But I just didn't like the feel of it. And I had my pride and I was stubborn. 'I'm sure you're right. But I'll manage. And, as you say, I hope I'll be able to pay it down over the next few years.'

Eduardo shrugged. 'Suit yourself. But if there's anything else we can do to help you out, anything at all, please come and ask. OK?'

Another warm smile.

I was just leaving when he called out to me. 'Oh, Nick?'

I stopped at the door and turned to him. 'Yes?'

'Isabel Pereira sent me the fax you received for Martin Beldecos yesterday.' He lowered his voice. 'You know what happened, I take it?'

I nodded.

He grimaced. 'It was a terrible thing. Terrible. But if you do receive any more messages for Martin, give them directly to me, won't you? And please don't mention them to anyone else in the firm. Martin was working for me on something that was very sensitive. Do you understand?'

It was a request, and on the surface it was a request made with charm and politeness. But lying just below the surface, unsaid, and undefined, was a threat.

'I understand,' I said, and left.

Jamie was waiting. 'What was all that about?'

I told him of Eduardo's offer to take over my mortgage, and my response.

He raised his eyebrows. 'Why did you say no?'

'I don't know. I just didn't like the feel of it. And once I had said no, I didn't want Eduardo to change my mind. Do you think I'm crazy?'

Jamie hesitated. 'Maybe not. Eduardo's right, there would be no strings attached. But if you work here you end up being dependent on them, one way or another.'

'What do you mean?'

'Oh, the bonuses and employee trusts are the most obvious example. But if you're in trouble Ricardo will help you out with money or contacts or whatever. You owed him five thousand pounds before you'd even started, remember?'

'You're right. But somehow it seemed different coming from Ricardo than Eduardo.'

'Maybe. They're very different people. But they are brothers. You owe one, you owe the other.'

'Are they close?'

'You bet. Most Latinos are pretty close to their family. But it's more than that with them.' Jamie lowered his voice again. I got the impression he enjoyed this conspiratorial gossip. 'There are some pretty dodgy rumours about Eduardo.'

I leaned forward, eager to encourage him. 'Oh, yes?'

'Yeah. Apparently he killed someone once. Pushed him over a balcony. It was when he was a student in Caracas. They'd had an argument over some girl. Ricardo hushed it up, and Eduardo walked free.'

I shuddered. 'I can imagine him killing someone.'

'I know what you mean. And he leads a pretty fast life. Girls, drugs. That kind of thing. You know there was even a rumour that he was screwing Isabel.'

'Eduardo?' I glanced over to Isabel's desk. I could just see the top of her head, bowed, a telephone pressed against her ear. 'I'd have thought she'd have more taste.'

Jamie shrugged. 'I suppose Eduardo's attractive to a certain sort of woman. I did warn you about her.'

'You did.' I was disappointed. I wouldn't have

44

believed that of Isabel, but since I didn't actually know her, had barely ever spoken to her, I realized I had no grounds to be surprised. A nascent fantasy dashed. Oh, well.

'Eduardo has his uses, though,' Jamie continued. 'He's intelligent. Cunning. And he can get things done.'

'What sort of things?'

'Things. He can make important people change their minds about things. He can influence people.'

'What, you mean bribery?'

'I'm not sure that it's as straightforward as that,' said Jamie. 'Ricardo's squeaky clean on bribery. In our market, either you're incorruptible or you bribe everyone. These days, it's better to have a reputation for being incorruptible. Less risk. But Eduardo has his methods, and Ricardo is probably happy not knowing exactly what they are.'

I resolved to have as little to do with Eduardo as possible.

I stayed late again that evening. I was engrossed in my reading: research reports and back copies of *IFR*, the bond market gossip sheet. Beside me was a pile of materials to read for the SFA exam, which I would have to pass before I could sell any bonds myself.

Eventually the room began to empty. Jamie said goodbye at eight thirty to go back to Kate. Isabel drifted off at nine, leaving a trace of musk in the air around my desk that quickened my pulse. By ten thirty, Ricardo was the only one left. He put down his phone, and strolled over to my desk. I looked up from my research, and smiled at him nervously.

He still looked as fresh and cool as he had at the morning meeting, although at some time during the day his top button had come undone, and his shirt cuffs had been rolled up once. He lit a cigarette. 'Coffee?'

God knows how many I had had that day. But it was good stuff. I nodded. 'Please.'

He strolled off, leaving me waiting uncomfortably. The boss was getting me coffee. Shouldn't I be fetching it for him? In a moment he was back with two cups.

'Well, what do you think? Fun, isn't it?'

'I didn't realize this stuff could be so intellectually interesting.'

Ricardo chuckled. 'You thought it was all screaming down telephones.'

'I suppose so.'

He looked at what I was reading, a piece panning Mexico. 'What's your view on that?'

'It's well written. Persuasive. It makes sense to me.'

'I know. Charlotte has that rare ability as an analyst to take facts and speculation, mix them up, and come up with an opinion that will make money. And I can assure you I value that opinion.'

He took a drag on his cigarette. 'Take Mexico. Charlotte's worried about it. She sees another currency devaluation coming in the next month or two, and she thinks this one will scare investors almost as much as the last one. And I agree with her.'

'So you sell Mexico and buy Argentina?'

Ricardo smiled. 'You're catching on. That would be the right trade. Argentina's a good choice, too. The bonds are much too cheap. But it's not that simple.'

'Why not?'

'Because Mexico want to borrow a billion dollars. And that's a deal we have to win.'

'I see. But you don't want to sell a billion dollars of

Mexican bonds to investors when they're scared about a devaluation?'

'Dead right.'

I thought about it. 'Can't you let someone else do the deal, then?'

'Normally I would consider it. Of course, we'd have to be involved. This is our market, we're always involved. Those are the rules. But maybe we could share the transaction with a couple of other houses and reduce our risk. The trouble is, Bloomfield Weiss are bidding for the whole deal. And I just can't let them win it.'

'They're the people who stole your Eastern European team, aren't they?'

'That's right. They're aiming for us. They want our number-one position. Until recently they couldn't give a damn about emerging markets, but in the last few months they've changed their ideas.'

'You can see them off, surely?'

'Not so easy. They're the top trading firm on Wall Street when it comes to the conventional markets. And they have ten times our capital. They'll use that to buy their way in.'

'So, what are you going to do?'

'I really don't know.' He pulled on his cigarette thoughtfully. I let him think, flattered that he felt able to share a problem like this with me on my second day.

Eventually, he spoke. 'So you like Argentina?'

'Yes,' I said.

'Why?'

I took a deep breath and answered him. 'Their policy of fixing the peso to the dollar really seems to be working. And the bonds have come off a few points just because a big American money manager has been selling. They're good value.'

'Uh-huh. And which bond do you like in particular?'

'The Discounts.' These were one of the classes of Brady bonds that had been exchanged for old bank debt when Argentina had renegotiated its borrowings a few years earlier. 'Am I right?'

Ricardo smiled. 'Did you know my father was Argentinian?'

'Jamie told me.'

'Well, I have an old rule. Never let a trader trade his own country's bonds. He can't be objective. Now, I usually break my rule in my own case, but this time . . .'

He picked up the phone.

'Who are you calling?'

He looked at his watch. 'US Commerce have a San Francisco office that should still be making markets. Hold on. Brad?' Pause. 'Ricardo Ross. Where are you in Argentina? The Discounts . . . In twenty million? . . . Of course, I'll wait.'

He grinned at me. 'The guy's panicked. But I know him. If I ask him to make a market in size, he'll do it. He has to prove himself. Especially to me.' Then back to the phone. 'Sixty-seven to a half? That's a wide market, isn't it, Brad? . . . OK, I know it's late. I'll take twenty at a half.' He hung up and turned to me. 'Now, you remember to tell me when to sell, won't you?'

I nodded, my heart suddenly beating rapidly.

'It's about time you went home, isn't it? We start again in eight hours. Don't you sleep?'

'Not much. Do you?'

'Not much.' Ricardo grinned. We were kindred spirits. It was rare to come across someone else who genuinely didn't need a full night's sleep, and it was a pleasure when it happened. I was used to staying up into the small hours reading, or researching. Five hours' sleep was all I needed. Especially when I was absorbed in something.

'Get on your bike,' he said.

So I did. I pedalled home fast, my emotions neatly poised between fear that my first bond position would all go wrong, and excitement that it would all go right.

4

Wednesday morning was foggy. I couldn't see the Tower as I rode my bike through the East End. Old warehouses loomed up on either side of Narrow Street. With London's haphazard modern skyline obscured, I could almost believe I was in Victorian England, until a van ran a red light and forced me on to the pavement.

But the trading room was surrounded by blue sky. I was drawn to the window. We were just above the fog, a choppy white surface stretching out on all sides beneath us. The tip of the NatWest tower broke through the clouds like a rock a few miles out to sea. We ourselves were an island far from England, closer to New York and Buenos Aires than Primrose Hill and Shoreditch. I looked around at my colleagues. We were a small band of colonists, immigrants from all over the world, come to seek our fortune in this strange new land.

Well, that was fine, but where were the Argy discos trading?

I switched on Jamie's screen. Sixty-seven and a quarter bid. I wasn't in the money. The rest of the market was up a point, leaving my bonds behind them. Oh, God. Maybe I'd picked the wrong issue, after all.

Jamie was out that morning. He had to make a presentation to a large insurance company that was considering investing in emerging-market bonds. It was an important meeting; as Jamie had put it, when these boys played, they played in size. So I spent the morning at my desk.

Except it didn't feel like my desk. It felt like Martin Beldecos's. To say that he was haunting it would be too strong. But when I was sitting there, I had a powerful feeling of his presence, even though I'd never met the man, didn't even know what he looked like. A desk is a private space. In a trading room, it is the only private space, a tiny island of security. I felt as though I was a usurper of someone else's territory. It wasn't a comfortable feeling.

Just then, the fax behind me chugged into life. Most of the faxes were for Isabel, but she was engrossed in one of her mammoth phone calls. So I strolled over to the machine, and picked up the two sheets of paper.

It was for Martin Beldecos. From United Bank of Canada. My curiosity got the better of me. I took it back to my desk – Martin's desk – and began to read.

Dear Mr Beldecos

Following your recent request regarding the beneficial ownership of International Trading and Transport (Panama), I thought you might be interested in the findings of a recent investigation at this branch.

You may recall that the only name on our records associated with International Trading and Transport (Panama) was Mr Tony Hempel, a Miami lawyer. Our investigations into another of our clients have shown that this Mr Hempel is closely connected with Francisco Aragão, a Brazilian financier under investigation by the United States Drug Enforcement Agency for drug-related money-laundering activities.

While we make every effort to assist the international agencies in their investigations into money-laundering and drug crimes, we also owe a duty of confidence to our counterparties, so we have not yet passed on your inquiry to the DEA. However, if you have information you would like to share with them, please call me, and I will give you my contact's name and number.

Yours sincerely

Donald Winters
Vice President

I stared at the fax.

Money-laundering. That meant, I believed, the recycling of illegally obtained cash through the financial system. Now I remembered from the first fax that this company, International whatever, Panama, had transferred some funds to a Dekker Trust account. And the lawyer who had ordered the transfer was an associate of a suspected money-launderer. Which meant that one of the Dekker Trust accounts might contain laundered money.

So this was what Martin Beldecos had been working on before he died! No wonder Eduardo wanted to make sure that he received Martin's messages personally, and that no one else saw them.

I picked up the fax and walked over to Eduardo's corner office. I knocked on the door, and tried to open it. It was locked.

'He's not in today,' said a middle-aged woman, presiding over a corral of desks just outside his office. 'Should be in tomorrow. Can I help?'

I dithered over giving her the fax. Eduardo had said I shouldn't let anyone else see any of Martin's messages.

But she was his secretary. But, then, this was clearly an important message. I remembered the implied threat in Eduardo's voice, and decided the safest thing was to wait until I could give Eduardo the message personally.

'No, that's all right,' I said, and made my way back round the square of trading desks to my own seat.

'One nil!' Dave flung his phone down on his desk, and stood up in triumph, his arms in the air, his stomach thrusting out in front of him. He attracted only a quick glance from the other traders around him. Another small victory over the market. Another dollar made.

Suddenly I felt cold. Perhaps Dave had been right. Perhaps Martin had been murdered by a contract killer. If he knew about money-laundering at Dekker, someone might have wanted to shut him up.

No. I was just being fanciful. I returned to my desk clutching the fax tightly. I should just give it to Eduardo and forget about it. He could sort it out.

But Eduardo? Perhaps he already knew all about it. If someone was laundering money through Dekker Ward, it wouldn't surprise me if Eduardo did know all about it.

What the hell should I do?

I looked round for Jamie, but he was still out at his meeting.

Then I saw Ricardo moving towards me.

'Still want to keep that Argentine position? They're lagging the market a bit, aren't they?'

I dropped the fax on to my desk, and wrenched my brain back to the market. 'The reasons we bought the bonds still hold good,' I said. 'So yes.'

'OK, fine. We'll see what happens. Now, what are you doing at the moment?'

The fax to Martin Beldecos was right there, face up

on my desk, partially covered by my left arm. Now was the time to tell Ricardo about it. Just give it to him, and forget it.

But something made me hold back. I think it was because I couldn't foresee the consequences, although I was sure they would be important. I needed time to think it through first.

So, keeping my arm on the desk, covering Martin Beldecos's name on the title sheet, I said simply, 'Reading.'

'Uh-huh. Don't you think it's about time you got involved in a real deal?'

'Yes. That would be great.'

'Good. Isabel is going down to Rio tonight to sort out this *favela* deal. She'll need some help. Can you go with her?'

'Of course.' My pulse quickened at the prospect of working closely with Isabel. Besides, this was a great opportunity; my first business trip at Dekker, and a big deal. One that Ricardo was personally interested in. Although I had to admit he seemed to be personally interested in every deal.

I glanced towards her. She was leaning back in her chair talking on the phone, but she had seen Ricardo with me, and gave me a quick smile of encouragement.

'Good. I'd like you to see how we operate in the markets we know well before I set you on to Russia,' Ricardo said. 'See what you can do.'

A voice interrupted. 'Ricardo! Vasily Ivanov from the Russian Finance Ministry on twelve!'

'Ah, the Russians are coming.' Ricardo smiled, and returned to his desk to take the call.

Isabel put down her phone. 'Pull up a chair,' she said. 'I'll tell you what we're doing.'

'Just a second,' I said. I picked up the fax, and looked at it once again. Then I opened the bottom drawer of my desk, which was still empty, and tossed the fax inside. I'd deal with it later, when I had had a chance to think about it.

I pulled over the chair from my own desk, and sat next to her. I could just smell her perfume. Concentrate!

'I said all this would get easier once you started doing it, rather than just reading about it, didn't I?' She smiled, a shy flash of teeth that came and went. 'Well, I may be proved wrong. This deal isn't a good one to start on.'

'I'll do my best.'

'OK. Let me tell you the story. First of all, do you know what a *favela* is?'

'It's some kind of a slum, isn't it?'

'That's right. In Brazil there's been massive migration from the countryside to the towns over the last forty years. People arrive in the cities without anywhere to live. So they find some empty ground, and build a shelter there. They make them out of pieces of timber, corrugated iron, things like that. As more people come, their homes become a bit more substantial, and these areas grow into large communities, some of them with thousands of inhabitants. These are the *favelas*.'

'They sound grim.'

'They are,' said Isabel. 'They have no sanitation, open sewers run through the streets. No running water. No garbage collection. If there's a fire, the fire service can't get in to put it out. There are very few schools or clinics. There are drugs and gang wars. They're horrible. No humans should be allowed to live in those conditions.'

'So why don't the authorities do something about them?'

55

'They've tried. Whenever they move the residents on, they just build a *favela* somewhere else. Sometimes the city will build cheap housing for some people, but then these are replaced by thousands more. And you know how little money Brazil has to spend on anything, these days.'

'OK, so what's the solution?'

'Well, the Municipality of Rio de Janeiro think they've found one. It's called the Favela Bairro project. *Bairro* means neighbourhood. The idea is that instead of trying to move or replace the *favelas*, they will try to change them. Turn them into proper neighbourhoods. So they will build roads, health centres, schools, parks, water systems, electricity. But, most important of all, they'll give the inhabitants of the *favelas* title to their properties.'

'What, ownership?'

'Not quite. But a long leasehold, which is more or less the same thing. This should make a big difference. Once these people know they're not going to be turfed out of their homes they'll improve them. And, just as importantly, they will have an incentive to stop new-comers building on their land. It should make a big difference. They should turn into proper *bairros*.'

I'd heard this argument before somewhere. 'Sort of like Margaret Thatcher selling off council houses in this country?'

Isabel smiled. 'That's right.'

I thought about it. 'Will it really work?'

'It should do,' said Isabel. 'It's certainly worth a try. We have to do something.'

'And how will all this be financed?'

Isabel leaned forward, eager to explain. 'That's where we come in. Although the World Development Fund are happy to help, organizing the financing for these projects can be quite a problem. Usually it has to go through the Municipality. There, it can be mixed up with funds for other projects, and all kinds of budget-related bureaucratic restrictions have to be met. In the past there have also been accusations of contracts being awarded at inflated prices in return for kickbacks. Also this project could be partially self-financing from taxes raised from the *favelas*, but the Municipality is not allowed to pledge tax revenues to any specific source. So the whole idea got bogged down.'

'Sounds like a nightmare.'

'It was. Until we thought of the idea of a trust.'

'A trust?'

'Yes. A trust will be set up to fund the project. It'll be called the Rio de Janeiro Favela Bairro Trust. It'll be funded with one hundred million dollars from the Municipality, and two hundred million dollars from a ten-year bond issue guaranteed by the World Development Fund.'

'And arranged by Dekker Ward.'

'Precisely.'

'And this trust is responsible for financing the project?'

'That's right. There will be trustees from the Municipality, from the *favela*, and from the World Development Fund.'

'Very neat.' I thought a moment. 'How will the money be repaid?'

'The trust will receive the rental payments under the long leases. Because they're rental payments, not taxes, they can be applied to the bond issue. Of course, if that isn't sufficient, then the Municipality or the World Development Fund will make up the difference.'

'I see. But won't the Rio authorities be unhappy about losing control of the funds?'

'That's been the problem,' said Isabel. 'But the current mayor of Rio really does want to do something about these places. And he and the new Finance Secretary are quite strict about not awarding contracts to political allies. This will help them clean the whole thing up.'

'So everyone gains?'

'That's the intention. Brazil needs foreign capital. This is a way of making sure it gets to where it's needed most.'

I was impressed. 'Was this your idea?'

'Yes. Or, at least, the trust structure was. I've wanted to do something like this for a long time, but no one took any notice. Then Ricardo put his support behind it, and it looks like it will finally happen. If we can squeeze it through the Brazilian bureaucrats, that is.'

'What are they like?'

'You'll see.'

I left the office at about six, early by Dekker standards. I had to go home and pack before making my way out to Heathrow airport. I was excited at the prospect of the trip, but also nervous. Things were moving fast. Only three days into the job, and I was already on my first trip! Normally, I was confident in my ability to pick things up quickly, but I was afraid that I would be way out of my depth in Rio. I hoped Isabel would be patient.

I caught sight of Jamie at his desk on my way out. He waved me over.

'How did it go with the insurance company?' I asked.

'Great! They're going to commit a hundred million pounds to the emerging markets. And that's just for starters. If they like the experience they'll stump up more. And, have no doubt about it, I'm going to make this a wonderful experience for them.'

Then he noticed my jacket was on, and my battered briefcase bulging. 'Where are you off to?'

'Brazil. Ricardo asked me to help Isabel with the *favela* deal.'

'That should be interesting. Isabel's good. You can learn a lot from her. Her father's some big-shot banker out there, so they all listen to her. But remember. Don't touch.'

I smiled.

'Oh, Jamie. Just before I go. I got a fax for Martin Beldecos I wanted to discuss with you. I'm not sure what I should do with it –'

Just then Jamie's phone flashed. He picked it up. 'Robert, hallo. It was a good meeting this afternoon, don't you think?'

As he listened to the response, he mouthed to me, 'Later.'

I could tell the conversation would last a while, and I didn't want to hang around and risk missing my plane, so I waved goodbye to him and left.

5

Humberto Novais Alves, the Finance Secretary for the Municipality of Rio de Janeiro, leaped to his feet and held out his arms. 'Isabel!' he said. '*Tudo bem?*' He kissed both her cheeks and rattled on in Portuguese.

Isabel broke free and turned to me. 'Humberto, this is my colleague Nick Elliot. He doesn't speak Portuguese, but I know English isn't a problem for you.'

'No problem at all!' said Humberto, pumping my hand. His round face broke into a grin. 'Sit down, sit down.' He gestured to a group of sofas and armchairs. 'Some coffee?'

As Humberto organized it, I looked round his office. It was large and well furnished, no doubt befitting his status. The walls were adorned with diplomas and photographs of gleaming new housing projects. The big desk was devoid of paper. The room smelled of new carpet. Every few seconds a pneumatic drill burst into life in the street below. I glanced out of the window. We were ten floors up. The dark flanks of the Mayor's office rose up a hundred yards away, a tower block just taller than the finance department. And behind that, the sea, mountains and the crowded buildings of Rio de Janeiro.

We had come here straight from the airport, through the chaotic grime of Rio's northern suburbs into the shabby administrative centre of the city. Our taxi had parked in what looked like a wire-fenced building site surrounding the finance department, and we had negotiated four sets of security guards, receptionists and secretaries before finally reaching the inner sanctum of Humberto's office.

A woman entered with a tray and three small cups of coffee, which she handed to each of us. Humberto added several spoonfuls of sugar to his, and Isabel some drops from a little blue plastic bottle. I took mine straight, and sipped the gritty black liquid carefully. It was strong and bitter.

'And how is your dear father, Isabel?' Humberto asked, taking a seat at the conference table. He was about fifty, and looked to my eyes more English than Brazilian. Pale and a little pudgy, with thinning dark hair, he wore a smart grey suit and striped tie. He would have blended in well in Whitehall.

'He's fine,' she replied. 'Working hard as usual.'

'With some results. Banco Horizonte is doing very well, these days, I hear. It has quite a reputation. When was it established? Eight years ago?'

'Ten years in October.'

'Well, he has achieved a lot in ten years. Give him my good wishes, won't you?'

'I will.' Isabel's smile was a bit strained. I got the impression that many of her business conversations in Brazil started off with her father.

Humberto took a sip of coffee, and lit a cigarette. 'Well, Isabel, my dear, we have good news. Very good news. Everything is finally coming together. The Rio de Janeiro Favela Bairro Trust was formally established yesterday, with myself as chairman.' He placed a hand on his chest and gave a mock bow.

'The Mayor is completely behind the idea, I mean completely. We have had ten departments working on this.' He counted them off on his stubby fingers: 'Finance, Health, Urbanism, Education, Housing, Fire, Water, Environment, Social Development and the Attorney General's Office. And they are all working together. That, as you know, is quite an achievement.'

'Great!' Isabel's face lit up. This was better than she had expected.

'You have the documents I sent you?'

'They're right here,' said Isabel, patting her briefcase. 'I have some comments. Nothing substantial, but we need to make a few changes just to be sure the mechanism works correctly. And then, of course, we've got the meetings tomorrow with the rating agencies. They shouldn't be a problem. They just have one or two final questions.'

The rating agencies were responsible for assessing and publishing a credit rating for each new deal brought to market. Given the complexity of Isabel's structure, this had required quite a lot of work on their part, but they were almost comfortable with it.

'Good. Let me get Rafael. One moment.' He picked up his phone and spoke quickly in Portuguese. 'He'll be here in five minutes.'

He placed his hands on the desk in front of us and beamed. 'But once we have agreed those documents, and satisfied the agencies, there's nothing at our end to stop us from going further.'

'Then we can launch the deal at the end of next week, as we planned?'

'As far as we are concerned, yes.'

Isabel caught something in the civil servant's tone. 'Humberto?'

'There is one small problem. It's probably nothing.'

'Yes?'

'Jack Langton at the World Development Fund has to check some small details with Washington. He says he'll get back to us at the beginning of next week.'

'What details?'

Humberto shrugged.

'I'll call him,' said Isabel.

'Good. Isabel, we are going to do this deal, I promise you.'

Isabel smiled. 'We certainly are.'

There was a quiet tap on the door, and the lawyer, Rafael, entered. We retired to a meeting room where we went over the documents Isabel had brought with her. I had read them through several times until I thoroughly understood the structure, and I was able to make some useful suggestions. It was good to contribute something for a change.

In the taxi back to our hotel, I asked Isabel how she thought the meeting had gone.

'I'm pleased. After a year, it looks like we're almost there. Humberto has always been enthusiastic about the deal. He said there would be no problem getting all the authorizations, but I admit I didn't believe him. And now it looks like he's done it.'

'What was all that about the World Development Fund?'

Isabel frowned. 'I don't know. I'll find out when we get back to the hotel. Oh, by the way, thanks for your help in that meeting. You certainly have picked up a lot.' She gave me a shy smile, a smile to die for.

'Thank you,' I said, my voice hoarse.

The taxi lurched on through the Rio traffic, accelerating through red lights, swerving round holes in the road, cursing and hooting its way through the jams. Eventually we entered a tunnel and the traffic speeded up. We emerged in front of a broad lake. Apartment buildings sprouted up around it, and behind them on all sides rose tall, green, rounded mountains. On top of one of these stood the statue of Christ, arms outstretched as he embraced the city below him. We skirted the lake at a crawl again, barely overtaking the parade of joggers and walkers. Two double sculls glided across the water, their oars moving in perfect time. Surrounded by these breathtaking walls of green, it was difficult to believe we were in the heart of a city.

These next few days in Rio were going to be difficult. Not the business. I had been pleased with the meeting and my performance in it. No, Isabel. Her presence was disconcerting. She didn't have to do anything, she could just be sitting next to me leafing through a magazine, and that would be enough to distract me. The way she bit her lip as she read, the way her hair caressed her elegant neck, the two knobs of collarbone peeking out of the top of her dress.

I thought I was good at ignoring pretty women when necessary. I had taught a number, eager twenty-year-olds, falling in love with a great literature, and easily impressed with their guide. But tutor–student relations were now frowned upon in the academic world, and I had successfully shown no interest in any of them.

I had tried to strike up a conversation with Isabel on the plane. She hadn't been rude, but she hadn't exactly been talkative either. She had shown a sort of shy self-possession that finished each conversation almost as soon as it had begun but which made her, if anything, more appealing. It would have been easier if she had just said, 'Shut up and leave me alone.' Eventually I had given up and read loan documents through the night, until the suburbs of northern Rio de Janeiro appeared through the window with the dawn.

In a few minutes the taxi pulled up outside the Copacabana Palace, nestling in the middle of a row of characterless hotels and apartment blocks that faced the famous beach of the same name. It was a squat white building, whose elegantly etched art-deco features recalled its heyday as the leading hotel for the rich and beautiful of the 1930s. Here, I had read, Fred Astaire and Ginger Rogers had danced, and Noël Coward and Eva Peron had gambled. As our taxi rolled to a halt, a man in a crisp white uniform opened the door, and another whisked away our bags. We checked in, and were led through a courtyard past a swimming pool, shimmering coolly blue against the white glare of the hotel walls. A solitary swimmer cut through its lightly ruffled surface as she forged up and down. Two couples, one a pair of bankers and one a pair of middle-aged tourists, drank coffee in the shade of a large, broadleafed tree. Quite simply, I was overawed. I'd travelled before, to India, Thailand, Morocco, but I had never stayed in anywhere that cost more than twenty pounds a night. The Copacabana Palace cost significantly more than that. Isabel, of course, knew the hotel well, and took it all in her stride.

I went up to my room, took a cold beer out of the minibar, and walked out on to the balcony. Below me was the pool and beyond that, outside the calm confines of the hotel, past the constant stream of traffic on the Avenida Atlântica, was the bustle of Copacabana beach itself. At its near edge, walkers strode purposefully up and down, occasionally pausing to perform a ritual twisting and stretching of limbs. The beach itself was dotted with brown and black bodies. This was a beach where people did things: played volleyball or soccer, sold ice creams or funny hats, milled about, or sat and watched everyone else. Then, beyond all this, there was the sea, swelling gently until a few feet from the shore, when it suddenly erupted into white fluffy waves, which broke tidily and prettily on to the pale sand.

I shed my jacket and tie, took a sip of cold beer, closed my eyes and pointed my face towards the soft heat of the late-afternoon sun. The complementary roar of traffic and waves lulled me. I began to relax.

The turmoil of the last few days began to sort itself out in my brain. The first week at Dekker and my attempts to absorb all the new information thrown at me; the complexities of the *favela* deal; Martin Beldecos's fax.

I still didn't know what to do about that. I wished I'd had a chance to discuss it with Jamie before I'd left. It seemed very likely that money was being laundered at Dekker Trust. Whether Ricardo and Eduardo knew that, I had no idea. But I also had no idea what it had got to do with me. My instincts told me to ignore it, at least until I got my bearings at Dekker. It could safely wait until I returned.

There was a knock at the door. It was Isabel.

'Come in,' I said. 'Do you want a beer?'

She shook her head. I wandered back out to the balcony and she followed me.

'This is amazing,' I said.

'Rio is beautiful,' she said, matter-of-factly. 'And if you work for Dekker, you tend to end up in the nicest hotel rooms.'

She was wearing a simple black summer dress. She leaned back against the railing of my balcony. My throat went dry. I had another swig of beer.

'I tried to get hold of Jack Langton, my contact at the WDF, but no luck,' she said. 'I've left a message for him to call me tomorrow at the Ministry of Finance.'

'OK.'

'I'm going to dinner with some old friends tonight. Will you be all right here by yourself?'

'I'll be fine.'

'If you do go out, don't carry much money with you, and if anyone asks you for it, just give it to them.'

'Yes, Mum.'

She smiled and blushed. 'I'm sorry, but this town can be dangerous for strangers.'

'That's OK. Don't worry, I'll be careful.'

She moved to leave and then hesitated. 'I'm having lunch with my father on Saturday. Would you like to come? He's always enjoyed reading Russian novels. I think he'd like to meet you.'

I tried to hide my surprise. 'Thank you very much.'

'Good,' she said, and was gone.

I sat and watched evening descend upon the beach. Then I grabbed a few *reais* and joined the evening promenade along the Avenida Atlântica.

The meetings with the rating agencies on Friday went well. They seemed to be satisfied that everything hung together. The only slight worry was that we didn't hear from the WDF. So during a break for lunch Isabel called them, and discovered that Jack Langton was out all day and would call back on Monday.

On Saturday morning I called Pedro Hattori at the office, on the off-chance he was in. He was. My

Argentine Discounts were down a point following an unsubstantiated rumour of a general strike the following week. Pedro told me not to worry, there was nothing in it. But I did.

I spent the morning exploring Rio. It overwhelmed my senses. It was an extraordinary city, physically the most beautiful I had ever seen. It was an absurd mix of sea, beach, forest and mountain, all four in such close proximity that it seemed impossible to fit a city in among them. Everywhere you went there seemed to be a beach in front of you and a mountain behind. The buildings themselves were nothing special, anything old in Rio was run down and shabby, but even the starkest modern building was overwhelmed by the beauty surrounding it.

I returned to the hotel at one o'clock to meet Isabel. We jumped into a taxi to Ipanema where her father lived. Ipanema beach was subtly different from Copacabana. It had the same white sand, and it was surrounded by similar lush green mountains, but the apartment buildings seemed newer and better kept, and the beachgoers were different, more relaxed. Phone booths like giant motor-cycle helmets in yellow and orange sprouted up in clusters every hundred yards or so. In most of them girls in shorts and bikini tops laughed and chatted. On my walk the other night along Copacabana the girls had looked like hookers; here they looked like middle-class schoolgirls fixing up the day's entertainment on the beach. Ipanema had sun, sea, sand, and money.

But, at the far end of the beach, behind a rectangular hotel, I could see a jumble of small buildings, little square boxes clinging to the edge of a mountain, looking at any moment as if they would tumble into the sea below. They were packed tightly together, no line was quite straight, no building quite complete. A *favela*.

'It's extraordinary to see the two so close together,' I said. 'The rich and the poor. It's almost obscene.'

'It is obscene,' replied Isabel.

We pulled up a side-street and stopped outside some iron gates adorned with a small video camera and an electronic combination lock. Above us rose a sand-coloured apartment building. The gates whirred and opened, and the taxi drove us up to the black smoked-glass entrance.

We walked into a cool lobby, and a uniformed doorman greeted Isabel with a grin. A boy, also in uniform, ushered us into a wood-panelled lift, and we headed up to the fifteenth floor. The doors opened, into a hallway.

'Isabel!' a deep voice cried. A tall middle-aged man with a slight stoop stood waiting for us. He opened out his arms.

'Papai,' she said, and gave him a hug.

Isabel's father had her long Roman nose, which on him looked distinguished. He peered at me over the half-moon glasses.

'I'm Luís. Welcome.' He shook my hand and smiled. He was very tall. Even with the stoop I had to look up at him, and I'm six foot three. His hair was still black, but was thinning. He had a good-humoured face, wrinkled by sun and laughter. 'Come through, come through.'

He led us in to a large living room. The furniture was low, and either of dark wood or cane. Bright colourful paintings covered the walls on large canvases. The sun streamed in from big windows that looked out on to a balcony. Beyond that stretched the shimmering blue sea.

Suddenly there was a clattering sound followed by heavy thumping from the hallway behind us. 'Isabel!' screamed a hoarse voice, and a large black woman wearing a dark uniform and an apron charged into the room. She grabbed Isabel and kissed her hard on both cheeks, breathing deeply from the exertion of her gallop. Isabel beamed and spoke to the big woman rapidly. They exchanged laughs and hasty comments, and then the woman caught sight of me. She whispered something that made Isabel blush, and turn and hit her playfully on the shoulder.

'Maria has been my maid since I was a little girl,' Isabel said. 'She still thinks she can tell me what to do.'

I held out my hand to her. '*Tudo bem?*' I said, using up fifty per cent of my Portuguese vocabulary. Maria's grin somehow widened further, and she regaled me with a torrent of Portuguese. I settled on '*Obrigado*' or 'Thank you' as an answer, which sent her into hysterics.

Luís looked on in amusement. 'Can I get you a drink? Have you tried a *caipirinha* yet?'

'Not yet.'

'Well, then, you must try one now.' He spoke quickly to another maid who was hovering at the door, and she disappeared.

Luís led us out on to the balcony. Although the table and chairs were in the shade, the glare of the midday sun reflecting off the nearby white buildings hurt my eyes. We could look over them, to Ipanema Bay, an astonishing blue, dotted with lush green islands. Brightly coloured tropical flowers spilled out of tubs on the terrace, and a bougainvillaea, in full purple bloom, framed the view. The gentle murmur of traffic, sea and people drifted up to us on the breeze. Directly beneath us were a couple of tennis courts and a swimming pool in a green compound. A private club, presumably.

The maid returned with the drinks. The *caipirinha* turned out to be some kind of coarse rum in lime juice. The sweetness of rum, the sourness of lime juice, the coldness of the ice, and the kick of alcohol created a delicious mix of sensations.

Luís was watching me and smiled. 'How do you like it?'

'It goes down very well.'

'Be careful,' said Isabel. 'You should always treat a *caipirinha* with respect.'

Luís chuckled.

'It must be hard to take London after this,' I said to Isabel, with another look out at the bay.

She laughed. 'It's true. As a Brazilian, you need courage to get through a London winter.'

'Isabel tells me you work with her at Dekker Ward,' said Luís.

'That's right. I have nearly one week's experience in banking. But you're a banker yourself, aren't you?'

'Yes. My family were landowners in the state of São Paulo. Through the generations they have shown a consistent ability to turn a large fortune into a smaller one. I suppose you could say I've changed that record.' He glanced at Isabel. 'In fact, it looks as if banking is now firmly in the blood.'

Isabel flushed. 'Papai, I enjoy it, OK? I have a good job, I do it well.'

'I'm sure you do,' said Luís, with just the barest hint of condescension. Isabel noticed it and scowled. 'Isabel tells me you used to teach Russian.'

'That's right. At the School of Russian Studies in London.'

'Ah, I wish I could speak the language. I have read many Russian novels, all the greats, but I think it would be wonderful to read them in the original.'

'It is,' I said. 'Russian prose is a marvellous thing. It seems almost like poetry. The sounds, the resonance, the nuances which writers like Tolstoy and Dostoevsky can achieve are extraordinary. Beautiful.'

'And who is your favourite?'

'Oh, Pushkin, undoubtedly, for just that reason. He does things with the language that no one has managed before or since. And he tells a good story.'

'I often think Brazil is a little like Russia,' said Luís.

'Really?'

'Yes. Both countries are vast. Both peoples seem to live for the present. We're both used to poverty, corruption, great potential that is always just beyond our reach. You know, they say about Brazil that it is the country of the future and it always will be.' He chuckled. 'But we don't give up. We have a drink, a dance, we enjoy ourselves, and perhaps the next day we die.'

I thought about what he had said. He had described exactly the strange mixture of exuberant good humour and melancholy that had attracted me to Russian literature in the first place. 'Perhaps you're right. I'm afraid I don't know enough about Brazil. But I suspect the climate's better.'

Luís laughed. 'That's true. It makes enjoying life easier.'

'It's a fascinating country. I'd love to find out more about it.'

Luís took my arm. 'Do you know Tolstoy's story, "Master and Man"?'

I smiled. 'I was teaching it just three weeks ago.'

'That could apply perfectly to Brazil.'

'What's that, Papai?' Isabel asked.

'You tell her,' Luís said to me.

'A nobleman and his servant are stranded in a snowstorm. The nobleman rides off to safety with their only horse, leaving his servant to walk. After a while the nobleman is thrown off his horse. As he trudges through the snow, he reflects on the uselessness of his life, and probably his death, spent alone and in selfishness. So he returns to find his servant lying freezing in the snow. The nobleman spreads himself on the servant like a cloak. In the morning, when the storm has blown over, they are discovered. The servant survives, but the nobleman is dead.'

Isabel's large dark eyes were watching me, following every word. 'That's beautiful.'

'It expressed Tolstoy's beliefs in the obligations of the nobility,' I said.

'Beliefs that we would do well to heed in Brazil,' said Luís.

'Unfortunately not many of Tolstoy's contemporaries took much notice either. Forty years later there was a revolution.'

'We won't have another revolution here. Just anarchy, violence and poverty.'

'Has Isabel told you what we're doing here?' I asked.

Isabel looked embarrassed.

'My daughter doesn't like to talk to me much about her work,' he said. 'My bank and hers often find ourselves rivals, so it's probably best that way.'

I wasn't sure whether I was about to give away a trade secret, so I glanced at Isabel. She shrugged. So I told him about the *favela* deal. He listened intently, glancing occasionally at Isabel who avoided his eyes.

There was silence when I had finished. Finally, he asked a question. 'When do you say the bond issue will be launched?'

'In two weeks, we hope,' answered Isabel.

'Well, have your people give me a call. I will make sure that the bank buys some.'

'But, Papai, you never deal with Dekker!'

'I know. But this is different. I think it's important for Banco Horizonte to support initiatives like this.'

Isabel's mouth hung open.

'Don't look so shocked, my darling.'

'Papai, you're not doing this just to humour me, are you?'

'No, of course not. It's a good idea. It deserves support. I'm glad to see you are doing so well. Ah, here's lunch.'

We sat down as a maid brought us some steak and salad. The meat was tender, with a much stronger taste than its British counterpart. The salad included all kinds of vegetables I had never seen before. It looked very good.

There was silence as we set about our food. Then Luís broke it. 'Isabel, I've been thinking. Would you like to come and work at the bank?'

Isabel looked at me anxiously, then at her father. 'Doing what, exactly?'

'Oh, I don't know, I'm sure we could find you something. You have lots of experience now. You could be very useful doing lots of things.'

'Papai – '

'It would be good for you. You could come back to Rio. Settle down – '

'Papai!' Isabel glanced quickly at me and then glared

at her father. She launched into a torrent of angry Portuguese. Luís tried to protest, but was cut off. Finally, they both lapsed into silence.

I cut my steak slowly and with great concentration. Luís began to speak. 'I must apologize for my daughter – '

'Don't worry about it,' I said. 'There's no point in having a family if you can't have a lively discussion every now and then. I was wondering,' I continued quickly, 'would it be possible to see a *favela*?'

I said it for something to say, a way of breaking the tension. And I was intrigued by these communities that I had heard so much about, but had not yet actually seen.

'You could take him to see Cordelia,' said Luís.

Isabel was still sulking, but she stirred herself. 'Yes, we could do that if you want.'

I coughed. 'Good,' I said. Then, 'Who's Cordelia?'

'Oh, Cordelia's my sister. She helps run a shelter for street children in one of the *favelas*. She should be working there this afternoon. We can go after lunch.'

'OK,' I said.

'By the way, Cordelia has some news,' said Luís to Isabel.

Isabel thought a moment, and then looked at her father. 'She's not pregnant, is she?' The corners of her mouth twitched upwards.

Luís shrugged, but couldn't suppress a smile. 'You'll have to ask her yourself.'

Isabel grinned broadly. 'That's wonderful news! She must be so happy. You must be so happy. I think I can see you as a grandfather.'

Luís beamed. It was clearly a role he was relishing.

'Well, we definitely have to see her this afternoon,' Isabel said to me.

'I don't want to interfere in anything. Perhaps you should go by yourself.'

'No. I'd like you to meet her,' said Isabel. This caught me a little by surprise. Why should she care whether I met her sister? 'I mean, it would be good for you to see the shelter.'

'That's fine, then. I'll come.'

6

I was sweating like a pig as I trudged up the dusty path under the mid-afternoon sun. I panted hard, each breath pulling in the foul smell of human waste, sweetened occasionally by the aroma of stale food or alcohol. In England I would be described as tall, dark and thin. Here, clambering up this hill of dirt and slime, I felt like a big, white, fat, rich man.

We had left Luís's car and driver well behind to begin the ascent of the hill. Most of the *favelas* are on hills, land too steep to build real houses. Makeshift dwellings crowded together on either side of the path. They were constructed from all kinds of different materials, although brick and plywood seemed to predominate. Small holes in the walls served for windows, and occasionally I heard a mysterious rustle of movement from the darkness within. Washing hanging from window ledges added splashes of colour to the red-brick or grey-plastered walls. There were children everywhere, most of the boys wearing nothing but shorts. One group was playing with a hoop; another was kicking a football, a difficult business on this slope. A two-year-old staggered in front of us crying, his hair a shock of yellow. A black woman trotted after him and picked him up.

We passed a small row of stalls selling vegetables and fruit. Behind one of them, a nut-brown man sported a yellow T-shirt proclaiming in English, *Who dies with the most toys wins.* Where the hell did he get that, I wondered.

A group of older kids eyed us with cold, proud eyes as we climbed past. They were passing round a bag: each one breathed deeply from it with an air of solemn concentration.

'Are you sure it's not dangerous here?' I asked.

'No,' said Isabel, puffing a few steps ahead.

'So it is dangerous?'

'Yes.'

'Oh.'

It hadn't rained for a couple of days, but every now and then the ground underfoot changed from dust to mud. An open sewer ran along the side of the path. I tried not to think what I was stepping in.

Eventually we came to a small plateau, which supported a tiny white makeshift church, and a larger rectangular structure, decorated with brightly coloured murals. I turned and paused for breath. Beneath me was one of the most spectacular views I had ever seen. The white buildings of the city snaked between green-clad hills down to the sea glistening in the distance. I looked for the statue of Christ, visible from almost anywhere in Rio, but it was lost in a cloud that clung to the mountains behind.

'You would think someone would pay a lot for this location,' I said.

'Believe me, you pay to live here. And with more than just cash.'

We approached the entrance of the building, stepping carefully through a small but well-kept garden. The splashes of red, blue, yellow and white were a welcome relief from the reddish-brown dirt.

The door opened, and a woman rushed out, hugging Isabel. There was a family resemblance, although Cordelia was heavier, older and tougher. Her face was lined, marks of both compassion and strength.

We shook hands.

'Cordelia, this is a colleague of mine, Nick Elliot,' Isabel said in English. 'I've brought him along to show him what you do here. You don't mind, do you?'

'Not at all,' said Cordelia, with a warm smile. 'The more people who see, the better.'

Isabel glanced towards Cordelia's stomach, and asked her something in Portuguese. Cordelia's smile widened and Isabel gave a cry and flung her arms round her sister's neck. They chatted excitedly for a couple of minutes, and then turned to me, both beaming.

'I'm sorry about that, Nick,' said Isabel.

'That's OK. I think I got the general idea,' I said, smiling myself. It was impossible not to be infected with their excitement. I nodded to Cordelia. 'Congratulations.'

'Thank you,' she said. 'So has Isabel told you what we do here?' Her English was slow and precise, her accent much more pronounced than her sister's.

'Not really. Something about running a shelter for street children?'

'That's right. It's a place for them to come to get a proper meal, to talk to someone, to feel that they belong somewhere.'

'Do they stay the night?'

'We only have room for a few. Those children who are genuinely afraid for their lives.'

'Who are they afraid of?'

79

'The police, mostly. Or the death squads. Groups of men who promise the shopkeepers they will keep the children off the streets. They beat them up or kill them.' Cordelia said this without emotion.

'Why? What have they done?'

'All kinds of things. Stealing, mostly. Although it doesn't even have to be that. A nine-year-old boy called Patrício used to come here. Last month he was killed, strangled. His body was found on the beach with a note: "I killed you because you didn't go to school and had no future." '

I recoiled. I looked closely at Cordelia's face. I could hardly believe what she was saying. In a way I didn't want to believe her. I looked for signs of exaggeration. But her face was blank. She was stating fact.

'How do they get away with it? Don't the police do anything?'

'It's the police who do most of the killing. Either in uniform or out of it.'

'But what about ordinary people? How do they put up with it?'

'They ignore it. They pretend it doesn't happen. Or they even praise the police for clearing up the streets.'

I grimaced. 'I can't believe it.'

She shrugged. 'Do you want to see some of the children?'

She led us into the building. It was dark, cool and clean, after the chaotic dust and heat of the *favela*. We walked along a long corridor, dodging children of all shapes and sizes. Paintings in bright unsteady colours covered the walls. We entered a kind of classroom where a number of children were playing, talking, or just sitting silently, staring.

'Don't these children have parents?' I asked.

'Many don't know their fathers. They might have a dozen brothers and sisters who all live together in one of those shacks down there, in one dark room. They're beaten and abused by stepfathers. Often the mothers spend their days in a drunken stupor. For these kids life on the street is better. They go down into the city during the day to work or beg or steal, and in the evening they stay down there if they can, or come up here.'

We came to another room where a group of boys were talking to a teacher. I wasn't sure if it was a lesson, or just a conversation. One kid, about twelve, saw me.

'Hey, meester,' he said. 'You got a dollar?'

I looked quickly at Cordelia, who gave a tiny shake of her head. 'No, sorry,' I said.

'What your name?'

The boy had a big smile, but his eyes were hard. They rested on me for a couple of seconds, and then darted about the room, as if he was expecting danger to appear at any moment from a window or a corner. Sores ran up the side of his left leg. His chin was lifted aggressively towards me.

'Nick,' I replied. 'What's yours?'

'Euclides. You have a gun, meester?'

'No.'

'I have a gun,' and with that he burst into a cackle of laughter. The other kids joined in.

We left the room. 'Was that true?' I asked Cordelia.

'We don't allow guns or knives here. Euclides is hiding here, he says the police are going to kill him. He says he stole a chicken. But now we don't think that's true. Suzane, there, thinks that he might have shot someone, for money.'

'A twelve-year-old hit-man?'

'That's right.'

'So what are you going to do?'

'We'll keep him here. These children need to know that we will shelter them whatever they have done, otherwise they won't trust us. Anyway, the police will get him one day. I'd like to pretend that these children are all angels, but they are not. What we are trying to do here is break a circle of brutality.'

Cordelia sighed, for the first time letting the emotion show. 'Do you know what Euclides wants to be when he grows up?'

I shook my head.

'A policeman.'

By the time we reached the car, I was hot, sweaty, dirty and tired. I was also profoundly dispirited. I felt sick.

'You know your *favela* deal isn't going to change that,' I said. 'A few roads and a lick of paint won't help those kids.'

Isabel sighed. 'I know. But it's a start. And we have to start somewhere.' She looked back up the hillside through the smoked windows of the car. 'Deep inside the soul of this country, there is a disease. It's some kind of brutality. It's like a virus. It replicates itself through generations, from child to drug dealer to policeman to child. Cordelia deals with its symptoms. I'd like to think that something like the Favela Bairro project deals with its causes. But after seeing kids like Euclides I just feel like giving up. Sometimes I wonder why I shouldn't just ignore the problem like everyone else. But we have to try. We absolutely have to try.'

I recalled the tough little boy with the big smile, and tried to imagine what adulthood would hold for him. If he ever made it that far.

'Euclides is a funny name for a kid, isn't it, anyway?'

'Brazilians can be very imaginative in naming their children,' Isabel replied, 'especially in the *favelas*. Cordelia looks after a skinny five-year-old called Marcos Aurélio.'

I smiled briefly at this, but only briefly. The *favela* had depressed and angered me. How could something like that exist in a supposedly civilized country like Brazil? How *could* so many fabulously wealthy people live so close to such poverty? You couldn't really blame the Brazilians – indeed many, like Cordelia and Isabel, were doing their best. Yet I was still angry with them, and angry with myself as well for accepting what I saw around me. But what could I do? What could anyone do? I longed for the simple answers of my more naïve past.

We drove on out of the *favela*, and into a green suburb of white houses hiding behind high walls and electronically laden iron gates.

'I admire your sister,' I said.

'I admire her. And I love her. But I think she's stupid. Stupid!'

I glanced over to Isabel. Her cheeks were flushed. 'I know she's doing good, a lot of good. But she's going to end up dead. God, I hope she gives it up when she has the baby.'

'Do you think one of the kids will kill her?'

'No, not them. She's a sitting target to be kidnapped. That's a popular sport here in Rio. And you heard all that stuff about the police and the death squads. How do you think they feel about their victims escaping? Cordelia's had death threats. They've tried to burn down the shelter.'

'But she won't give up,' I said. I'd seen the determination in Cordelia's eyes.

'No,' said Isabel. 'She says that they wouldn't dare do anything to her. Because of who our father is, and the high media profile she has, it would be counter-productive for the death squads to do anything. It would start a public outcry against them.'

'Do you think she's right?'

A tear glistened in the corner of Isabel's eye. 'I pray she is. But one day some off-duty policeman is going to decide that enough is enough.'

'Can't your father stop her?'

'No one can stop her. Not him, not her husband. Don't get me wrong. If she wasn't my sister, I'd think she was doing a tremendous thing. But she is my sister . . .' Isabel rubbed her eye.

'I think I would be very proud of her if she were mine,' I said carefully.

Isabel glanced at me for a moment, and gave me a small smile.

'Um, Isabel?'

'Yes?'

'Would you have dinner with me tonight?'

Isabel met me in the lobby of the hotel wearing the simple black dress she had worn when she had gone out with her friends a couple of nights before. It suited her perfectly, complementing the smooth graceful glide of her body as she walked.

'Let's have a drink by the beach,' I said.

'Fine. Lead the way.'

Outside, the Avenida Atlântica was lined with hookers in skimpy tops and tight shorts leaning against the backs of parked cars, hoping to entice passing trade. We stopped outside one of the many little kiosks that lined the edge of the sand and ordered a couple of beers.

We sat and watched the world go by. We exchanged a few words, but it was difficult. I wasn't sure whether Isabel was shy, or being evasive, or both.

A little boy of about four came up and stood beside us, offering us chewing gum. He had a delicate face, and large brown trusting eyes. '*Não, obrigado*,' I said, and tried to shoo him off, but he took no notice. Then Isabel spoke some sharp words of Portuguese to him. Wordlessly he turned away from us and approached the next table. The barman left his post, clapped his hands and sent the child on his way.

We fell silent. The boy was Oliver's age. I wondered

if he would turn into another Euclides, a twelve-year-old hit-man with attitude.

Just then a woman with a puffy face and dyed blonde hair, who had been drinking a *caipirinha* sloppily at the table next to us, staggered to her feet. She lurched a few yards and threw up on the sand.

'Let's go,' said Isabel. 'I knew there was a reason I preferred Ipanema to Copacabana.'

We ended up at a fish restaurant just back from Ipanema beach. It was crowded and lively, with a menu I couldn't understand but wine I could.

'I liked your father,' I said. 'He's a nice guy.'

'Yes, he is. He just drives me crazy sometimes.'

'Did you always want to be a banker like him?' I asked, pouring her a glass of wine.

She glanced up at me. Her large liquid eyes considered me, weighing up how much to tell me. I held her gaze, although it was difficult to maintain a dispassionate expression rather than just stare.

Then she gave me that quick smile, and replied, 'No. I hated banking when I was a student. I thought the last thing I would ever do would be to become a banker. I was sickened by what I saw around me. Poverty surrounded by wealth. So I wanted to do something about it. Attack the root causes, not just treat the symptoms like Cordelia.' She was relaxed now, talking much more freely. 'You know how it is when you're twenty. You think that if only the world knew what you knew, then it would be a better place. So your job is just to explain to everyone how stupid they are.'

'I know just what you mean,' I said. 'I used to be convinced that if the government ran the economy for the benefit of all the people, not just the rich gits, everyone would be better off. Then I went to the Soviet

86

Union for two years. It was quite difficult to stay a socialist after that. In the end I just gave it all up and read books instead.'

'I was fascinated to hear you talk to my father about that,' Isabel said. 'I mean I like reading books, but you're in love with them. Just like Papai.'

'Yes, I do love literature. Especially Russian literature. It seems to speak directly to the soul. Economics is all bullshit. It's all about understanding money, and no one ever gets the right answers anyway. But when I read a poem by Pushkin, I feel that I have glimpsed some deeper truth about humanity. And I can read the same poem again and again, and learn something new each time.'

I had always loved reading. When I was a child, I had friends enough to play with outside the house but no one within its four walls. So I read. It became more than just a pastime, or even an escape into an imaginary world. Books became my security, my family, my home.

A waiter hovered on Isabel's elbow. She ordered.

'So what on earth are you doing here, now?'

I smiled. 'I need the money. And I want to see if I can do it. Don't get me wrong, I don't want to spend the rest of my life in the City. Just a few years, enough to earn a lot of money. And then I'll go back to reading and teaching.'

'And will you be able to do it?'

'I think so. What do you think?'

Isabel studied me for a moment. 'Perhaps. But I'm not sure you'll want to.'

'What do you mean?'

'Well, you're intelligent, you pick things up incredibly quickly, and you do well with people. But to succeed in this business you need a killer instinct. And I'm not sure you've got it.'

For some reason, this criticism bit into me deeply. It was what I had half feared, and it was what I was out to prove was wrong.

'Believe me, when I want to do something, I do it,' I said. I meant it as a bold statement, but it came out a bit like a whine.

The corners of Isabel's mouth twitched. Her eyes mocked me. 'You're just too nice a guy for this game.'

'Grrrr. Cancel the fish. Give me a raw steak.'

Isabel shook her head. 'You don't convince me.'

'Well, what about you, then? Do you eat government officials for breakfast?'

'I surprise myself sometimes. And them.'

'So how did you end up in this business? I mean Dekker isn't exactly the World Development Fund, is it?'

'You're right. After I left university here in Rio, I studied development economics in the United States. At Columbia. And I guess I came to the same kind of conclusions as you. There was very little real difference that I could make.'

'But why banking? I mean, wasn't that a total sell-out?'

'It was to do with my father.'

'He put pressure on you to go into the family business?'

'No. Far from it. Now, if I had been a son, that would have been different. Papai always wanted a son, I'm sure, but my mother died before she could give him one.'

I had wondered about Isabel's mother, but I hadn't liked to ask. 'I'm sorry,' I said.

Isabel shrugged. 'I was only two. It would have been nice to have known her, but . . .' Her eyes wandered off into space for a moment. 'Sorry. Anyway, I was a girl, and girls of my father's class get married before they are twenty-five to men of good family. Education is OK, and perhaps a job for a couple of years, but not a career.

'Now in the States I saw women who were making careers for themselves in all sorts of different fields. They were becoming lawyers, bankers, doctors. But not me. I wasn't supposed to do any of that. And then I found out that the man I was supposed to marry, Marcelo, was messing around with one of my friends while I was in New York!'

'Oh dear.'

'Yes. Oh dear. So I decided to make my own career in banking, in my father's business. I joined Banco Evolução in São Paulo. But it's difficult to be a woman and a banker in Brazil, especially if you have a father like mine. So I went to work for Dekker three years ago. Since then, I've won them fifteen bond mandates in Brazil.'

'Not bad.'

'I must sound terrible,' Isabel said. 'I'm not really a radical feminist. I'm just proud. And stubborn.'

'And you like to annoy your father?'

For a moment I thought I had gone too far. 'I love him,' said Isabel defensively.

'I know that. I could see that when you were with him. And he adores you. Maybe that's why you rub each other up the wrong way.'

Isabel smiled. 'That's exactly why. My poor father. Somehow he has no control over us. He must wish we were ladies of leisure like all his friends' daughters. Could you believe it when he offered me a job in the bank? "I'm sure we could find you something," he said. I mean, I know Horizonte is one of the most successful investment banks in Brazil. But Dekker dominates the whole of Latin America, for God's sake! And I'm responsible for most of their Brazilian business. And he thinks he can find some corner for the boss's daughter!'

Actually, I was jealous of Isabel for her father. His deep affection for her was evident. He was a banker yet, unlike my father, this did not seem to automatically exclude all interest in other things. It's true that his love of Russian literature appealed to me, but I was sure Luís could speak knowledgeably about a wide range of topics that would leave my father looking blank and uninterested. You don't choose your parents. But Isabel seemed to have taken hers for granted.

'You are pretty good at this banking business,' I said. 'I'm very impressed with this *favela* deal.'

Isabel blushed. 'Thank you.'

'It's good to see a case of international capital genuinely providing a solution for poverty.'

'We don't know whether it will work yet but, yes, it is. It's probably the most satisfying thing I've done in my career so far. But that's the exception rather than the rule. You just wait till you have to gouge a competitor's eyes out to win a deal providing finance for a local bank to dodge taxes. And you won't have to wait long.'

'We'll see.'

At Isabel's suggestion I ordered a fish I had never heard of and that neither she nor the waiter could translate.

'You've seen my father,' she said. 'What about your parents?'

'I don't see them much,' I said. 'My father was in finance too.'

'Well, then,' she said. 'You know what it's like.'

'I'm afraid my father's a very different kind of man from yours,' I said. 'Or, at least, he seems that way to me.'

'What do you mean?'

'Well, he worked for an old British stockbroker. Much like Dekker Ward used to be, I would imagine. He had lunches with his friends, gave his customers good tips, and then when his firm was bought out by the Americans in 1986, he retired to a small village in Norfolk. You know, on the east coast.'

'I've been there,' said Isabel. 'It's cold.'

'It certainly is.' I smiled. 'He spends all day in his garden or reading the paper. I think at first he tried investing his retirement money on the markets, but he lost most of it so he stopped. I've never found it easy to talk to him, and I suppose I've given up now.'

'What does he think about you joining Dekker Ward?'

'I don't know. I haven't told him.'

'You haven't told him!'

'No. Awful, isn't it? He always wanted me to go into the City, and I always refused. I can't face telling him I've finally succumbed. I'll tell him next week. Or the week after.' I took a gulp of wine. 'I'd love to have the relationship you have with your father. But we find it difficult to talk. My father doesn't understand my life at all, and although I'm sure my mother could if she wanted to, she chooses not to discuss it. So I gave up.'

We were silent for a moment. I watched Isabel expertly parting the white flesh of her fish from the bone, biting her lower lip in concentration. Her skin glowed in the candlelight.

Then she spoke. 'Nick, I'm sorry about being a little

cold with you earlier. It wasn't very fair of me. And it has nothing to do with you. Nothing. It's just that I've got myself in trouble with men at Dekker before, and I don't want to let it happen again.'

'I understand.' I thought of what Jamie had told me about her and Eduardo. How could this woman possibly have had anything to do with him?

'Your friend Jamie, for example.'

'Oh, yes?'

'Yes. He kept on trying to ask me out. He made a pass at me twice.'

'Oh, that's nothing,' I said, laughing. 'He was just flirting. He's very happily married. You've nothing to fear from him.'

'I don't know about that. I'm Brazilian. I know all about flirting. I can tell when a guy is just having fun, and when he really means it. And, believe me, your friend Jamie really means it.'

I looked at her sharply. She must be mistaken. 'No. He always used to chat up women. He just wants to make sure he can still do it, that's all.'

'Nick, I think he wants to prove that he can do more than just chat them up.'

I shook my head. 'I'm sure you're wrong.'

'OK. He's your friend. You know him best. I'm just glad I'm not his wife.'

Despite my protests, Isabel had planted some seeds of doubt. I hadn't been able to understand what Jamie had against her when he had warned me about her. Had he tried his luck and been rejected? It did fit. But Jamie was a good friend, and so was Kate, and I just didn't want to think that there was any infidelity there. If that meant I had to bury my head in the sand, so be it.

Isabel could see my doubt and irritation. She put her

hand on mine. 'I'm sorry, I shouldn't have told you that. It's just that after Marcelo, and um – ' She broke off. 'After Marcelo, I'm not very impressed with unfaithful men. I probably judged Jamie too quickly. Please forgive me.'

That wasn't difficult. 'I forgive you.'

And so our conversation eased gently into the night.

Some time after midnight we spilled out of the restaurant, and headed for the sea, only a couple of blocks away. We crossed the road, pushed our way through the throng of people along the pathway, and headed down to the water itself. The beach was floodlit, and a game of foot volleyball was in full swing. The skills of the players amazed me, rally after rally of three touches, with head, chest or feet.

We walked all the way down to the water, watching the foam beat rhythmically on to the sand, the flecks of salt water picked out brilliant white by the floodlights. We took off our shoes and padded along the strip of wet sand at the water's edge, letting the strongest, most adventurous waves wash over our toes. On one side was the dark sea, on the other the life and lights of Ipanema. We didn't speak. The beauty of the night hung around us. I wanted to walk for ever with Isabel along that beach.

We were approaching the *favela* I had seen tumbling down into the sea the day before, a mass of pinpricks of individual electric lights. It was quieter and darker at this end of the beach, down by the shore.

Suddenly we were surrounded by figures, small, thin and lithe. I don't know where they came from. There were four of them, I think. Instinctively, I tried to move in front of Isabel, but I was stopped by a long thin knife, an inch from my chest.

I glanced at Isabel. She was standing still. 'Don't move!' she said, in a voice of surprising calmness. 'Give them what they want.'

A kid of about fourteen waved his blade in front of me, and said something in Portuguese.

'OK, OK,' I said. Slowly, I reached into my trouser pocket, and produced some notes. It was a healthy bundle. Fortunately I had left my wallet at the hotel, with my passport, as Isabel had suggested.

The kid snatched the money. Isabel was carrying a cheap shoulder bag, and she slowly handed that over.

I began to relax. They'd got their money. Now they'd let us go.

The kid in front of me tucked the notes into his pocket, keeping his eyes on me all the time. He didn't move, standing there, still. He was half my age, much smaller than me, but he had a knife, and he certainly knew how to use it.

I sought his brown eyes with mine, but they flicked away. Then his thin shoulders tensed. I knew what he was going to do. I started to turn, but I was too late. The knife flashed, and I felt a hot piercing pain in my chest. Isabel screamed. My hands flew to the hilt of the knife. The kid tried to pull it out, but I clung on to it, determined not to let the blade leave my body. My chest was on fire. It hurt to breathe, but I kept trying, short gasps, each one agony. My legs buckled underneath me, and I sank to the ground, pulling the knife and the kid with me. He yanked a couple of times, and then gave up, letting me slip down to the sand.

'Nick! Nick . . .' Isabel's voice faded into darkness.

8

I had my own room in the hospital, and it was clean. Isabel had made sure of that. She had secured a well-qualified doctor who had pronounced that the knife wound, although deep, wasn't dangerous. It had missed my heart, but nicked my lung. There had been some internal bleeding, but this had been minimized because the knife had not been withdrawn. The lung itself had not been badly damaged, and would heal quickly. He had stitched me up carefully, so the scarring would be minimal. Rio doctors were, apparently, experts with a needle and thread. I had woken up with a tube down my throat, which they soon took away, but my breathing was still painful. The doctor wanted to keep me in hospital for a couple of days to make sure no infection took hold, and to give me time to recover from the shock of the attack.

I needed it. There was a steady, dull, persistent pain in my chest, but that wasn't the problem. I felt weak and my brain was fuzzy. My body was telling me to lie still.

Isabel was in and out all the time. I got the impression she was organizing everything in the background. A plain-clothes policeman came to see me. Isabel translated. She had obviously already given him all the information she could, and there was nothing I could add. She said that the police were particularly tough on locals who attacked foreigners: it was bad for the tourist trade. Someone would suffer for this crime. Whether it would necessarily be the kids who had committed it might never be known. The Rio police's justice was arbitrary.

Her father also came to see me. He said he felt guilty that this had happened to me in Rio, his city. It was comforting to know that Isabel and Luís were looking after me. The thought of dealing with the Rio police and medical system alone, wounded, and speaking no Portuguese, scared me.

Ricardo called me on Sunday evening to wish me well. He said I was lucky to be in Isabel's hands. I agreed with him.

They let me out of hospital at lunch-time on Monday, on condition that I spent the afternoon at the hotel. I was beginning to feel much stronger. Isabel suggested I stay at the hotel on Tuesday and fly home that evening, but I asked her if I could join her at the Ministry of Finance. The deal was nearly finalized, and since I had come all this way, I wanted to see it through. Or so I told her. More than that, I had enjoyed having Isabel around, and I wanted to prolong the experience as long as possible.

We were supposed to be meeting Humberto Alves at nine thirty on Tuesday morning, and we arrived ten minutes early. By eleven he still hadn't seen us. Isabel was becoming agitated.

'Half an hour late is OK. It's normal. But an hour and a half? I don't know. Something's wrong.'

And it was.

Eventually Humberto called us into his office. He

bade us sit down, and began to pace up and down. He fussed over me, which was fair enough, but he took much longer than necessary.

'Humberto. What's wrong?' said Isabel in the end, in frustration.

He ran his hand through the remnants of his hair, and glanced at Isabel nervously. 'We've decided to appoint Bloomfield Weiss as lead-manager of the *favela* deal. We've asked them to invite you into the deal as a co-lead-manager, and they've agreed.'

'You've what?' shouted Isabel, leaping to her feet.

Humberto edged round behind his desk, and glanced down at its sparkling top. 'We've asked Bloomfield Weiss to lead-manage the deal.'

Isabel shouted at him in a stream of Portuguese. He tried to answer, but it was no good. Eventually he sighed. He glanced at me. 'OK,' he said, in English. 'You deserve an explanation.'

Isabel perched on the very edge of Humberto's small sofa, poised at any moment to leap off and go for his throat. Humberto sat uncomfortably opposite us.

'Well?' Isabel's eyes were alight.

'OK, I know this deal was your idea all along. And we had given you the mandate. We'll reimburse all your expenses.'

'I don't care about the expenses, it's the deal I want!' cried Isabel.

'I know. If it was up to me, I would have gone ahead with you.'

'Don't give me that bullshit. It *was* up to you!'

Humberto winced. 'Not exactly.'

'So who has a problem with us? The Mayor? The Governor? We know them well. We've done a lot for them over the last few years.'

'No, not them.'

'Who then?'

'The World Development Fund.'

'Jack Langton?' Isabel paused. This obviously made more sense to her. 'What's his problem?' she said, in a quieter tone.

Humberto relaxed a touch. 'I don't know. He said that if the World Development Fund were to guarantee the deal, then Dekker Ward couldn't be the lead-manager.'

'Why couldn't we? Did he say?'

Humberto shrugged. 'He said it was policy. Something to do with the WDF's global funding strategy. He says they are worried about the monopoly Dekker Ward has in leading bond issues in Latin America. They think it would be a good idea to have a choice of several sources of funds, and the best way of doing that is to insist on another lead-manager.'

'But why Bloomfield Weiss?'

'Apparently, they are the biggest lead-manager of the WDF's global deals. And, besides, no one else was willing to take the deal from you. Which sort of underlines Jack Langton's point, don't you think?'

'No, Humberto, I don't think! No one else took the deal because it would be completely unethical to do so when we had done all the work. Bloomfield Weiss were the only firm dirty enough to try.'

'Look, Isabel, I fought for you. I pushed hard. But Jack wouldn't move. And you know we can't possibly do this deal without the WDF guarantee.'

Isabel stood up. 'Humberto, I'm disappointed in you,' she said, her voice quivering.

'There's one other thing Jack said that I didn't understand,' said Humberto.

Isabel waited.

'Apparently the WDF have information that Dekker Ward has a relationship with some of the narco-traffickers that control the *favelas*. That makes it difficult for them to use you, they say.'

Isabel turned on her heel and stormed out of the room.

I was a bit slow following her. I was just about to nod and smile at Humberto when I realized that this would be inappropriate, so I gave him a sort of stiff little bow instead, and rushed off to catch up with her.

Our taxi fought its way back towards our hotel.

'Bad news,' I said.

Isabel put her head in her hands. 'Very bad news. I can't believe it!'

'But they did ask us to be co-lead-manager.'

Isabel shook her head. 'That's an insult. We'd never go into a deal Bloomfield Weiss took from us. Ricardo will be furious. Once Bloomfield Weiss show the market they can steal a deal from under our noses, everyone will be doing it.'

'Can we talk to the World Development Fund?'

'There's no point. Bloomfield Weiss will have more influence with them than we have.' She stared glumly out of the window.

'If I ask you something, will you promise not to kill me?'

'No,' she said, 'I'll promise no such thing.' But she looked at me curiously.

I went ahead anyway. 'Aren't they right? I mean, isn't it better for the World Development Fund to have a choice of investment banks to lead their deals in Latin America?'

'Don't worry, I won't kill you,' said Isabel, with a

small smile. 'Yes they're absolutely right. And, in fact, I'm surprised this hasn't happened before now. We couldn't dominate this market for ever. Nevertheless this is a bad day for us. If only it had been anyone else but Bloomfield Weiss!'

'There's something else I don't understand,' I said. 'What was that at the end about how Dekker deals with narco-traffickers in Rio?'

Isabel snorted. 'That's rubbish. I know about all Dekker's Brazilian business and, believe me, we don't go anywhere near drug dealers.'

I thought about Martin Beldecos's fax and Francisco Aragão, who according to United Bank of Canada was a Brazilian money-launderer. But I decided not to contradict her just then.

I joined Isabel in her room as she rang Ricardo. I had never seen her so tense. She explained what had happened, and answered some questions concisely. Then there were some monosyllabic yesses and nos, and she hung up. She sat on the chair by the desk in her room, and rubbed her face in her hands.

'I take it he wasn't pleased,' I said.

She looked up. 'I've never heard him so angry.'

'What's he going to do?'

She frowned. 'He's getting on a plane down here tonight. He'll be in Rio tomorrow morning. He says he'll sort everything out.'

'Oh.'

'Not exactly a vote of confidence, is it?' Isabel muttered. 'But I can't blame him.'

'How can he sort this out?'

'I've no idea. We'll just have to see.'

Isabel and I waited for Ricardo in the lobby. Isabel had

checked whether his plane had landed on time. It had. We waited in silence, Isabel clearly nervous. I didn't feel quite so bad – after all, I was so inexperienced that I could hardly be held to blame. But I felt for Isabel, and every now and then I gave her a smile of encouragement, which she seemed to be grateful for.

It felt odd, sitting in this smart hotel, five thousand files from the School of Russian Studies, waiting for a bollocking. It was cool in the lobby, and it was the cool that made it feel exclusive. Outside it was hot, sticky and noisy. Outside was where ordinary tourists and ordinary *cariocas* fought their way through the fumes, noise and heat of the city. Outside was also where people were attacked with knives. Inside was where the people with money sat, safe and dry in their suits in the cool.

A car drew up, and the tall slim figure of Ricardo stepped out. He didn't look at all as if he had spent the night on a plane. His tie was neatly knotted over a crisp white shirt, and his suit looked as if it was on its first day out from the tailor's. A doorman brought in his two cases, a small overnight bag and a large briefcase.

Isabel and I stood up nervously.

Ricardo saw us and smiled. 'How are you, Nick?'

'OK. A bit sore. A bit shaken.'

'I bet. You were very lucky, I hear.'

'Yes, I was. Although it was bad luck to be attacked in the first place.'

Ricardo shook his head. 'First, Martin in Caracas, and now you here. Travel really is getting dangerous, these days.' Then he moved over to the reception desk. 'Just wait here a minute while I check in,' he said. We did as we were told.

He spent a moment filling in forms, and then he returned. 'Let's get a cup of coffee, shall we?'

Breakfast was almost over, but they let us have a table with some coffee. Ricardo took his jacket off, sat back in his chair and sighed. He closed his eyes and stretched. Then he leaned forward and looked Isabel in the eye.

'OK. First thing. I want you to know that I was very impressed with your work on the Favela Bairro deal. It's just the sort of creative work that we want to do at Dekker.'

'Thank you,' whispered Isabel, surprised and relieved.

'We've lost the deal because of those arseholes at the World Development Fund. I don't know if there's anything you could have done to prevent that. In any case, it's too late to worry about it now. But I do not like the way Bloomfield Weiss stole the deal from us. They have to know that I, personally, will not let them get away with it.'

Isabel and I both nodded. Whatever you say, Ricardo.

He looked at his watch. 'Let's see, it's ten o'clock now. I've arranged a meeting with Oswaldo Bocci at ten forty-five. That just gives us time to finish our coffee.'

Oswaldo Bocci's office was on the top floor of a cylindrical glass building with the words *TV GoGo* emblazoned over the entrance. It had one of those great Rio views that I was beginning to get used to, this one was of Guanabara Bay peeking out behind other prestigious offices. The chairs were light blue leather, and abstract art adorned the walls in a profusion of tropical colour. A few Indian artifacts dotted the large room, many of them figurines with pendulous breasts or prominent genitalia. They were all pretentiously displayed and labelled.

Bocci himself was a powerfully built fifty-year-old with jet black hair and a forceful chin. He wore an open-necked silk shirt, which stretched tight over his well-defined torso. Gold glittered from his hands, his neck and his left ear. The scent of his aftershave clashed with the fragrance of the exotic flowers in a tall vase by his desk.

Ricardo had told me about Bocci in the taxi. Apparently he was one of a number of Brazilian media entrepreneurs who wanted to challenge Roberto Marinho's Globo empire for dominance of the hearts and minds of the people. So far he had successful papers in Rio and Minas Gerais, and he had launched a TV station from scratch in the Rio area that was ahead of plan. He had done all this with money provided by Dekker.

He was pleased to see Ricardo, was polite to me, and leered at Isabel. She ignored him vaguely.

After a quick discussion of Flamengo's chances of winning the state soccer championship, Ricardo came to the point. 'We need your help, Oswaldo.'

Bocci's eyes lit up, and he smiled. It wasn't a generous smile: he scented a trade of favours, a deal. 'Anything I can do for you, my friend.'

'You've heard about this Favela Bairro project?'

'I have.'

'And what do you think of it?'

'I'd say it's boring. I think we are against it, but I forget why. Wasting taxpayers' money, adding to imprudent borrowing, that kind of thing.'

'I have some interesting information about the deal.'

'Really?'

'Yes. The Finance Secretary has been in discussions with the local drug gangs that control the *favelas*. Most of the money will end up going to them although, of course, Humberto Alves will get some. A scandal, don't you think?'

Bocci rubbed his large chin. 'Maybe. I don't know. Where's the evidence?'

'Oh, you know. Anonymous sources in banking circles.'

'So you knew about this?'

'We discovered it,' said Ricardo. 'And so we pulled out of the deal. We left it to another house who were prepared to turn a blind eye.'

'Who was that?'

'Bloomfield Weiss, the American investment bank.' Ricardo paused, watching the other man. 'So, what do you think?'

'It's a scandal, sure. But it's not a really big scandal. And there's no hard evidence. I don't know.'

'OK, I understand,' said Ricardo. He pulled out a cigarette, and offered one to Bocci who took it. They both lit up. 'So, how's business?'

Bocci blew some smoke to the ceiling and smiled. 'Great, great. TV GoGo's doing very well. The format is really working – popular commercial TV for the people. Viewers understand that. And so do advertisers. After twelve months we're way ahead of the figures we gave you in our forecast.'

Ricardo smiled. 'I know, I've seen the numbers. It's always nice to see people exceeding their projections. It doesn't happen very often, I can tell you.' He took a thoughtful drag on his cigarette. 'Tell me, do you think this format would work in, say, São Paulo?'

Bocci's eyes locked on him. Ricardo held them, unblinking.

'I'm sure it would. Of course, we'd need the finance.'

'How much?'

'Fifty million dollars.'

Ricardo nodded. 'I'm sure we could raise that for you. You'll need some time, of course, to draw up detailed plans. But give Isabel a call when you're ready, and we'll sort something out.'

'I'd need to be sure we could raise the finance. Don't you have to talk to investors and so on?'

Ricardo waved his arm dismissively. 'Oh, of course we'll have to do all that eventually. But I'm certain I can get you the money, Oswaldo. And my word is better than any piece of paper. You know that.'

Bocci smiled broadly. 'Good.'

'Now,' said Ricardo, 'have you decided what editorial line to take on this *favela* business?'

So, it was all settled. The *favela* deal was destroyed. Bloomfield Weiss had learned their lesson: you don't steal a deal from Dekker and get away with it. With our mission accomplished we could all go home now.

I was seething. I couldn't believe what Ricardo had just done. I could see Isabel was angry too. But she couldn't exactly say anything: if she hadn't let Bloomfield Weiss win the *favela* deal it would still be alive. Ricardo must have been aware of the way his two colleagues felt, but he seemed to take no notice.

We left Bocci's office, picked up our bags from the hotel, and made our way to the airport in painful silence. We were, of course, in first class. Ricardo checked us in. I was dismayed to see I was sitting next to him. Isabel was in the aisle opposite.

Dinner on the plane passed in silence. Ricardo read through a stack of papers. He had one of those extra-large briefcases that lawyers often use. A standard-sized briefcase wouldn't give him enough fuel for a two-day business trip. I stared out of the window at the black sky. I realized that Ricardo hadn't even spent one night in Brazil. It had only taken him an hour to finish off what Isabel and Humberto had taken a year to create.

After the attendant had cleared away my dinner, I eased my chair back and pretended to go to sleep. It was difficult: my chest was sore, and I could hear the gentle rustle of documents and the insistent scratch of pen on paper next to me.

Suddenly banking had become brutal. An idea that would improve the lives of thousands had been squashed because of jealousy over who would take the credit for it. I stewed, and my agitation grew. Eventually I couldn't stand it any more. I opened my eyes, and reached into my own briefcase for a book. It was *Islanders* by Yevgeny Zamyatin, a Russian writer who had spent a couple of sad years in exile in Newcastle building ships just before the First World War. I was lulled by the music of the prose; in my mind Zamyatin was the closest the twentieth century had come to Pushkin's mastery of the language, although he lacked Pushkin's absolute precision. *Islanders* was a satire of the hypocrisy and moral emptiness of the capitalist industrial England he had found. He didn't know the half of it. He should have got a job in a bank.

Then I remembered Zamyatin had ended his life in abject poverty in Paris.

'How's your Argentine trade going?'

'What?' I lifted my head from my book, and blinked at Ricardo.

'I said, how's your Argentine trade doing?'

I didn't give a damn how the Argentine trade was doing. Actually I did. I hoped it was losing Dekker lots of money. But I had just the sense not to say that. I knew that not taking a trading position seriously would be tantamount to quitting, and I hadn't decided whether I wanted to do that yet. 'It hasn't moved all week.'

'Do you still believe in it?'

What a ridiculous question. I could believe in God or Marx or even Thatcher. But how could I believe in bonds?

I took a deep breath. 'From what I knew at the time, the Argentine Discounts seemed good bonds to buy. But since I only had two days' experience upon which to make that judgement, I have to say that I have very little confidence that it was the correct one. The only thing that makes me feel I might have got it right is that you bought the position yourself. I trust your judgement. If you haven't sold the position, I still believe in it. Have you sold it?'

Ricardo smiled. 'I like the fact you're aware of your own limitations. But it was a good choice. And you're right, I wouldn't have put on the position if I hadn't agreed with you. As a matter of fact, I haven't sold it, I've bought more. A lot more.'

'That's good. I hope it works out well,' I muttered, and turned back to my book.

We sat in silence for a while, but I was aware of Ricardo's eyes on me. 'It's been a tough week for you, hasn't it? First being attacked, and then losing the *favela* deal.'

'It has,' I mumbled.

'It must be very frightening to be attacked like that.'

I glanced up at Ricardo. His eyes were sincere. So sincere. As though he had been knifed himself.

'It was,' I said. 'First we were just walking along the beach. And then suddenly I had a knife sticking out of my chest.'

Ricardo nodded. 'Brazil's a cruel country. It has this wonderful exterior, but underneath it can be brutal. It's a great shame. That's one of the reasons the *favela* deal was such a good idea.'

I hadn't wanted to be drawn on this, but I couldn't help myself. 'Then why did you destroy it?'

'I had no choice. I couldn't let Bloomfield Weiss win that mandate. It would have meant the end of Dekker Ward.'

'Oh, come on. We would still have had the largest share of the market. And something would have been done about those *favelas*. Now, all those people will just be left to crawl around in their own garbage.'

'I'm not responsible for the social conditions of Brazil, or any other country for that matter,' said Ricardo, calmly. 'Over the last hundred years Brazil has had the same access to capital, natural resources and labour as Canada and the United States. The reason it's a poorer country is entirely to do with the Brazilians and how they have decided to use or misuse those resources, not with me.'

I listened, making no attempt to hide the cynicism I felt.

'My responsibility is the success of Dekker Ward,' he went on. 'I've built it into one of the most successful investment banks in the world, but the moment I sit back, the moment I let anyone else take the initiative, it will all be over. Oh, of course, we all make out it's a friendly market, and that all the other guys are happy to let us run things. But they'd love to see us trip up. They'd love it even more if they could take over from us. My biggest fear is that we get complacent.'

His blue eyes bored into mine. 'There comes a time when you have to play tough. Bloomfield Weiss should not have stolen the deal from us like that. They were playing tough. I had to show them, and everyone else, that I could play tougher.'

'And what about the children in those *favelas*?'

'If the Favela Bairro idea is as good as we think it is, it will get financed eventually. And, remember, it was Dekker who brought international capital back to Latin America when every other bank in the world had turned their back on it. We've organized more than twenty billion dollars of finance for the region. You know how badly these countries need that capital. And they're using it properly now, investing to create jobs, and improve infrastructure.'

He saw the doubt in my eyes.

'OK, I won't pretend that's the main reason why I've built up Dekker into what it is now. But it's an important result of what I've done, and I'm proud of it.'

'And what about all the money you make?'

'Oh, come on, Nick! You told me that was the reason you wanted to join us.'

'Yes, but – '

'But what?'

'I wanted money to do something. To buy myself freedom to do what I wanted with my life.'

'And?'

'And . . .' I hesitated, trying to find the right words. 'I just think that, at places like Dekker, money seems to be an end in itself.'

Ricardo rubbed his chin. 'I know what you mean.

But it's not quite what it seems. As I keep saying, I like people who are hungry, people who *need* to make money for themselves. Then they end up making it for the firm as well, and the firm grows. And that's good. But I don't think it's greed, exactly.'

'What is it, then?'

'Money is the score. I suppose I just want to have the highest score when it's all over.'

'And when's that?'

Ricardo smiled. 'Good question. I'm not sure. I suppose for me it's a game without end.'

We fell silent for a moment, thinking about what the other had said and both surprised at how personal the conversation had suddenly become. I remembered the T-shirt I had seen in the *favela*: *Who dies with the most toys wins*. Ricardo's game was played all over the world, by rich and poor.

He waved to an attendant, and asked for a Cognac. I ordered a whisky. We both sat back in the huge first-class seats, and sipped our drinks.

'My father played the game and lost,' Ricardo said.

'Jamie said he's a businessman in Venezuela?'

'Was. He died about fifteen years ago.'

'I'm sorry.'

'He was a deal-doer himself, in the oil industry. He came to Caracas from Argentina in the fifties, and built up quite a portfolio of interests. But then he over-stretched himself. It was nineteen eighty, just after the second big oil-price hike. He thought oil was going to forty dollars a barrel. It went down to six. He always used to drink, but after that he drank more. He died four years later. He left us with very little in the end, so we had to make our own way. Which I'm proud of.'

'Did he teach you much?'

'The truthful answer is no. We didn't really see much of him, he was always away doing deals, and I was away at school in England. But I think I inherited his nose for a deal. I just hope I know when not to go too far.'

'So you think you're competing against him?'

Ricardo thought this over for a moment. 'In a way, yes. I would have liked him to have seen what I've achieved. He never gave me much praise when he was alive, perhaps he would now.'

'And your mother?'

'Oh, I don't think my mother knows what I do, or cares. As long as I have enough money to keep her bank balance healthy.'

'What about Eduardo? Does he take after your father too?'

Ricardo smiled ruefully. 'Eduardo inherited a different set of characteristics from our father.'

I desperately wanted to ask Ricardo what those were, but there was something in his tone that suggested I had already gone far enough. He was a fascinating man, and I felt privileged that he had allowed me to learn more about him. But was he just manipulating me with his frankness? If so, I could feel it working.

Ricardo put down his glass, and turned to me. 'Look, I know you find what you've seen difficult to take. I know you're questioning the whole premise of what we're doing. And I respect that. Honestly. I would rather have people who question first principles than those who blindly do what everyone else does. So think about it. But don't pretend that you can work in finance, take the rewards and avoid the tough decisions.'

His blue eyes held mine. They were sincere. I knew he believed in what he was saying. And those eyes were inviting, persuasive, almost hypnotic. Join me, they said.

'I want you to work for Dekker. You'll be right in the middle of the most exciting market in global finance today, and you'll have a hell of a lot of fun too. I think you can do a lot for us. But you need to be committed. If you don't buy into what we're doing, then go back to your Russian books. You decide.'

I swallowed. I remembered that when I had originally taken the job at Dekker I had played through this dilemma in my mind. Then I had decided that if I was to succeed in finance, I would have to accept the ethical system that came with it. And it wasn't immoral, just amoral. As Ricardo had said, the reason that Brazil was in such a mess was that the Brazilians had made it that way. The same could be said of Russia, that other great sprawling, chaotic country. Isabel's father had liked Tolstoy's story of the Master and Man, and its nobility was appealing. But the Master had been foolish to insist that he and his servant drive on in the snow instead of waiting at the inn for the storm to clear. And, in the real world, masters just didn't give up their lives for their servants.

Then I thought of Cordelia, and the tense little boy with the big smile and the hard eyes, and I turned my back on Ricardo towards the dark mid-Atlantic sky.

9

I received quite a welcome when I arrived at the office late on Friday morning. Dave, Miguel, Pedro, Charlotte, people whom I hardly knew, all came up to ask how I was. Although I had been at Dekker less than two weeks, and had spent barely three days in the office itself, they treated me as one of their own. I had to admit, it was a good feeling.

The plane had landed at lunch-time the previous day and, unlike Isabel and Ricardo who had gone straight into work, I had returned to my flat. I saw my GP first thing the next morning. She was impressed with the Brazilian doctor's work, changed my dressing and told me to take a week off work. There wasn't a chance of that, but in deference to her I left my bike at home and took the tube and the Docklands Light Railway into Canary Wharf. I hated it, and vowed to cycle in on Monday, however much my chest hurt.

I was disappointed to see that the desk next to me was empty. Isabel was out somewhere.

But Jamie was in the office and it was good to see him.

'What a trip! Are you OK? Where did you get stabbed? Can I look?'

'No, you can't!' I said. 'I just got it strapped up this

morning and I'm buggered if I'm going to take it all off for you.'

'OK.' Jamie feigned disappointment. 'What happened?'

He, of course, had none of the reticence of the others about asking me that question, and I didn't mind answering him.

'Jesus!' He shook his head. 'One inch one way or the other and that would have been that.'

'I'm afraid so.'

'So how are you feeling?'

'I'll be all right,' I said. 'Or, at least, the knife-wound will be. But did you hear what Ricardo did?'

'About the *favela* deal? He killed it, didn't he?'

'Yes. I couldn't believe it. After everything that Isabel had done. I saw one of them, you know. A *favela*. Someone's got to do something about them.'

'I know,' said Jamie. 'It must be tough for her. This game gets rough sometimes.'

'And there's something else.' I reached down into my bottom drawer to dig out the fax to Martin Beldecos. It wasn't there.

'That's funny,' I said.

'What is?'

'I left a fax just here before I went to Brazil. I'm sure I did.'

Jamie made as if to get up and go.

I held up my hand. 'No, wait. It's important.'

Jamie watched me as I ransacked my desk. Not there. I thought about whether I might have put it somewhere else, or taken it home, or to Brazil.

No. It had definitely been in that bottom drawer. And now it was gone.

'What was it?' asked Jamie.

I stopped my search and sat up. 'It was a fax from United Bank of Canada in the Bahamas to Martin Beldecos. It said that the man behind one of the accounts he had been investigating was linked to a suspected money-launderer.'

'Really? Did it say which account?'

'Something about International Trading and Transport (Panama). Or, at least, they were the company that had paid the money into a numbered account at Dekker Trust in the Caymans.'

'That makes sense,' Jamie said. 'It would have been very difficult to trace.' He appeared thoughtful.

'What exactly is money-laundering?' I asked.

'It's the washing of dirty money,' replied Jamie. 'The money might come from drugs, or smuggling, or organized crime, but it's mostly drugs related. It's often easier for the police to trace the cash rather than the drugs, so criminals have become very sophisticated at hiding the source of the money and then investing it anonymously. They usually use shell companies in offshore jurisdictions.'

'Like the Cayman Islands?'

'Like the Cayman Islands. Or Panama, or Gibraltar, sometimes even the Channel Islands or Switzerland. There are dozens of possibilities. Some of the money-trails get very complicated.'

'I see,' I said. 'And Martin Beldecos discovered one of these money-trails.'

'Perhaps.'

'So what do you think?'

'About what?'

'What should I have done with the fax? Which has now disappeared, by the way. Eduardo said if I received any more messages for Martin Beldecos I should give them to him personally. I'm just not sure about giving him this one.'

'Why not?'

Jamie's lack of concern unsettled me. Maybe I was imagining things. 'Well, in case he already knows about it,' I said uncertainly.

'Hmm.' Jamie was thinking. 'I see what you mean. And, anyway, he'll have a fit if you then tell him you've lost it.'

'I haven't lost it!'

'Then where is it?' asked Jamie.

'Jamie, I promise you I haven't lost it. Someone must have taken it while I was in Brazil.'

That shut him up. He thought for quite a while. Finally, he said, 'If I were you I would forget all about it.'

'Why?'

'I fear you may be right. It wouldn't surprise me if Eduardo has some money-laundering business going on the side. It's common enough in our world. And the last thing he would want is for you to pop up and cause trouble for him. He would not be very happy.'

'But what if he doesn't have anything to do with it?'

'Then it won't do any harm to let things lie.' Jamie saw the doubt in my eyes. 'Look, millions of dollars of drug money is laundered through the banking system every day. There's some in every bank everywhere. The only time there's a problem is when a bank gets found out. It's not like anyone's being hurt or anything. It's not even a fraud. No one's losing money. Just let it drop. This is going to bring nothing but trouble if you talk to anyone about it.'

'But I don't want to cover anything up,' I said doubtfully.

'What are you covering up?'

'The fax.'

'What fax? You haven't got a fax. If there was a fax, it wasn't to you. Look, Nick, forget it. I'm going to.' He stood up.

'Jamie?'

He paused.

I hesitated before putting words to the thought that was forming in my mind. 'Martin Beldecos suspected that there was money-laundering at Dekker. He was murdered in Caracas. Then I begin to suspect it, and I nearly get killed in Rio.'

As the words came out, I felt stupid. Paranoid. And Jamie's scornful look made me feel worse. Then his face softened. 'Nick. After what happened to you, it's natural you'll feel nervous. I'm sure they'll understand if you don't want to travel to South America for a bit. And who knows? Maybe there is some dirty money tucked away in a corner at Dekker somewhere. But don't blow it out of proportion. Calm down and do your job. You'll be OK.'

With that he walked off, leaving me feeling uncertain, embarrassed, and a little silly.

10

Ricardo's house was a rectangular Georgian manor, built of yellowish stone, with smooth lines. It stood on the brow of a small hill, with a cluster of cottages and a church bowing at its feet. I wondered what the locals thought of the new people in the big house. Jamie drove us up a long drive, which cut a swath through a wide expanse of lawn. The gardens were designed for ease of upkeep rather than beauty. There were shrubs and trees, but few flowers. Some of the finest cars that Germany could produce fought for space on the gravel apron in front of the house, and Jamie nosed his British Jaguar in among them, next to the only other interloper, Eduardo's Ferrari.

Ricardo was having a party for everyone at the office. These were apparently regular affairs, and this one had been planned weeks in advance. Jamie told me it was a three-line whip, but I was happy to go anyway. He and Kate had agreed to pick me up from a nearby station.

Inside, the house was furnished in the traditional way but the walls of the hallway and drawing room were adorned with large brightly painted pictures of Brazilian scenes. Most of the flat surfaces supported weird and exotic sculptures, which seemed to combine Amerindian and modern abstract styles. It worked. They filled

'Hallo,' she said, in a husky, almost cracked voice, holding out her hand to shake mine. 'Are you Jamie's friend?'

'That's me, I'm afraid.'

Ricardo turned to Kate. 'Of course, you must have known Nick for quite a while.'

'Nearly ten years. In fact, I've known Nick for longer than Jamie.'

'Oh, really? You met at Magdalen?' Trust Ricardo to remember my college.

'No, the Cowley Road.'

Ricardo laughed. 'I remember it well. Was Brett's Burgers still around when you were there?'

Kate smiled. 'It certainly was.'

'Well, we can't quite compete with that. But grab yourself a burger, or anything else you'd like.' He waved towards the barbecue, rather incongruously tended by two men in white coats. 'There's some good red wine somewhere about, or you can stick to champagne if you prefer.'

He noticed Kate's glass half filled with water. 'Or there's a man somewhere with elderflower *pressé*. Try some. It's good.' With that he drifted off.

'How the hell does he know about Brett's Burgers?' I whispered to Kate. 'He wasn't at Oxford, was he?'

'No,' she replied. 'But he knows everything. And I mean everything. You'll get used to it.'

Then Kate turned to Isabel, and Luciana to me. 'I hear you had an unpleasant first visit to my country,' Luciana said. She stood very close to me. Although she was well made-up, I could see the lines round her mouth and eyes. They were hard eyes. But at this range her chest was impossible to miss by any heterosexual male over the age of twelve.

I scrambled my brain into order. 'Yes, it was. But Rio's a beautiful city. The most beautiful I've ever seen. Are you from there?'

'No, São Paulo. But my father had business interests in Rio, and we have a house there. My brother spends much of his time there now.'

'What does he do?'

'Oh, I'm not sure. Francisco calls himself a financier, but I don't know what that actually means. I have two others – one runs the family businesses in São Paulo and the other is a candidate for the state government.'

So, Luciana had a brother called Francisco who was some kind of financier. Interesting.

'Don't you miss Brazil?' I asked.

'Of course I do. And I go back quite often. But what can you do? I met Ricardo when we were young, in America. We were in love. We got married.' She smiled. 'It's not so bad. And I have my business.'

'What's that?'

'Interior decoration. I have clients in London, Paris, New York. Normally they are from Latin America. They want to decorate their houses with things that remind them of home. I like to create a sophisticated modern interior with a Latin theme. Something that reflects the personality of the Latin in northern Europe. You saw the drawing room?'

'I did. I liked it. You couldn't do something with my flat, could you?' I said.

'I'd love to. But I'm afraid you couldn't afford me.' She grinned teasingly at me over the rim of her champagne glass.

I blushed. I couldn't help it. 'Yes, well,' I said. 'Perhaps I'll stick to Ikea and Dulux.'

She laughed. 'Tell me what you saw in Rio.'

So I told her. And I told her honestly, about the *favelas*, about Cordelia's shelter, about the kids who had attacked me. She listened. She was interested. She certainly wasn't stupid. I was flattered to have such a beautiful, sophisticated and, let's admit it, voluptuous woman hanging on my every word.

Suddenly I was interrupted. '*Oi*, Luciana, *tudo bem*?' Isabel leaned in front of me, and kissed Luciana on both cheeks.

'*Tudo bem*,' she replied. 'You know, Nick, obviously.'

'Yes, we've just come back from a trip together,' Isabel said.

'Oh, you went together, did you? You didn't say it was Isabel who showed you all this, Nick.'

It was true I hadn't. I shrugged.

'Well, I'll leave you to him,' Luciana said, flashing me a coy smile, and she drifted off to entertain someone else.

'It looked like you two were having an interesting conversation,' said Isabel.

'We were, actually.'

'She was all over you. She's old enough to be your mother.'

'No, she's not.'

'She's forty-two.'

'So? My mother's fifty-eight.'

'She'll eat you alive.'

'Hold on,' I said. 'Isn't she Ricardo's wife?'

'Yes. When she sees him. Which, given his working hours, is virtually never. The rest of the time she is her own woman.'

'So you say.'

'So a significant number of the younger men here say. Just ask your friend Jamie.'

'Isabel!'

'Sorry.'

'It's a bit risky fooling around with the boss's wife, isn't it?'

'You're right. Most of them turn down her charms. They know what would happen if Ricardo ever found out.' She looked at me pointedly as she said this.

'Well, thank you for the careers advice.'

I smiled to myself. Beneath the banter she was jealous. I hadn't meant to provoke her, but it felt good to think that she cared about me. I looked up and saw she was smiling at me. I wanted to pull her to me and kiss her. The problem was there were forty other people standing around. Another time. Another time soon.

'How's your chest?' she asked.

'Still a bit sore, but healing fast,' I answered.

'Good.'

'Thank you for looking after me so well in Rio. I don't know how I would have managed without you there.'

She smiled. 'If you live in Brazil, you need to know how to work the system. There is always a *jeitinho* to get things done. I'm an expert.'

'Well, I'm very glad of that.' I looked around the English garden and up at the back of the house. 'This isn't the kind of place I would expect Ricardo to own at all.'

'It's not so surprising. Many people in South America like to have a farm in the country. We have one, for instance. And you know what they say about the Argentinians?'

'What do they say?'

'They're all Italians who speak Spanish and pretend to be English.'

'Ross is hardly an Italian name, is it?'

Isabel's eyes twinkled wickedly. 'No, but Rossi is.'

'Huh? No!'

'Just a thought.'

I switched my empty glass for a full one from the tray floating past, and grabbed an orange juice for Isabel. She was driving. So were at least half of the other people at the party, I thought, but that didn't seem to make much difference to them. They liked to break the rules in that as in everything else, I supposed.

'Can you believe the women here, Nick?' It was Dave, the Romford trader, waving a can of beer. Miguel, the tall Argentinian, was at his elbow. 'Oh, sorry, Isabel, present company included, of course. I don't know where they get them from. Miguel thinks that that Danish bit with Carlos is his au pair.'

To my disappointment, Isabel slipped away, out of my peripheral vision.

'So where's his wife?' I asked.

'At home with the children, I imagine,' said Miguel. 'Someone has to look after them, after all.'

'Are you getting one of them, Mig?' Dave asked.

'What, an au pair? But I haven't got any kids.'

'So she'll have more time to devote to her other duties, then.' Dave leered, and lifted the can of beer to his lips.

Miguel shook his head. 'I pity Teresa. That's Dave's wife, you know,' he explained to me. 'A perfectly nice woman, she just has this little problem with her eyes, that's all.'

'Oi!' Dave squawked loudly.

Miguel winced. 'And her ears.'

The party warmed up, and I began to enjoy myself. Dave and Miguel were an unlikely double act, but very funny once they had a few drinks inside them. Eduardo even honoured us with his presence, bringing in tow a German model, barely out of her teens, who didn't seem to speak much English or Spanish. This didn't seem to bother Eduardo overmuch. He, too, was charming and friendly, but I noticed that everyone tensed in his presence.

A good while later Kate swayed over towards me. Or she might have walked in a straight line, and I might have been swaying.

'I've had enough,' she said. 'I'm off. I can't stand much more of this, and if I leave now I'll get home in time to put Oliver to bed. Jamie says he's staying. He'll take the train back. Will you look after him?'

I frowned, trying to decide whether I should go with her.

She saw what I was thinking. 'No, you stay here. You shouldn't leave early, but I can. And I'd be happier if you kept an eye on Jamie.'

'That I've done before.'

'OK, see you.' She put a hand on my arm. 'Isabel's nice,' she said, winked and was gone.

An hour or so later, as people began to disperse, I phoned for a taxi to take us to the station, and then I went in search of Jamie.

He wasn't inside from what I could see, nor was he in the garden. I caught sight of Isabel. 'I'm off now. See you tomorrow.'

'Oh, goodbye. It was nice to talk to you.'

It was a polite thing to say, but I was sure she meant it. 'Yes, it was nice,' I said. And then, 'Have you seen Jamie?'

'Oh, yes,' she said. 'He went that way to look at a statue with Luciana. That was about half an hour ago.' She gave me an amused glance.

'A statue?'

'Yes. Apparently there is a statue of Hercules in the wood. One of the Victorian owners of the house removed his equipment. Luciana has had a replacement specially made. I believe she's very proud of it.'

Christ! Kate had said keep an eye on Jamie and I hadn't. But to try to do something with the boss's wife at a party with everyone from work would be foolhardy. Insane. Just the kind of thing Jamie when drunk *might* do.

I hurried out of the back garden round the side of the house, trying to make as much noise as possible, so as not to surprise them doing something I didn't want to see. A little copse of trees stood discreetly back from the house, with a path winding through it. It was beginning to get dark.

'Jamie!' I called. Too loud. Someone might hear. Someone other than Jamie.

I found the statue. No sign of Jamie or Luciana. But I wasn't surprised to see that Luciana hadn't stinted in returning Hercules his manhood. He was now a very proud statue indeed.

'Jamie! It's Nick! Come on.' I crashed through the undergrowth, and eventually spilled out in front of the house. There was Jamie in a little group with Luciana, Eduardo and Pedro, standing right by the taxi. They were all smiling, all tipsy.

'Ah, Nick! There you are!' he called, with a broad grin. 'I've been looking for you everywhere! Our taxi's here.'

I was too embarrassed to go back in and say goodbye to Ricardo, but I thanked Luciana, who drew me close to her for a kiss on both cheeks.

'It was very nice to meet you, Nick,' she purred. 'Come and see my designs some day.'

'I'd love to,' I said, and bundled Jamie into the taxi.

The *favela* deal was dead. Bocci's papers carried the scandal over the weekend. It harmed Humberto Alves and the Mayor, but there wasn't enough in it to do them serious damage. Brazilians had found a new enthusiasm for rooting out corruption; they had even successfully impeached a president. But there was nothing that really surprised the city in this story: everyone assumed that this kind of thing was still going on. Besides which, Rio's mayor, assisted by Humberto, had done much to clean up the municipal finances and the city was not about to throw them over because of one unsubstantiated scandal.

For Bloomfield Weiss things were different. International banks dealing in Latin America have to be scrupulous about keeping their reputations clean. Gringo financiers make easy targets for accusations of corruption, as Bloomfield Weiss were finding out. They couldn't risk more damage to their reputation by going ahead with the deal. So they pulled out.

The Dekker machine continued to operate as if nothing had happened, bringing bond issues to market, spreading rumours, buying, selling. I watched Jamie work: it was all beginning to make more sense to me now. But we were both subdued. We didn't mention the *favela* deal, money-laundering or where he and Luciana had got to at the party the previous day.

But our activities in Brazil were not only marked by Bocci's newspapers. A small article in *IFR* caused a ripple round the dealing room when it was first noticed. It was in the gossip column, where the following week's events often first appeared as unsubstantiated rumour.

An English banker working for London-based Dekker Ward was in Brazil last week. Nicholas Elliot was walking on Ipanema beach in Rio de Janeiro late at night when he was attacked by a gang and stabbed in the chest. Elliot is understood to have recovered well from his ordeal.

Not so his colleague, American citizen Martin Beldecos, who was murdered in his hotel room in Caracas last month, ostensibly by thieves. Two such attacks so close together demonstrate the increasing dangers facing bankers travelling to South America. However, there may be a more sinister explanation. Sources inside Dekker Ward say that Martin Beldecos was working on verifying the origin of funds received by Dekker Trust, Dekker Ward's Cayman Islands affiliate. There are rumours in Caracas that Beldecos's murder was not the result of a random burglary gone wrong, but a contract killing. A spokesman for Dekker Ward denied this, and spoke of the shock felt by the whole firm over the tragedy, and their sympathy for Martin Beldecos's family.

Jamie scanned the article and threw me an anxious glance. 'That wasn't you who talked to them, was it?'

'No,' I said. 'But it's interesting, don't you think?'

'It's just gossip. The real trouble will come when Eduardo finds out who has been talking to *IFR*. Watch out, here he comes.'

Eduardo was walking across the square to Ricardo's desk, clasping his yellow copy of *IFR*. They conferred for a few minutes, and then Eduardo broke away.

'Shit! He's coming this way,' whispered Jamie.

He was indeed, a large dark presence, brows knitted in anger.

'Follow me,' he growled at me, barely pausing to slow down as he passed Jamie's desk.

I did as he asked, into the opaque corner office.

'Sit down,' he said.

I sat.

He strode round his desk and sat facing me, his large shoulders hunched over the plain white pad of paper in front of him.

'Well?'

Initially cowed by his presence, I now began to feel angry myself. I had done nothing wrong. I wasn't a schoolboy. I shouldn't be intimidated like this.

'Well, what?' I replied, looking him in the eye.

'Did you talk to *IFR*?'

'No.' I kept my voice calm.

Eduardo leaned back in his chair and fixed his eyes on mine. They were large, dark and angry, but like Ricardo's they seemed to bore straight into me, threatening me to tell the truth, daring me to lie.

'No one is allowed to talk to the press at Dekker Ward without permission,' Eduardo said. 'And to spread this kind of rumour is a betrayal to everyone who works here. Dekker Ward has worked hard to keep a spotless reputation in Latin America. This kind of rumour can do us untold harm. Do you understand?'

'I understand very well,' I said. 'As I said, I haven't spoken to any journalists. I don't even know any financial journalists.' The anger rose in my chest, and seemed actually to cause my wound to throb. 'A week ago I was stabbed in the chest while I was on business for Dekker Ward. I deserve your trust. In fact, I expect your trust.'

Eduardo watched me with his thick lips pursed. 'I hope you're telling the truth,' he said, 'because if you're not – '

I'd had enough. 'Of course I am!' I said. 'Now, if

you'll excuse me.' I stood up and left the room, feeling Eduardo's glowering eyes on my back.

Jamie was right. There was no way I was going to tell Eduardo about Martin Beldecos's fax.

During the morning, a number of other people were called into Eduardo's office, including Jamie. The atmosphere in the office changed noticeably. I was not the only one who was angry.

Just before lunch, Ricardo emerged from Eduardo's office and perched himself on Jamie's desk.

'Nick, I suspect Eduardo was a little rough on you this morning,' he said.

I nodded. 'He was. And without cause. He has no reason to think that I talked to the press. And it was me who was stabbed.'

'I know. And I'm sorry. I appreciate that. I trust you and Eduardo trusts you too. It's just it doesn't look good for the firm to be linked to a drug-gang murder, and I think my brother was a little angry about it. Don't worry, you're doing a good job and we know that. Let's just forget it, shall we?'

He patted me on the shoulder, and walked over towards Dave and Miguel, who both looked like they had had a hard time too.

I glanced at Jamie. 'Eduardo does this every now and then,' he said. 'Loses his rag and throws his weight around. Then Ricardo has to calm things down. At least this time it looks like no one got hurt.'

I was still angry. But soon something happened which took my mind off money-laundering, Martin Beldecos's murder, and Eduardo. The Brady battle.

11

The battle started at seven fifteen on Wednesday morning. We started it. Or rather Ricardo did.

The battlefield was my Argentine Discount bond issue.

These bonds had been born out of Argentina's Brady plan, named after the US Treasury Secretary, Nicholas Brady, who had sponsored the original idea. During the early 1990s, the banks who had lent billions to Latin America agreed to swap their defaulted loans for bonds, which could then be traded. These became known as Brady bonds. In the next few years most of the major Latin American countries had undergone a Brady plan, leaving over a hundred billion dollars of Brady bonds outstanding. Needless to say, Dekker had a lot of fun trading them. The Argentine Discounts, or 'Argy discos' as they were known, were one of the three classes of bonds created out of the Argentine Brady plan in 1992.

After the usual round of comments from everyone, Ricardo told us his idea. 'As you guys all know, Argentina has been cheap for a while, and it's getting cheaper. There's no good reason for it. Cavallo's peso plan is working and their banking crisis is under control. We're not going to see another Mexico meltdown down there.' He was referring to the crisis that had hit Mexico after the disastrous devaluation of its currency in December 1994.

'The discos are cheap. We know that the Shiloh Fund has been offloading a ton of them into the market. So that's where we'll move. Pedro and I have picked up two hundred million so far, but that's just a start.'

I caught my breath. Two hundred million! Ricardo hadn't been exaggerating when he had told me he had bought a lot of bonds. I couldn't help feeling a little proud. Of all the bonds in all the world, Ricardo had picked mine to do a number on. I listened in anticipation.

'Now, the Discounts are the smallest of the three Argentine issues with just over four billion dollars outstanding. That's still quite a lot of bonds, but we think that up to three billion is locked away by people who won't sell at these prices, mostly because they'd have to book a loss. So if we pick up four or five hundred million we should really move the market. Get these bonds trading where they should be.'

There was a chuckle from the assembled group. 'I like it,' said Dave.

'Do we cut in our customers yet?' asked Jamie.

'Not quite yet,' said Ricardo. 'We'll edge up our bids on the discos today to see what we can pick up. But don't encourage your accounts to sell unless they really have to. You don't want to look fools tomorrow. Any other questions?'

Nothing.

'Anything else?'

Carlos Ubeda, the head of Capital Markets, spoke up. 'Yes, one thing, Ricardo. We need to bid for the Mexican deal tomorrow. Two billion dollars, five years.' Carlos meant that Mexico wanted to borrow two billion dollars from the markets through a bond issue, and they had asked us to quote them a price at which we would lead it.

'Two billion! I thought they only wanted one. That's huge. Why so much?'

'They've got a lot of debt to repay this year. And you know the Mexicans. They like to show the world that they can do bigger deals than anybody else.'

'This is hardly the time for it. What price do you think will get it?'

'I think we might need to go inside ten per cent.'

Ricardo winced. 'That's tight.'

'The competition's tough.'

'OK, everyone. Ask your customers what they're hearing about Mexico. See if we can find out what price the competition are talking. But make sure that they know we think it should be at least ten per cent.'

The meeting broke up. I followed Jamie to his desk.

He grinned at me, his eyes twinkling, and rubbed his hands. 'We're going to have some fun today.'

He picked up the phone to his old regulars. He was calm as if this was just any other day, but the calls were crisper than usual. Less chat.

He ran through our prices with Chris Frewer of Colonial and Imperial, a London-based fund manager.

'Heard anything about a new deal for Mexico?' Jamie asked.

'Yeah. Bloomfield Weiss say they might be bringing a big one.' Frewer was English, and he sounded the same age as Jamie and me.

'Oh, yes? Any price talk?'

'A touch over ten per cent. Are you involved?'

'Are we involved?' Jamie snorted. 'Of course we are. I'll let you know when I hear more.'

'Hold on! Before you go, did you say sixty-eight and a half bid for the Argy discos?'

'That's right.'

'Is that good for ten?'

'Good for ten, good for fifty,' Jamie said. He dropped his voice to a whisper. 'But if I were you I wouldn't rush into anything this morning.'

'Oh, yes?' A note of interest had entered Frewer's voice. He wasn't stupid. 'And why not?'

'Well, I could give you a lot of economic bullshit, but I don't want to waste your time. Let's just say they're going up.'

Frewer thought for a moment. 'OK. I'll hold off and watch.'

'Sound decision. But, Chris?'

'Yes?'

'You won't go off and *buy* any yet, will you?'

Frewer laughed. 'Of course not. Keep me posted.'

As Jamie put the phone down, I asked him something that had been bothering me. 'Are we being fair?'

'What do you mean?'

'Building up a position in a bond issue before recommending it to our customers.'

Jamie smiled. 'We're not trading British Telecom on the London Stock Exchange. You're on the wild and woolly shores of the emerging markets here. This is the law of the frontier. That's exactly how guys like us make money.'

'Ah.'

The sandwich man came round, and I grabbed a bacon and avocado on ciabatta. I fetched us both a cup of coffee. But we didn't stop dialling and talking. Then, at about one, I heard the familiar hand-clap. I looked up. Ricardo was standing in the middle of the square of desks, making a T sign with his hands. Time out. The hubbub swiftly died down as all the phones went on hold. Everyone turned to watch him.

'OK, *compañeros*, we've got three hundred and forty million of the discos at an average price of sixty-eight and a half. It's time to go public. Tell your most favoured accounts first. Charlotte will release a research report in an hour's time. Any bonds Pedro gets from now on he'll use to fill customer orders. We want to cut our friends in. By now we should have hoovered up all the bonds dumped by the Shiloh Fund. From now on we'll be taking the Street short, so the price should start to move.'

The group stirred in anticipation.

'Now, anything on Mexico?' Ricardo asked.

'They're talking a smidgen over ten per cent,' said Jamie.

'And who's in the market?'

'Bloomfield Weiss, apparently. They say they're confident they'll get the deal.'

Ricardo frowned. 'Well, keep your ears to the ground. And don't let anyone even *dream* of a yield of less than ten per cent.'

The meeting broke up and Jamie went straight on to his favoured customers. Chris Frewer chuckled and bought twenty million. By this time New York, Miami and all the South American cities were in. Andrea Geller at a small New York hedge fund bought another twenty. And Alejo bought fifty.

Alejo was Jamie's biggest account. He was a serious punter. He worked out of Miami, but he ran the money of one of Mexico's wealthiest families. Needless to say the deals were booked through one of the Dekker Trust numbered accounts. Jamie had apparently cultivated

Alejo as a client during his previous job at Gurney Kroheim, and had taken him with him to Dekker.

Alejo's fifty was done at a price of sixty-eight and a half.

'I thought you said the price would go up,' I said to Jamie.

'Don't worry,' he said. 'Give it time. This is good. We've got our people in at a good price.'

I looked round the room. It was buzzing. People were buzzing, phones were buzzing, bonds were buzzing. It was intoxicating. The Dekker machine was in action and it seemed unstoppable.

But it turned out Dekker's wasn't the only machine in action that day.

'I'm sixty-eight offered in the discos!'

It was Pedro. We turned to look at him. He was talking rapidly to Ricardo, who was frowning.

'What's going on?' Dave shouted.

'I don't know!' said Pedro, running his hands over his close-cropped hair. 'I'm getting hit with bonds from all directions!' He grabbed a phone. I watched as he hunched over it, and slammed it down.

'Hey, Pedro! Where do you offer ten discos?'

Pedro rubbed his chin. 'Sixty-seven and a half!'

The price tumbled. Pedro kept lowering his price, and he kept being sold bonds. We could see the green figures on the screen in front of us winking. Sixty-seven and a half. Sixty-seven. Sixty-six and a half.

'Jesus!' whistled Jamie. 'We've got to own five hundred million by now.'

Five hundred million! And a two-point loss. I did the sums. 'That's ten million we're down.'

Jamie nodded grimly.

Ricardo strolled over. He leaned down next to Jamie.

'I don't know what's going on here. Kent has spoken to the Shiloh Fund, and they're definitely cleaned out. Someone is selling a lot of these bonds. We need to find out who.'

'I'll see what I can do,' said Jamie. He thought a moment and then called Frewer at Colonial and Imperial.

Chris Frewer was angry. 'What's going on? I wanted to sell some bonds this morning, and somehow I seem to have ended up with twenty million more than I started with, and the price is off two points. I hope I haven't made a mistake here.'

'Relax. Ricardo's on to it, I promise. But look, do me a favour.'

'Fat chance,' said Frewer. 'I want out of Argentina.'

'You will be out. In a couple of days. I just need to work out what's going on.'

'You should bloody well know what's going on!'

'Chris. Trust me. Ring Bloomfield Weiss, and ask them what they think of the discos. Say you're considering buying some.'

There was silence as Frewer thought about it. Jamie clung tight to the receiver and winced. 'OK, OK,' Frewer said, finally. 'I'll be back.'

'I hope this one doesn't blow up in our faces,' said Jamie. He sat still, staring at the phone, not touching it. Nothing was more important than Frewer's call. We waited for five minutes. It seemed like an hour. Then the direct line to Imperial and Colonial flashed and Jamie pounced. 'Yes?'

'Bloomfield Weiss hate it. They told me they've got some bullshit computer model that shows that the discos yield half a per cent less than they seem to. The guy's faxing it over now.'

'You couldn't fax me a copy when you get it, could you?' Jamie asked.

'All right,' said Frewer. 'But what am I going to do with my discos?'

Jamie winked at me. 'Well, they're two points cheaper. Why not buy some more? Off Bloomfield Weiss.'

'Are you sure about this?' Frewer asked.

'Course I'm sure. As I said, Ricardo's on the case.'

So Frewer trotted off to buy twenty million more bonds from Bloomfield Weiss.

But first he sent through his fax. I was waiting by the machine, and took it over to Jamie. It was written by a Ph.D. and used all kinds of arcane mathematical language to prove that the method that everyone was using to calculate the yield on Argentine Discounts was all wrong. I didn't understand a Greek letter of it. But I did understand that Bloomfield Weiss were trying to screw us.

'This is all crap!' Jamie said.

'Do you understand it?'

'Of course not. That's the whole point. Let's show it to Ricardo,' Jamie said.

We crossed the square to Ricardo's desk. He was on the phone, but when he saw the look on Jamie's face, and the way he was holding the fax, he put it down. Pedro, too, hung up. Pedro's short dark hair was plastered to his forehead. He was not having a good day.

'What have you got?' Ricardo asked.

Jamie handed him the fax.

'*Carajo*!' Ricardo muttered, and handed it on to Pedro. Then to me. 'Can you give a copy of this to Charlotte? We need one of her people to come up with a response. The quants out there will want some numbers to get into.'

I nodded, but hovered. I wanted to hear what Ricardo was going to do. He let me stay.

'OK, so Bloomfield Weiss are doing their best to screw us,' he went on. 'They're flooding the market with bonds, and bad-mouthing the deal to try to get their customers to sell. They want to hurt us. And they have ten times our capital to do it with. Where are the discos trading now, Pedro?'

'Sixty-six and a half to sixty-seven.'

'And we've got what, eight hundred and fifty million?'

'Eight hundred and fifty-six.'

This was turning into a gigantic struggle. We were buying hundreds of millions of dollars of bonds and Bloomfield Weiss were selling even more. The price was going down. That meant there were more sellers than buyers. It meant Bloomfield Weiss were winning.

And Bloomfield Weiss had more fire-power than us. With ten times our capital they could afford to carry a much bigger position than we could. We couldn't afford to buy discos for ever. Bloomfield Weiss could afford to sell them.

Now, for the first time, Ricardo looked worried. He was frowning deeply, and I noticed his wedding ring flying from finger to finger of his left hand. He called together some of the other traders, and told them what was happening. 'We can't let them win this one,' he said. 'It's much too public. The world can see what's going on here. That's why Bloomfield Weiss sent out this note. They want everyone to know that this is a struggle between us and them. Those bonds *have* to go up.'

'Can't we just keep buying?' asked Dave.

Ricardo shook his head. 'We're way over our limits already. We can hide some of it in Dekker Trust, but we can't carry a bigger position for any length of time. If we buy more, we have to know it will work.'

Jamie had explained to me that the regulators placed limits on the maximum size of any bond position. Dekker had developed all sorts of ways round these limits, but apparently Ricardo was only willing to go so far.

'This doesn't make sense,' said Dave. 'It's a four-billion-dollar issue, and we know three billion is locked away with accounts who will never sell. That leaves a billion, and we've got most of that. So where are Bloomfield Weiss getting their bonds?'

'They have to be selling short,' said Pedro. 'I would have known if they'd been sitting on that many bonds.'

'So they're borrowing them,' said Ricardo. 'From whom, I wonder.'

There was silence. Bloomfield Weiss had flooded the market with bonds, bonds they didn't own. Pedro thought they must have done this by *selling short*, which meant borrowing bonds from a friendly holder to sell. Of course, when this friendly holder wanted his bonds back, Bloomfield Weiss would have to buy them out of the market. Bloomfield Weiss's bet was that by then the price would have fallen so that they could make a large profit. And by that time, they might have forced Dekker out of the market, too.

It wasn't just fifteen to twenty million dollars at stake here, although that was important enough. It was the future of Dekker Ward in Latin America.

My brain raced. Over the previous couple of days I had read some back copies of the trade press from 1992 when Argentina had negotiated its Brady plan. I had particularly focused on the genesis of the Discounts.

'It might be US Commerce Bank.' My voice was hoarse, almost a squeak.

They all turned to me. They were listening.

I cleared my throat. 'US Commerce Bank. They were the biggest holders of Argentine bank debt in 1992. During the Brady plan negotiations, they insisted on swapping all their bank debt for Discounts, which they preferred to the other classes of bonds for some accounting reason. They may still have them.'

There was silence. Ricardo was watching me closely.

'Hey, Carlos! Over here!' Carlos Ubeda stuck his head up from his desk, and hurried over. 'US Commerce have been trying to break into our market for a while now, haven't they?'

'Yes. But they have no credibility. They were only in two deals last year.'

'So how would they respond to co-lead-managing the biggest deal of the year?'

'I think they'd jump at it.'

'I hope you're right,' said Ricardo grimly, and he picked up the phone.

I rushed off to make a copy of the Bloomfield Weiss fax for Charlotte. She was sure it was crap and she said she had a pet nuclear physicist who would be able to prove it. I went back to the square, to find everyone subdued, waiting. Frewer and Alejo called back, asking what was going on. Jamie stalled them charmingly. Pedro was getting hit with more and more bonds. The rest of us were lying as low as we could.

It took Ricardo several phone calls. Pedro was holding his price at sixty-six, but he was hurting.

Then, at about six o'clock, Ricardo put down his

phone and clapped his hands. The room fell silent, as all phones went on hold.

'It turns out Nick was right. US Commerce Bank have seven hundred million dollars of Argentine Discounts, all of which they've been happy to lend to Bloomfield Weiss. Until today, that is. In an hour, Bloomfield Weiss will receive a demand to deliver seven hundred million dollars of discos back to US Commerce by twelve o'clock tomorrow. And there's only one place they can get them. Here.'

You could feel the glee around the room.

Dekker Ward bought bonds long into the night.

Seven fifteen the next morning. I had slept little and I suspected few of the others had. But we all felt fresh, and ready to work. We gathered round Ricardo.

'OK, *compañeros*, we're up to a billion two,' he said. You could hear the collective intake of breath. This was big, even by Dekker's standards. 'The bonds are still sticking at sixty-seven. Bloomfield Weiss have been happy to sell us all we can buy, until just before the market closed last night in New York. Then they suddenly went quiet. We'll see what happens this morning.'

There were grins all round

'Now what about this Mexican deal?'

'The price talk seems to be ten and a quarter per cent,' said Miguel. 'And Bloomfield Weiss sound confident.'

'Well, we need to win this one,' said Ricardo.

Charlotte coughed slightly.

Ricardo held up his hand. 'Don't worry, Charlotte. I know Mexico's looking a little precarious right now. And this isn't the time I would choose to sell two billion dollars of their debt. But we're splitting the deal with US Commerce, which reduces our exposure. And today might just be the day we finish off Bloomfield Weiss in Latin America for good. So we go in at nine and three-quarters and we win the deal. OK?'

I saw Jamie wince. He would have to sell this Mexican deal. Even I realized it would be difficult at that yield. He half opened his mouth and then closed it.

'Good.' Ricardo rubbed his hands. 'Now, let's make some money.'

There was a lot of noise and activity in the room that day. But only two phone calls mattered. The first came through for Ricardo at eleven thirty. It was Bloomfield Weiss's head trader. It was rare for head traders to talk to each other like this, but he had no choice. He wanted to know where Dekker would offer seven hundred million dollars of the Argentine Discounts.

The room knew instantaneously what was happening. We were all quiet, all watching Ricardo.

'Seventy-two.'

A pause.

Then Ricardo put down the headset. 'Seven hundred million Argentine Discounts sold at seventy-two!'

A huge cheer met his announcement. In that second, thirty-five million dollars flowed into Dekker Ward's profit and loss account.

The second call was much later, about seven o'clock London time. Dekker Ward and US Commerce Bank had been awarded the mandate to sell two billion dollars of five-year United Mexican States eurobonds at a yield of nine and three-quarters per cent. The issue was to be launched the following Wednesday.

The Marketmaker had shut Bloomfield Weiss out of his domain. And we had a lot of bonds to sell.

12

The Brady battle tempted Lord Kerton out to Canary Wharf to inspect his victorious troops. He was Chairman of Dekker Ward, a post he had effectively inherited from his father twelve years previously. He and Ricardo had come to an arrangement. Ricardo had independence, his own offices in Canary Wharf, and fifty per cent of the profits he generated for himself and his people. Kerton had the other fifty per cent, and the satisfaction of seeing Dekker Ward grow to be the most successful brokerage firm in London. He and Ricardo treated each other with a mixture of civility and circumspection.

They strolled round to where I was sitting with Jamie.

'Jamie you know,' said Ricardo. 'But I don't think you've met Nick Elliot, one of our new hires. He was the one who worked out where Bloomfield Weiss were borrowing their bonds.'

My chest swelled with pride. I couldn't help it.

Lord Kerton shook my hand, and looked me in the eye. He was a tall, athletic man of about forty, with fair hair that curled over his ears and down the nape of his neck. He wore a double-breasted suit with a broad stripe. 'Jolly well done, Nick. Good to have you on board.'

'I'm enjoying it here.'

'Excellent, excellent,' he said, and then he was off, looking around curiously, as if he would suddenly discover the key to our extraordinary profitability lurking under a desk, or behind a screen, if he only looked hard enough. He was gone within half an hour.

'That was a bit like a royal visit,' I said to Jamie.

He laughed. 'That's about it. Kerton is just like a monarch. A useful figurehead with no power, who knows that if he makes a nuisance of himself he'll be overthrown. He's no fool. He realizes if he leaves Ricardo well alone he can just sit back and watch the profits roll in. Nice job, if you can get it.'

The phone light flashed. It was Alejo. He sold his Argentine Discounts back to Jamie for a four-point profit. Although most of the conversation was in Spanish, Alejo didn't sound very grateful. Chris Frewer had been much more enthusiastic that morning.

'Alejo's a miserable sod, isn't he?' I said.

'Yeah,' said Jamie. 'But he does some pretty big trades so I don't complain. You've seen what we've done over the last few weeks.'

It was true. Alejo had been in and out of the market many times in size. Big size. Like two hundred million sometimes. A customer well worth keeping sweet, however grumpy he was.

It only took me a few minutes to pedal the mile or so from the office to the bar where I had agreed to meet Isabel. It wasn't exactly a secret assignation. Isabel just didn't want to draw attention to us by leaving together, or by meeting up at the more convenient Corney and Barrow, a wine bar in Canary Wharf that some of the Dekker crowd used on a Friday night.

The bar was big and noisy, converted from a warehouse during the yuppification of the Docklands. It was full of young men and women in suits drinking designer beers. Some of them were on their way home west from Canary Wharf, and some were the new inhabitants of the area who had moved into the speculatively priced waterfront apartments. No sign of a true East Ender of course.

Even though I was wearing one myself, I still felt uneasy surrounded by this sea of suits. I was more used to the pubs around Bloomsbury or Kentish Town, where scruffier men and women talked in quieter tones over pints of bitter.

Isabel arrived a few moments after me. We hadn't spoken much during the week. I had spent most of the time at Jamie's desk, and Isabel had been very busy.

I was still pretty sure she really was nervous of starting a relationship with someone from work. This I could understand, even though I didn't necessarily like it. But I knew, with Isabel, there was no point in pushing my luck.

I ordered two extortionately priced bottles of Budvar, which seemed to be the local beverage of choice, and we perched on stools at the end of a crowded table.

'That was a long week!' I said, taking a swig of the malt-laden beer. 'In fact, so was last week. I feel like I've been at Dekker a year already. Is it always like this?'

'Basically yes,' Isabel said. 'There's always something going on.'

'Are you working on another *favela* deal?'

'Yes. São Paulo sound as if they might be interested.' She sighed. 'But it's hard to motivate myself to put in all that work after what happened to the Rio deal.'

'It must be,' I said.

'I still can't believe it!' Isabel's face reddened with indignation. 'Or I can believe it of Ricardo. That's just the trouble. OK, so I blew it. I lost the deal. But that's no reason to destroy it for the people of Rio!'

'I agree,' I said. 'I spoke to Ricardo about it on the plane.'

'What did he say?'

'He said that he knew the *favela* deal was a good thing. But he had to teach Bloomfield Weiss a lesson. He had no choice.'

'Bah!'

'I find it difficult to get used to,' I said. 'What I was doing before had a purpose that had nothing to do with making money. We were teaching something important. And we were trying to understand a bit more about literature and language. We were paid just enough to be able to do that. But now everything we do is to make money for us and our firm. So if it makes money we do it, if it doesn't, we don't, and if it makes money for a competitor, we destroy it.'

'What did you expect?' muttered Isabel.

'I suppose that's what I expected. It just takes getting used to.'

'It's a dirty business,' Isabel said. 'I hoped with this one deal I would finally be able to do something good as well as make money for the House of Dekker. Stupid of me.' She sighed. 'Still, there's no point getting depressed about it. We've just got to go on to the next deal. It's a mistake to question what we do too closely, Nick. You'll never like the answers.'

I knew she was right. In a perverse way it encouraged me that someone like Isabel, who seemed to share some of my misgivings about the money business, should have found a way to come to terms with it. I found the work at Dekker Ward fascinating, and I was determined to succeed. If Isabel could deal with her conscience, so could I.

But there was still one thing I wanted to ask her.

'Do you think Dekker is involved in money-laundering?'

She thought for a moment before replying. 'No, I don't,' she said. 'Ricardo sails very close to the wind, but he knows when to stop. Money-laundering is illegal. It can get you into too much trouble if you're caught. Ricardo has worked hard to maintain a reputation for being aggressive but always legal, and I don't think he would jeopardize that.'

I listened to her words closely. She seemed convinced of what she was saying, and I trusted her judgement.

'Why do you ask? That article in *IFR*?'

'Yes. And there was Jack Langton's comment about Dekker and the Rio drug gangs,' I said.

'I *know* there's nothing in that,' said Isabel. 'I know everything we do in Brazil.'

'Well, it's not just that,' I said. 'Do you know Luciana's maiden name?'

It was a question I had been meaning to ask someone ever since I had spoken to her at Ricardo's party. With all that had happened over the last week, I hadn't quite got round to it. Now I wanted to know the answer.

Isabel was puzzled, but she answered my question. 'Aragão. Luciana Pinto Aragão.'

'I thought so,' I said. 'So her brother is Francisco Aragão?'

'Yes. That's right.'

I had guessed as much. The Brazilian financier who had been mentioned in Martin's fax. The one under investigation by the DEA for drug-related money-laundering activities.

'What is it, Nick?' Isabel asked.

I told her about the second fax for Martin Beldecos, and about my suspicion that it had been taken from my desk while I was in Brazil. I also mentioned Eduardo's insistence that I tell him and only him if I received any more messages for Beldecos.

Isabel listened closely to every word.

'So what do you think?' I asked her, when I had finished.

'I don't know what to think.'

'Well, is something going on?'

'From what you've said, yes, there must be. But I still can't believe Ricardo is involved. It's not like him.'

'Francisco Aragão is his brother-in-law.'

'That's true. But Ricardo goes to great lengths not to deal with him. It's a policy I have no trouble with. Francisco has a bad reputation in Brazil. My father told me he's rumoured to be dealing with the narco-traffickers. Dekker have always steered well clear of him.'

'In public, yes. But couldn't Ricardo have set up an account at Dekker Trust in secret?'

Isabel looked doubtful. 'It would certainly be possible for him to do that easily enough. But I still don't believe he would. It would be against the way he does business. I know it sounds ridiculous, but Ricardo has his own set of rules, and he never breaks them.'

'What about Eduardo?'

Isabel thought for a moment. 'That's more likely. Eduardo doesn't believe in any rules.'

'And he's responsible for Dekker Trust, isn't he?'

'True. It would be easy for him to set something up.

There's just one thing not quite right with that, though.'

'What's that?'

'He and Luciana don't get on at all.'

'Hm,' I said. 'But this could be a strictly business arrangement. I can imagine Eduardo getting over his dislike of someone for money.'

'Maybe,' said Isabel. 'But he'd know his brother wouldn't approve.'

'If he ever found out.' Our beers were empty. 'Another?' I asked.

Isabel nodded distractedly. She was deep in thought over what I had said.

I procured two more Budvars from the bar, and returned. 'So what should I do?' I asked, as I took my seat. 'I haven't told Eduardo. Jamie says I should just forget the whole thing.'

'Difficult,' said Isabel. 'I think Jamie's right that you shouldn't tell Eduardo. There's too big a chance he's involved, and then you might get yourself into quite a dangerous situation.'

'You mean if he knew I suspected him of money-laundering?' I was concerned I had already got myself into that position already.

'Yes. But I think I *would* speak to Ricardo.'

'Wouldn't he just tell his brother?' I protested.

'He might. But I'd trust him on this. I don't think he's involved, and I think he'd want to know.'

Trust Ricardo? I wasn't quite ready to do that.

'What about going to the authorities?' I suggested.

Isabel inhaled through her teeth. 'Now that's something Ricardo would never forgive. If you spoke to them without speaking to him first, he'd feel betrayed. And he'd be right. No, I think you should talk to him.'

'Hm.'

'What will you do?' Isabel asked.

'I'll think about it,' I said. And I would. But I was pretty sure now that the wisest thing would be to keep quiet, at least for the time being.

My fears about Martin Beldecos's death and my own stabbing seemed more grounded. But I didn't want to discuss them with Isabel. She might think it all a bit melodramatic, and while I could live with looking silly in front of Jamie, I didn't want to appear paranoid in front of her.

But I did want to ask her about the man whom I was increasingly thinking of as my predecessor.

'What was Martin Beldecos like?'

'He was nice enough,' said Isabel. 'He was quiet, almost shy. Very dedicated to his work.'

'He was American, wasn't he?'

'That's right. From Miami. He had worked for one of the branches of the big US banks there, which deal with Latin American private clients.'

'And do you know what he actually did?'

'Not precisely. I think technically he was employed by Dekker Trust. He spent half his time here, and half his time in the Caymans. He was working on some project for Eduardo, which he tried to keep confidential, but it obviously had something to do with Dekker Trust. He asked us all about clients of ours who had accounts there.' Isabel paused. 'It's terrible what happened to him. He was only thirty.'

'Any family?' I asked.

'Parents. And a brother and a sister, I think. They're all in Miami. He wasn't married or anything.' She looked at me sharply. 'And the same thing nearly happened to you.'

I nodded. Now she knew what I was thinking.

13

'I've left the School of Russian Studies.'

A piece of overdone pork hovered on my fork. I shoved it in my mouth and chewed. And chewed. My mother was not a good cook.

'Really, dear?' she said, raising her eyebrows.

'Good God! When was this?' thundered my father.

'About a month ago.'

The obvious question for most families would have been 'Why didn't you tell us sooner?' But not in our family. I had long since stopped discussing anything important with them, and they had stopped expecting it.

We were sitting in the small square dining room in the flint cottage that my parents had bought in Norfolk after my father had retired. Even though it was the end of April, it was cold. When the wind came from the north or east, it was always cold; there wasn't much between the cottage and the North Pole. Both my mother and I were wearing thick jerseys, and my father an old sports jacket.

I had inserted this remark into a pause in the conversation. Although it wasn't really a conversation, more a monologue as my father droned through his staple topics: Europe, old friends from the City, Lady Thatcher (always with the 'Lady'), and cricket. The subjects hadn't changed much since my youth, although he had substituted Europe for the unions as his principal object of hatred. He would eat and talk at the same time, his large florid face bulging as he chewed. These conversations required no participation at all from my mother and me. I sometimes wondered whether they occurred when there was just the two of them. I concluded something much more depressing. Days, months, years of meals eaten in silence.

'So, what are you going to do?' my father demanded.

This was the bit I wasn't looking forward to. I chewed some more, and finally managed to swallow the lump of pork, and felt it force its painful way down my throat.

'I'm going to work for a company called Dekker Ward,' I said.

'Dekker Ward! Not the stockbroker?' My father put down his fork, and broke into a huge grin. 'Well done, my boy! Well done!' And then, much to my embarrassment, he leaned over and shook my hand. 'Know them well. Old Lord Kerton was a pal of mine. Must be near retirement age by now. They specialized in plantations, I think. Now there was plenty of money to be made there if you could get the timing right. Oh, yes. Plenty of money.'

'I think the old Lord Kerton died, Father.' He liked to be called Father. 'It's his son, Andrew, who's chairman now.'

My father tucked into his burnt pig with renewed gusto. I had made his day. 'Don't remember a son. Probably still at school when I knew him. Sorry to hear about old Gerald, though.' He took a gulp of the tap water in the glass in front of him. 'Well, old man! Whatever made you finally do it?'

'Money, Father. I needed the money.'

'Well, you should make plenty of that. The City's rolling in it, these days. A smart young man like you will make a fortune. Let me get a bottle of wine. We need to celebrate.'

My mother had been watching me all this time, wearing a slight frown. 'Why?' she mouthed.

'I'm skint,' I mouthed back. She nodded. She understood that. When we had lived in Surrey, we had lurched from having plenty of money to having very little. For a while I had thought it was my fault. I had gone to a local grammar school that had become independent. I had enjoyed it. The teachers were excellent, the rugby team won more often than it lost, I made some good, like-minded friends, and it got me into Oxford. But somehow I was made to feel guilty that I was there. It was to do with the fees. The termly demands for payment were met by frowns and barbed comments from my father. I was never quite sure why: he was a stockbroker, like many of the other boys' fathers, fees should not have been a problem. I'm pretty sure now that my father's distress was a result of inept stock-market speculation, but at the time he left me in no doubt that the family's money worries were down to me.

He returned with a bottle of Argentine red. Very appropriate. He prattled on, talking a lot about the old colonial stocks in which Dekker Ward used to ply their trade.

After several minutes I decided to correct him mildly. 'Actually, Father, they concentrate a lot on Latin America now. And they're thinking of doing business in Russia. That's why they want me.'

'Oh, I see. Jolly good.'

My father talked on, about the deals he'd done, the

people he knew, and he trotted out some aphorisms such as 'Sell in May and go away,' and 'Never trust a man whose tie is lighter than the colour of his shirt.' I studied the surface of the dining table, where the imprint of my school homework could still just be picked out. 'Oct 197' and '$= 5x + 3$' were the most prominent marks.

After coffee, I asked my mother if I could look at her latest paintings. She smiled and led me to her studio. We left my father behind with the washing-up.

The studio was a large room that took up half the length of the cottage. It had big windows that provided plenty of natural light. But to walk in there was like walking into a hurricane.

Five years ago her pictures had been open landscapes of the Norfolk shoreline, in an impressionist style. Since then they had become steadily darker, wilder, swirls of cloud enveloping lonely figures on beaches that never ended. Individually they were highly unsettling. When surrounded by dozens of them at once the effect was downright frightening. The nearest thing I had felt to it was walking through the Edvard Munch exhibition at the National Gallery several years before.

My mother's painting worried me. It was probably brilliant, but it had taken over her life.

'Have you tried any more galleries, Mum?' I asked.

'I've told you, dear, none of the galleries round here will touch them.'

'How about London?'

'Oh, don't be ridiculous. They wouldn't be interested in this.'

I wasn't so sure. I suspected that someone somewhere would jump at her work. But these pictures were for herself, not other people.

We were looking at a particularly haunting painting of the blackened shell of a wreck being slowly sucked down into the sand flats off Brancaster beach.

'I'm sorry you're giving up Russian literature, Nick,' she said.

'I'm not. I'll still read. And, once I've made some money, I'm sure I'll go back to it in some form.'

'Hmm. Just promise me one thing.'

'What's that?'

'Don't marry a banker.'

I couldn't answer. The sadness of it wrenched my gut. I glanced at her profile. She had a broad, intelligent face, beneath thick hair only now beginning to go grey. She was still attractive, and was striking in the wedding photograph that had been in the sitting room for as long as I could remember. They must have been in love when they married, although I could only remember sniping in my childhood that changed to major rows in adolescence. Then, since I had left home, this had lapsed into silence.

My father gave me a lift to King's Lynn station. Just as I was getting out of the car at the station entrance, he called after me, 'Oh, Nick?'

'Yes?'

'If you hear any good tips, don't forget to let your old man know, eh?'

He winked.

I smiled quickly and slammed the car door shut. It was with a huge sense of relief that I felt the train lurch away from the platform.

As the fens dashed past the grimy train windows, I thought of the City as my father saw it. Lunch, drink, talk, helping out old pals, getting on to a good thing. It was a long way from the efficient activity of the Dekker machine, high up in its gleaming tower, whisking billions round the world. But there were some shared assumptions. In both the deal was all. You helped out your friends and screwed your enemies to get the best deal. And then you felt clever about it.

A heavy shower scurried across the fen, and hit the train in a tantrum, splattering the window with angry raindrops. I slumped back into my seat, and didn't feel very clever at all.

14

It was a slow cycle into work on Monday. The weather was still foul, and my heart wasn't in it. By the time I made it up to the fortieth floor, still dripping, the meeting was already well under way.

As if on a signal from my arrival, Ricardo cleared his throat. 'I'm sure you all read the article in last week's *IFR*,' he began. 'The content of the article itself doesn't concern me, it was obviously rubbish, and a gross insult to Martin and his family. What does concern me was that one of us spoke to a journalist, and gave him information that was highly detrimental to the firm. This person has been fired.'

There was a murmur from the gathering. Everyone looked round at everyone else to see who was missing. Quickly, the murmurs took shape into a recognizable word. Dave. Dave! Why had he done it? What had he said?

'This person will not only not work for Dekker again, but he will also not work in the bond markets,' Ricardo continued in a clear voice. 'He has breached the confidentiality agreement you all signed as part of your contract when you joined Dekker Ward. As a result he has lost all of his interest in the employee trusts. He has been warned not to talk to the press any further. The market will be told that he made large trading losses, and that he covered them up. I expect all of you to back this up if asked.'

We were all silent now. Dave was a popular member of the team. The mood of the room felt finely balanced between sadness at his dismissal and shock that he had betrayed the rest of us.

'Some of you may think this treatment is harsh. But we're all a team here. If you're not with us, you're against us. There are many people out there who don't like Dekker and what it has achieved. Together we can win. But if any one of us betrays the others, as this man has, then we're all vulnerable. I will not allow that to happen.'

Ricardo glanced round the room. His eyes, which were usually so cool, were angry now. But even his anger drew us in. We were all angry.

The meeting broke up, and we exchanged glances. Many eyes rested on the empty desk where Dave had worked. Alberto, the sixty-year-old 'coffee boy', was putting his belongings into a couple of boxes. Under Ricardo's stern gaze, we returned to our desks and picked up phones, but over the course of the morning the room buzzed with speculation.

And so did the outside world. Word had already gone round the market that Dave was one of that most dangerous of animals, a trader who not only made losses but lied about them. The rumour echoed back into the Dekker trading room, where to my surprise it was confirmed. Even Jamie told Chris Frewer it was true.

'Why did you do that?' I asked him, shocked. 'Couldn't you just say you don't know why he left?'

Jamie sighed. 'In these situations you have to follow the party line. Ricardo will be watching. This is a test of loyalty for all of us. And he's right. We'll only succeed if we stick together.'

I listened in mounting disgust to what was happening around me. The initial shock and sadness at the loss of a friend was already changing, as Dave's character was rewritten. Just as the Dekker machine could persuade itself that a lousy bond issue was the investment opportunity of the year, so they came to believe that Dave was an incompetent fraud. They did it with determination and purpose, and without looking each other in the eye.

I watched, stunned. I had no idea whether Dave was a good or bad trader, but I knew that he was not what these people were portraying.

The man leaning against the bar lifting his second pint of bitter to his lips seemed very different from the boy I had known at Oxford. First he was a man. He had a grown-up suit and briefcase, but then so had Jamie and I, and that didn't mean anything. But he also had a receding hairline poorly hidden with wisps of blond hair, a wife and baby, and a way of talking that made him sound closer to forty than twenty.

Stephen Troughton had studied PPE with us. He had always been precocious, capable of discussing knowledgeably mortgage rates, house prices and unit trusts, when the rest of us would have nothing to do with such bourgeois concerns. He had talked his way into the City with no difficulty, and had been one of the lucky few that Bloomfield Weiss had plucked from British universities during the 1988 milk-round. He had taken to Bloomfield Weiss like a duck to water, and had done very well.

Even though he was the same age as Jamie and me, he looked thirty-five at least, and used this to his advantage. Stephen Troughton had gone far.

Jamie saw him once or twice a year for a drink, to 'catch up'. I had tagged along this time, even though I hadn't seen Stephen since university. We were in an old pub in a mews in Knightsbridge, touristed by day, besuited in the evening.

I was beginning to realize that 'catching up' meant comparing careers. I watched them at it.

'Did you hear about that big Brady trade we did last week?' asked Jamie, at the first opportunity.

Stephen laughed. 'Oh, that, yes. We were just dipping our toe in the water.'

'Got a bit wet, didn't you?'

'A little, but we can take it. We're the biggest trading house in the world. That kind of loss just gets hidden in one day's profits.'

'Oh, yeah?'

'Oh, yes,' said Stephen. He lowered his voice, as though he were about to impart something of great importance. 'You'd better watch yourselves, Jamie. Bloomfield Weiss are serious about the emerging markets. And when we get serious about a market we tend to make our mark. Don't get me wrong, Dekker are a clever little firm, but when a market matures, then it's only natural that the big boys will take over.'

Stephen said this in a tone full of fake reasonableness designed to irritate Jamie. It succeeded. He rose to the bait. 'And there's that big Mexican mandate that you lost,' he said. 'That must have been a bit of a blow.'

'We do those kinds of deals every day for the likes of the World Development Fund. It won't be long before we're doing them for Mexico as well.'

Jamie snorted.

'So, tell me about this trader you sacked,' Stephen said. 'Dave Dunne, wasn't it? He must have lost you a packet.'

Jamie shrugged.

'He asked for a job at Bloomfield Weiss,' Stephen went on. 'We didn't give him one, of course. We can't be seen taking Dekker cast-offs.'

'He was a good trader,' I said. It was my first foray into the conversation. Jamie threw me a warning glance.

Stephen ignored my comment as though it had no validity, given my short experience. Which was, of course, true. But I had drawn attention to myself.

'Well, I never would have imagined you in the City,' he said. 'What's going on?'

'I need the money.'

'Fair enough. And I suppose Dekker wanted your Russian expertise?'

'That's right. Although Ricardo wants me to see how they operate in South America first.'

'Russia's a huge growth area for us at the moment. We picked up your Russian team, of course.' Stephen shot a glance at Jamie when he said this. Touché. 'Actually, that's something I'm curious about,' he went on. 'A couple of them are suddenly having problems with their visas. Ricardo doesn't have anything to do with that, does he?'

Jamie spluttered into his beer.

'So he does?'

'I don't know,' said Jamie. 'But serves 'em right, that's what I say.'

Stephen raised his eyebrows and turned to me again. 'Tell me, Nick, what's this guy Ricardo Ross really like?'

This was the question I had been asking myself ever since the first time I met him. I decided to give Stephen a straight answer. 'I honestly don't know.'

'He has quite a reputation. All this stuff about being "The Marketmaker" and everything. Is he that good?'

'Oh, he's good. And he does treat the market as if he owns it. That's why he's so pissed off about you guys muscling in. He has great judgement. He always seems to know exactly what to do when things get tough. Don't you think?' I turned to Jamie, who was watching me closely.

'Absolutely,' he said. 'He's easily the most astute person I've worked with in the City.'

Stephen was watching me. He had blue watery eyes, but they were intelligent. 'So, if he's that good, why did you say you didn't know? What's wrong with him?'

'I'm not sure. He might be a bit too aggressive. Sometimes I wonder if he goes just a bit too far, but then later it turns out he's judged it just about right.'

Stephen clapped my shoulder. 'Quite honestly, it's hard to go too far in this business. As long as you don't get caught.' He put his glass down on a nearby ledge. 'I've got to go. Nice to see both of you again. Cheers.'

'Cheers, Stephen,' Jamie said. Stephen left, but Jamie and I stayed for another.

'Jerk,' said Jamie.

'I don't know why you bother seeing him.'

'He's not always as bad as that. And he's bright. It's good to stay in touch. You never know.'

'But he's such a grown-up. Balding, wife, kid.'

'But I've got a wife and kid.'

'Jamie, you *are* a kid. And you don't look forty.'

'It's funny getting older,' said Jamie. 'I mean, I do feel it sometimes. I've got a big mortgage. I do have a wife and kid to look after. And I've got to take my career seriously. Things have changed.'

'I suppose they have.'

'Whatever happens, I don't want to turn into my parents.'

'Why not? They're nice people.'

Jamie snorted. 'They might be nice but they're broke, aren't they? My grandfather was a big landowner. And now my father drives a mini-cab. If I carry on the great family tradition, Oliver will have a career in McDonald's.'

'Anyway, you will become your father. You're just like him. You can't avoid it.' I meant it as a joke, but Jamie shot me a dark look.

'I'm serious. It's about time somebody made some money in my family.'

I had visited Jamie's parents a number of times over the years. I was always made to feel welcome as Jamie's intellectual friend from Oxford. The first couple of times I'd stayed it had been at a lovely farmhouse, which presided over a livery stable. Shortly after Jamie had left Oxford this had gone, and now his parents lived in a rented lodge at the bottom of someone else's grand drive.

Jamie's grandfather had owned a small estate at the foot of the Quantocks, and the after-tax remnants of this were still farmed by his uncle. His father had tried to make money out of horses and failed. Jamie told me he now drove a mini-cab, but I wasn't to mention this to anyone, especially to him.

Whatever their past glories or future worries, Jamie's parents were unfailingly hospitable. His father was the old rogue that Jamie might one day become, with a winning smile, rugged features and a twinkle in his eye.

His mother was tall and striking, even now, and had not lost any of her charm. Jamie was the apple of their eye. He could do no wrong. His every pronouncement was met with rapt interest, his minor successes with applause, his major successes with studied indifference, as if his parents never doubted that he would achieve great things.

And Jamie hadn't let them down. Head boy of his public school, entrance to Oxford, an occasional place in the university rugby team, and a job in the blue-blooded merchant bank, Gurney Kroheim. Jamie's move to Dekker Ward had taken his parents a little by surprise, but once Jamie had explained it they understood. Their son was one of the new generation of entrepreneurs they had read about.

I don't mean to mock this attention. I would have loved half of it. But whenever I achieved something, my father never quite understood exactly what it was.

I drank my beer thoughtfully. 'I still don't know what I'm going to do with my life.'

'Aren't you going to stay at Dekker?'

'I don't know. Sometimes it gives me a great buzz. Like that Brady battle. But then I think about what they did to Dave, and the *favela* deal, and the drug money.'

'Oh, forget that,' said Jamie.

'But I can't forget it. It bothers me. Doesn't it bother you?'

Jamie paused for a moment. 'I think it might if I stopped to think about it. So I don't stop to think about it. For Kate and Oliver's sake, I have to make this a success. I could be really good at this stuff, you know.'

He looked at me for reassurance. I was able to give it. 'You could.' From my brief time at Dekker, I could tell Jamie was good. 'Sorry,' I said. 'I didn't mean to be ungrateful. Thank you for getting me this job.'

Jamie smiled. 'Don't worry about it. Ricardo likes you. I get Brownie points.'

'Was that true about those Russian traders' visas? Do you think Ricardo arranged that?'

'I hadn't heard about it, but I wouldn't be at all surprised,' said Jamie. 'And if it wasn't Ricardo who fixed it, it was Eduardo. They don't like people letting them down.'

'I can see that.'

We were on to our third pint. The edginess that surrounded Stephen had left with him, and I was slowly enveloped in that special type of warm glow that you can only get from three pints of good bitter with an old friend.

Jamie and I had been through a lot together over the years. In taking the job at Dekker, I had trusted my future to him. But I could rely on Jamie.

'Kate told me you were quite taken with Isabel,' Jamie said.

I could feel my cheeks reddening. Which was strange, because normally I found it quite easy to talk to Jamie about women.

'She's a nice girl, Jamie.'

'Oh, really? Nice girl, eh? Now that's serious. Not just "She's got fabulous tits," or "She's desperate for it."'

'No. Neither of those things, actually.'

'Is there anything going on between you?'

'No.'

'But you'd like it if there was?'

'I can't deny that. But I don't think it's likely.'

'Why not?'

'Oh, I don't know. She just doesn't seem that keen.'

'Well, be careful. She's a strange woman.' He was struck by a thought. 'You didn't talk to her about this money-laundering business, did you?'

I nodded. 'I did. She agreed with you about not telling Eduardo. But she thought I should speak to Ricardo about it. I'm not going to, though.'

'Oh, Nick! You shouldn't even have spoken to her. I told you about her and Eduardo, didn't I?'

'You did. But that was only a rumour. I don't believe it.'

'You don't want to believe it, you mean. You saw what happened to Dave. You'd better forget this money-laundering stuff or the same thing will happen to you.'

'I can trust Isabel,' I said.

'The truth is, Nick,' Jamie said, 'in this business you can trust no one.'

I wanted to argue, but I didn't. Partly because I had an uncomfortable feeling he was right.

'Come on, it's late, let's go,' Jamie said, draining his glass.

'Yeah.' I finished up my pint. We spilled out of the pub, Jamie to hail a cab and me to find the tube station. I'd left my bike at Canary Wharf.

The next day was grey and cold, as spring went into remission. High up in the Canary Wharf tower, the Dekker dealing room felt crammed against the ceiling of dark cloud just a few feet above it. The euphoria of victory over Bloomfield Weiss in the Brady battle died down quickly as the reality of trying to sell two billion dollars of Mexican bonds sank in. This was a time to call in favours.

I listened to Jamie perform. He was good. He started with his best customers. He was a different person with each. With some he discussed football and TV, with others modified duration and stripped yields. Sometimes he talked non-stop, sometimes he just listened. But he cajoled and begged and blustered his way to an order from each of them. The orders were large: ten or twenty million in some cases, but they weren't large enough. It would take a miracle and a few hundred-million orders to shift two billion dollars of bonds.

Ricardo was working the phones furiously himself. The really big orders would come from calling in the really big favours, and that was something only Ricardo could do. Every now and then he would get up and pace the room, checking up on us. Despite the pressure that we all felt, he was encouraging, praising a five-million order from a difficult account or commiserating if a client failed to bite. We were all in this together, he took our commitment as given.

But Ricardo was capable of dealing with more than one problem at once. That afternoon, I felt a tap on my shoulder, as I was sitting hunched listening to Jamie at work. 'How much do you know about Poland?'

'Not much. I've been there once. To the University of Kraków.'

'What do you think are the chances of a devaluation?'

Honesty was always the best policy with Ricardo. 'I have no idea.'

'Do you know anyone who might have an idea? A good idea?'

I thought a moment. 'As a matter of fact I do. There's an economist I know who's at the LSE. He taught the finance minister fifteen years ago. I know they keep in touch. I could talk to him. I'd have to drink a bottle of vodka to find out, though.'

'Excellent!' Ricardo said. 'Drink a gallon. And put it on expenses.'

15

Wójtek was happy to hear from me, and invited me round to supper. I had first met him when I was studying the Soviet economy, and it was through him that I had gone to Kraków. He had long been a critic of the command economies of Eastern Europe, and he had built up quite a following in his home country. I had told him I was now working in the City, and needed to find out something about Polish economic policy.

I arrived at his flat in Ealing with a bottle of Bison Grass, his favourite vodka.

'Wonderful!' he said. 'Come in! Come in!'

The flat was exactly as I remembered it. Those portions of wall that were not covered by books displayed posters announcing obscure Polish, Russian and French exhibitions. I was sure that each one was carefully selected for its street cred, rather than its direct importance to Wójtek. In an indiscreet, drunken moment he had told me that *When Harry Met Sally* was his favourite film. But I had been sworn to secrecy on that subject, and there was no sign of that poster.

Although Wójtek was in his late forties, he did his best to look and act like an angry postgraduate student. He sported a full black moustache, he had bushy, tousled hair in a pony-tail, with only the slightest hint of grey, and a white-filtered cigarette dangled from his lips. Despite his appearance, businessmen, politicians and the International Monetary Fund all loved him. He preached an economics that was fiscally and monetarily prudent, and yet didn't insist that unless unemployment was running at twenty per cent the government were a bunch of wimps. He was one of those teachers who took a strong personal interest in some of his students. I had been so favoured once, as before me had the current finance ministers of Poland and the Slovak Republic.

I liked him. Although he was older than me, and I didn't see him often, I counted him as one of my friends.

'So how is the lovely Joanna?' he asked.

'In America with the obnoxious Wes.'

'Good, I never liked her, and whoever he is, I'm sure he deserves her. I've cooked a ratatouille, I hope that will do?'

'Of course,' I said.

'Now, let's get that bottle open.'

We hit the vodka. Wójtek told me about his latest girlfriend, a twenty-three-year-old American student. Wójtek liked girls until they reached the age of about twenty-five whereupon he lost interest. He had married a couple of them, but soon stopped that idea, since the marriages had no chance of lasting more than a few years and ending them was an administrative nightmare.

He served supper in his large kitchen. The ratatouille was excellent, the vodka strong, and within less than an hour we were quite drunk.

As expected, he berated me for going into the City, and then asked me what I wanted.

I cleared my throat, tried to clear my head, and

answered him. 'I was recruited by Dekker because of my knowledge of the Russian language and economics. Now all of a sudden I'm supposed to know about Poland too, but I haven't followed it for years. I was hoping you could give me a clue so I don't sound like an idiot.'

'Ah, Nick, there is very little chance of you sounding like an idiot about anything. But I will tell you.'

Then he proceeded to explain to me clearly and succinctly the story of Poland's economy since the days of Solidarity. I understood it, it sounded clever, and I hoped I would remember it in the morning.

'And what about a devaluation? Isn't the currency too high at the moment?'

'You're right!' said Wójtek, almost in a shout. He stood up. 'I keep telling them! Devalue now, before the economy is completely ruined. It is better to stay in control and be seen to be choosing when to devalue than wait until an international crisis forces it upon you.'

'So, do you think they will?'

Wójtek stopped pacing, glanced at me, smiled and said, 'I don't know,' with such a dollop of mock innocence that I didn't believe him for a moment. He knew what the Poles were going to do, and what they were planning to do made him happy.

We got drunker and drunker, until I thought it was safe to escape.

'But it's only ten o'clock!' protested Wójtek.

'I know. But I have to be in to work by seven tomorrow. And with what I've drunk, I'll feel bad enough as it is.'

'Well, great to see you, Nick.' He embraced me, and I left him alone with the dregs of the vodka bottle.

It was a tough cycle ride in the next day. My head hurt, and my mouth felt dry and furry. I stopped at a corner shop to buy a pint of milk, which I absorbed, rather than drank. Thank God it was downhill some of the way.

Ricardo laughed when he saw me. 'I see you did your duty last night.'

'Oh, God, does it show?'

'It does. Was it useful?'

'I think the Poles are going to devalue.' I explained my conversation with Wójtek, and his barely hidden excitement that the Polish government were following his ideas.

'Are you sure this guy has the influence he thinks he has?' asked Ricardo.

'I'm sure.'

'Then well done!' He smiled and clapped me on the shoulder. 'Time to adjust our Polish position.'

He went back to his desk and picked up the phone.

'Not bad,' said Jamie. 'I'm impressed. Don't tell me, you play rugby with Boris Yeltsin's doctor.'

''Fraid not,' I said. 'Wójtek is about the full extent of my influential contacts.'

'Well, you are an important person. But by the way . . .'

'Yes?'

'You look like shit.'

'Thanks.'

I was pleased with myself. It was good to be useful to Dekker. Maybe Ricardo would make some money. If he did, he would be bound to remember my part in the profits. That was the good thing about Ricardo. He gave credit where it was due.

The phone rang.

'Nick? It's Wójtek.'

His voice sounded thick and horrible. It was a fair bet that he had drunk much more than I had by the time he had passed out.

'How are you?'

'Fine,' he said. I smiled. Liar. 'Yesterday, Nick. When we talked about Poland. And the devaluation. You remember?'

'Yes, I do. Thanks, Wójtek. It was very useful.'

'Yes, well. I like to help you, Nick. But when you asked about whether the Polish government would devalue, I didn't answer you, did I?'

Oh, God. 'No,' I said, trying to sound bright. 'No, you didn't say anything at all.'

'Good. Because if the financial markets found out about the devaluation through me, that would be a real breach of trust on my part.'

'Of course, I understand.' My ears were singing. I could feel the blood rushing to my cheeks.

'So will you give me your word you won't tell anyone at your work about what we ... didn't discuss last night.'

Shit! Shit! Shit!

'Nick?'

What to do? Lie, of course.

'No. Don't worry, Wójtek, I won't guess anything. You just gave me useful background, that's all.'

I think my voice sounded steady. I was just glad he couldn't see my face.

'Good.' He sounded relieved. 'It was great to see you again. Keep in touch, OK.'

'OK, Wójtek. See you soon.'

I slammed the phone down, and took a deep breath. I looked up and saw Ricardo coming towards me.

'Well done, Nick,' he said. 'We're all set up now. I just hope you're right.'

'I'm right,' I said. But I felt very wrong indeed.

'Oh, we're taking some clients out tonight. Very important clients. Would you like to come along?'

Oh, God. More drinking. The last thing I felt like was being nice to people I didn't know. I wanted to go to bed early. Very early.

But it was clear that I should feel flattered to be asked. So I summoned up a smile, and said, 'Great.'

I grabbed a cup of coffee from the machine, and reached for the paper. I laid it out on my own desk away from the square. I had earned myself some peace and quiet. The coffee didn't really seem to help. My head still hurt, and my stomach was queasy. I felt hot. I was sweating gently. Vodka was an occupational hazard of studying Russian. I could see that it would become a problem in this job too, once I became seriously involved with Eastern Europe.

I glanced at Isabel. She was reading through a pile of papers, her hair hanging down and hiding most of her face. God, she was attractive. Since our drink the previous Friday, we had exchanged a few friendly words, but nothing more. I guessed that she wanted to make sure that nothing developed between us. And that was a great shame.

I remembered Jamie's warnings about her. He was wrong, surely. I was certain I could trust her. But I had no intention of following her suggestion and talking to Ricardo about my suspicions. Prudence suggested I should do nothing, although that didn't seem right, either. My head hurt. I didn't come to any conclusion.

'Nick, what is it?'

'What?'

'You're staring.'

My eyes came back into focus. Isabel was looking at me with an amused smile on her face.

I could feel myself reddening. 'Oh, I'm sorry. My eyes and brain aren't well connected this morning. I was out drinking for Dekker last night.'

'Such loyalty is touching,' said Isabel.

Embarrassed, I cast my eyes down to the paper in front of me. I leafed through to the arts pages. I had to admit that the film reviews in the *FT* were pretty good. There was a new Polish film out by Krzysztof Kieślowski. It sounded interesting. I'd try and see it if I got the time.

Oh, damn! I hated having to lie to Wójtek. I had betrayed his trust. Of course, it was partly his fault. Mostly his fault. I had gone there telling him who I was and what I wanted. He had been stupidly indiscreet. He knew it: that's why he had just rung me in a panic. It was his fault. His fault that I had betrayed his trust.

No. It didn't work. Wójtek would be seriously upset with me if he ever found out what I had done. I would just have to hope that he never did.

Stephen's words echoed to me, in that pompous accent of his. 'Quite honestly, it's hard to go too far in this business. As long as you don't get caught.'

Ugh.

After a couple of glasses of wine, my brain began to clear, or at least the pain softened. We were in Vong's, a smart New York restaurant that had migrated to Knightsbridge. There were seven of us and five of them. Ricardo was there, with Eduardo, Jamie, Miguel, and a couple of others. Our guests were officials of a central bank. This trip to London had become something of an annual event, a thank-you from Dekker for business done in the past and to be done in the future.

I had to admit that, for civil servants, these people were quite fun. The food was delicious, the drink flowed, and with it the laughter.

I was sitting next to Eduardo, but we spoke little, until towards the end of the meal he leaned over to me. 'You'll learn a little about how business is done tonight,' he said, with a twinkle in his dark eyes.

'Oh, yes?'

'Yes. It's important to give your customers what they want. And that's not just the best prices or the best deal. Ricardo can do all that. But someone has to look at the broader relationship. That's my speciality. Do you know what I mean?'

He looked at me closely, his lips parted in a smile.

'I'm not sure,' I said.

'Well, you have to know what your customers like. Now, I happen to know that this group all like women. That's easy. Except for that man at the end of the table.' He pointed to a good-looking balding man, listening with great interest to a story Jamie was telling. 'I happen to know he prefers boys. His colleagues don't know that, nor does Jamie, but I'm sure he will appreciate being seated next to the prettiest one among us.'

I couldn't help myself smiling at this. It was true that Jamie's good looks could attract interest from either sex, which caused him intense irritation. He would go spare if he knew Eduardo was using him in this way.

'You won't tell him, will you?'

'I will one day,' I said. 'I won't be able to resist it.'

'OK, but not tonight. Tonight you will see why these people always deal with us, and never with Bloomfield Weiss.'

At about eleven, we left the restaurant, amid cries of 'Eduardo!'

'What happens now?' I asked Jamie.

'We go back to Eduardo's flat for more entertainment.'

I was intrigued. I had caught a second wind, and the exuberance of the crowd was infectious. I bundled into one of the three cabs we commandeered outside the restaurant.

Eduardo's flat was in Mayfair, not more than half a mile away. He had a large living room, with plenty of chairs and sofas, and heavy expensive curtains and carpets. The light was dim. We piled in, taking off jackets and loosening ties. There were bottles of champagne waiting on a sideboard, guarded over by a very attractive blonde waitress. I accepted a glass, and slumped into a sofa.

The man next to me, Felipe, was talking about a notorious conference that Dekker had set up in Acapulco two years before. I had difficulty following all of it because he was speaking fast, he had a thick accent, and in his excitement he didn't make much sense. But the others around him were nodding and laughing at the memories.

The champagne was excellent, the flat was warm, the chair very comfortable, and I sat back in a relaxed fug. I stopped trying to focus on the noise around me. This was really rather nice.

A light flashed in my eye, and startled me. I looked over to its source. It was a small mirror. Eduardo and two of our guests were hunched over it arranging some lines of white powder.

I smiled at the irony of the situation. Having spent the last ten years of my life in universities, I was used to seeing drugs around me and avoiding them. Things were obviously not much different here. I sank further into my chair, and hoped they wouldn't notice me.

The mirror attracted most of the men in the room, including Jamie. He caught my eye and shrugged. I knew Jamie wasn't a coke user. This was probably another one of those things he did to fit in.

I looked around for Ricardo. He had slipped away. Everyone else had stayed. His privilege, I supposed.

Then Eduardo caught my eye, and called across to me. 'Want some, Nick? You should try it.'

Damn. 'No, thank you,' I said, trying not to sound too prim.

'Hey, try it. It's good stuff. A little bit won't do any harm. Get you in the party mood.' His thick lips broke into a broad smile, but his eyes were hard, commanding.

'No, sorry.'

He moved over towards me. He sat down on the arm of the sofa. I could smell his eau-de-Cologne. The top two buttons of his shirt were undone, and I could see black tufts of hair and the glint of gold. He put his arm round me, and patted my cheek. I wanted to hit him so badly.

'Come on, Nicky, my friend. Enjoy yourself! Party! Hey, what you need is someone to play with.' Just then the doorbell rang. 'And here she is!'

He stood up and made an announcement to the group of expectant central bankers. 'These are some friends of mine. They all work in the modelling business.' He winked. 'I'm sure you'll like them.'

He opened the door to a procession of about a dozen stunning women, all with different colours of hair and skin, and all wearing revealing but expensive cocktail dresses. Immediately the men stood up, the noise level rose, champagne corks were popped. The excitement in the room was almost palpable.

I stayed stuck in my chair. Eduardo put his arm round the waist of a tall girl with red hair and extremely long legs, and steered her towards me.

'Nick, Melanie, Melanie, Nick,' he said. 'She's a beautiful woman, Nick, I'm sure you will like her.' Then he left us, much to my relief.

'Hi,' she said.

'Hallo,' I replied, smiled politely, and ignored her. She sipped champagne, making small-talk in an upper-middle-class accent, to which I didn't respond. I was very tired, and I wanted to go home. None of these women interested me like Isabel did, and the artificiality of the situation made me queasy. I looked around at the smartly dressed, wealthy men, all with wives and girlfriends, talking animatedly to these women whom they had never met before. Two couples, they were couples already, began to dance, slow and close. I felt ill.

I stood up, smiled politely at the redhead next to me, retrieved my jacket, and headed for the door.

'Nick!'

Jamie extricated himself from a blonde, and rushed up to the door. I waited.

'Nick, where are you going?'

'Home.'

'Look. Stay here. Eduardo won't like it if you go now. Come on. You're not even married.'

'Maybe that's why I don't want to stay,' I said. 'And screw Eduardo.'

I woke up late the next morning – nine o'clock. I brewed some fresh coffee, made some toast and read the paper. The Polish devaluation was on page eight. More money for Dekker. I finished my coffee, left the flat and strolled up Primrose Hill, with its stunted black lamp-posts, and its daffodils neatly trussed up now they had finished blooming. It was a cool day for May, and a breeze bit into my skin. It felt good, refreshing.

Just below the brow of the hill, I sat down and looked out over London. In front of me was the extraordinary polyhedron that was the aviary at London Zoo, and beyond that St Paul's and the skyscrapers of the City. Even further away, barely visible through the new leaves of the trees on the hill, was Canary Wharf.

The Dekker people would be there now, toiling hard, pretending that they could function normally after the night before. They would be exchanging knowing glances with each other, lying to their customers about what a wonderful place Mexico was, ticking up the trades, ticking up the profits.

I considered the last few weeks. The *favela* deal, the money-laundering, Dave's sacking, my own lying to Wójtek, the sleaze of the previous night. All of these things I could handle individually. But together they made me feel sick.

I didn't fit. I could pretend that I did, but only for so long. Or I could change, as Jamie had. Change so that I could lie happily, ignore what needed to be ignored, do what needed to be done. If my conscience couldn't hack it, then I should just change my conscience.

Or leave.

Was I running away? Was it just that I couldn't take the real world, the commercial world?

I honestly didn't think so. There was no doubt that the attack on Ipanema beach had shaken me. But I was sure I wasn't letting that affect my judgement. I would have to face up to the fact that I had made a mistake in joining Dekker. It was a real cock-up. I was proud, and I didn't like admitting to mistakes. But there was no hiding from this one.

Still, as Ricardo would say, a good trader knows when to take his losses. And the time had come.

It was eleven o'clock by the time I made it to my desk. I nodded to Isabel.

'Have a good night, did you, last night?' she said coolly.

'No, actually. I found it pretty unpleasant. I left early.'

'Oh, I see,' she said, and returned to her work. She didn't believe me, of course. I was just telling the same sort of lie that people at Dekker always did. That made me angry.

I considered telling her what I was going to do, but then decided against it. She would probably say I was foolish, I should accept what I saw. And she'd have good reasons. I'd made up my mind, and I didn't want to have it unmade.

Jamie rushed over to me. He seemed on edge.

'Nick, what time do you think this is? We've all been in since seven. You've got to show you can take a heavy night.'

'No, I haven't,' I said.

Jamie looked at me as though I was just being difficult. 'Anyway, about last night,' he said, low enough for no one else to hear. 'You know I normally don't do drugs. Only when I have to. Like last night.'

'I know,' I said grimly.

'And those girls. I didn't do anything with any of them. Just talked, you know.'

'I'm sure.'

183

'You won't tell Kate, will you? I mean, you should have stayed too.'

I now realized why Jamie had been sorry to see me go. He wanted me to be an accomplice in crime. Then he would feel better about it.

I sighed. 'I won't tell Kate,' I said. And I wouldn't. Even in my current negative mood, I wouldn't stuff a friend like that.

Jamie seemed relieved. 'Good. I'll see you later.'

As he left, Ricardo approached. He pulled up a chair next to my desk, and sat down.

'In a bit late this morning, aren't you?'

'Sorry,' I said.

'Whatever you've been doing the night before, you have to be in by seven. It's an unwritten law here. A point of pride, almost.'

'It was two nights,' I said.

'Oh, yes, I forgot about your Polish friend. By the way, I was very pleased to see the devaluation come through so quickly. Good work. But the point is, sometimes you'll have to do seven consecutive nights like that, especially when you travel.'

It was just a mild ticking-off. A preliminary warning. But it didn't matter any more.

I had to tell him now. While I was determined. Before I thought too hard about it. It was strange, with Ricardo here in front of me, the decision suddenly seemed more personal. I was letting him down.

Enough of that. Tell him now.

But he had started talking again. 'It's about time you did some real work. Isabel is going down to Brazil, and I'd like you to go with her.'

I shut up and listened.

'The City of São Paulo are very keen to go ahead

with their own *favela* deal. And it will be a good opportunity to persuade our friends in Brazil of the merits of Mexico. You've heard Jamie talk about the deal all week, so you should have the story down pat.'

Go to Brazil. With Isabel. That seemed like quite an attractive idea. Perhaps the resignation could wait until I returned.

'That is, if you're OK with that,' Ricardo said. 'After what happened last time, I'd understand if you were a bit reluctant.'

I was nervous. But I'd be OK down there as long as I was careful. And, even though I was planning to resign, I didn't want to show Ricardo, or myself for that matter, that I was a coward.

'No, that's fine. When do we go?'

'Tonight.'

'Tonight!'

'What's the matter? You had a lie-in this morning.'

He smiled and went back to his desk. I looked across to Isabel, who had been listening. 'Is that OK with you?' I said it without thinking. I suspected she had been distancing herself from me for the last week, and clearly she was not impressed with my participation in the previous night's events.

But she smiled. 'Of course it is. It makes a lot of sense. You know the details of the Rio deal, and Ricardo's right, you know a lot more about the wonders of Mexico than I do.'

I caught the irony in her voice. 'A fine investment opportunity,' I said.

She gathered together a pile of paper on her desk and handed it to me. 'Here, copy that. Read it. And I'll see you at the Varig lounge at Heathrow, Terminal Three, at eight thirty. The flight leaves at ten. I'll have the tickets.'

'OK,' I said, and toddled off to the photocopier.

Later, on my way out of the office, I stopped at Jamie's desk.

'I'm off. I'm going to Brazil tonight.'

'Really?' He frowned. 'Be careful this time.'

'Don't worry,' I said. 'I will be.'

'Are you going with Isabel?'

'Yes.'

'Well, have fun.' He grinned.

I was about to answer, 'I will,' but I stopped, confused. 'We'll see,' I said in the end.

16

The plane began its descent to São Paulo. I looked out of the window at the second greatest metropolis on earth. Twenty million people live in Greater São Paulo. Low red-roofed houses sprawled as far as I could see. Sprouting out among them like the white shoots of early spring were hundreds, if not thousands, of skyscrapers. They were grouped in clumps, as if handfuls of seed had fallen together from the hand of a careless sower. On the horizon, between the brown and red of the city, and the blue of the sky, stretched a thick dark grey band of smog. As we descended, the landscape was broken up by a grey ribbon of river, and dozens of industrial sites. We passed low over a lake of the most extraordinary lime green. God had created Rio in a fit of inspired imagination, man had created São Paulo with a total lack of it.

São Paulo is the business and financial centre of Brazil. *Paulistas* are proud to compare their city with New York and, indeed, the long avenues flanked with skyscrapers did look impressively commercial. People in suits dashed back and forth, and the traffic moved urgently through the vast network of São Paulo's highways. There was money to be made and work to be done and, although it was eighty-five degrees and humid, the *paulistas* would do it.

We met Humberto Alves's equivalent in the São Paulo Finance Department. The *paulistas* had a different approach to dealing with *favelas*, which they called the Cingapura project. It was an idea that had supposedly been developed in Singapore, hence the name. It involved what they called 'verticalization'. That meant tearing down the temporary structures and replacing them with modern high-rise hous-ing. It sounded to me more heavy-handed than the Rio project.

They were hot to trot. The Cingapura project had been under way now for several years, but the City was having problems finding the funds for more construc-tion. Isabel's ingenious trust idea was just the way to unlock the World Development Fund cash that was desperately needed to move on to the next stage. And now Rio's deal had fallen through, São Paulo's would be the first out in the market, which made the whole idea even more attractive.

It was a Friday, and we had meetings planned for that day and for Saturday, which showed how eager they were. As the day wore on, Isabel and I became progres-sively more excited as we realized that a deal might actually happen. Bloomfield Weiss were nowhere to be seen: after their humiliating withdrawal from the Rio deal, São Paulo wouldn't take them seriously.

It was a hard day, but we worked well together. I had read the pile of documents Isabel had given me on the plane, through the night. I was well prepared, and we operated brilliantly as a team. I quickly got the hang of how her mind worked, and she treated me like a valuable partner. Although I had lost any loyalty to Dekker, I didn't want to let Isabel down, and besides, her enthu-siasm had infected me. I believed in what she was doing.

At last, at eight thirty, we finished, with a promise to

be back in the municipal offices at nine the next morning. We flopped into a taxi, feeling both tired and excited at the same time.

'Did you know that São Paulo has the best Japanese restaurants outside Japan?' Isabel said.

'No, I didn't know that.'

'Would you like to try one?'

'Sure.'

She leaned forward to the taxi driver. 'Liberdade.'

We were dropped off next to a bustling street market. The smell of spices and fried food mixed in the warm night air. Black, white and brown Brazilians mingled with the Japanese and Koreans. It was good to see people wandering around on foot after driving from place to place by car all the time. A statuesque black woman walked past with her little four-year-old son. She caught me looking at them. 'Hey, how are you?' she said in English, with a leer. Embarrassed at my innocence in not realizing that a mother and a hooker could be the same thing, I looked away.

Isabel led me down a street daubed with Japanese characters. Over one million Japanese are supposed to live in São Paulo. So do many people from the Middle East. I noticed a sign for Habib's Fast Food, written in English and Japanese. Somehow it seemed typically Brazilian.

We came to a crooked wooden gateway, behind which was a tiny Japanese garden. Inside was a restaurant, divided into cosy booths. A large Japanese man was ostentatiously wielding huge knives. I winced as he twirled the blades round his hands, expecting at any moment to see a human finger added to the raw fish on the slab in front of him.

The place was bustling with Brazilians of all shades,

189

but after a short wait we were squeezed into a tight booth for two and ordered beer.

'Well, it looks like a *favela* deal is finally going to happen,' said Isabel.

'Yes. And so it should. You deserve it.'

'Thank you. I like working with someone else on this. I normally do all this stuff by myself. But I think we make an excellent team.'

She smiled at me, an innocent smile of encouragement.

'We do. It's a shame I won't be able to see it through with you.'

'You won't? Why not?' I was pleased to see the disappointment in Isabel's face. Actually, I was disappointed too.

'I'm going to resign as soon as I get back to London.'

'Really? Why?'

'You know. We've talked about it before. I just can't put up with Ricardo's way of doing things.'

Isabel lowered her eyes. 'I understand,' she said.

A waitress came round for our order. After a minute's consideration of the menu, I ordered tempura, and Isabel sushi.

'What are you going to do?' she asked.

I shrugged. 'Finish my thesis, I suppose. Try to get a job.'

'You don't sound very optimistic.'

'I'm not. I needed the job at Dekker. And the money. I won't be able to sell the flat for as much as the mortgage. So I'll have to let it, although I'll be lucky to get enough to cover the mortgage payments. And there aren't any jobs. But I must admit it will be good to get back to my thesis.'

Isabel nodded in sympathy. It must have been difficult

for her to understand my position, what with a father worth millions and her own substantial income. But she seemed to.

'I'm sorry it didn't work, Nick.'

'So am I. I screwed up.'

'I think you've taken the right decision, though. I know it's easy for me to say, because I haven't any money problems, but I don't think you could have carried on at Dekker and been happy with yourself.'

'And what about you?'

She smiled. 'That is a very uncomfortable question.'

'I'm sorry. I shouldn't have asked it.'

'No, that's OK. I guess I'm still trying to prove to myself that I can do this well. I don't want to give up. And every now and again, like on days like today, the job seems worthwhile.'

'Well, good luck with it,' I said, raising my glass.

'And good luck to you,' she said, raising hers. Then, 'I shall miss you.'

The words hung in the air. For a brief moment, she looked embarrassed, as though she wanted to take them back, but then she left them there, defiantly, looking directly at me, so that I knew what she meant, and that she didn't care that I knew.

My heart leaped. The bustle of the restaurant receded from my peripheral vision, and from my ears. There was just Isabel, there in front of me.

Neither of us said anything. I think I grinned stupidly. Isabel looked down as a bowl of soup was placed in front of her, and then looked up at me again and smiled. I felt as though I was falling into that smile, into those big dark eyes.

Then she giggled, we both relaxed, and delved into our soup.

*

The taxi journey back to our hotel took half an hour. It was late, it had been a long day, and we were both tired. Isabel let her head slump on to my shoulder, and shut her eyes. I sat motionless, unable to relax, totally aware of her body next to me. Her shoulders and head rested on me with the lightest of pressures. A hint of her perfume, a scent that I already associated strongly with her, surrounded us. A strand of her dark hair crept up and tickled my chin. I left it there.

She opened her eyes as the taxi lurched to a halt outside the hotel. It was midnight. The lift was waiting for us. This time, both our rooms were on the same floor. As the lift slowly eased upwards, Isabel held my eyes, and smiled shyly.

A breathless minute later, we were in her room. She watched me undress. My hands were trembling with anticipation, nerves, excitement. It was hard to concentrate on unbuttoning my shirt and trousers, pulling off my socks.

She laughed. Her clothes slipped off easily, and she sat on the bed, naked. One leg was tucked under her buttocks, and her small round breasts pushed out towards me. I kissed her. Her lips were soft and pliable, her tongue quick. She touched me, and I ached. I pulled her towards me, her body light under my hands. My hands moved over her, gently searching, stroking. She trembled under my touch.

Then she was on me, her body flowing over mine, shimmering pale in the reflected lights of the street outside. Eventually our muscles relaxed. She gazed down at me, her eyes dark pools half hidden behind strands of hair flopping over her face. She sighed and rested her head on my thumping chest, her body as light as before.

I held her.

'That was nice, Nick,' she said, some time later.

'Mmm.'

She ran her finger over the scar on my chest, which was healing nicely.

'Don't go away.' She rolled off me, and climbed out of bed. I watched her as she moved across the room to the bathroom. Naked, her body was supple but lithe as she walked.

She returned two minutes later, poured a glass of mineral water from the bottle on the desk, and sat cross-legged next to me.

'Don't stare!' she said.

'Sorry. It's hard not to.'

'You'll give me a complex.'

'Don't be silly. You're perfect.'

'Look, I'm about the only woman in Rio who hasn't had cosmetic surgery.'

'Really?'

She nodded. 'Everyone does it.'

'So what would you do?'

'Oh, I'd sort this out first.' She pointed to her nose. 'And then my bottom needs lifting. Here. My breasts are OK.'

'Yes, your breasts are OK. That's something,' I said, with heavy irony. She hit me with a pillow.

I sat up next to her and drank some of her water. 'You know, over the last couple of weeks, I couldn't work out what you thought of me.'

'I liked you,' she said.

I smiled. 'Well, I hoped you did. But you seemed to be keeping your distance. I didn't think I had much of a chance.'

'Sorry. You're right. I mean, I did want to see more

of you, but then I really didn't want to start something with someone at work again. So . . . I was confused.'

I almost felt like asking her if my resignation was why we were where we were, but that was unfair, and I most certainly did not want to be unfair to her. Not then.

She had said 'again'. 'Start something with someone at work again.' What was that?

'Jamie told me something that makes no sense,' I said.

'That doesn't surprise me.'

'It was about you and Eduardo.'

Isabel held back her head and laughed. 'You didn't believe that, did you?'

'It didn't make much sense to me. Now Ricardo I could have believed.'

For an instant Isabel tensed. In more usual circumstances, I wouldn't have noticed it. But after what we had experienced a few minutes before . . .

'You didn't?'

I could see Isabel's first reaction was to deny it. But she realized it was too late.

'I did.'

'Oh.'

'It didn't last long.'

'That's OK. You needn't tell me. It's none of my business.'

'No, I'd like to. I'd like to tell someone about it.'

'All right. I'll listen.'

'It was just after I'd joined Dekker. Ricardo and I were invited for a weekend's skiing in Aspen by the chairman of one of the São Paulo banks. Ricardo was in a great mood. Dekker had just had the best year of their history. Our host insisted that we ski'd and didn't talk business, so we did as we were told. Ricardo and I clicked. I know Ricardo has that effect on just about everyone, but with me I truly do think it was different.'

She looked at me to see whether I believed her. I did. 'Go on.'

'I mean I was completely taken with him. I guess that's not so surprising. But the way he looked at me. It was . . . I suppose it was like the way you look at me.'

'I'm not sure I like the sound of that.'

She ignored me. 'Well, we slept together. And over the next few months we went on a number of trips together.'

'And what did Luciana think about that?'

'She never found out.'

'Lucky for you. I wouldn't want to be on the wrong side of her temper.'

'But she cheats on him! Everyone at the office knows it. Apart from Ricardo. Just ask Jamie.'

I frowned.

'OK, you're right. I was wrong to do it. And I'm definitely not going to do it again. Especially after what happened.'

'What happened?'

'He dumped me.'

'Did it hurt?'

'Yes. A lot. I think it still does.' I squeezed her hand. 'He said he had been wrong to start it. He said it was the first time he had been unfaithful. He was risking his marriage, and he was risking his working life as well. Sleeping with one of his team was not the right way to do things.'

'I suppose not.'

'You know how self-controlled he is. Usually he

wouldn't put anything before Dekker. And he talks a lot about the importance of family life although, of course, he hardly ever sees Luciana. I think it's some sort of fiction he has created for himself.'

'Did you believe him? That it was the only time?'

'Yes. Of course that's what every dumb mistress wants to believe, but in this case I think it really is the truth. I think he was scared that he'd let his self-control slip. It certainly hasn't happened again.'

I stared up at the ceiling, considering the concept of Isabel and Ricardo. I didn't like it. There may have been an element of jealousy, but there was more to it than that. I wanted to get Ricardo out of my life, but here he was getting even closer to me.

'How's your relationship now?' I asked.

She sighed. 'Oh, he's very professional with me. He's friendly, he treats me just like the others. I try and be the same way with him, but I can't quite manage it.'

'So how did the rumours about you and Eduardo start?'

'I think the others realized that there was something going on with me. They just guessed the wrong Ross, that's all.' She shuddered. 'Yeuch. Just the thought of it makes me ill.'

'And since Ricardo?'

'No one. Until now.' She turned to me and smiled. I melted.

'You know, I definitely shouldn't be doing this,' she said, bending over to kiss me.

But she did. Twice more.

We were booked into a business hotel located between the metallic-smelling river Pinheiros and a highway. The dawn rose red in the São Paulo smog. From our window

I could see a patch of wasteland that had been turned into a soccer pitch, and a small *favela*. Isabel's theory was that there weren't any nice locations in São Paulo anyway, and this hotel had good facilities and was convenient for the airport.

I went back to my own untouched room to dress, and returned a few minutes later to pick up Isabel.

She laughed when she saw me. 'You look dreadful.'

I looked in the mirror. Dark patches edged with yellow surrounded my eyes. I glanced at Isabel. 'You don't exactly look fresh yourself.'

She yawned and stretched. She looked delectable. Tired but delectable.

'What will they think at the municipal offices?' I said. 'Maybe they'll assume we've been up all night working on the project.'

Isabel laughed. 'They might if they were English. But they're Brazilian. They'll assume we had sex all night.'

'Oh dear.'

Isabel laughed. 'Don't worry. It won't matter. In fact, I think they'll rather like the idea.' And she put her arms around me and gave me a long, lingering kiss.

I suspected they could tell, but they didn't seem to mind. We put in another hard day's work, but it was fun, and we made good progress. We finished at six, and Isabel and I spent Saturday night in São Paulo in bed, with room service to provide us with sustenance.

To Isabel, a *carioca*, the prospect of a weekend spent entirely in São Paulo was appalling so she suggested flying to Rio on Sunday morning, and taking the shuttle back to São Paulo first thing on Monday. She would show me the beach, and then we could have dinner with her father.

Initially I was reluctant; I wasn't sure I wanted to return to a Rio beach. But Isabel promised me that the beach she went to was completely safe, and that we would probably have dinner with her father at the Rio Yacht Club, which had armed guards. I agreed to go, ashamed at my nervousness.

I thought I knew Rio's beaches, but I didn't. The Point was a quarter-mile stretch of the Barra de Tijuca, a beach just down the coast from Ipanema. I brought my towel and my book, and a plan that would involve turning my pale body a delicate shade of pink. That wasn't how it worked.

The beach was crowded, crowded with beautiful brown bodies. All the men had terrific muscular definition, the result of regular workouts, and the women had smooth, tanned soft skin, displayed to great effect by bikinis that revealed almost everything. In Brazil, the buttock was all, and swimming costumes were designed to show them off in all their glory.

Isabel was wearing one of these dental-floss bikinis, and she looked stunning. It was very hard not to stare. In fact it was impossible, so I did.

But the extraordinary thing about the Point was that no one was lying down basking in the sun or reading a book, as people would on a European beach. They were sitting, squatting or standing, and talking. It made quite a racket. I shut my eyes, and the chattering, shrieking and continuous chirruping of mobile phones sounded as though I was in the midst of a crowded café.

Everyone seemed to know Isabel, and they were friendly to me. Despite my absurdly pale skin, I was quickly made to feel at home. There were plenty of bottles of the local beach beer around, and I soon relaxed, mellowed by the friendly charm of *carioca* hospitality.

I watched Isabel and her friends with interest. She seemed much more relaxed than she ever did at Dekker. She smiled, laughed, gossiped and argued in a free and uninhibited way that I found enchanting. It was as though the real Isabel, the Isabel I had glimpsed privately before, had suddenly emerged from under the long shadow of Dekker Ward.

At four we left and headed back to the Copacabana Palace Hotel. We stopped at an intersection. On the corner, two policemen slouched by their blue and white car. They wore baseball caps and dark glasses, and their first names were taped on to their chests. Right in front of them two small girls were attempting to wash windscreens, with little success. Behind them a tall, scruffily dressed man leaned against a parked car, relieving himself on the passenger window. The policemen smoked cigarettes and posed.

The traffic moved us on, past Ipanema beach, and the spot where I had been stabbed. The *favela* on the cliff above the beach looked alive but peaceful. In there, somewhere, were our attackers.

Isabel saw me tense and squeezed my hand. 'Try to forget it,' she said.

'It's difficult.' I swallowed, and we spent the rest of the journey in silence.

When we reached the hotel, Isabel joined me in my room. Eagerly, we made love again. It was long and slow, our bodies tingling from the sand and the sun. Afterwards, with Isabel's black hair spread across my chest like a soft, lightweight blanket, I asked her a question that had suddenly become very important to me.

'Isabel?'

'Yes?'

'Can I see you again? I mean, when we get back to London.'

She lifted her head, and smiled into my eyes. 'Of course.'

I pulled her back down on to my chest. 'Good.'

As I stroked her hair, I thought about what we might be getting into. My relationship with Joanna had been the only serious one of my life. It had lasted five years, five years which to me now seemed wasted. Of course we had had some good times, but I didn't remember them well. What I did remember were the daily power struggles over small things, power struggles that I always let Joanna win. She hadn't been worth it, and when she had run off to America with Wes, I had savoured my new-found independence.

Since then I had avoided another relationship. I had dated women, but had never let things progress. I was afraid of a serious attachment, and jealous of my independence.

Until now.

Isabel was completely different from Joanna, or at least Joanna as I remembered her. She was a strong, independent woman, but she was also natural, kind, warm. And she was very beautiful.

She was well worth the risk, I told myself, as though I was in control of my emotions towards her. Of course I wasn't. I had lost myself to her long ago. I looked forward to the months ahead with her with optimism.

But, of course, there was the job. Although Dekker seemed a long way away, we'd have to get back to work the next day in São Paulo. And then we'd return to

London, and I would resign. I wondered how Ricardo would take it. Not very well, I imagined. And Eduardo? I shuddered.

'Is it true Eduardo killed someone once? A student?' I asked.

Isabel didn't answer immediately, her head lay motionless on my chest.

'No, it's not true,' she said at last.

'It wouldn't have surprised me if he had. But I suppose it's just another myth.'

'Not entirely.'

I stayed silent, waiting for her to continue.

'It was Ricardo who killed the student.'

'Ricardo?'

She propped herself up on her elbow. 'Oh, it was a complete accident. It was at a party in Caracas. The other guy was drunk and took a swing at Ricardo, who was chatting up his girlfriend. Ricardo hit him harder than he meant to, and the guy fell back over the balcony, four floors up. Apparently it was very messy.'

'So Eduardo had nothing to do with it.'

'Not quite. There were witnesses, and they were the student's friends, not Ricardo's. The police came and Ricardo was soon in jail. They were about to work on him for a "confession", when Eduardo sorted it all out.'

'How?'

'I don't know. Even then Eduardo had a flair for that sort of thing. And Ricardo walked free.'

'Ricardo told you this, presumably?'

'Yes. He still feels guilty about it. And grateful to Eduardo.'

'I bet he does.' I sympathized with the guilt. I clearly remembered one night in Oxford when Jamie had become involved in an argument with a six-foot-six-inch University of Cape Town rugby player. Height never bothered Jamie: it just made his head-butts more effective. The South African had staggered back into the road. A van was driving fast down the empty High Street, and braked hard. It hit the South African, but only gently, and no damage was done. But if the van driver's reactions had been just that little bit slower . . .

'Eduardo and Ricardo seem to have a very strange relationship,' I said. 'That must be why.'

'It's not just that. I think a lot of it has to do with their father. Apparently, he was quite a successful businessman. The brothers never saw much of him, or of their mother who made a career out of spending the money her husband earned. Ricardo worshipped his father. He said he was always trying to prove himself to him, but his father never took any notice so Ricardo just tried harder.'

'Yes. He told me something similar himself. But what about Eduardo?'

'I think that Ricardo is the Argentinian and Eduardo the Venezuelan. From what I understand, their mother wanted Eduardo to be educated in Venezuela. Ricardo never lived there as an adult, but Eduardo spent a lot of time there. The flashy clothes, the cars, the speedboats, the girls, the apartments in Miami. He's a typical Venezuelan rich kid.'

'That's quite a car he owns,' I said.

'What, the "Testosterone"? The amount of times he's tried to get me into that thing!'

I grinned. I couldn't really blame him.

'Anyway,' Isabel continued, 'Ricardo's father drank. In the early eighties his businesses fell apart when the oil price crashed, and he tried to drink his way out of it. He died at the age of sixty-two. Ricardo was twenty-seven.

'You know how seriously Ricardo takes things. I think he saw it as his responsibility to look after his mother and his brother. Especially his brother. Eduardo was getting himself into all sorts of trouble with drugs. Ricardo found the money for some fancy detox clinic in America and persuaded Eduardo to go.'

'So Ricardo has always helped Eduardo out?'

'It's a two-way thing. They both owe each other a lot of favours. I'm not sure they even like each other. Eduardo thinks Ricardo's too squeamish, and a control freak. But he's jealous of Ricardo's success and wants to be a part of it. Ricardo thinks Eduardo has no self-discipline and is a danger to himself as well as other people. They're both right, of course. But as a result they both think they have to be around to help the other out.'

'So they need each other?'

'That's what they think. I think they'd both be better off having nothing to do with each other.'

She swung out of bed, and walked, naked, to the window. I followed her with my eyes.

'Oh, look,' she said. 'I think you're going to see a classic Rio rainstorm.'

I joined her, and wrapped my arms round her. A thick line of black lurked on the horizon. As we watched, it grew, gathering itself into a dark blanket that moved swiftly over the sky towards us. The breeze, blowing in through the open window, became softer, heavier. The city, still in sunshine for a few moments more, cowered in front of the enveloping clouds. Then the blanket reached us, blacking out the sky and dropping itself upon us in a torrent of water. We let the giant drops splash into the room through the open window. Below us, the courtyard erupted into thousands of tiny fountains as the rain struck it, and the surface of the swimming pool was shattered into a myriad of angry whirlpools.

'God, what a sight,' I said.

'We'd better get going. The traffic in Rio becomes a nightmare in a storm like this.'

We showered, dressed, and then scurried to a taxi beneath one of the hotel's white umbrellas. As I scrambled into the back seat after Isabel, I thought I caught sight of someone I recognized. I turned to look as we pulled off.

'What is it?' she asked, a drop of water dangling appealingly from her nose.

'I thought I recognized the driver of the car behind. I could have sworn he was waiting for someone at the airport this morning.'

'Where?' She turned to look behind us.

The rain fell heavily on the rear window and created a curtain of water behind us.

'I can't see him now. Or his car. It was a Fiat, I think. Blue.'

We both strained to see through the rainstorm. Nothing.

'Are you sure?' Isabel asked.

'To be honest, no. I might just be imagining it.'

She squeezed my hand. 'You're getting jumpy after what happened last time. Rio isn't that dangerous, you know.'

'You're probably right,' I said, but nevertheless I did check behind every now and again. I didn't see anything.

We were meeting Luís at the Rio Yacht Club. The journey took about three-quarters of an hour. The traffic slowed to a crawl. Torrents of water gushed down any small incline, often reaching up to the tops of the struggling cars' wheels.

It was dark by the time we reached the Yacht Club. Luís was already there, and gave Isabel a huge hug, which she returned warmly. He seemed genuinely happy to see me too, which pleased me. The club was, of course, next to a small marina, and we could just make out the sailing boats, bobbing in the rain-lashed sea. Eventually, the downpour softened to a more recognizable rain, and it was possible to see the buildings of Botafogo across the bay, and the imposing shape of Sugar Loaf mountain, looming high up above us.

I drank the compulsory *caipirinhas* – I was beginning to realize that no foreigner could avoid them in Brazil – and ate some glorious fish whose name I didn't quite catch. Luís and Isabel both did a good job of avoiding any difficult subjects, and I didn't witness a single argument. Isabel seemed happy, very much alive, and she glowed in the attention of her father and me.

'So, you didn't want to spend the weekend in São Paulo, Nick?' Luís asked, with a smile.

'Isabel didn't seem very keen on the idea.'

'Where did you take him?' he asked Isabel.

'The Point,' she said.

'Ah, very good. Did you like the view, Nick?'

'Oh, Papai!'

I grinned. 'One of our poets once said, "Water, water everywhere, nor any drop to drink."'

This Luís seemed to find very funny. Isabel just looked cross.

'Well, I'm glad you found a few minutes to spend with your old father,' he said.

'I'm sorry I'm not staying with you tonight,' Isabel

said, 'but we're leaving for the airport tomorrow morning, and I knew you were in Petrópolis today, and we are leaving very early, so I thought it made sense to stay at the hotel with Nick. So I can show him to the airport.'

This explanation was all a bit breathless. It sounded forced to me. I think it did to Luís, to judge by the way he glanced at me. I pretended not to notice.

But then he shrugged. 'No matter. I quite understand. You often stay at the Copacabana Palace when you're here on business. It's just nice to see you for dinner.'

Isabel blushed becomingly and concentrated on her food.

'I'm very sorry about your Favela Bairro deal,' Luís said.

'Yes, I know. The whole scandal was set up by Ricardo. All that stuff linking the drug gangs to the deal was ridiculous. Ricardo just wanted to make sure Bloomfield Weiss didn't steal the mandate.'

'I thought it must be something like that. I never believe what Oswaldo's papers say. Not that I ever read them.'

'Still, we have another chance. São Paulo are very interested in doing a similar deal.'

'Good. Well, good luck with that. So you're going back there tomorrow?'

'Yes,' said Isabel.

'Well, remember Nick, in São Paulo you can breathe out but don't breathe in.'

I laughed. 'I'll remember.'

Finally, at twelve, we left. The rain was steady now, and had clearly set in for the night.

'Would you like a lift back in my car?' Luís asked.

'Oh, no,' Isabel said. 'I've ordered a taxi to meet us

from the hotel. It's probably been waiting for us half the night. We'd better take it.'

Another suspicious glance from Luís, which I ignored.

'Oh, well, see you soon, my dear.' He bent down to kiss his daughter. Then he straightened up and shook my hand. I met his eye, which I was relieved to see was still friendly. 'Nice to see you again, Nick. Please drop in and see me when you are next in Rio.'

'Thank you,' I said. 'I will.'

He ran through the rain to his chauffeur-driven car, and we jumped into the taxi.

'Why didn't we go with him?' I asked.

'I suppose we could have. It's just I would have felt pretty bad having him drop us off together at the hotel.'

'I think he suspects something,' I said.

'Do you?' Isabel fell back in the seat. 'Oh, well, never mind. I think he likes you.'

'I like him.'

Isabel smiled, and rested her head on my shoulder. 'I'm *so* tired.'

With the drink and the fatigue, my eyes stared ahead without focusing properly. The road was empty apart from the car in front, which was driving slowly. Suddenly it stopped.

Our driver swore under his breath, and braked also. He hit the horn. Just then there was movement in the windows all around us. The driver saw it, and hit the button by his shoulder. The central-locking system clicked in all the doors. He slammed the gears into reverse, and there was a crash as he hit something behind us. I turned. Another car had driven up to block our escape. The taxi leaped forward and hit the vehicle in front as the driver tried to shunt out. Then his window shattered in an explosion of broken glass. A gun pointed in, and a voice behind it shouted urgently. The driver took his hands off the wheel and pushed up the lock to his door.

Isabel screamed.

I turned to my door, which was flung open. A gun was thrust in my face. A man in a Balaclava shouted at me in Portuguese. I can still remember his eyes. They were brown, the pupils huge, and they stared in frightened panic. I could see bushy eyebrows beneath the Balaclava, and the remains of a couple of spots between his eyes. The mask was dripping with water.
The gun was silver. It was the same style as a Colt .45. The fist that held it was clenched so tight it was shaking. It was a miracle the trigger finger hadn't pulled already.

This guy was as jumpy as hell.

The shout turned to a scream. I kept perfectly still and stammered, '*Não entendo.*' The man kept screaming. I felt a kick in my back as Isabel was dragged out of the car, but I couldn't take my eyes off the gun.

Then he reached into the car and grabbed my jacket, still shouting. I let him pull me out into the rain. He pushed me towards the rearmost car. I could hear Isabel screaming behind me as she was dragged towards the vehicle in front.

Swift panicky hands pushed me down into the well between the back and front seats, but I didn't fit. Then the front seat lurched forward, and my face was shoved down on to the floor. It smelt of dust and cigarettes. One of them sat in the seat beside me, I heard the car door slam, and felt the cold barrel push into the nape of my neck. It was wet, and drops of water dribbled down my back.

Someone shouted something in Portuguese, and we lurched off. The car screeched round some tight bends, and then seemed to reach straight road. We were moving fast and steadily, in what direction I had no idea.

17

I began to think through what had happened. We'd been kidnapped, that much was obvious. I hoped Isabel was OK. I wondered where they would take us, what they would do with us. If they'd kidnapped us, they would want to keep us alive. Remember that. Help them. Keep them happy.

But who would pay our ransom? Luís would pay Isabel's. Would Dekker pay mine? God, I hoped so. Ricardo had a reputation of looking after his own. Thank God he had no idea I was about to resign.

How long would the process take? Maybe Isabel would know. I had heard kidnappings were pretty common in Rio, so she probably knew something about them.

I was in a very uncomfortable position, with my back twisted and my face jammed down into the floor. I tried to move, but this prompted a shout and the gun barrel jabbed hard into the back of my neck. So I decided to stay exactly where I was.

Suddenly the car slowed, and turned off whatever road we were on. We were moving more slowly now, stopping and starting. After a few more minutes we began to climb, turning left and right up a steep hillside.

We drove like this for half an hour, or maybe an hour,

it was hard to tell. Then we made another turn and the car began to bump and judder. A dirt track. My cheek was driven into the car floor at each jolt. We drove up an even steeper incline, which eventually levelled off. Finally, we came to a stop.

My back and shoulders ached like hell. I tried to move, but the gun jabbed my back again, and I stayed still. Then some black fabric was tied round my eyes, and I couldn't see.

I heard voices, car doors opening and shutting. A hand grabbed my collar and tugged. Willingly I pulled myself up out of the well, and allowed myself to be dragged from the car. I stood up straight and stretched.

I could see nothing through the blindfold. It had stopped raining. And the air was filled with noise: the sound of crickets, cicadas, frogs, and all kinds of night creatures. It made quite a din.

'Isabel?'

'Yes!'

'*Cale a boca*!' screamed a voice in my right ear.

I felt a gun jab my ribs. But at least I knew she was alive and with me.

There was some heated discussion around me. I heard four voices. Rope was tied round my hands until it bit into my wrists. Then I felt a push behind me, and an order in Portuguese that I took to mean 'Move!'

The ground was wet and muddy underfoot. Soon we were moving up a steep hill along a narrow path. I could tell that because of the vegetation brushing at my ankles. Behind and below I heard the two cars driving off. With the blindfold on I couldn't protect myself from the branches and tendrils that brushed my face. Pushing through an unknown jungle blindfolded raised all kinds of primeval fears about snakes, and unseen precipices.

I tried to move slowly and carefully, but a hard metal object jabbed me in the back whenever I hesitated.

I heard movement ahead and behind. I didn't call out for Isabel this time. I didn't want to push my luck.

After an hour or so, the ground began to level off, and the going became much easier. Ten more minutes, and I heard the command *'Pare!'* and then 'Stop!'

With relief, I stopped. I stood up straight, and the blindfold was removed.

We were in a very small clearing in a forest. It was still night, but after the blindfold it almost seemed like daylight. A canvas tent had been rigged up between three trees, and there was another, ten yards away from it. I could see Isabel, and two men. Both of them wore Balaclava-type masks. The one who had taken off my blindfold was standing a few feet away, with the gun pointed straight at me. Dark suspicious eyes peered at me through the mask. The other man was taking off Isabel's blindfold.

She looked round for me and caught my eye. She seemed OK, although when I looked closer, what I thought was a shadow turned out to be a bruise on her cheek. The bastards had hit her.

One man pulled out some handcuffs and a chain from a sack on the ground, while the other man covered us with the gun. Without blindfolds, we had a few seconds of relative freedom before being chained to something, although of course our hands were still tied. And a gun was pointing at us.

Isabel must have seen the opportunity, because as the man stood up with the handcuffs, she kicked him hard in the groin.

The other man immediately jerked his gun towards Isabel.

'No!' I shouted, and leaped at him.

He hesitated before pulling the trigger. Perhaps he didn't want to shoot a woman in cold blood, I don't know. I chopped down hard on his gun arm, and he dropped the weapon. His hands were nearer to it than mine, and I just managed to kick it into the undergrowth, before he could reach it.

'Run!' I shouted to Isabel.

There were two paths out of the clearing, one leading in from the way we came, and the other heading downhill on the opposite side. Isabel chose that path, and I followed her. One of our captors was still clasping his groin, moaning, and the other was scrabbling about in the undergrowth for the gun.

The path led sharply downhill, and we half slid, half ran down it. It was difficult keeping balance with our hands tied, and we both kept falling, and landing awkwardly. I rolled, hopped and jumped down the hill, but Isabel was slower. I paused to wait for her. She tumbled down a steep slope towards me, but was suddenly pulled up short. She had snagged her tied hands in a bush. I scrambled up the hill to help her.

There was a crashing above us as one of the men slid down the hill. It was the one Isabel had kicked in the groin; he didn't appear to have a gun.

Isabel's hands were wedged tight into the branches of the bush. The rope and wood were slippery with the wet, and I couldn't free them.

'Run, Nick!' she shouted.

I took no notice, and scrabbled frantically at the rope.

'Nick. Run! Leave me!'

I stood up to see one of our captors only a few feet above us. Then I heard a shout from his friend behind him, and the sharp crack of a pistol.

I glanced at Isabel. Her eyes pleaded with me to run. Should I stay with her? Would I be better able to free her if I was with her or if I escaped?

God only knew.

'For God's sake, go!' she screamed.

I ran.

I tumbled further down the path, and glanced back. I could see both men had stopped by the bush where Isabel had snagged her hands. I prayed she'd be all right.

I ran on, scratching myself on branches and stones, following the faint path downwards. After about ten minutes I paused to listen.

I couldn't hear anything above the nocturnal din of the forest. I wasn't being followed. I slumped down by a tree trunk and caught my breath.

Above me, tall trees obscured the night sky, vines dangling down from their thin branches. The floor of the forest was dark, murky and damp, with all kinds of mysterious vegetation crammed thickly together. There was no question of venturing off the path. I couldn't go far with my hands tied like this. But if I followed the path to its end, perhaps where it spilled out on to a road, wouldn't they just be waiting for me? I had no choice. I had to press on before they got themselves organized.

I was relieved to see that the path continued downhill. I knew that if you became lost walking in the Scottish Highlands, the thing to do was head downhill. Eventually you would reach civilization that way. The theory should hold in the Brazilian forest, shouldn't it?

I was pretty sure we must be in the Tijuca forest, a swath of Atlantic rain-forest to the west of Rio. It couldn't be that big. I must hit a settlement at some point. Mustn't I?

After about half an hour, I came to a gully. It was strewn with huge looming boulders, through which ran a stream. The rocks were the product of some earlier flood. No wonder there were powerful floods with rains like those I had witnessed the evening before. That was just what I needed now, a flash flood.

I decided to leave the path and follow the stream downhill, on the basis that I would avoid a reception party waiting for me at the end of the path. It was tricky picking my way through the rocks in the dark, and I made slow progress.

Just as the sky began to lighten, I saw a bridge below me. I paused for breath beside one of the giant boulders. Perhaps they were waiting by the bridge? If I joined the road, would the kidnappers find me? I didn't know. I decided not to follow any roads. I would carry on under the bridge, and down the stream bed until I found some habitation.

I was getting tired. My legs were scratched and bruised, and my muscles ached. I stopped for a rest on a stone. Dawn comes quickly to Brazil, and the landscape around me was fast revealed in the grey morning light. I was surrounded by forest and steep hills, rising behind me into clouds. The night-time noises had died down, and it was oddly silent. It was eerie, this damp gloomy forest, clad in moisture. Ahead, down below, I could see nothing but grey. As I rested, I began to feel cold.

Then down to the right, I noticed wisps of a lighter shade of grey. Smoke!

I stood up, and stumbled down the stream bed. The smoke came from quite a substantial building, which backed on to the stream. I clambered up a path from the stream to the building, my muscles aching. I could barely make it to the top of the bank.

I staggered round to the front of the building. It was some kind of restaurant. I pushed a bell and waited.

18

The owner of the restaurant spoke English, and insisted on giving me some food before driving me himself back to the hotel. It took two hours, most of it through the Rio rush-hour traffic. He had no problem agreeing to my request not to tell the police. I wanted to talk to Luís first. The Brazilian police were an entirely unknown quantity. I was worried that I might be putting Isabel's life at risk by contacting them.

Eyebrows were politely raised as I swept through the hotel lobby in my dishevelled state and went straight up to my room. I found Banco Horizonte's number, dialled it, and asked for Senhor Luís Pereira.

'Yes, Nick, what can I do for you?' The deep voice was friendly but tinged with a mild curiosity as to why I should be telephoning him that morning.

'Isabel's been kidnapped.'

There was silence.

'Where are you?' he said eventually, his voice still outwardly calm.

'At the Copacabana Palace Hotel.'

'Can you go directly to my apartment? I'll meet you there in half an hour.'

I showered quickly, changed into some clean clothes,

and arrived at Luís's apartment thirty-five minutes later. He was already there, pacing up and down the large living room. He gestured for me to sit down in a low cane sofa, while he took the chair opposite. He leaned forward in his seat, his eyes fixed firmly on me. He seemed cool, businesslike.

'Tell me what happened?'

I told him all about the kidnapping, our escape, and Isabel's recapture.

When I had finished, Luís sighed. 'Kidnapping is a fact of life in Rio. I had expected it to happen some time, but frankly I assumed either myself or Cordelia might be the victim. I thought Isabel would be safe.'

He paused for a moment, his eyes looking into the distance over my shoulder. Then he focused back on me. 'There's a man called Nelson Zarur who has advised me about these matters, taking precautions and so on. He's a security consultant. He helped a friend of mine's family when he was kidnapped. I'll give him a call.'

'Shall I wait here?' I asked.

Luís smiled. 'I'd like you to, if you can. We will have to talk to Dekker Ward about this. And I'll have to tell Cordelia.' His expression clouded. 'It will be good to have a friend of Isabel's here.'

Luís probably didn't know how good a friend. I was glad of the opportunity to stay.

Luís made some phone calls. I couldn't understand what was said. Most were calm and controlled. One involved lots of listening with a pained expression on his face – Cordelia. Then he left the room. A few moments later I heard a loud keening – Maria.

It was hard to sit there, doing nothing, watching while Luís calmly put things in motion. I felt shaken, physically and mentally. My muscles were tired and ached, and the bruises and scratches I had picked up on the hillside were making themselves known. Details of the kidnap came flooding back, and of Isabel's reckless attempt to escape. If the gunman hadn't hesitated she could well have been shot. Or perhaps she had calculated that they wouldn't shoot a kidnap victim unless they absolutely had to.

And then the moment when I had left her, tangled up in the bush. She had wanted me to go, but I still felt I should be with her now, wherever she was.

How were they treating her? Had they hurt her? Punished her for escaping?

And then the most important question of all. Would we get her back alive and unharmed?

Luís finished and gestured to the phone. 'Why don't you get in touch with Dekker?'

Relieved to be doing something, I dialled Ricardo's number in London.

'Dekker.'

'Ricardo. It's Nick.'

'What's up?' There was concern in Ricardo's voice. He could pick up the concern in mine.

'Isabel's been kidnapped.'

'How?'

I told him.

Ricardo took it coolly, like a big trade going wrong. 'OK, Nick. Now don't worry. Kidnapping's a local pastime in Rio. It nearly always ends in a ransom being paid and the victim being set free.'

A thought suddenly struck me. I knew how ruthless Ricardo could be. Surely even he couldn't . . .

He answered my unspoken question. 'Don't worry. If they ask us for a ransom, we'll pay. All Dekker employees are insured against kidnap at Lloyds.'

'I didn't know you could do that.'

'Well, you can, and we have. We've never had to use it before. But there's a procedure. As soon as we hear of the demand, then we'll get a negotiator on the case. But since it's Isabel, they're more likely to go to her father.'

'I've told him. I'm at his apartment now.'

'Good. How's he taking it? Does he know what to do?'

'He seems to have thought all this through before-hand. He's got hold of some kind of security consultant.'

'Excellent. Now, can you stay in Rio until things become clearer?'

'I'd be happy to.'

'OK. Keep me informed.'

I was comforted as I put down the phone. Both Ricardo and Luís were taking the situation calmly. I began to hope that Isabel's life was safe in their hands. Knowing that this was a common event made me feel better. If we just stuck to the rules, and so did the kidnappers, then Isabel should go free. Eventually. After being kept locked up in some hole somewhere for God knows how long. And I wasn't quite happy with the idea of Ricardo using his tough negotiating tactics for Isabel's life.

I tried to calm myself down too, to be useful. It was difficult. The tide of worry threatened to over-whelm me. Would she be hurt? Would they let her go? Would they treat her well? Why hadn't I stayed with her?

Nelson Zarur was at the apartment within half an hour. He was an odd-looking man, short with a round orange face and bulging eyes. He wore a bright green short-sleeved shirt and tan trousers. Luís had mentioned he was a retired policeman, although he didn't look much over forty-five.

Luís introduced us, and asked Nelson to speak in English for my benefit. I was pleased to be included.

Luís asked me to describe the kidnapping itself. Nelson took notes in an old notebook with a cheap biro, occasionally asking detailed questions.

'That area is a favourite place for kidnappings,' he said. 'There have been three there in the last year. Quiet streets next to a highway. Perfect. And the Tijuca forest has been used before as a staging post to keep the victims for a couple of days while they get somewhere else ready.'

'So what can we expect now?' Luís asked him.

'The most important thing to remember is that this is a business transaction,' Nelson began. His English was fast and accurate, although his accent was strong. He sounded confident, and his confidence was infectious. He clearly knew what he was talking about.

He went on: 'The kidnappers have goods of value to you, which they want to sell. They can only do that if the goods are in good condition. So that is why it is in their interest to keep Isabel healthy.'

'I'm not sure I like the idea of thinking of my daughter as goods to be traded,' said Luís.

'Of course not. And that's what the kidnappers will be playing on. They will use everything they can to make you think that they are callous sadists who are just about to harm your daughter for no good reason. But they're not. Kidnappers in Rio are usually very rational. All they want is the ransom. My job is to help you remember that, to try to keep this a commercial transaction, and to ensure that Isabel is returned safely for the smallest sum of money.'

He leaned forward and touched Luís's arm, his round orange face sincere. 'I've advised on sixteen kidnaps so far. In all but two the victim was returned alive. The odds are heavily on our side.'

Luís frowned. 'That's good to know. But will she . . . I mean will they – '

Nelson interrupted, 'We have no way of knowing what conditions she will be kept in. That depends entirely on the kidnappers. But they won't touch her. In my experience they never do.'

Luís's frown lightened. Rape hadn't occurred to me, thank God. But it would have done eventually, and I was very pleased to hear what Nelson had to say.

'You have to decide whether to tell the police,' Nelson went on. 'I would strongly recommend it. They will keep their distance and won't interfere with the ransom negotiations. And if we are open with them there is less chance of them stumbling blindly into the middle of something.'

Luís hesitated. 'But what if the kidnappers tell us not to contact them?'

'It's quite likely that they will say that, but the police will keep a low profile. However, we should try to keep the press out of it if we can. The fewer people who know about this the better.'

'How big's the forest?' I asked. 'Do you think the police will find them?'

Nelson shook his head. 'There is no chance of that. As soon as they realized you had escaped, the kidnappers would have moved on. But the police might learn something if they find the remains of the camp you saw.'

Luís nodded. 'OK. We'll tell the police. What happens next?'

'We wait for the kidnappers to get in touch. It may be quick, or it may take several days.'

Just then Cordelia burst into the room, and ran to her father. He held her, his tall frame stooped over her, protecting her. I could see his expression, it was still firm, but they clung to each other for a long time.

Nelson caught my eye, and we left the room. We moved into a smaller sitting room with a TV in it.

Nelson turned to me. 'He's taking it well at the start. Some of these tough businessmen do. But it won't last. It's hard when it's your daughter.'

'I'm sure it will be.'

'Are you a good friend of hers?'

The question was innocent, but the look that accompanied it was not. I nodded, letting Nelson draw his own conclusions.

'I work with Isabel,' I said. 'I believe our firm has some kind of kidnap insurance.'

'That's technically illegal in Brazil. But I know some of the firms in London who operate in that area. Tell your employer to get their insurers to contact me here.'

'OK,' I said. We were trusting a lot to this man's judgement, I thought. But Ricardo had said there was a procedure, and I was glad we had someone on our side who knew it.

There was one thing I had to ask him. 'When I escaped, I left her with the kidnappers. I feel bad about that. I think I should have stayed with her. To help her.'

Nelson took hold of my arm.

'One of the most common reactions to kidnapping from the relatives or friends of the victim is guilt. Guilt that they should have done something to prevent their loved one from being taken. It's always a waste of time, and it can get in the way of thinking rationally about how to set the victim free.'

'But I could have cheered her up if I'd stayed with her. Helped her through it.'

Nelson lowered his voice. 'Frankly, Nick, you are lucky you did escape. Isabel is safe. She has a rich father willing to pay a fair ransom. You? You could easily have been killed to show that they mean business. You're better off here.'

I shuddered. Perhaps Nelson was right. But I would do anything, *anything* I could to get Isabel out.

I spent the day at the Pereira apartment. A policeman came, a detective called Da Silva wearing the same sort of bad suit and loud tie that detectives all over the world wear. As Nelson had suggested, he promised to keep a low profile. Apparently, by focusing on the methods, or *modus operandi* of the kidnap gangs, the police were having some success in making arrests. Certainly more than they had in surprising a drop with all guns blazing. Da Silva interviewed me for an hour, asking me for every conceivable detail I could remember. Then he organized a tap on the phone, and asked to be kept informed on a daily basis.

The waiting was difficult, and it had only just begun. Luís tried to carry on with the bank's business, but he couldn't concentrate. So he paced around restlessly, picking up papers and documents, occasionally talking to me or Cordelia.

Cordelia insisted on staying. She too tried reading, but in the end she turned on the TV in the small sitting room, and sat staring blankly at it.

I was very tired: I hadn't slept at all the previous night. But I couldn't sleep now. I spent the time trying to control the agitation inside me. I wanted to scream, shout, *do* something. But, of course, there was nothing to do.

I became morbid, I couldn't help it. I found myself snatching at the memories of things Isabel and I had done together as if they would be the last. This was ridiculous. The most likely thing was that she would be released unharmed, and I would see her again. But I could only force my brain to think of the most probable outcome for a few minutes. It would always drift back into thinking the worst.

Nelson stayed too, but remained inconspicuous. I spoke to Ricardo and put Nelson in touch with the kidnap insurance broker at Lloyds who had written the Dekker policy. They seemed to know of Nelson, which was encouraging. Under the policy the insurance company would cover a ransom paid by the family or Dekker up to a limit of a million dollars.

The phone rang on and off all day. Luís wanted to keep in touch with the office. He told them his daughter was ill and needed him. He wasn't very specific and it didn't make much sense, but he was the boss so no one could argue.

I stayed for supper, and then went back to the hotel. It seemed empty without Isabel. I went up to her room, and packed her stuff. I felt uncomfortable, gathering together her small personal belongings. It seemed a strangely domestic thing, as though at the moment we had been torn apart, we were making a step closer. The irony made me feel sick.

I returned to my room with her case, and got ready for bed. The phone rang. I looked at my watch. Eleven o'clock. I picked it up. 'Hallo?'

'Mr Nicholas Elliot?'

The voice was harsh, the accent so strong I could

barely distinguish my own name. My heart-rate quickened.

'Yes?'

'I have your friend. You give me one million dollars. I let her go.'

My mind raced. I knew I wasn't the person to carry out this negotiation. I needed to get them on to Luís and Nelson.

'I am not her friend. I just work with her,' I said.

'If you not give me one million dollars, she dies!' the voice said. The accent was so pronounced and the words so melodramatic that it hardly seemed real. But it was.

'No, wait! You telephone her father. This is his number,' and I read it down the phone. 'He will talk to you.'

'OK,' said the voice, and the phone clicked.

I hung up and raced to dial Luís's number before the voice. He answered, tense. I told him what to expect. I said I would be right round.

It took me fifteen minutes to jump in a taxi and get there. Luís and Nelson were deep in conversation, with Cordelia listening.

'They want a million dollars,' said Luís. 'They want it dropped off on Wednesday morning at two a. m. They say if I don't pay, they'll kill her. I told them to call back in the morning.'

It was Monday night. Wednesday morning was just over twenty-four hours away.

I could see that there was some tension between Nelson and Luís. 'What's the problem?' I asked.

Luís glanced at Nelson. 'A million dollars is nothing for Isabel's life. I want to pay it.'

'And I feel we should ask for proof of life. Something to show that they've got her, and that she's alive,' the little man said. 'And then we should negotiate the price down from there. They will expect it.'

'But we know she was alive when they took her. I don't want to anger them. Believe me, I can afford a million dollars.'

For the first time, Luís was showing signs of strain. Nelson paused to defuse the situation, and then spoke calmly. 'We don't know they've got her. It might be a hoax.'

'How can it be a hoax? No one knows she has been kidnapped, do they? Just us and the police.'

'What is this proof-of-life business?' I asked Nelson. 'Do you want a photo of her with a newspaper?'

'No, that can be faked. The best thing is to ask them a question that only Isabel will know the answer to. If they call back with the correct response, then we know they have her and she is alive.'

Both Luís and Nelson were looking at me. They wanted my advice. I wasn't going to duck the responsibility.

'Why don't you do what Nelson suggests? If they have Isabel, it can't hurt, can it?'

Luís sighed, and rubbed his temples. 'OK' He nodded.

I slept in the guest room at Luís's apartment that night. Or, rather, I didn't sleep, but I lay down under some covers and let my brain tumble.

The kidnappers called at nine the next morning. Luís told them he couldn't raise the cash that day, he would need more time. He also asked them to tell him the name of Isabel's favourite teddy bear when she was a girl. I could hear the abusive threats down the phone at this.

Luís was white when he put the receiver down. 'They

said that if we don't drop off the money at two o'clock tomorrow morning, Isabel will die. They won't wait another day.'

I began to think that I had given him the wrong advice.

Only Nelson was unconcerned. 'If they have her, we will hear back from them soon,' he assured us.

'But what about the two o'clock deadline?'

'Ignore it. They can't be serious.'

But we didn't hear back from them all day.

I stayed the night again. Luís seemed to want me there with him when the deadline passed, and I was happy to oblige. We were both up and awake at two o'clock. Of course the phone didn't ring. We exchanged grim glances as the kidnappers' deadline ticked away.

The waiting was beginning to take its toll. Both Luís and I were suffering from lack of sleep, although by now I was so exhausted that at last I could begin to doze for short periods. Luís just walked around, looking gaunt. And it was only day three. Cordelia had gone home the day before, but insisted that we call her with any news. By Wednesday night we had still heard nothing. Nelson had returned to his own home that afternoon, with instructions to be contacted if anything happened.

Supper was an omelette and salad. Luís didn't eat much of his. During the last few days he had managed to keep his outward composure, apart from the show of tension with Nelson just after the kidnappers had given their first demand. Then, suddenly, as the two of us sat in silence round the dinner table, his lip quivered, and he put his head in his hands. He began to sob.

I watched in silence. Tentatively I stretched out a hand and touched his sleeve.

'She's dead,' he said.

'No, she isn't. Maybe they'll call later.'

'Why should they? It was a simple question. All they had to do was ask her and call me back. They said if I didn't pay them by two last night she'd die. And she's dead.'

'Perhaps it's a hoax. Maybe they aren't the real kidnappers.'

'How can that be? We've been through that. Nobody else knows.'

We had been through that. Then a thought struck me.

'Why did they call me at the hotel?'

'They followed you from there,' Luís said. 'They knew you were staying there.'

'Yes, but they could have got your number from Isabel. Why didn't they?'

Luís was silent for a moment. He brightened. And then his face clouded over. 'Unless she's dead. Then she couldn't tell them.'

'Luís, there's no reason for them to kill her!' My brain, which had been turning somersaults for the last three days, suddenly settled. 'I know! It was the taxi driver. He saw the kidnap and drove off. He must have told some friends about it, and tried his luck at a ransom demand.'

Luís listened.

'I'll call Nelson and see what he thinks.'

But before I could reach the phone, it rang. I froze. Luís grabbed it.

I picked up the second earphone Nelson had attached. It was a different voice. Younger, calmer. Luís spoke for about two minutes. I couldn't understand what was said, but Luís smiled as he put the phone down.

'Well?'

'It was another man. He said his name was Zico. He says he has Isabel. He wants a ransom. I asked the teddy bear question, and he didn't seem concerned. He said he would call back with the answer.'

I felt a surge of relief. So the first voice had been a hoax. I much preferred Zico's voice. He sounded calmer, more rational.

'Zico? Isn't that the name of a soccer player?'

'Yes,' Luís smiled grimly. 'He was brilliant. He used to play for Flamengo. My club.'

'How much does he want?'

Luís frowned. 'Fifty million dollars.'

'Fifty million! Christ! Have you got that much?'

'Technically my stake in Horizonte may be worth that much, but there's no way I could get at it without selling the bank, which would be difficult. No, impossible.'

'Still, it's a start,' I said.

Luís smiled. 'Yes. It's a start.'

19

The next couple of days were a relief. Zico called back within half an hour with the correct answer to Luís's question – Lulu. He made threats about how Isabel would die if fifty million dollars wasn't paid by the end of the week, but Luís didn't believe him and neither did I. We were just glad that the process had begun which would lead eventually to Isabel's release.

We sat round the breakfast table with Nelson. Luís was almost smiling.

'Now we have to discuss tactics,' Nelson said. He was wearing a particularly bright purple shirt. Tufts of grey chest hair peeked through its open neck. He spoke carefully and rapidly, very much in control. He had proved himself to us with his suspicion of the hoax ransom demand; it was becoming easier to trust him.

'OK,' said Luís.

'We must decide how much you are prepared to pay for Isabel.'

'That's ridiculous!' Luís protested. 'The answer is everything.'

'No, that's not the answer,' said Nelson. 'Remember, this is a commercial transaction. The answer is the lowest amount you can get away with. Look, the kidnappers can't know exactly how much money you have.

We will come to a point where we have to say this is our final offer. Then, provided the kidnappers believe us, they will hand over your daughter.'

Luís took a deep breath. 'OK.'

'Good. Now, how much do you think you could get your hands on? In cash.'

Suddenly I felt awkward. Here I was about to hear all about the personal business of a man I hardly knew, in fact the owner of a rival bank to my employer. I began to stand up. 'Perhaps I should leave you to it . . .'

Luís held up his hand. 'No. Stay. Please.'

I paused. He meant it. Nelson nodded. 'OK,' I said, and sat down.

'I can probably raise up to five million dollars,' said Luís. 'Maybe a little more. But it will mean talking to some of my colleagues. I'll have to borrow money.'

'Good,' said Nelson. 'I'd hope to get away with a lot less than that.' He pulled out his notebook and biro. 'We should think about some numbers. The average settlement at the moment in Rio is about two hundred thousand dollars. But I think they know how wealthy you are, or at least they can make a good guess. The first demand was high.'

'I can't pay fifty million,' said Luís.

'Nor will they expect you to. Another rule of thumb is that the final settlement is about one tenth of the initial sum offered. In this case that's five million dollars. But that's still too high for the market in Rio right now.'

'I could pay it if necessary. Somehow.'

Nelson held up his hand. 'No. I think two million should be fine. You should be able to claim a million back from Dekker's insurers anyway, although you will probably have to put up the cash to start with.'

'Perhaps Dekker could provide it?' I suggested.

Luís's eyes narrowed for an instant. 'No, thank you. I don't want to borrow money from Ricardo Ross.'

The speed of his reaction surprised me, but in a way I was pleased to see that he could still think shrewdly.

Nelson and Luís argued back and forth on the target figure, and eventually settled for three million dollars.

'OK. We have a number,' said Nelson. 'We can't expect to come to an agreement of the price too quickly. We have to let the kidnappers string things out a bit, feel that they've had a proper negotiation. Otherwise they won't believe three million is our final offer.'

Luís opened his mouth to protest.

'Offering more money won't get Isabel released any faster, believe me.'

Luís saw the logic and nodded.

'I suggest we start off with a million dollars, then move it up in half-million chunks until we get to two million. Then we need to raise our offer in ever smaller amounts so that it seems as though each rise is a struggle. We will aim to stop the negotiations just short of three million.'

It seems a long way to come down from fifty million to one million,' said Luís doubtfully.

'Believe me, one million is a big first offer for a kidnapping.'

We believed him. Zico called on Thursday night. He treated Luís's offer of one million dollars with derision. He said he knew that Luís owned Banco Horizonte. Luís explained that he only owned part of it, and that he couldn't sell his stake. He performed well. He sounded cool at the beginning, and then as the conversation went on he displayed more tension. His assertion that he couldn't raise more than a million sounded credible to me.

I listened to the tape played back. Although I couldn't understand what was said, I was fascinated by Zico's voice. Calm, measured, cold, intelligent. The compulsory threats to Isabel had none of the mindless violence of the first hoax caller. But the coldness was menacing in its own way. Zico wouldn't kill Isabel unless it suited him. But if it suited him . . .

The police came. They took the tape of the conversation away for analysis of Zico's voice. They had traced the call to a mobile phone somewhere in a crowded shopping street in the northern zone. Mobile phones were common in Rio. The land-line system was so bad that its citizens had been driven to using them instead. And they were virtually impossible to trace.

A dozen policemen were searching the Tijuca forest but so far they had found nothing.

Maria fussed over both Luís and me. She seemed to be taking it well, until she would suddenly run from the room, trying to hold back tears. Cordelia would come round for a couple of hours every day, but she found the waiting stressful. She had become withdrawn, a different person from the tough woman I had met at the children's shelter. She had stopped going there. Just for the time being, she said.

I stayed at Luís's apartment during the day, and my hotel at night. A couple of times I went out for walks through the wealthy streets of Ipanema. It was good to get out into the world, to see people shopping at the expensive boutiques, to wander past the up-market stalls selling flowers or rugs or Indian jewellery. Ipanema was a forest of luxury apartment buildings crammed together between the beach and the lagoon. Every now and then an old colonial-style building squatted among them, but old by Ipanema's standards probably meant less than fifty years. I found a pleasant bar in one of these and stopped for a beer. I had read somewhere that 'The Girl from Ipanema' had been written by a man who hung out in a bar somewhere round here, watching the local talent go by. There were indeed many young, tanned and lovely girls who walked past. But they just reminded me of Isabel.

I tried to imagine where she was, what kind of state she was in. Was she well fed? Was she allowed to wash? It was hard for us here, it must be harder for her there. But she was a strong woman mentally. If anyone could cope with an ordeal like that, she could.

I shouldn't have left her alone. *I shouldn't have left her alone!*

I avoided Ipanema beach. After the kidnap, I had forgotten my stabbing there. I wanted it to stay forgotten. My fears of money-laundering and concerns about Dekker were pushed to the back of my mind. I just wanted Isabel to be freed.

I spoke to Ricardo regularly, keeping him informed of the progress of negotiations. It was comforting to hear Ricardo's calm voice every day. He seemed impressed with Nelson as a negotiator. He was happy to continue footing the bill for the hotel. He had spoken to Luís, who had made a firm request that I be allowed to stay.

I spoke to Jamie, too. He was sympathetic. He said the whole office was in shock. But life had to go on. In particular, selling the Mexico deal had to go on. It wasn't going well, and there were still a lot of bonds on Dekker's books. The situation in Mexico itself was looking rocky: people were beginning to ask questions about whether the government would be able to refinance its borrowings that were maturing this year.

I didn't care.

The police came again. They had fitted Zico's voice to two previous recordings they had taken of kidnappers. In both cases the victims had been treated well and eventually released. This lifted Luís's spirits. And mine.

But the waiting began to weigh heavily on us. It had been only four days since Isabel had been kidnapped, but it seemed much longer. Nelson warned us to be prepared for a long wait. These cases took weeks, sometimes months to resolve, not days. Nonetheless every time the phone rang, Luís, Cordelia and I thought it would bring an agreement for Isabel's release. Of course it didn't.

At Cordelia's suggestion, we went up to Luís's *fazenda* near Petrópolis for the weekend. It was what the family usually did, and she felt a change of scene would be good for Luís. He was worried that Zico wouldn't be able to get in touch with us, but she pointed out that if he called the apartment and someone gave him the number in Petrópolis, he could hardly object.

Luís picked me up from the hotel late Friday afternoon. His chauffeur took us to the compact Santos Dumont airport in the centre of the city. I was surprised, Petrópolis was only forty kilometres away, no one had explained we would be flying. Luís was distracted as he led me through the airport and into a little van that took us to a blue helicopter. It had five seats, and Cordelia and her husband were already waiting for us. I climbed in too, pretending that this was the most natural thing in the world. Within a couple of minutes the helicopter had eased itself into the air and we were scudding across Guanabara Bay.

*

Twenty minutes later we were up above the mountains. Below us roads and buildings wriggled like snakes through the folds of the hills. We descended so that the forest-clad mountainsides rose on either side. We burst round a corner and there, beneath a sheer rock-face, was a large white house surrounded by a lush garden dotted with trees and a lake. Behind the house was a patch of flat grass with a large white H painted on it.

The *fazenda* had been the focal point of a substantial coffee estate. Its rooms were large and cool. The furnishings were tasteful without being opulent: dark colonial Brazilian wood, oriental vases, French nineteenth-century paintings. It was a few degrees cooler than Rio, but it was still warm by my standards. Nevertheless a huge fire roared in the sitting room.

As soon as we arrived, Luís relaxed visibly. I could understand why Cordelia had insisted on it. It was his routine to come up here and unwind on a Friday evening; and unwind was what he needed to do now.

That evening the atmosphere was almost normal. Cordelia's husband, Fernando, was good company. He was a lawyer who had a wry sense of humour, and an inability to take himself, or Brazil, too seriously. He doted on Cordelia, though.

We were laughing, actually laughing, at dinner, clustered round one end of a ridiculously long dining table, when the phone rang.

There was an extension in the dining room. We could tell from Luís's reaction who it was. Luís was prepared. He acted distraught but in control. The conversation lasted less than two minutes. Zico said one million dollars was insulting. Luís said fifty million was absurd. Zico wouldn't budge. Luís upped his offer to a million and a half. He wanted Zico to know that he understood the game, and he was playing.

Immediately afterwards, Luís called Nelson, who said he would be up the next day. Once again, he was encouraging. According to Nelson, everything was going to plan.

The next morning, Saturday, Luís showed me round the garden. It stretched up a gentle incline from the house for what seemed like half a mile, until it merged into a forest. It took my breath away. On either side and in front loomed large, absurdly shaped mountains, obviously with the same geological provenance as those that surrounded Rio. One had a sheer rock-face, the others were covered with trees on their lower slopes and meadows higher up. The garden itself was a valley of lawns, trees and shrubs, with a long lake down one side. The air was cool and clear, though a little damp, and filled with the sound of running water and birds squabbling. There were swans, both white and black, flamingos, exotic ducks and a variety of other types that I didn't recognize.

'It's beautiful,' I said.

'It was designed by Burle Marx, a German who came here during the war. It is extraordinary. There are over two thousand species of plant in this garden. And it has seen some wonderful parties in its time.'

I glanced at Luís. He didn't seem a great entertainer. He seemed a tall, lonely man, standing up well to adversity.

'How long have you owned it?'

'About five years.'

It must have cost serious money. I knew that Isabel came from a wealthy family, but I had no idea what that wealth translated to. It was strange to me to see a house and garden like this being used as a home. In England it would have been dotted with nice ladies in tweed skirts gently ushering visitors This Way.

Luís read my thoughts. 'We didn't always have money. Or, at least, I didn't. I come from an old family, one of the *quatrocentonas*, the Portuguese families that came over to Brazil four hundred years ago. My great-grandfather had plantations in the state of São Paulo that were as big as some European countries. He had thirty thousand slaves. Then came emancipation. Then the collapse of coffee prices. Then the crash of 'twenty-nine. My grandfather wasn't astute. My brother still runs the rump of the property, a small coffee plantation. But I left.'

There was a kerfuffle as a white swan tried to mount a black one. Luís laughed. 'True Brazilians. You see!'

'You came to Rio?' I prompted.

'Yes. I went to university there, and joined a big bank. I found money fascinating. For many years now Brazil's financial system has been pretty complex. With inflation and interest rates at several thousand per cent a year, there were opportunities to make a lot of money. In nineteen eighty-six I decided to make some of that money for myself, and so I started Banco Horizonte. As you know, it's now one of the biggest investment banks in Brazil, and in fact we're beginning to think about expanding overseas. So that's how I can afford all this.'

Luís made no attempt to hide his pride, and indeed he had a lot to be proud of. 'But it's a shame to build this up and see it die with me. We wanted a son, Vivian and I.'

'Vivian was your wife?'

He nodded. He turned back and looked at the

fazenda. 'She never saw all this. All that I have created. Or perhaps she can see it now.'

'There's Isabel,' I said.

Luís snorted. 'Isabel! What chance have I of getting her to work for the bank? She's far too stubborn. You heard her. My daughters! I suppose no father understands his daughters. But I just don't know why Isabel and Cordelia won't for once do something sensible. Maybe this episode will make them think again.'

'It might. But I'm not sure that's a good thing.'

He turned to look at me, listening closely.

'They're just like you, aren't they? They want to go their own way. Do their own thing. The fact you disapprove just encourages them. I'm sure that's true of Isabel.'

Luís gave a brief, dry laugh. 'I suppose you're right.'

'That's one of the reasons I like her.'

There was a pause. He studied me. 'You are close, aren't you? More than colleagues. More than friends?'

For a moment I panicked, imagining myself accused by an indignant Latin father of deflowering his daughter. But Luís's gaze was warm, encouraging.

I nodded.

Luís turned to continue up the hill. '*Bem*,' he muttered, I think. I couldn't quite hear.

We decided to stay at the *fazenda*. It was tough on Nelson; he had to make the hour and a half drive up from Rio every day. But it was good for Luís, and good for me. We were optimistic. As long as we could put up with the waiting, Isabel would be free.

On Sunday night Cordelia and Fernando left for the city by helicopter. Zico called again. I listened in to the conversation. I heard what I thought were the words thirty million, and then a bit later Luís countering with two million. We were still a long way apart, but we were drawing ever closer. At this rate, one day in the next few weeks, Isabel would be released. I thought about returning to London. Things seemed to be on track, and there was little more that I could do to help. And there was a limit to how long I could stay.

We were beginning to get used to the slow tempo of the negotiations. But on Tuesday, day eight, all that changed.

20

Nelson came up in the morning for breakfast. He seemed excited.

'I have some news.'

Luís looked up from the tiny roll on his plate. He still wasn't eating much. 'About Isabel?'

'Yes. The police have received a tip that they're taking seriously. You know the Disque Denúncia?'

Luís nodded.

Nelson explained for my benefit. 'It's an anonymous phone line the public can use to tip the police off about criminal activity. Apparently, about a week ago, a blindfolded woman was seen being led from a car to a small shed in the middle of the night. The shed is in Irajá, in the north of the city. The police are going to check it out this morning.'

'They will be careful, won't they? They're not going to storm the place or anything?'

'Da Silva assured me they won't. If they find Zico and his friends, they'll just watch them, and arrest them after Isabel is released.'

'Are you sure?' Luís glanced at Nelson suspiciously.

'I've known Da Silva for fifteen years. He's given me his word.'

Luís looked worried, and I shared his unease. Nelson

was an ex-cop so he would say we could trust the police, wouldn't he? But, on the other hand, they would be more likely not to lie to him. We would see. In any case, there was no doubt in my mind that a dramatic rescue attempt was not the best way to release Isabel. The anxiety grew the more I thought about it.

Nelson could see Luís's reaction as well.

'The shed will be under surveillance now,' he said. 'Da Silva said he would telephone us here this morning.'

The detective was as good as his word. The police had found the shed empty. It had a basement, and there were plenty of signs that this had been used to hold a kidnap victim. There were marks where a tent had been erected in the middle of the floor. This was apparently a common way of holding kidnap victims so that they couldn't see their captors. There were food wrappers, empty plastic bottles of mineral water, and some scraps of bread that was quite fresh. There were no signs of blood.

Someone had been held there, and had recently been moved.

Half an hour later the phone rang. But it wasn't Da Silva. It was Zico.

This time the conversation became quite heated. I could follow very little of it, but Luís was as angry as I had seen him. After a couple of minutes he slammed down the phone and turned on Nelson, eyes blazing.

They exchanged some sharp words of Portuguese, and Luís stormed out of the sitting room into the garden. I glanced at Nelson. For the first time he looked flustered and angry. I followed Luís.

He stood, staring out at the garden, breathing heavily. A cloud was gathering above the hill at the head of the valley, threatening to roll rain down towards us.

'What happened?' I asked.

'*Merda*,' he muttered. Then '*Merda! Merda! Merda!*' more loudly.

I waited.

'Zico wanted to know why we had told the police. I said that we hadn't, that they had just received a tip-off. He didn't believe me.' He sucked in his breath. 'Zico said I was lucky Isabel wasn't dead. He said he would give me just one more chance. I should pay ten million dollars tomorrow night or Isabel will die. He said now the police are on to him he can't afford to wait. He's going to call me back in two hours. He sounded serious.' Luís jerked his head back towards the house. 'I told that idiot that the police should have checked with me first before going to the hideout. I should never have trusted him!'

I let Luís stew for a minute. 'What are you going to do?'

'I don't know. Pay the ransom, I suppose. I can't risk Isabel's life further.'

'Can you get ten million dollars by tomorrow?'

'I don't know. It'll be difficult.'

'What does Nelson say?'

'I don't give a shit what Nelson says.'

We walked along the path towards the lake. A tree burned orange in front of us. The clouds at the head of the valley were darkening, although the garden itself was still in sunshine.

I took a deep breath. 'It looks like the police made a mistake. Maybe Nelson made a mistake in trusting them. But his advice has been good so far. He's objective, and he's seen all this before. Maybe we should listen to him. Then we can decide what to do.'

We walked on in silence. I was scared about Isabel.

But I thought our best chance lay in behaving calmly and following the rules. Zico was prepared to release Isabel alive; Luís was prepared to pay a ransom. As long as we kept our nerve, that's what would happen.

'OK, let's talk to him,' said Luís.

'Good,' I said, and we hurried back to the house just as the sky went dark and raindrops began to fall.

'Keep negotiating,' said Nelson. 'He has lowered his price so fast because he knows you are worried about the police. He hopes to close the deal quickly. Well, that's fine with us, but not at ten million. We were raising our offer by half a million at a time. We should reduce that, let him know we're getting close to our ceiling. Offer two million two hundred thousand.'

'No!' said Luís. 'I can pay more than that! Why don't I offer three?'

'Because he will think there is a lot further to go!' said Nelson, who was beginning to lose his patience. 'Don't you see that if your offer goes up in larger amounts, the whole negotiation will take longer?'

I saw what Nelson meant. So, in the end, did Luís.

Zico called back when he said he would. Luís gave him his offer of two point two million dollars. The conversation was short. Luís went pale, but stood his ground.

'What did he say?' I asked, as soon as Luís had hung up.

'He asked for five million,' said Luís. 'And he said Isabel would definitely be dead tomorrow night if I didn't pay up. I think I believe him. He'll call back in another two hours.'

I turned to Nelson, who looked thoughtful. 'He's coming down too quickly,' he said. 'I've never seen a demand drop so fast before. And he seems genuinely eager to get the payment through fast.'

'He thinks the police are on to him,' Luís muttered.

Nelson shook his head. 'I don't think that would bother him too much. Kidnappers expect the police to investigate them.'

We watched him. His face clouded over into a frown.

'What is it?' I asked.

He sighed. 'I think we should ask for proof of life again.'

Luís exploded. 'You heard him! He's not going to stand for that now. There's no time!'

I was silent. I felt sick. I knew what Nelson was thinking.

Luís saw my expression. 'What?'

I didn't say anything. I couldn't.

'What is it?' demanded Luís.

'Nelson thinks she might be dead,' I said quietly. 'That's why the kidnappers are so eager to be paid now.'

'No!' shouted Luís. 'We have no reason to think so. I won't accept that!'

Nelson held up his hands. 'You may be right. I hope you're right. But we should just be sure.'

'And I suppose you want me to make a tiny increase in my offer again?'

Nelson nodded.

'Well, I won't! I'm accepting their five million, and I'll have Isabel back here tomorrow night.'

I glanced at Nelson who was watching Luís closely. He shrugged. 'I can offer my advice, nothing more.'

'Good.'

'Luís?' I said, hesitantly.

He frowned towards me.

'I know you can pay five million dollars, and you

want to. That's fine. I'd like to see Isabel back soon too. But Nelson's right, we should just check to see that she is alive. So why don't you agree to five million provided they come back with proof of life? If they have her, and they know they will get their five million, then there's no reason for them to delay in replying, is there?'

I looked over to Nelson for support. He nodded.

'OK,' said Luís. 'But you think up the question.'

The question was, 'Which town does Dave come from?' Luís never got a chance to ask it.

When he suggested proof of life, Zico refused. Luís stuck to his demand, with no luck. Eventually the phone call ended, with Zico swearing he would kill Isabel.

Luís put down the phone. His face was fixed. Cold.

'You know what this means? She might be dead already,' said Nelson quietly.

Luís stood before me, tall and gaunt. The events of the last few days, and especially the last few minutes had aged him.

'I'm just going up to her room,' he said.

I pounded up the track, the trees and undergrowth of the Atlantic rain-forest on either side a mass of dark murky green. But I hardly noticed the profusion of life around me: my eyes were focused on the dirt under my feet. My brain was focused on Isabel.

My feelings were a swirl of contradictions. I hardly knew her, yet I felt as though I knew her better than any other human being in the world. The conversations we had had together played over and over again in my mind, especially those discussions we'd had long into the night about everything and nothing. I saw parts of her, now her huge eyes, now her shy smile behind a strand of black hair. I remembered the time I had first seen her, leaning against a desk in the Dekker Ward trading room, sexy, instantly attractive.

I burst out of the forest into the sheep meadows above. Behind me, I knew, was a spectacular view of the *fazenda* and the outskirts of Petrópolis. But I didn't look at it. My head was bent, my eyes down.

I was angry, angry that Isabel might now be dead. Angry with myself for abandoning her, angry with Nelson for not preventing the police from disturbing her kidnappers, angry with Luís for not being more in control. But worst of all, and this was something I could hardly admit to myself, I was angry with Isabel. She knew she was a kidnap risk, so why hadn't she been more careful? Why had she gone and got herself killed just now, just when I realized how much she meant to me?

Except I didn't know how much she meant to me. I was confused about that, too. We were only at the beginning of a relationship. How would it have developed? Would it have come to anything? I found my imagination fast-forwarding to a whole life together. Would she have fitted into my small flat in Primrose Hill? It was difficult to imagine her there.

It was absurd. It probably never would have worked. And now, because of Zico and his friends, I might never know what might have been.

But I couldn't accept that.

Was she really dead? Nelson thought she was. Luís thought she wasn't. We hadn't heard a word from Zico.

Logic suggested Nelson was right, and he had experience of these situations. But until we had proof that she was dead, I couldn't believe it. I was with Luís. I had to hope and pray she was alive, whether it made sense or not.

Finally, near the summit of the steep hillside, I stopped and sat down. I could just see the *fazenda* nestling in the valley below.

It had been a horrible couple of days. Luís had been like a ghost. Cordelia had gone into hospital: her doctors were worried about the effect all the stress was having on her pregnancy. Nelson Zarur had offered to waive his fee, but in the end Luís had paid it.

I had phoned Ricardo and told him that it looked as if Isabel might have been killed. It was difficult. He had tried to take it coolly, but his voice sounded dead, empty. I told him I would be coming back to London soon. He cut the conversation short. Isabel had been right: she had meant something to him.

'She's still alive, you know.'

It was evening. Through the french windows behind us, the last red embers of the sun were crumbling behind the mountain at the head of the valley. In front of us was a roaring fire. We had been sitting staring at it in silence for half an hour, each holding a glass of Ballantine's.

I nodded. 'I know.'

'We have to believe that, no matter what Nelson or Zico or anyone else says.'

'I know.'

Silence.

Then Luís stirred. 'What was she like? At work?'

'She was quiet. Serious. Very good at her job. She got on with things. I think people respected her.'

Luís shook his head. 'I'm surprised she went into banking. Disappointed, in a strange kind of way. She seemed so idealistic. Of course I disagreed with her, and we had arguments. But I respected her ideals. And then she went to the United States, and came back eager to prove to the world that she could be a better banker than me. Why?'

'I don't know. But she certainly was driven. She did want to prove something, and I think it was to you.'

'But she didn't have to!' said Luís. 'It was enough for me that she was my daughter. I didn't expect her to become a great financier as well.'

I thought about this for a moment. 'Perhaps it was the fact that you didn't expect anything of her that drove her on. I don't know. But don't blame yourself. You brought up a wonderful daughter. You should be proud.'

Luís just stared into the fire.

'She hadn't lost her ideals,' I said. 'That *favela* deal was a brilliant idea. And she believed in it. For her it was a chance finally to use her skills to do some good.'

'It was good. It's a shame it didn't work.'

'That was only because Ricardo Ross destroyed it.'

'Oswaldo Bocci is scum. Ricardo is a fool to have anything to do with him. I know Dekker Ward are very good, but sometimes they go too far. I wish Isabel had worked for someone else.'

'They have a bad name?'

'Yes, they do. They're not exactly corrupt, Ricardo isn't that stupid. But there is a . . .' he searched for the word ' . . . smell about them. They deal with people they shouldn't. Like Oswaldo Bocci. They bend the rules when they shouldn't.'

I wasn't surprised. 'Presumably Isabel knew this when she joined them.'

'Yes,' said Luís. 'I tried to talk her out of it, but that

probably only egged her on. She said that it was a great career opportunity for her and that *she* would be completely honest. And I think she has been. She has a good reputation in Brazil.'

The fire crackled and spat. It was almost totally dark now, and the room was illuminated by the glow of the flames.

'I'm going to resign when I get back to London,' I said.

'Are you?' Luís straightened in his chair. 'Why?'

'I don't like banking. Or maybe I just don't like Dekker. I had decided before I came out here with Isabel.'

Luís didn't answer. We lapsed into silence again. Our thoughts drifted back to Isabel.

'We can save her *favela* deal,' Luís said.

'How?'

For the first time in days Luís smiled. It was a small smile. The way he twitched the corners of his mouth reminded me of Isabel. 'Bocci is an upstart in the Rio media world. I have friends with bigger papers. We can turn Ricardo's strategy against him. It will hurt him. And it will be something we can do for Isabel.'

21

I went into work with trepidation on Monday morning. But there were smiles and nods, sympathy, questions delicately put. In a way it felt as if I was returning home. That wouldn't last long.

After the meeting had finished, I crept back to my desk. Paper had accumulated on it in the three weeks I had been away. I glanced over to Isabel's desk. Empty. Tidy. Waiting for its next occupant.

Ricardo drifted over, pulled up a chair and sat next to me. It was quiet here, away from the square of traders and salesmen who were already hitting the phones.

'How are you feeling?'

I just shrugged.

'It shook us all badly here,' Ricardo went on. 'It's been tense this last couple of weeks. And then, just as things were going so well, suddenly everything fell apart.'

I nodded.

'It must be tough for her father. He meant a lot to her.' Of course. Isabel must have told Ricardo all about herself and her family, much the same as she had told me. I wasn't sure I liked that idea.

'It is hard for him. Not knowing whether she's alive or dead.'

'And this man Nelson Zarur thinks there's no chance that she's still alive?'

'There's always a chance. But he's not optimistic. Neither are the police.'

We sat in silence. I didn't want to talk to Ricardo about all this. But, once again, there was something beguiling about his frankness. 'I liked her,' he said. 'And, if I'm not mistaken, you did too.'

'I did,' I said quietly. 'I mean, I do.' I hated to talk about Isabel in the past tense. To me she was still alive. She had to be alive.

'Sorry,' said Ricardo. 'You're right. I can't accept that she's . . . not alive either.' His voice held a gentleness I had never heard before. 'People respond to this kind of thing in all sorts of different ways. I don't know how you feel about it. Take it easy if you like for a bit. Or maybe you want to get stuck into the work to take your mind off it. You do whatever you think is best. We can be patient here.'

Until you read the Brazilian newspapers, I thought. Luís had said the story would come out at the beginning of this week. I began to feel second thoughts about that. In Luís's sitting room, in front of the fire, thinking about Isabel, it had seemed a good idea. Now, I wasn't so sure. I had to make sure I wasn't around when the story broke.

'Ricardo?'

'Yes?'

'There's something I want to tell you.'

He waited.

'I resign.'

'What?'

'I said I resign.'

Ricardo was about to say something, but saw

253

the expression on my face, and kept quiet. He settled himself, and his eyes sought mine. I held them.

'Why?' he said quietly.

'I was thinking about it when I went down to Brazil. And after what happened to Isabel . . . I just don't want to work here any more.'

'Nick, it's natural you're upset. Take some time off – '

'No, it's not just Isabel.' I took a deep breath. 'I don't think I can do things the Dekker way.'

Ricardo frowned. 'What things? What do you mean?'

I paused to collect my thoughts. I knew that, if I wasn't careful, Ricardo would talk me out of this. 'We talked about it on the plane back from Brazil. And there are other things I've seen since then that have made me more concerned.'

'You saw the Brady battle against Bloomfield Weiss, didn't you? Of course you did. You played an important part in it.'

'Yes, I saw it.'

'Didn't you enjoy that?'

'Yes, I did.'

Ricardo paused and looked at me. 'Do you know how much money you'll make this year, if you do as well as I think you will?'

'No.'

'Guess.'

'Well, nine months' work, that's a bit over twenty thousand pounds' salary. And a bonus.'

'Of how much?'

Damn him! I should just ignore his question. But it intrigued me. He was clever. I'd joined Dekker for the money. How much money had been left vague. Now I would find out.

'I don't know. Ten thousand pounds, maybe?'

'I would be surprised if you didn't get a bonus of a hundred thousand dollars this year.'

Jesus! I tried hard not to look excited or greedy. I could feel a smile creeping across my face, but I suppressed it. 'Oh,' I said, my voice strained.

'And, of course, we'll start making investments for you in the employee trusts. In three years you'll be worth at least half a million. In five, a million. Now, do you still want to resign?'

He was telling the truth, I could see. He wasn't bullshitting me. With a million quid I could give up and do what I really wanted to do for the rest of my life. If I left now, the boiler still wouldn't get fixed.

But I would lose myself. I would become a different person, a rich person, but a person I wouldn't like. A person Isabel wouldn't like.

'Yes,' I said.

Ricardo's face flushed. He looked angry. 'You really should take some time to think about it. Take a week.'

'No. I'd like to leave today.'

'If you're not with me, you're against me. I told you that before, didn't I?' There was a real edge to Ricardo's voice.

I held up my hands. 'Hey, I don't want to become Dekker's enemy. I'm just in the wrong job, that's all.'

'No, Nick. I have personally put a lot of trust in you. You have let me down. I won't forget that.'

His eyes looked straight into my soul, blue and piercing. I felt very uncomfortable. I wanted to bow my head, to say, 'Yes, of course, Ricardo, I'd be happy to stay.' But I held his eyes, and kept silent.

'All right. There's no need for you to go right away. It's not like you're going to a competitor or anything. Are you?' He glared at me.

I shook my head. There was no way I was going to make the same mistake twice.

'Good. Well, clear your desk and be out by this evening. Talk to Eduardo about your P45, and your loan.'

With that, he stood up, turned his back on me, and walked off.

I hung my head and sighed. I felt like shit. I felt disloyal, dishonest, cowardly. How did he do it? How could he make me feel like this?

A few minutes before he had treated me with genuine sympathy. And then . . . It was his single-mindedness, I supposed. Anything that threatened his beloved Dekker Ward threatened him personally, even if it was only the resignation of one of his most junior people.

His words returned to me. 'If you're not with me, you're against me.' No compromises.

I knew I had taken the right decision. While I had been in Brazil my doubts about the money-laundering, the way I had deceived Wójtek, and what had happened to Dave had all receded into the background. But they would come back. I had discussed my resignation with Isabel, and she had thought it a good idea. Besides, with the press story Luís had concocted, it was best to get out now. The whole Dekker experience had been a big mistake. The sooner it was behind me the better.

Slowly and deliberately I began to gather my things together.

I felt a presence beside me. It was Eduardo. He looked angry.

'Ricardo tells me you have resigned.'

'That's right,' I said.

'Well, I think you should leave now.'

'But Ricardo said I had until this evening,' I protested.

'And I say you leave now,' Eduardo repeated firmly. 'The security guards will be up in a couple of minutes.'

I shrugged my shoulders. Actually, that suited me. I had collected all my stuff in a cardboard box, there wasn't that much of it.

Eduardo's dark eyes bored into me. 'When you go I want you to forget Dekker, and forget all you saw here. But I won't forget you. I'll be watching you. And if I see you try anything, any tiny little thing, which might harm this firm, I will take the appropriate steps.' His voice was low, almost a whisper. It made my skin prickle, a physical reaction to the danger that loaded his words. 'Do you understand?'

My throat was dry. I knew Eduardo didn't make empty threats. But I didn't want him to see me swallow.

'What I do with my life is my own affair,' I said.

'Oh, no, it's not,' said Eduardo, leaning forward. 'It's mine now, too.'

I picked up my jacket from the back of my chair and put it on. Eduardo was right to be concerned about me, of course. As he would realize when he saw the stories in the Rio papers.

Two security guards arrived at my desk. They searched me, turning out my pockets, and patting my chest, arms and legs. Eduardo seemed disappointed when they didn't find anything.

The dealing room went quiet, as everyone watched me, jaws open. Jamie saw me from the square. 'What the hell?' he mouthed. He still didn't know I had resigned. I sought out Ricardo. His eyes met mine, emotionless. I felt the stares burning into me. Still, I thought, if they could turn Dave into a non-person so quickly, they'd have no trouble with me. The guards led me through the unnatural silence, out of the trading room to the lifts.

I plummeted forty floors down to the real world.

22

I felt elated as I pedalled rapidly back to Primrose Hill, leaving the Tower further and further behind me. No more worrying about Ricardo and Eduardo. I could forget money-laundering and murder. I had escaped!

By the time I reached home it was one o'clock, and I was hungry. As soon as I was through the door I checked the fridge for something for lunch. Nothing. There was a pint of milk, though, so I made myself a bowl of cornflakes. There were also a couple of cans of beer. I don't drink during the day. I took one. It turned out that beer and cornflakes don't go well together.

I was glad about leaving Dekker, although I felt a fool for going there in the first place. It would be a difficult mistake to unravel. I would have to go cap in hand to Russell Church at the School of Russian Studies, admit I was wrong, and ask if he knew of any jobs anywhere. I shuddered as I thought of applications, interviews, explanations of why I hadn't any formal Russian qualifications, if I even got far enough to be allowed to explain. My father would think I was crazy.

And money. I had received one pay cheque from Dekker, which helped a lot. But I still had the mortgage on my flat. Mr K. R. bloody Norris would be on my back again in no time. And I owed Ricardo his five grand, three of which I still had in the bank. Well, that would come in useful to tide me through the next few months. One day I'd pay him back. Maybe.

Sharp hammering started up somewhere above me, followed by the muffled crash of plaster pulled away from a wall. I remembered that the old lady upstairs had warned me that she was having some work done. I was never home during the day so I hadn't noticed before.

I finished the bowl, and prowled through to the tiny bedroom, stepping over my bag of rugby kit, which I still hadn't had time to wash after the last match of the season. My euphoria at escaping Dekker was swiftly evaporating as I faced the realities of life without a salary. The bed beckoned and I flopped on to it. I lay face down, eyes open, thoughts rushing through my mind.

I missed Isabel. The eagerness with which my brain had tried to deal with her kidnapping, the scrambling for memories, for causes, for culprits, had been replaced by a tiring, chronic despair. The uncertainty was hard to cope with. Most of the time I told myself she was alive. But in dark moments, like now, I felt she was dead, that I would never see her again. The question was always there. If she was dead, why hadn't they found her body? If she was alive, why hadn't Zico called back with the proof of life? Why would he want to kill her, when he was on the edge of making a fortune out of her? Why should he keep her alive, when it looked as though the police were on his trail? I needed to know one way or the other. And yet . . . At least there was still hope.

The phone rang. It was Jamie. The noise and chatter

of the Dekker trading room came through strongly in the background.

'What the hell have you done?'

'Resigned.'

'I know you've resigned. But why? It's put Ricardo in a hell of a bad mood. He rated you, you know. And why didn't you tell me?'

I should have told Jamie, but I hadn't. I just couldn't face explaining it to him, and then having to explain it to Ricardo. I hadn't seen him at all since I had returned from Brazil.

'I'm sorry, Jamie, but you know I've had questions about Dekker ever since I joined. It's not for me.'

'Are you all right? The theory here is that you've lost it since Isabel's kidnap. Are you sure you know what you're doing?'

'I'm sure. I am upset about her, but I'd planned to resign before I went out to Brazil in any case.'

'Well, we're busy doing a Dave on you here. Although it's a bit easier in your case.'

'Yeah, well. I'm not surprised.' But I was a little hurt. I liked the other guys. I didn't want to be erased from their consciousness.

'You must feel awful, mate. Shall I pop round for a drink? I can't make it this evening, but tomorrow?'

'Yes, Jamie. That would be good.'

I had never doubted that Jamie's friendship would survive my resignation. He had stuck his neck out for me with Ricardo, and I had made him look a fool, something Jamie never liked. But I knew he would stick with me. It would be good to see him tomorrow.

I drank the other can of beer, then went out to the off-licence and bought some more. I put on some of Joanna's old CDs. I suppose I hoped that they would remind me of her, and push Isabel to the back of my mind for a moment. They didn't. I ordered a pizza and ate it. Then I rang Luís and told him I had resigned. No news of Isabel. At some point, as the day dragged to an end, I went to sleep.

I went to sleep thinking of Isabel, and I woke up thinking of her. But I also woke up determined to pull myself together. I cleared up the debris of the day before, bought some real food from the supermarket, and made myself a proper breakfast: bacon, sausages, fried eggs, fried bread, the works. And I made a pot of fresh coffee.

Feeling fat and a little happier, I sipped my coffee and stared out of the window at my small garden. It was a mess, with weeds bursting upwards, overwhelming the few perennials that had survived the winter. The grass was looking more like a miniature hayfield than a lawn. Perhaps I would get stuck into that after breakfast.

I should call Russell Church at the School of Russian Studies. But not today. Tomorrow.

The phone rang.

'Hallo.' It was the first word I had said all day. It came out thick and hoarse.

'Nick. It's Father.'

'Oh, hallo.'

'Are you all right?'

'Yes, sorry, I'm fine, Father. What's up?' My father never phoned me. Never. My mother rang very occasionally, on my birthday, perhaps, or when she hadn't heard from me for a couple of months, but not my father.

'I telephoned you at the office last week, but they said you were in Brazil on a business trip. Sounded interesting. Then when I rang this morning, a nice chap said I could find you here.'

'Well, here I am.'

'Listen, Nick. I thought I'd come down to London for the day next week. Catch up with a few old pals. I wondered if I could drop in and see you?'

Oh, God. Just what I needed.

'Fine,' I said.

'I think I can remember where Dekker's offices are. They haven't moved, have they?'

'I don't work there any more.'

'What?' He sounded shocked.

'I resigned. Yesterday.'

'Whatever for?'

I groaned inwardly. How could I explain this?

'The City is just not for me, Father.'

There was silence. 'OK. I see.' His voice blew cold down the phone line from Norfolk. 'It was a terrific opportunity for you to make something of yourself, Nick.'

'It's not a good place, Father. Honestly. I'm better off out of it.'

'Well, your mother will be most disappointed,' he said. Actually I thought she'd be quite pleased.

'I'd still like to see you,' I said, almost to my surprise.

'Um, yes, well. Maybe another time. I was hoping to see you *in situ*, as it were. But if you're not working, then there's not much point, is there?'

'I suppose not.'

'Goodbye, then.'

''Bye.'

I put the phone down. Despite myself, I felt guilty and angry. Guilty that I had disappointed him, angry that he hadn't wanted to see me.

I felt alone.

My thoughts turned back to Dekker. Jamie had said they were doing a Dave on me. I wondered what had happened to Dave. I hadn't had time to get to know him very well, but I had liked what I had seen of him. And now I felt some kindred spirit with him. A fellow ex-Dekker non-person.

I dug out the phone list I had been given when I had joined Dekker. It listed all home numbers, Dave's included. Dekker employees were expected to be able to deal round the clock.

He answered the phone. 'Nick! All right, mate? That's a blast from the past. I thought I'd never speak to another Dekker man again.'

I explained my situation, and I asked if I could come round and see him.

'Course you can. Come round this afternoon, if you like. It's not like I've got anything to do. Have you got wheels?'

'Only two.'

'Motor- or pushbike?'

'Pushbike, I'm afraid.'

'Well, never mind. Take the tube to Theydon Bois, and give me a ring from the station. I'll pick you up.'

Dave met me in an old Ford Escort. We drove through a succession of well-kept suburban roads to a large modern house at the end of a private road. Two 'For Sale' signs guarded the short driveway. He fiddled with a remote control to open the doors of a huge empty garage, and then drove the Escort into the middle of it.

'Lots of room for this little car, isn't there?'

'Don't,' said Dave. 'I had a Porsche 911 I parked just

there, and a four-wheel drive just there. And the missus had a little MR2. All gone now.'

He led me through a door in the garage into the house. 'Have you met my wife, Teresa?'

She was big, like Dave, with dyed blonde hair and a wide smile. 'Hi,' she said. 'Do you want a cup of tea?'

'Love one.'

Dave led me through a couple of miles of corridor to a huge lounge, with picture windows overlooking a large lawn and a swimming pool. Now Dave was about my age. And this place had cost a packet.

'Nice place, innit?' he said, following my eyes. 'Shame it's not mine.'

'Oh, you mean the building society own it?'

'Worse. Dekker. If I can't meet next month's mortgage payment, which I can't, they'll repossess. I'm desperate to sell it before then.'

'Don't you have any savings?'

'All tied up in the employee trusts, aren't they? I can't get hold of them if I'm dismissed for bad faith. So, you could say I'm up shit creek.'

'Have you tried to get another job?'

'Yeah. I tried. No chance. I don't know how Ricardo did it, but you'd think I was Nick Leeson, the way they treat me.'

'So what are you going to do?'

Teresa came in with two mugs of tea. 'Thanks, love,' said Dave, taking his. He sipped it and then answered my question. 'Sell this place. I've got some old mates from my forex days who'll back me to buy a pub. Then Teresa and I'll run it. Quite honestly, I'm looking forward to it. I've had enough of the City.'

'So have I,' said Teresa.

'I know what you mean,' I said.

'So you got the boot too?' Dave asked.

'Not quite. I jumped.'

'Why?'

I told him about my reservations about Dekker, and about Isabel's kidnapping. He was shocked.

'She's a nice chick. Bright, too. So, they don't know whether she's still alive?'

'No.'

'Nor who the kidnappers are?'

'No, again. Kidnapping is an industry in Brazil. This kind of thing happens all the time.'

'Like bankers getting topped for their wallets?'

I looked at him sharply. 'You told *IFR* you were suspicious about that. Why?'

'It was no more than that, a suspicion. But a strong one. There are all those numbered accounts at Dekker Trust, supposedly overseen by Eduardo. Ricardo says he knows where all that money comes from, but I'm not convinced he does. And you know Eduardo. He'd happily turn a blind eye.'

'OK, so there might be some dodgy money there. But that's not proof, really, is it?'

'No. But there's talk in the market.'

'Talk?'

'Yeah. Everyone knows Chalmet handles dodgy money, and they own twenty-nine per cent of Dekker Ward. Now they're beginning to talk about us, too. Ricardo doesn't hear that stuff, of course, no one would dare to say that kind of thing to his face. But I've heard stuff down the pub over a few pints.'

'And you think it's true?'

'I wasn't sure at first. I ignored it. But I thought it was interesting when that bloke Martin Beldecos started rooting around. He was asking difficult questions, and waiting till he got answers that made sense. Then he was conveniently murdered. And when you got yourself stabbed, it was too much of a coincidence.'

'So you talked to someone at *IFR*?'

'Yeah. Big mistake.'

'Why?'

'Because he wrote about "sources inside Dekker Ward", didn't he? Then he spoke to me on the phone here. I reckon Eduardo was tapping it somehow. That's how they caught me.'

'But why did you talk to him? You knew Ricardo wouldn't like it if he found out.'

Dave sipped his tea, and glanced at Teresa. 'I dunno. It just seemed wrong. A bloke murdered, another guy attacked, everyone wringing their hands, no one asking the right questions. I'd been thinking a lot about it, and it didn't make sense. I'd probably have kept my trap shut but we'd had a few beers, and I thought, What the hell? It just sort of slipped out. I didn't think it'd blow up in my face like that.'

I nodded. Maybe I should have asked more questions.

'I went to the police, you know,' he said.

'Really?'

'Yeah. After they fired me. I was so pissed off I wanted to get back at them somehow.'

'And what did the police say?'

'It was a complete waste of time.'

'Why?'

'Well, a murder in Venezuela is hardly their jurisdiction, is it? And Martin Beldecos was an American citizen, technically resident in the Cayman Islands. I mean, it was a total non-starter.'

'What about the money-laundering? Weren't they interested in that?'

'They was. Sort of. But Ricardo's clever. You see, most of his activities are not really regulated by anyone.'

'Why not?'

'Well, to start with, Dekker Ward, the stockbroker, is regulated by the Securities and Futures Authority, not the Bank of England. The SFA is less worried about money-laundering. Then Ricardo's biz is all run from Canary Wharf, and the SFA deals mostly with head office in the City. Most emerging-markets trading is unregulated anyway, it's not like trading on the London Stock Exchange. They keep a close eye on that. Anyway, many of Ricardo's trades are booked through Dekker Trust in the Caymans, which is a legally unrelated company, so it's outside the UK authorities' control.'

'I see.' Ricardo had woven a compliance web that it was nobody's job to untangle.

'So, they keep a watching brief. As long as money isn't being laundered in London, which it isn't strictly speaking, there's not much more they'll do.'

'And what about the police?'

'Not much better. If I can come up with a "suspicious transaction", they'll bung it on a computer somewhere. Apparently they have banks reporting hundreds of dodgy transactions all the time.'

I thought all this over. 'Last month I came across a fax for Martin Beldecos from the United Bank of Canada. It said that the US DEA are investigating Francisco Aragão and that they'd traced a payment from him to Dekker Trust. Maybe they'll tie him in with Dekker. He is Ricardo's brother-in-law, after all.'

'Francisco Aragão, eh?' Dave rubbed his chin. 'Well, that would make sense. He sounds very dodgy.' He sighed. 'You could try telling them, I suppose, but don't hold your breath.' Dave saw my frown. 'The best thing to do is to forget it, Nick. There's nothing you or I can do to get back at Dekker. Look, when I get my pub, will you come in for a drink?'

'Of course,' I said. 'If you let me know where it is.'

'I'll do that.'

I stood up to leave. Dave gave me a lift to the station. As I was getting out of the car, he called to me. 'Nick?'

'Yes.'

'Be careful. When Dekker Ward have it in for you, they can get nasty.'

'I will.' I smiled grimly, shut the door, and turned into the station.

Despite Dave's scepticism about the DEA, I thought it worth trying them. Now I had left Dekker there was nothing to lose. So, doing my best to ignore the damage it would do to my phone bill, I asked International Directory Enquiries for the number of United Bank of Canada in the Bahamas, and dialled it. I soon got through to Donald Winters.

'Good morning. It's Nick Elliot here, from Dekker Ward in London. I'm a colleague of Martin Beldecos's.'

'Oh, yes. What can I do to help you, Mr Elliot?'

Luckily, it seemed that Winters hadn't heard about Martin's death.

'You sent a fax to Martin last month mentioning that you had linked a payment to our Caymans affiliate with Francisco Aragão.'

'That's right. That was something to do with a lawyer called Tony Hempel, wasn't it?'

'I think so. You said something about Francisco Aragão being under investigation by the US Drugs Enforcement Agency?'

'Yeah. I'm not sure what became of that. We haven't

heard anything more from them. But I can give you the number of my contact there if you're interested.'

I wrote down the name and number, thanked Winters, and hung up.

I dialled the new number. It was somewhere in the United States, but I wasn't familiar with the city code so I didn't know exactly where.

The phone was picked up on the first ring. 'Donnelly.'

'Good morning. This is Nicholas Elliot from Dekker Ward in London. Donald Winters at United Bank of Canada gave me your name.'

'Oh, yeah.'

'I have some information relating to Francisco Aragão, who I believe you're investigating.'

'Shoot.'

So I told him about Martin's fax, Martin's death, and my own attack. I could hear the scribbling on the other end of the line.

'Do you have a copy of this fax?' Donnelly asked.

'No, but you can get the information from Donald Winters if you need it.'

'OK.' More scribbling. 'Have you reported your suspicions about this Martin Beldecos's murder, or the assault on you?'

'No,' I said. 'I'm not sure who to talk to about it.'

'I understand. Well, thank you very much for the information Mr, ah, Elliot. Can you give me a number where I can reach you?'

I gave him my home number. But I didn't want him to disappear without telling me what he was going to do.

'Are you going to investigate this?' I asked.

There was a moment's pause, a pause of impatience.

'This may be useful intelligence, Mr Elliot. We are

pursuing a number of investigations at the present time, and this might help us.'

'But will you investigate Dekker?' I asked, unable to keep the exasperation from my voice.

'I'm sorry, I can't disclose who or what we're investigating. But thank you for the information, Mr Elliot, and we know where we can reach you. Now, goodbye.'

I put down the phone. I was disappointed. I supposed I had hoped that squads of agents would fly out to London immediately to question Ricardo and Eduardo. But that obviously wasn't going to happen.

I tried to think of it from the DEA's point of view. They probably had a target in mind. Perhaps it was Francisco Aragão. Presumably they would use any information they could to help them nail that target, but they wouldn't necessarily allow themselves to be sidetracked by suspicions that were, I had to admit, unsubstantiated.

In some ways I felt better, though. I had done my duty, I had reported what I knew to the proper authority. Maybe now I could forget Dekker.

But I couldn't forget Isabel.

'Well, you have caused a stir, haven't you?'

We were in my local, the Pembroke Castle. Jamie had dropped by for a quick pint, as he had promised.

'Tell me.'

'There's the story in the Rio papers. But you know about that, presumably.'

'I knew it was coming. What did it say?'

'It said that last month's finance scandal involving Humberto Alves and narco-traffickers in the *favelas* was entirely fabricated by Dekker Ward. That Oswaldo

Bocci agreed to publish the story in return for finance to expand his empire.'

'Sounds accurate to me,' I said.

'Well, it certainly touched a nerve. Ricardo is disturbed. Seriously disturbed. And Eduardo is positively raving. He's not a happy bunny.'

I smiled. I liked the idea of niggling Eduardo.

'You've got to watch it, Nick,' Jamie went on. 'These are powerful enemies you're making.'

'I don't care,' I said. 'The way Ricardo torpedoed the *favela* deal was outrageous, you know that. All Luís is doing is setting the record straight.'

'Well, Ricardo holds you responsible.'

'That's absurd.'

'You tell him that.'

I sipped my pint. 'I saw Dave today,' I said.

'How is he?'

'Pissed off. Ricardo has dumped on him. He hasn't been able to get another job in the City.'

'So what's he going to do?'

'He's got some mates of his to buy a pub somewhere. He plans to manage it with Teresa.'

'Not a bad job for him.'

'Yes.' I paused a moment. 'You know, he thinks there's something going on at Dekker. That Martin Beldecos was murdered because he stumbled across something at Dekker Trust.'

'Does he have any proof?' asked Jamie.

'No. He spoke to the police, but they weren't interested. And I spoke to the DEA in America today.'

'You did?'

'Yeah. They took down the details, but they didn't seem that interested either.'

'Ricardo doesn't know you've been talking to Dave and the DEA, does he?'

I shook my head. Then I thought about Dave's suspicion that Eduardo was tapping his phone. Oh, no.

'Well, make sure he doesn't find out,' Jamie said. 'I don't know whether there is anything in this money-laundering stuff. And I don't want to know. But I do know that Ricardo is angrier than I've ever seen him. It's scary.'

'Can you keep your eye out for anything suspicious?'

'No, Nick, I can not. I will keep my head well down on this one. Here, let me get you another beer.'

23

I was woken by the sound of glass shattering and wood splintering. I sat up in bed, and tried to get my bearings. There was loud banging from the sitting room. I threw myself out of bed, and lurched through the door, still wearing only my underpants.

There were three of them, big, hard men dressed in T-shirts and jeans. I threw myself at the nearest one, sending him crashing into a bookshelf.

'Get him!'

Strong hands pulled at my arms. I clung on to the man underneath me, trying to force my arm round his throat. He bucked and kicked. The two others broke my grip free, and hauled me to my feet. The man I had jumped on, staggered upright and kicked me hard in the balls. I cried out, and felt sick. Then there was a blow to my back that just missed my kidney, and a knee came smashing up into my face. My cheek stung and I tasted blood, but it was my groin that still hurt most. I tried to double up but they wouldn't let me. Then something hard hit me on the side of the head and it all went black.

'Ambulance! Quick!'

The crackle of a police radio. Someone kneeling down

next to me. 'He's breathing. Hit on the head. Check the bedroom!'

I lay there, playing dead. I didn't have the energy to move, even to open my eyes. My body hurt all over. There was the continued sound of movement around me, the gentle weight of a blanket laid over my semi-naked body and then the wail of a siren. Strong arms lifted me on to a stretcher. I felt cold air against my face. I opened my eyes.

I was in the street outside my flat. Although it was night, there seemed to be lights everywhere, orange from the street lamps, flashing blue from the ambulance.

A man dressed in bright green overalls leaned over me. 'Hang on. You'll be all right, son.'

They slotted me into the back of the ambulance. The pain screamed throughout my body. I was enormously tired. Everything went black again.

My second visit to hospital was briefer than my first. I was let out late the next morning with instructions to come back if my headache got worse. There was a sore spot on my skull, but my head felt fuzzy rather than in pain. I had bruises all over me; one in my back and one in my thigh really hurt.

I took the taxi home with trepidation. The flat was a mess. They had stolen a couple of things, some gold cuff-links my parents had given me for my eighteenth birthday, and the video recorder. And my Apple Mac.

Oh, shit! There was three years' worth of unfinished thesis on that. I fell into the sofa and stared at the space on the desk where it had sat. Now, think. It can't be that bad. Under the desk were three cardboard boxes. My notes. Please God, let me have kept the rough printouts!

I rushed to the boxes and tore them open. My notes were all there and drafts of three of the chapters. But the rest? All gone. I put my head in my hands. It would take months just to re-create what I had written.

I sat on the floor, surrounded by the debris of the attack. Books were everywhere, drawers were opened. My body hurt, my head was befuddled. I had no job. I had months of boring rewriting ahead of me. And Isabel was either dead or shut up in some flea-pit thousands of miles away.

The phone rang. I crawled over to the patch of floor where it lay, and picked it up.

'Hallo.'

'Nick?'

I felt cold. I recognized the deep voice. It was Eduardo.

'Yes?'

'How are you getting on?'

'You know damn well how I'm getting on. You just had me beaten up and my flat wrecked!'

'You've been attacked? Oh, I'm so sorry to hear that.' Eduardo made no attempt to hide the mockery in his voice. 'There was a very unfortunate piece in the Brazilian press yesterday. Very unfortunate. Now, remember, I'm watching you. And I want you to keep quiet, do you understand me?'

'Fuck you!' I shouted, and slammed down the phone.

Tidying up took me a long time. I was dispirited, stiff and slow. I was interrupted by a police constable, who came round to take details of what was missing. I told him. I also told him about Eduardo's phone call. Why the hell not? I doubted very much that they would be able to find any evidence to link him to the attack, but it might make his life a bit difficult. The constable treated me a bit like a paranoid ex-employee, which of course I was, but he promised to look into it further.

I finally finished clearing up and rang Russell Church, the head of my old department at the School of Russian Studies.

'Nick, how are you? I was just about to phone you to thank you.'

'Oh, really?' What the hell was he talking about?

'Yes. For the Dekker Ward sponsorship.'

My heart sank. Bloody hell! 'What sponsorship?'

'I've just been on the phone with a man called Ross. He says that Dekker Ward would like to provide substantial commercial sponsorship to SRS. They'll start with a trial period of a year, and then see how it goes from there.'

'In return for what?'

'Well, they will want access to some of our people and our contacts. They say they're planning to do more business in Russia. But they're willing to pay good commercial rates for any consulting work they commission. It's perfect. It's just the sort of external funding we need! Well done.'

'Actually, I knew nothing about it.'

'Oh. I rather assumed you were responsible. You must have made a good impression at any rate. So, how are things going there?'

'Well, they're not.' I tried not to let my voice sound sulky, but I couldn't help it. 'I've left. You said I should give you a call if I decided the City wasn't for me.'

Russell was full of enthusiasm. 'Well, now we might be able to find something for you here. We haven't thrashed out the details of the sponsorship deal yet but perhaps you could take up some sort of liaison role.'

I stopped him. 'Wait a second, Russell. I'm not sure

that would work. Dekker and I didn't see eye to eye when I left.'

'Oh.'

'What would be useful for me is if we could carry on our conversation about openings at other universities. And I'd like to use you as a referee, if I may.'

It clicked. Russell's voice became more cautious. 'OK. Let's have a chat.'

'Tomorrow?'

'All right. Say eleven? See you then.'

I was nervous as I knocked on Russell's half-opened door; as nervous as I had been the first time I met him for that interview five years before.

'Come in.'

I could see that Russell had spoken to Dekker as soon as I entered. Neat, with thinning grey hair, he usually greeted me with a beam. This time he rose awkwardly from his desk and shook my hand, not meeting my eyes.

'Oh, hallo, Nick. Have a seat.'

It was almost as though he wasn't expecting me. I perched on the small chair crammed against his desk. I recognized much of the debris that cluttered it. Most of it was under the School of Russian Studies headed memo paper. Admin. Piles of it. There was not a single page of Cyrillic script to be seen.

He removed his glasses, and wiped them, frowning. 'Now, what was it you wanted to talk about?'

'I need a job. I wondered if you knew of anything?'

'I haven't heard of much since you left here. I think the post at Sheffield might still be open. There's a chance something might come up soon at the University of Surrey. Apart from that, not much.'

This was my mentor, almost my friend over the last

five years. The man who had gone out on a limb for me, despite my lack of formal qualifications in Russian. He could do better than that.

I had to know. 'You will be able to provide me with a reference, won't you?'

A reference from Russell was crucial. He was well respected in the academic community in the UK. Worldwide, for that matter. Without a good one, I had no chance of getting a job.

The glasses came off again for another polish.

'That might be difficult,' said Russell. 'I can provide you with something, of course. But it will be difficult for me to make it enthusiastic.'

'Why? What's wrong? What have they said to you?'

'Mr Ross at Dekker Ward explained to me the circumstances under which you left their firm.'

'Which Mr Ross?'

Russell hesitated. 'I think he said it was Eduardo Ross. I'm not sure.'

'Oh, yes. And what did he say?'

Russell shifted in his chair. 'He told me that you had been caught bribing the authorities in Brazil over a transaction there, that this had become public knowledge, and that they'd had to let you go.'

'That's bullshit!'

'I've seen the newspaper article, Nick.' He pulled out a photocopy of the article from Bocci's newspaper.

'But Dekker Ward planted that. I can show you another article that says the opposite!'

'Ross told me you had gone to the press behind their backs as well.' Russell's demeanour had changed. He was leaning forward, his jaw jutting out, ready for confrontation.

'But don't you want to hear my side of the story?'

'OK. Fire away.'

So I tried to explain. It was difficult without going into too much detail, but I thought I did a pretty good job of it. But Russell wasn't listening. He didn't hear; he didn't *want* to hear.

When I had finished, he tapped his pencil on his desk. 'Basically, Nick, it's your word against Dekker's, and the Rio press.' He tapped the Bocci article in front of him. 'And at this moment Dekker Ward are crucial to this institution's future. I can't afford to doubt them.'

I'd had enough. 'Russell! You're being bought!'

'That's an absurd accusation!'

'No, it's not. If I had come to you from a faceless City institution and said I wanted to go back into academia you wouldn't have asked any questions. It's only because these people are promising to pay you money that you're listening.'

'I can't give you a reference in good faith when I know you've been involved in bribing government officials.'

'You know no such thing. All you have is Eduardo Ross's word, that's all. This sponsorship comes with strings, and the first string is to ditch me. Your first commercial sponsorship deal, and within a day you're letting it compromise your independence!'

Russell held up his hands. 'Now, calm down, Nick. Let's talk about this Surrey post, shall we?'

'Forget it!' I said, and stormed out.

I pedalled back to Primrose Hill in record time, ignoring the pain in my aching back and leg. Russell's reaction was all too predictable but nonetheless severely disappointing. Since he had become head of the department three years ago, he had made commercial sponsorship the central plank of his strategy for preserving the funding base of the department. Until now, he'd had little concrete success. His position internally within the School was not yet secure. And he was ambitious. So why give it all up for some promising Russian lecturer who still hadn't got his Ph.D. under his belt?

Because that would have been the right thing to do. Because he was my friend and supporter. Because the School of Russian Studies wasn't Dekker Ward.

Bastard!

So why had Dekker done it? Was I really that important to them that they wanted to shell out a million or two to keep me out of work? I supposed it was an intelligent move on some level. The School of Russian Studies did have good contacts and knowledge of Russia that Ricardo could tap. And, of course, all Russell had at the moment was promises. Dekker would have plenty of opportunity to back out before they actually put up hard cash.

I stopped at the pub just round the corner from my flat, and bought a pint and a ham sandwich. I thought practicalities. It would be very hard to get a job teaching Russian in a university now. And I probably couldn't get another job in the City even if I wanted it. I still had six months or so to go on my Ph.D., not including the three or four months it would take just to get me back to where I'd left it. I should probably get my head down and finish that. I had three thousand pounds in my bank account, mostly the residue from the money Ricardo had lent me for clothes. I would try to live on that.

The mortgage payments on my flat were once again going to be impossible to meet. There was still no chance of selling it for more than the amount of the loan. I would have to let it and try to find somewhere cheap to live. Very cheap. Like a squat or something. I looked at the ham sandwich in front of me. I wouldn't be able to eat out like this in future.

And what future? I looked towards it with an almost total lack of interest. If Isabel were around, or even if I knew she were alive, things would be different. But the uncertainty surrounding her disappearance weighed on me, dragging me down into a sort of pessimistic apathy. I was losing the ability to believe in her survival and, without that, the future looked unbearably grey.

I went back to the flat. It was almost tidy now. Workmen had put up a temporary door where the french windows had been. They would install something more permanent in the afternoon. Luckily the insurance covered that.

I paced through the four small rooms: kitchen, sitting room, bathroom and bedroom. It would be a shame to leave. When Joanna had first bought it, the flat had seemed extravagant, and then it had become a millstone. But there were all those bookshelves that I had spent hours, no, days putting up, shelves that ingeniously held two thousand books. There was the tiny garden: I knew every plant, every weed.

Suddenly, unexpectedly, a rush of anger swept through me. I was losing my flat because of Dekker. I had screwed up my career because of them. They had arranged to have me beaten up. Who the hell did these people think they were? Couldn't I do something to stop them? Or at least something to hurt them? I wanted revenge, and I wanted it right then.

But what? Exposing Ricardo's manipulation of Bocci had hurt them, but not enough. They would recover soon. I wanted to do something that would cause them permanent harm.

But what could I do? One unemployed investment

banker with two months' experience. I'd have loved to have been able to blow this money-laundering thing up in their faces. But it would require an extensive international investigation to uncover more, and it didn't look like the DEA were about to start one, at least not into Dekker itself. I believed Dave when he talked about the indifference of the authorities.

I hated the feeling of powerlessness. There had to be something I could do.

My brooding was interrupted by the phone.

'Nick? It's Kate. I heard the terrible news. I was just phoning to see how you were.'

'Which terrible news?'

I caught the hesitation on the other end of the phone. 'Well, both things, I suppose. Isabel. And then you losing your job. It must be awful.'

'It is. And I've been broken into and beaten up.'

'Oh, God! When?'

'The night before last.'

'Were you badly hurt?'

'I was knocked out. My head still hurts. And my back. And leg,' I said, moving my stiff leg into a more comfortable position.

'What are you doing now?'

'Thinking about renting out the flat.'

'Can't you get another job?'

'No. Dekker Ward have suddenly decided to sponsor the School of Russian Studies. My continued unemployment is the condition.'

'Oh, no! Where are you going to live?'

'I don't know. I'll find a squat somewhere. Camden's a good area for that sort of thing, I believe.' I could tell my voice must sound weary, low.

Kate was silent for a moment. Then she said, 'Well,

stop moping. Pack a suitcase and come round here now. You can stay with us until you find the squat of your dreams. You need people around, even if it is only me and Oliver.'

Suddenly there was nothing I wanted more than to do what Kate suggested.

'OK,' I said. 'I'll see you this evening.'

I took my bike, weighed down with saddlebags, on to the train, and arrived at the station at eight o'clock. It was on the edge of an old market town thirty miles from London, which had lost the battle to avoid becoming a dormitory community. Jamie and Kate's house was three miles from the station, on the outskirts of the village of Bodenham.

It was still light as I rode along the narrow lanes. Chestnut trees were everywhere, bedecked with white candles. It wasn't quiet, the birds were making a racket, and farm machinery was returning to base for the evening. I plunged down a steep hill into Bodenham and swerved left at the bottom by the duck pond, narrowly avoiding a mallard strutting importantly across the road. Even here cyclists didn't get proper respect.

Their house was at the end of a straight half-mile stretch of lane. I didn't hear the car until a loud horn sounded a couple of feet behind me and almost sent me out of my seat. I turned to see Jamie's Jaguar XJS whispering along in my slipstream. He tried to overtake, but I slowed to walking pace and weaved across the road in front of him. Some people just don't grow up.

They lived in Dockenbush Farm, an old farmhouse that was still surrounded by working buildings used by a neighbouring farmer. It had half an acre of garden, an appealing mess of unkempt roses and shrubs. On one side was a small orchard with a purple and green carpet of uncut grass and bluebells. A confused yellow rose scrambled across the front of the house, and I had to duck as I walked in at the front door to avoid a heavy branch of thorns and flowers.

'I must tie that back,' said Jamie. 'Although at least it keeps out lanky gits like you.'

'I'll do it,' I said. 'In fact, I might give the whole place a good haircut.'

They had moved in two years before, just after Jamie had joined Dekker. The house had seemed to me absurdly large for the two of them plus small child, especially since I was used to seeing them in a cramped one-bedroomed flat in Chiswick. It reminded me a little of the house Jamie had grown up in, which I had seen on my first couple of visits to his family before his father had been forced to sell it. That was no coincidence, of course. I also suspected that it was no coincidence that Ricardo, too, had a nice house in the country.

Kate came through and stepped up on her bare toes to give me a kiss. 'Hallo. Supper's almost ready. It's only stew, I'm afraid.'

The large old kitchen was warmed by an Aga, and pleasingly cluttered with toys and iron pots and pans. The stew was delicious. We downed a bottle of Chilean red between the three of us and talked and laughed. Then, over a spread of French cheeses, Jamie touched on the subject we had all been avoiding. 'Ricardo talked about you this morning.'

'Oh, yes?'

'Yes. He gave us a little speech. He told us why you'd left. He said that he didn't mind people disagreeing with the Dekker ethos, and that he had given you a chance to resign, which you hadn't taken. He wouldn't tolerate any member of the team betraying the rest of us. He said you'd never work again, not in the City, nor in a university.'

'Jamie! Didn't you say anything?' Kate protested.

Jamie shrugged.

'He couldn't,' I said. 'Ricardo isn't that sort of person.' Then I asked Jamie, 'What do the others think?'

Jamie sighed. 'It's impossible to tell. Everyone's a bit down after Isabel. And this Mexican deal is becoming a real problem. They know I'm a good friend of yours, so they wouldn't talk to me about it anyway. But I suspect they'll keep quiet. The message from Ricardo is clear. Stick with me and I'll look after you. Leave and you're in trouble.'

Kate looked at Jamie with concern. Jamie avoided her glance, and studied the debris of cheese and crumbs on his plate.

'I thought it was a bit extreme sponsoring the School of Russian Studies just to keep me out of a job,' I said.

'It was. And that's why it was effective. It's a warning to the rest of us of how far Ricardo will go to punish people whom he thinks have betrayed him. But also it's a good idea. We'll need information and contacts to get into Russia. Your old place can provide us with useful introductions.'

'And beating me up? Wrecking my flat? Did Ricardo tell everyone about that too?'

'I doubt he even knows. That has all the marks of Eduardo.'

'Jamie, you've got to get out of there!' said Kate. 'Especially after what they did to Nick. You should leave before it's too late.'

Jamie sighed. 'It is too late. Especially now. Ricardo will be watching me for signs of disloyalty.'

'Screw him!' said Kate. 'Just leave.'

'It's not that easy,' said Jamie. 'This house needs to be paid for. I'll need two years' good bonuses to make a dent in the mortgage. And if I leave, what will I do then? Ricardo isn't a good man to have as an enemy. The Latin American market is small: everyone knows everyone else.'

'You could work for Bloomfield Weiss,' said Kate. 'They'd have you like a shot.'

'Yeah, and if they lose their war with Dekker, which it looks like they will, they won't need me any more and I'll be out on the street.'

'Oh, Jamie!' growled Kate in frustration. She threw down her napkin and left the table.

The two of us sat in awkward silence. Finally Jamie broke it. 'I'm sorry,' he said.

'Don't worry about it. I'm free to screw up my own career. There's no need for you to screw yours up in solidarity. You've got Kate to look after, and Oliver.' And your ambition, I thought. That was the real problem, and both Jamie and I knew it. He was doing well at Dekker, and if he kept his head down he could be making millions in a few years' time. That was something he desperately wanted to do.

But he was an old friend of mine. I didn't want him to give up his ambitions on my account.

I helped Jamie wash up, and went to bed. I didn't see any more of Kate that evening.

I spoke to her the next day. Jamie had gone to work, and she had taken Oliver to school. The weather was glorious, sunny with a gentle breeze. We sat in the back garden drinking mugs of coffee.

'Did you know your godson has a girlfriend?' Kate said.

'Really? He's a bit young, isn't he?'

'I think they're quite keen on the opposite sex at this age, and then they go off them when they get older.'

'What's her name?'

'Jessica.'

'Is she pretty?'

'You'll have to ask Oliver. She looks a bit dumpy to me. But she plays rockets with him, so I don't think he minds. He asked me if she could come round to play. He was terribly shy about it. It was quite sweet.'

'Well, I look forward to a formal introduction.'

We lapsed into silence, sipping our coffee. Something disturbed the rooks in a nearby copse, and they rose in a complaining black swirl, before eventually settling down again.

'Do you think they'll find her?' Kate asked.

'Isabel?'

'Yes.'

I thought for a moment. 'Yes, I do. I have to believe that they will.'

'She seemed very nice.'

'She is.'

'But I hate women with figures like that. They look good in anything.'

I smiled. I remembered how she looked, how she felt, her scent, her voice. She *had* to be alive. She just had to be.

Kate reached across and squeezed my hand.

'I'm sorry about last night,' she said. 'It's just that Jamie drives me mad. His life seems to have been taken over by Dekker. I sometimes feel like he's sold his soul to Ricardo.'

'I know what you mean. Ricardo likes to control the people who work for him. He lets them go about things their own way, but he makes sure their interests are tied up completely with his. But I can understand Jamie's point of view. He needs to pay for all this.'

'No, he doesn't!' said Kate with surprising forceful-ness. 'We don't actually *need* all this. Of course it's very nice, but we could quite happily live in a small flat in Chiswick. And that stuff about providing for me is crap, too. I had a perfectly good job in a City law firm. I could earn a decent salary again. Of course I want to spend the time with Oliver while he's young, but I don't have to.'

I was quiet. I didn't want to get involved in an argu-ment between Kate and Jamie. Especially when I thought one of them was right and the other wrong.

'Do you know, he was angry with me for letting you stay here?' she said.

I shook my head.

'He said it would look bad at the office. I told him not to be so absurd.'

'I don't want to stay if – '

'You stay,' said Kate firmly, her eyes blazing. I was surprised. Kate was normally calm, unflappable. I had never seen her so worked up as in the last twelve hours.

The shock must have shown in my face. 'Don't worry,' she said, with a slight smile. 'Jamie wants you here too. I think he realized he was being stupid.'

She took a sip of her coffee, and stared out towards the hill behind the garden. 'He's changing, you know.'

I didn't answer at first. I didn't want to talk too deeply about Jamie with Kate. But, then, she clearly needed to talk to someone about him. So I stepped delicately into the minefield.

'Is he?'

Kate shot me a glance. She sensed my reluctance to talk, but went on regardless. 'You remember him at university. He never took anything too seriously. He was always fun, he was always kind, he was always, well, affectionate. And afterwards, too. He was great when my father died.'

I remembered when Kate's father had been killed in a car crash. She had been devastated. Jamie had done all that could be expected of a husband, and done it very well. He seemed to know exactly when to cheer her up, and when to let her be alone.

'He's always been a good friend to me,' I said. 'He got me the job at Dekker, didn't he? I know that didn't work out too well, but he stuck his neck out for me.'

'Yes, he did.' Kate smiled briefly, but she still wore a frown. 'But what about Oliver? When he was born, Jamie was wonderful. And now he hardly ever sees him.'

'He doesn't have any choice, Kate. I've been inside Dekker. You have to work hard, ridiculously hard. Jamie spends no more time there than anyone else. In fact he probably spends less.'

'But why does he have to work there in the first place? After all it's done to you. After all it's doing to him.'

There was a note of anguish in Kate's voice. I knew the answer. I had played rugby with Jamie. He was one of the most competitive people I had ever come across. And he never gave up. If he had decided to make his fortune at Dekker, there was nothing that Kate or I could do to change his mind.

'You know,' she said, 'I really admire what you did.'

'What? You mean resigning?'

She nodded, looking straight ahead, her coffee mug half an inch from her lips.

'I had to. I didn't have any choice.'

'That's what I mean.'

She turned to me and smiled her warm friendly smile. The sun shone off her short brown hair. She was wearing a white T-shirt and a long cotton skirt, light summer clothes that gently rested on the soft roundness of her body.

Jamie didn't deserve her.

So I stayed with Kate and Jamie. I spent a couple of days sorting out my flat. This involved talking to letting agents, getting a plumber in to fix the boiler, tidying up, packing, and hiring a van for a morning to move my stuff, eighty per cent of which was books. The agents were optimistic that they would find a tenant at a rent that would almost cover the mortgage.

I began work again on my thesis. I had thought that resurrecting the missing chapters would be desperately tedious, but actually it wasn't. I could remember quite well what I had written, and although I needed to dig around in my notes a lot, even that I enjoyed. And the thesis was taking better shape second time round. But I hadn't made adequate notes of all the references I needed. For these I would have to spend a couple of days at the School of Russian Studies' library in London. Most of the rest I could do from Dockenbush Farm.

It was a very pleasant place to work, especially in May. There was a guest room at the top of the house. I fixed up a table and chair in front of the window, which supported the brand new Apple Mac I had bought in anticipation of insurance money. The view was over the top of the apple trees to a couple of fields of young barley and a low wooded hill beyond. It was idyllic. I worked a full day, eight till eight, with an hour off for lunch with Kate and Oliver. I was able to throw myself into Pushkin's world and forget my own. Ricardo, Eduardo and Dekker were still there, but they seemed a long way away.

The only reminder was Jamie, who brought with him the smell of Dekker as he returned each evening. It soon wore off: he didn't want to talk about it; neither did Kate nor I. The atmosphere in the house had improved since their argument on my arrival. We had fun in the evenings: we stayed up late drinking and talking. It felt almost like a holiday.

I phoned the police station in Kentish Town to see how they were getting on in solving Crime Number 1521634/E. I wasn't surprised to hear that they had got nowhere. None of the stolen goods had turned up. They had interviewed Eduardo, who had denied all knowledge of the burglary, and they had been unable to find any connection between him and it, apart from my suspicions.

I thought intermittently about Isabel, rather than constantly. I felt guilty about this, although I realized it was probably a good thing. Because when I did think of her, I felt anxious, guilty, worried, uncertain, angry. We had spent so few days truly together, and it had been so far away. I kept on asking myself whether the relationship would have worked, and I kept on telling myself it would. Very well. And then I got angry that I'd been prevented from finding out.

I phoned Luís to see if there was any news. He was pleased to hear from me. He said he had introduced KBN, a large Dutch bank with good Brazilian connections, to Humberto Alves, and suggested they talk about *favela* financing. It would take a couple of months to resurrect the deal, but Humberto was confident something would come out of it. I was glad Ricardo hadn't been enraged for nothing.

'No news of Isabel?' I asked.

There was a heavy silence. 'No,' he said. 'Nothing.'

'Have the police found anything yet?'

'No.' He paused. I let the silence hang there. 'She's still alive, you know. They haven't found a body yet. If she was dead, they would have found her. I know she's alive. I can feel it.'

'I hope you're right,' I said. And I had to believe he was.

One evening, in my second week at Dockenbush Farm, Dekker intruded. Jamie was tense when he returned home, and this time the tension didn't leave after the first glass of wine. It was time for our taboo to be broken.

'What's up?' asked Kate.

'Things aren't good at work.'

'What is it?'

Jamie glanced at me. 'Nick'll probably love this. I think we've got big problems. The market's been in free-fall all last week, and it looks like it's continuing this week.'

'What happened?' I asked. I had deliberately stopped reading the Latin American news in the papers.

'Mexico is up shit creek. Banks are going bust all over the place, the government has a huge debt-refinancing burden to deal with this year, and everyone's scared.'

'And Dekker is still long that two billion Mexican deal they led last month?'

'Yes, that, and a lot more besides. Mexico is off twenty points and Ricardo keeps buying more. You see, his theory is that the US bailed out Mexico in nineteen ninety-five, and they'll do it again. As far as he's concerned, it's a great opportunity to buy into a panic at the bottom. He's got extra funding from Chalmet, you know, the Swiss bank that owns twenty-nine per cent of us. We have enough Mexican paper to fill the entire Canary Wharf tower.'

'Exactly how much is that?'

Jamie winced. 'We're long four billion of Mexico, and two billion of other stuff.'

'Jesus! What happened? Is Ricardo losing his nerve?'

'Ricardo isn't. The US Congress is. Have you heard of the Pinnock Bill?'

'No.'

'It's a new piece of legislation that will require Congress to approve any emergency-aid package above a certain size. It's specifically designed to prevent the US government bailing out Mexico again.'

'Will it get through? Won't the President veto it?'

'Maybe, maybe not. There are deals within deals to be done on this one. Let's just say that it has made Mexico's situation more uncertain. Some of the Bradys are down in the thirties.'

Whew! I remembered they were trading in the sixties and seventies a month before. 'So, no bonus this year?'

Jamie sighed. 'It's worse than that. Our capital was one and a half billion dollars at the beginning of this year. At today's prices our losses are bigger than that now. Technically we're insolvent. Of course, all the losses are unrealized. And no one outside the group knows about it, not even Lord Kerton. There's still a chance that the market can bail us out. But until then, we're relying on money from Chalmet and creative accounting.'

Jamie was right. I was pleased. But I did my best not to show it. He was worried. He didn't want Dekker to disappear before he had received his first truly fat bonus.

But when I sat down to work the next morning, I found I couldn't concentrate. The notes that had so absorbed me yesterday now lay spread out on the desk in front of me. My eyes were drawn to the window, and the apple trees below.

So Dekker were in deep shit? Great! My only regret was that I hadn't put them there. I did feel slightly sorry for Jamie and some of the others who stood to lose their bonuses after all the work they had put in to get them. But Jamie was lucky enough to have Kate. What did he want with all that money?

Dekker would probably wriggle out somehow. Prices of Mexican bonds would bounce. Who knows, maybe Dekker would end up making a fortune instead of losing it? But right now they were weak, vulnerable. If I wanted my revenge, now was the time.

And I did want revenge. Ricardo and his brother had destroyed my career, stolen my thesis, beaten me up and forced me out of my flat, all with apparent impunity. The arrogance of it rankled. I couldn't let them get away with it. What had Ricardo said? 'If you're not with me, you're against me.' Well, I was against him all right.

But what could I do?

I remembered Kate suggesting Jamie should get a job at Bloomfield Weiss. That would annoy Ricardo a little, true. But he wouldn't much care if I joined them. Not that they'd have me, with my experience in finance stretching to less than two months.

Wait a moment. I'd got it. It seemed absurd at first,

but the more I thought about it the more sense it made. I pushed Pushkin to one side, and scribbled thoughts down on a clean sheet of paper, smiling broadly to myself.

I would need some luck. But, if I pulled this off, Dekker was finished. And I would be responsible.

24

That afternoon, I asked Kate if she minded whether I made a couple of international calls. She didn't. I started off with International Directory Enquiries for Bloomfield Weiss's number in New York. Then the Bloomfield Weiss switchboard for the name of their chairman and the number of his office. Then the chairman's office itself.

It turned out Sidney Stahl was in London. What luck! I got the London number from his secretary in New York. I tried that.

'Mr Wolpin's office,' a woman's voice answered.

'Can I speak to Mr Stahl? I believe he's in London.'

'He certainly is. But he's in a meeting with Mr Wolpin at the moment. Who's speaking?'

'Nick Elliot. From Dekker Ward.'

'Can anyone else help you, Mr Elliot? I think Mr Stahl will be tied up for a while.'

I was being screened out. Unsurprising.

'No, I need to talk to Mr Stahl myself. Can you tell him it's about Dekker Ward's losses on their Mexican position. And can you tell him I'm calling in an unofficial capacity. I'll give you my number.' I gave her Kate and Jamie's.

'Certainly, Mr Elliot. I'll tell him,' said the woman,

managing to carry the suggestion that there was not a chance in hell that Mr Stahl would call me back. I had considered going to Bloomfield Weiss through Jamie's friend Stephen Troughton, but after some thought, I'd rejected that idea. I didn't trust him, and I would quickly have lost control of events. Much better to hold out for direct access to the top man.

I sat by the phone in the sitting room, reading the newspaper. Kate was in the garden playing with Oliver. She breezed past to get him a drink. 'Taking a break?' she asked, with a hint of surprise. I never usually took a break for more than ten minutes or so at a time.

'I've just finished a chapter,' I said. 'I'm rewarding myself with the newspaper.'

I was half-way through the sports section when the phone rang. I grabbed it.

'May I speak with Nick Elliot?' said a quiet young American voice.

'Speaking.'

'This is Preston Morris. I work with Mr Stahl. I believe you called him earlier.'

I looked around. Kate was still in the garden 'I need to speak to Mr Stahl personally,' I said.

'I'm afraid that won't be possible today, sir. Perhaps I can help?'

The screening was in full working order.

'OK. Listen. I'm a former employee of Dekker Ward. I have details of their recent losses in emerging-markets trading and a suggestion to make. I'd like to discuss it with Mr Stahl tomorrow. It'll only take fifteen minutes. If he doesn't like what he hears, he can throw me out.'

'I'll check with Sidney and call you back.'

I tried to stay closer to the phone than Kate all afternoon, but didn't quite manage it. At last, just after six, it rang. Despite my efforts, she got to it first. 'Preston Morris,' she said, handing the receiver over to me. She watched as I agreed to a meeting at nine forty-five the following morning.

'What was that all about?' she asked.

'Oh, just someone who wanted to see me,' I answered.

'Sounded like a banker to me.'

'Do you think so? I'll tell him that,' I said, as I drifted out of the room, feeling Kate's puzzled gaze on my back.

Bloomfield Weiss's offices were in Broadgate, a modern complex of brown marble offices behind Liverpool Street station. I negotiated security guards, reception and secretary, before being directed to a sofa outside a closed door. As I was waiting, I remembered Isabel and my visits to Humberto Alves's office. I smiled as I recalled the going over she had given him for awarding Bloomfield Weiss the mandate for the *favela* deal. I would need all her audacity if I was going to pull this off. I felt almost that she was there with me, and I resolved not to let her down.

After half an hour, the door opened and a small, birdlike man in a white shirt and braces came out. He took me in in an instant, and wasn't impressed. I could almost see him deciding there and then that this was going to take five minutes, not fifteen.

He held out a hand, 'Sidney Stahl. Come in,' and he ushered me into a large plush office with a huge desk and a suite of cream sofas and chairs. Two men, who had been perched on the edge of a sofa, stood up. One young, tall and preppy, one older and more world-weary. Stahl waved towards them. 'My assistant Preston

Morris, who I believe you've already spoken with, and Cy Wolpin who heads our emerging-markets unit in London.'

We shook hands briefly. Stahl's voice was rough New York. He really was very small, scarcely taller than five feet, and he can't have weighed more than nine stone. He seemed dwarfed by the two men next to him, but you could tell he was the boss. They stood back from him, giving him space, as though they were uncomfortable looking down on him.

'What can we do for you, Mr Elliot?' Stahl sat down, and the others took their cue from him, as did I. Stahl's eyes looked my way, but they weren't focused. He was thinking of his last meeting, or his next.

I came straight to the point. 'I worked for Dekker Ward for just over a month. I left a couple of weeks ago.' So what? said Stahl's face. 'I happen to know that Dekker have taken on huge positions in Mexican bonds over the last few weeks.'

'The whole market knows that,' said Cy Wolpin. 'Dekker did that Mexican deal that bombed, and they've been buying back bonds ever since.'

I ignored him. I had got half of Stahl's attention. His eyes were at least focused, and pointed in my direction. 'Dekker's positions are much bigger than that. They own four billion dollars of Mexico paper, and two billion of other stuff. Their losses on these positions are so great that they're technically insolvent. They're relying on funding from their Swiss shareholder, Chalmet, to keep them afloat.'

Now I had them. 'Go on,' said Stahl.

'Well, I know that Bloomfield Weiss want to expand into emerging markets. And everyone knows that that's Dekker's market. So my suggestion is that Bloomfield

Weiss acquire Dekker. Then it will be your market, not theirs.'

Stahl laughed. It was a kind of extended cackle that worked its way up through lungs thickly coated with mucus or tar. The other two men's expressions instantly switched from scornful seriousness to mild amusement.

'D'you hear that, guys? That's balls for you. The kid's pitching for an M and A mandate.' He reached into his pocket for a cigar and lit up. It looked huge compared to his tiny body. Despite the laughter I was encouraged. Stahl's cigar deliberations were giving him time to think.

'Isn't Dekker a private company?' he asked. 'Doesn't that guy they call "The Marketmaker" own most of it? What's his name? Ricardo Ross, that's it! He's not gonna sell to us, is he?'

'You're right, it is a private company,' I replied. 'But Ricardo owns very little.'

Stahl raised his eyebrows. They were pencil thin, as if they had been plucked.

'Ricardo finds other ways to take cash out of Dekker,' I said. 'Lots of it.'

The eyebrows fell back to their normal position. 'So who does own it?'

'Fifty-one per cent is owned by Lord Kerton and his family. His ancestors founded the firm a hundred and thirty years ago. Chalmet et Companie, the private Swiss bank, owns twenty-nine per cent. They picked that up in 1985 just before Big Bang. And the remaining twenty per cent is owned by other directors.'

'And Ross is one of those?'

'No, actually. Ross refuses to go on the board. He wants his Emerging Markets Group to be as separate as possible from the rest of the firm.'

Wolpin and Stahl exchanged glances, Wolpin's I-told-

you-so, Stahl's irritation. I realized I had briefly tres-
passed on a political battlefield. But in a moment Stahl's
attention was back on me. 'Well, how can we buy the
company if it's that tightly held?'

'Kerton doesn't know what a hole Ross has got him
into. If we tell him, he may want to sell. Especially if,
once we've hit him with the problem, we give him the
solution.'

'Which is?' asked Stahl, puffing on his cigar.

'Bloomfield Weiss taking on the Dekker portfolio and
trading their way out of it. There can't be many firms
in the world that could do that. They'd have to be big,
they'd have to know how to trade, and they'd have to
know emerging markets. That means Bloomfield Weiss
and about nobody else.'

'That would be one hell of a position,' said Wolpin.
'The risks would be substantial.'

I looked straight at Stahl. 'I thought that's what you
did. Take risks.'

Stahl cackled again. 'I like this guy. Of course we can
handle the risk, Cy. We're gonna be buying the bonds
for peanuts. But what about the Swiss?'

'I don't know. I've no idea what Ross has told them
about his position. It's also impossible to tell where
their money is coming from. You can get very little
information on Chalmet. Theoretically it's a small bank
based in Geneva, but it has undisclosed billions under
management, and I think that it's using its clients' money
to fund Dekker.'

Wolpin interrupted, 'Chalmet have a reputation in
South America as a good place to park dirty money. I'll
bet they've got all kinds of drug dealers and corrupt
politicians on their client list.'

This was a subject I wanted to steer well clear of. I

didn't want Bloomfield Weiss to scare themselves off with talk of money-laundering.

'There must be a lot of loyalty to Ricardo Ross at Chalmet,' I said. 'But if they think they're going to lose everything, they might be prepared to change their minds. And, once again, the best way for them to get their money back might be to have Bloomfield Weiss take over Dekker's portfolio and trade out of it.'

'Interesting,' said Stahl. 'So, what do you want, kid? A two per cent fee? We have our own people who know about this corporate-finance stuff, you know.'

I smiled. 'I'm sure you do. And I don't want a fee. I know you wouldn't pay me one anyway. All I ask is that you keep me informed. Tell me what happens.'

'So what's in it for you?'

'Dekker Ward treated me very badly,' I said, the intensity of my voice surprising even me. 'I want them to pay.'

Stahl smiled quickly. He understood revenge as well as greed. A more noble motive would have raised his suspicions. 'Well, they will. That is, if we decide we want to go along with your idea,' he added quickly. But there was something in his voice that made me feel sure he would. I couldn't help smiling. He caught it, and his quick brown eyes twinkled. 'OK,' he said, standing up. 'We'll be in touch. Soon.'

'So where were you going this morning in your nice little suit?' asked Kate. We had just sat down to supper, a salad I had thrown together. 'Interview?'

Both Kate and Jamie looked at me expectantly. I had been worrying about how to deal with this all day. There was no way I could tell them the truth. It would be expecting too much of Jamie for him to keep quiet, and it would be hard to stay in his house.

I was betraying him, and I felt bad about it.

'Yes,' I lied. 'It was with a management consultancy. They're looking to start some operations in Russia.'

'Oh, which one?' asked Jamie.

'KEL,' I said. 'It's only a small one.'

'Oh, I know KEL! Christian Deerbury works there. He was at Oxford with us. Do you remember him?'

Damn! I did vaguely. 'No, I don't think so,' I replied.

'Well, I could give him a call. Get him to put in a good word.'

'No, don't bother. I'm sure they don't want me. Consulting's too much like banking anyway. I should never have gone.'

I felt uncomfortable, and Jamie and Kate could sense it. But I couldn't tell them what I was really doing.

They realized I didn't want to continue with the conversation, and fell silent.

I took a deep breath. 'Perhaps I ought to leave soon. I should start looking for a place of my own.'

'No!' said Jamie and Kate together.

'Stay here, Nick. Please,' Kate said.

I looked at Jamie. He nodded his own encouragement. 'OK,' I said, and smiled weakly.

I sat up at my desk that night, looking out over the shallow valley, illuminated by a full moon. Should I stay? It was very pleasant, and I had nowhere else to go. The estate agent had successfully let my flat. Kate's eagerness for me to remain was evident. Why? I wondered. I suspected it had something to do with Jamie. Perhaps she thought I could change him or, rather, prevent him from changing. I sighed. I feared there was little chance of that.

But, if I stayed, how would they react when they found out about the takeover, as they surely would? Well, Kate would probably approve. She thought as little of Dekker as I did. She was as angry as I was over the way they had treated me.

And Jamie?

It would be a shock. But it shouldn't be too bad for him. One of the main attractions of Dekker to Bloomfield Weiss was its employees, and Jamie was an important one of those. And continued employment with them would be preferable to Dekker going bust.

So that was how I persuaded myself that I wasn't letting down my friends.

And I would be giving Ricardo exactly what he deserved.

Stahl himself called me back at about eight the next morning.

'We're gonna go for it,' he growled. 'Be at our office in Broadgate at ten forty-five. We're gonna see Lord Kerton.'

I waited for him in the Bloomfield Weiss lobby. He was flanked by two besuited bankers. Although they were both of average height, they towered above him. In fact, as he swept out of the office with one each on either side and slightly behind him, he looked like a Mafia boss with his two heavies in tow.

And these guys were heavies. Bloomfield Weiss had a reputation for aggression that applied to its corporate-finance dealings as well as everything else. These two had personally been involved in the dismemberment of dozens of corporations throughout the world. Technically the activity was known as mergers and acquisitions, or M and A. But some of the jargon gave a better idea of the flavour of what actually happened: 'downsizing', 'giving value back to shareholders', 'shedding non-core activities', 'squeezing cash out of the business'. And then there was another set of phrases that dealt with the other side of the coin: 'golden parachute', 'executive incentive scheme' and especially that little three-letter word, 'fee'.

Stahl introduced me as 'the kid I was telling you about'. The bankers' names were Schwartz and Godfrey. We hurried across the paved squares in the centre of Broadgate to a cab that was waiting for us on one of the side-streets that adjoined the complex. Dekker Ward's office was in a small street just behind the Bank of England. It took us fifteen minutes to crawl there through the City traffic. It would have taken five minutes to walk.

Of course, I had never been to Dekker's City office before. It was where the traditional, non-Ricardo business of the firm was carried out: trading in British and ex-colonial stocks, some private client business, a small fund-management group, and corporate finance. At least, that's what I thought went on there. Sitting high up in the air three miles away in Canary Wharf, Ricardo's team neither knew nor cared much what anyone else at Dekker did.

The façade was an elegant Georgian four-storey building, painted light grey. We walked into what could have been the entrance hall of a country house. The man at the reception desk was more like a butler than a security guard. After having our credentials respectfully taken, we were ushered into a lift and led into a board-room one floor up. There, an assortment of Victorian financiers stared down at a long, polished table. I wandered over to look at the names. There was a Dekker, and a Ward, but most of them were Kertons.

Stahl, too, looked closely round the room. I could tell he liked it. He liked it a lot. 'Hey, Dwight, do you think we could fix up the thirty-eighth floor like this?'

I glanced at the two bankers and only just managed to suppress a smile.

'I dunno, Sidney,' said the one called Dwight. 'We'd need some old photos of your folks. I'm sure we could find an artist to add the necessary touches.'

Stahl laughed. 'I'd get them to put up my old grandma. You know she was a matchmaker? One of those *babushkas* who arranged marriages? Boy, did she know how to create a deal out of nowhere.'

Just then the door opened, and Lord Kerton strode in. With his tall frame, longish fair hair and his elegant suit, he was all poise and self-assurance. 'Morning,' he said, holding out his hand. 'Andrew Kerton.'

Stahl shook it. 'Sidney Stahl. This is Dwight Godfrey and Jerry Schwartz. And Nick Elliot I believe you know.'

'Actually, I don't think I do,' he said, but he shook my hand and smiled in a friendly way.

Stahl glanced at me strangely. 'Nick used to work for Dekker Ward until recently.'

Kerton frowned.

'In the Emerging Markets Group,' I added quickly. 'We did meet once.'

'Oh, I'm sorry. I do know many of the people over there but I couldn't quite place you. Jumped ship, have you?'

'You could say that, sir.'

Kerton's cool blue eyes studied me for a moment, and then he turned back to Stahl. 'Have a seat, gentlemen.' There was a knock on the door and a butler-type man brought in coffee. 'As you requested, I'm here alone. I haven't told anyone else in the firm about your visit, but I must admit I'm curious to know what it's about.'

'OK Mr . . . er . . .' Stahl hesitated, caught uncharacteristically off-guard. 'Andy OK?' he said.

Kerton smiled. 'Andy's fine, Sid.' I caught Dwight Godfrey stiffening a touch. I suspected Stahl preferred Sidney to Sid.

'OK, Andy. It's real simple. We'd like to make an offer for your company.'

Kerton leaned back in his chair. 'I'm flattered,' he said, looking it. 'But Dekker Ward is growing very strongly, and we expect this growth to continue. I don't think we're too keen to sell at the moment.'

'OK,' said Stahl, and waited.

'All right,' Kerton said, a pleased smile on his face. 'You've intrigued me. What price were you thinking of?'

'Ten million pounds.'

Kerton snorted. 'Ten million! That's absurd. I'm sure you've discovered we keep our results confidential, but our annual profits are substantially more than that. In fact our *monthly* profits are several times that.'

'Oh, we know,' said Stahl, fixing Kerton with his brown eyes. 'The thing is, we know you got a problem down there with your emerging-market guys. But we don't know whether you know how big a problem it is.'

This had caught Kerton's attention. 'You're referring, I take it, to the deal we launched last month for Mexico?'

'That, and some other things.'

'Well, the deal wasn't a success. It suffered from unfortunate timing. But when you dominate a market like we do, you have to take the rough with the smooth.

I can assure you we can handle it. Look, if you want to talk emerging markets, perhaps I ought to get hold of Ricardo Ross.' He reached towards a telephone.

'No, don't do that, Andy,' Stahl said. 'There's more. Nick?'

'Well, sir, I understand that Ricardo has bought four billion dollars of Mexican bonds, and two billion of debt from other Latin American borrowers. As you know, the market has fallen sharply in the last two weeks. My understanding is that Dekker's losses are more than one and a half billion dollars.'

Kerton didn't respond at first. His expression switched from polite attention to hostility. Of course he didn't know this. And he felt a fool for not knowing. He was cornered. He lashed out. 'Who the hell are you, anyway?' he said to me. 'Did we fire you or something?'

'I resigned before you had the chance, sir.'

He turned back to Stahl. 'I can't see how you can possibly listen to this man. He obviously bears a grudge. He's making it up.'

'It kind of fits with what we've seen in the market, Andy,' said Stahl. 'I believe him.'

'Well, I don't. And I think you should leave. There is no need for me to respond to such allegations.'

Stahl stood up. 'OK, Andy. We're going. But check out what Nick here is saying. And we'll be in touch to see if you change your mind. But do yourself a favour, OK? Don't tell Ross about our little talk. At least, not till you know he isn't hiding anything from you.'

Kerton showed us out of the building in icy silence.

Stahl called at lunch-time the next day. 'Kerton wants to talk. He wants to come to our offices. Can you meet us at three?'

'I'll be there.'

It was tight, but I changed into a suit, bicycled to the station, got the train to London and the tube to Liverpool Street, and arrived at Bloomfield Weiss at two minutes to three. We met in a conference room: Kerton, Stahl, the two corporate financiers, and me. It was a much blander room than the one we had occupied at Dekker Ward, but there was a nice view of a giant iron phallus that looked as though it had been blown down in the wind. Kerton was there with someone he introduced as Giles Tilfourd from Tilfourd and Co., a corporate-finance boutique. It was promising that he had his own independent adviser. It suggested he expected discussions to lead somewhere.

'OK, Andy,' said Stahl. 'Shoot.'

Kerton did well. He kept his cool. Although he seemed thoughtful, he didn't look like a man who had just discovered that his shareholding, which he thought was worth several hundred million pounds, was now worth just five.

But it was.

'Perhaps you could go through the details of your offer again . . .'

Negotiations proceeded quickly. They have to, in these situations. Any further deterioration in the market would make Dekker Ward worthless, worse than worthless. It would become a liability that even Bloomfield Weiss wouldn't be able to handle. Stahl left London, but Godfrey and Schwartz stayed, and kept me informed. Kerton was careful to keep Ricardo out of it. He sent a trio of his own people down to Canary Wharf under the guise of an internal audit. This apparently aroused some disquiet in Ricardo, but no suspicions. He was confident he could run rings round any internal auditors.

I bought the *Wall Street Journal* every day. Things seemed neither better nor worse in Mexico. It was unclear what would happen to the Pinnock Bill in Congress. It seemed to have become sidetracked somehow in a negotiation over which military bases would be shut down in the continental United States.

It was difficult to focus on my thesis, but I did my best. Sitting in my room at the top of Kate and Jamie's house, my mind kept drifting back to the deal. It was exhilarating. I spent many hours imagining the look on Ricardo's face when he heard that Dekker had been sold from underneath him. To Bloomfield Weiss, of all people! Surely even he wouldn't be able to keep his cool. He and Eduardo probably had plenty of cash stashed away for a rainy day, but this would hurt Ricardo much more than merely losing money. This would be a very public humiliation. A statement that the powerful Dekker machine that was so feared by the market was, in reality, nothing but a pile of worthless paper.

I thought of Isabel, and smiled wryly. I was sure she would appreciate it. If she was still alive. The familiar, chronic anxiety returned. I thought of calling Luís again to see if he had any news, but there was no point. I knew he would contact me as soon as he heard anything, if he ever heard anything.

I felt twinges of concern for the other people that worked at Dekker: Charlotte Baxter, Miguel, Pedro and, of course, Jamie. But Bloomfield Weiss intended to keep most of them, in fact it was the people they were really buying. They were good; even without Ricardo, they were the best in the market.

My musings were interrupted by a knock at the door.
'Come in!'

It was Kate. Her face was serious. She carried a brown envelope in her right hand. I recognized it immediately.

Shit! It was an internal report prepared by analysts at Bloomfield Weiss on Dekker.

'Where did you find that?' I asked.

'By the phone downstairs.'

Damn! I had rung Dwight Godfrey the day before, when Kate was picking up Oliver from his nursery school. He had wanted to know whether the Bloomfield Weiss report gelled with what I had seen at Dekker. It had, more or less.

'Have you read it?'

'Yes.'

Kate stood in the middle of the room. She had been a promising City lawyer. If she'd read it, she'd understood it. She was clearly rattled. I felt my cheeks redden; I had been caught.

'Why have you got this report, Nick?'

I took a deep breath. Nothing but the truth would do now. 'Because it was my idea.'

'Your idea?'

'Yes. I suggested to Bloomfield Weiss that they should buy Dekker.'

Kate sat on the bed, still clutching the envelope.

'Why?'

I swallowed. 'Ricardo deserves it,' I said, slowly and deliberately. 'And so does Eduardo. They've tried to ruin my career. They wrecked my flat, and destroyed my thesis. And it's not just me they've trampled on. They've done the same thing to Dave. And to the poor bastards who live in the *favelas*. And who knows why Martin Beldecos was murdered?'

I was getting quite heated now. 'Ricardo thinks that the rules of us lesser mortals don't apply to him. Well, I'm going to show him he's wrong. Let him feel what it's like to have his life's work taken away from him.'

Kate was looking at me hard.

'But what about Jamie? This will put him in an impossible situation.'

I sighed. 'I know. But Dekker's sinking. If Bloomfield Weiss do take them over, Jamie should still have a job.' I met her eyes. 'Are you going to tell him?'

'I don't know,' said Kate, and she stood up from the bed and left the room.

25

I spent the barest possible time with Kate and Jamie that evening at supper, before making an excuse about working on my thesis and escaping upstairs to my room. I sat at my desk, my notes in front of me, my mind elsewhere. Would she tell him? What would his reaction be?

Sure, I had my justification ready, the one I had given Kate. But Jamie wouldn't see it that way. I knew that Dekker was important to him. I was staying in his house, and I had betrayed him. And I did not want to betray Jamie.

I began to wish I had just left Dekker alone. Forgotten about it, as Dave had told me to. Let Ricardo get away with it, in the same way everyone else did. But I hadn't. And it was too late to go back now.

I missed Jamie the next morning. He left before the rest of the house was up, as usual. But I had breakfast with Kate and Oliver.

'Did you talk to him?' I asked her.

Kate turned to Oliver, who was still in his pyjamas chasing the last few Coco-Pops round his bowl with a spoon. 'You can get down and play if you want, Ollie.'

He was off like a shot. He hated getting dressed in

the morning, and this seemed like a possible reprieve.

'No,' she said, when he was gone.

I smiled with relief.

'But you could have told me what you were doing!' she protested.

'I couldn't,' I said. 'It would have put you in an impossible position.'

'Well, what kind of position do you think I'm in now?'

I winced. Fair point. 'Are you going to tell him?'

Kate shook her head. 'No. I thought about it a lot last night. He's better off not knowing. Then, whether Dekker survives as an independent firm or Bloomfield Weiss take it over, he should be all right.'

'I'm sorry, Kate. But I'm doing the right thing.'

She nodded. 'I know you are. And I hope you get the bastards!'

I called Stahl in New York that afternoon. Despite his elevated status, he seemed to like to talk to me directly. It angered his sidekicks, who resented the access I had to him.

'How are we doing?' I asked.

'Great, Nick, great. I just got back from Geneva yesterday. I met with the directors of Chalmet. Boy, I put a rocket up their asses! They have no idea what's going on at Dekker. In fact, I don't think they know what their own emerging-markets guys are up to. But they're scared. It's beginning to dawn on them that all this great new Latino business isn't as kosher as it might be. They didn't even know that Chalmet were using hundreds of millions of their clients' dough to fund Dekker!' Stahl chuckled. 'You should of seen their faces. It was like I'd dropped a whole cartload of shit right there on their pretty polished desks. Which I guess in a way you could say I had.'

'So what are they going to do?' I asked.

'They want outa there, fast. They'll sell.'

'Excellent. Does that mean we're there?'

'Just about. We're working to a deadline of June fourteen. There are still some numbers to be run, and Kerton's got to get the SFA and the Stock Exchange to approve the transaction, but that shouldn't be a problem. And then we have a done deal.'

The fourteenth of June. That was next Friday.

'Great!'

'Yeah. Nice deal, Nick.'

'Does Ricardo know about it?'

'Nope. He has no idea.' Another laugh like a rasping saw. 'I gotta go, Nick.' The phone went dead.

I stared at the receiver in triumph. Yes!

I really was working when Kate knocked on my door.

'Nick, phone. I think it's Isabel's father.'

I bounded down the stairs to the sitting room. Kate discreetly left me alone.

'Luís! How are you?'

'I don't know, Nick. I have news.'

'What is it?'

'Isabel is still alive.'

My heart leaped. I felt a rush of elation, that was tempered immediately by fear. This was too good to be true.

'Where is she? With you?'

'No, Nick,' said Luís. I knew from his tone what was coming next. 'I heard from Zico. He says they still have her.'

Disappointment. And then fear again. 'Have you proof of life?'

'Yes, I have. After our previous experience, I didn't want to contact you until I was sure she was really alive.'

'What happened? Why didn't they come back with proof of life before?'

'I don't know. Zico said that they gave up negotiations earlier because of the police raid. But it doesn't quite make sense to me.'

It didn't to me either. But Isabel was alive! 'So, how much do they want this time?'

'That's the interesting thing, Nick. They don't want money.'

'Then what do they want?'

'Zico said he wants you to call off the takeover of Dekker.'

I was stunned. How the hell did Zico know about the Dekker takeover? And what did he care?

'Nick? Are you there?'

'Yes, I am,' I said. 'It's just quite a lot to take in at once. But it's so good to know Isabel's alive. Now we just have to work out how to get her home.'

'What's this Dekker takeover?' Luís asked.

I took a deep breath and explained. Isabel's safety was far more important than any duty of confidence I owed to Bloomfield Weiss.

Luís, of course, followed everything. 'But why do the kidnappers care about Dekker?'

I thought aloud. 'I don't know. The one person I know who would be most concerned about Dekker being taken over is Ricardo.'

'So does that mean he's behind Isabel's kidnap?'

'I suppose so. Either him, or his brother Eduardo. It sounds more like something Eduardo would do.'

'*Filho da puta*!'

'But I didn't think Ricardo knew about the takeover.'

'Well, if Zico knows someone must have told him,' muttered Luís. 'And, by the way, he said something else.' Luís's voice was strained.

'Yes?'

'If we talk to the police, he will send us Isabel's head.'

'You mean . . .' My stomach turned. 'Oh, God.'

'I spoke to Nelson. In fact, he's here now.'

'Good.' I was glad that Nelson's calming presence was close at hand. 'What does he say?'

'He doesn't think we should tell the Rio police after what happened last time. He thinks there's a chance the kidnappers were tipped off by one of them.'

'That makes sense to me. What about going to the police in Britain? Ask him about that.'

I held for a time while Luís discussed with Nelson Ricardo and Eduardo's likely involvement with the kidnappers.

'Nelson thinks it's risky. He says this threat is different from the usual bluster in kidnappings. Especially if they know we can link the kidnapping to an individual. If Ricardo or Eduardo or whoever it is gets a hint of police involvement, then the kidnappers will carry out their threat. But maybe you can trust the British police not to intervene.'

I didn't have any idea what the British police would do. 'Let's leave them out of it, then,' I said.

'Good.' There was relief in Luís's voice.

'So Zico wants me to call off Bloomfield Weiss?'

'Can you?' Luís's voice was tentative, full of fear and hope.

'I don't know. How long have I got?'

'A day and a half. Thursday at midnight, Brazilian time.'

That was interesting. Bloomfield Weiss were due to put in their offer on Friday.

'And if I don't?'

Luís whispered, 'They kill her.'

'And if I do, do they let her go?'

'They say they will. But Nelson thinks they might hold out for a cash ransom as well. If they do, I'm happy to pay it.'

I thought it over. 'I suppose if Eduardo is behind it, he won't need the money. But he might want to keep her to stop us going to the police after she's released.'

'Maybe you're right. But unless you call Bloomfield Weiss off, I think they will carry out their threat.'

That, at any rate, was clear.

'OK, Luís. I'll do what I can.'

I put the phone down, and thought over what Luís had said. Could Ricardo or Eduardo be behind Isabel's kidnapping? Ricardo would go to almost any lengths to save Dekker. But would he go as far as kidnapping Isabel, his former lover? That I wasn't sure of. But I remembered Eduardo's threats to me and shivered. It would be no problem for him.

All that made sense now. But why had they seized Isabel in the first place? There didn't seem an obvious answer to that one.

I had no time to think about that now. I'd have to call Stahl back. What the hell would I say to him?

I looked out of the window for inspiration. A girl on a palomino pony was trotting along a bridle-path up the hill. It seemed absurd that I should be juggling negotiations over someone's life and a company's survival between three continents from this quiet spot in the heart of the English countryside. Except I wasn't juggling. The balls were up there in mid-air, and there was no way I could catch them all before they came crashing down round my head.

I couldn't order Stahl to call the deal off. I racked my brains trying to think of a financial excuse. There wasn't one. I would have to tell him the truth, and trust to his humanity.

Bloomfield Weiss was renowned as one of the most inhumane investment banks on Wall Street.

I called him. Got past his secretary, told Preston Morris this was urgent information on the Dekker deal, and within two minutes was talking to Sidney Stahl himself.

'Whaddya got, Nick? I'm in a meeting.'

I took a deep breath. 'I'd like you to call off the deal.'

'Why?' The response was immediate, sharp.

'One of Dekker Ward's employees was kidnapped in Brazil last month. The kidnappers have said that they will kill her unless we call off the takeover of Dekker Ward.'

'What is this shit? Is this for real?'

'Yes, it is.'

'I can't call off the deal now. Anyway, why should I? Dekker Ward's employees aren't my responsibility. If they want to kill their own people, I can't stop them. This makes no sense.'

'This woman means a lot to me, Sidney.'

There was silence at the other end of the phone. For a moment, my hopes rose. Maybe he was considering going along with my request.

But he wasn't. 'I'm sorry, Nick. You're an emotional guy and you've gotten yourself emotionally involved in this one. Look, I'm grateful you brought me the transaction, and it's a great deal. But this is business. This could be the most important deal in Bloomfield Weiss's history. I can't stop it now. It's time for you to step back, Nick. Tell 'em you've spoken to me and there's nothing I can do.'

'But she'll die!'

'This thing's too big to stop now. I'm sorry. 'Bye Nick.'

The phone went dead.

Jesus! I couldn't believe it. In the last few hours, I had discovered that Isabel was alive, only to realize that there was nothing I could do to keep her that way. I imagined her shut away in a room somewhere in Rio. God knows what she looked like now after a month in captivity. What was she thinking? Did she know about the threat? Did she know she would die unless I did something to save her? And did she realize that in fact there was nothing I could do?

I sat there, my head in my hands, feeling useless, worthless.

I thought about going to the police. They might arrest Eduardo, and the more I thought about it the more I was sure it was Eduardo, not Ricardo, who had ordered the kidnapping. But although it was clear to me that he was involved, there was no proof whatsoever. Even if the police arrested him, he would no doubt hire a top-class lawyer who would point out the lack of evidence. The British police would have to work with their opposite numbers in Brazil. In fact, as I thought about it, the crime had been committed there against a Brazilian citizen. There would be all kinds of legal limitations to what the British police could do.

I cursed myself. Getting Bloomfield Weiss to take

over Dekker had seemed like a just piece of revenge for all that Ricardo and Eduardo had done to me and others. It had been sweet at first, but now that it could lead to Isabel's death, it tasted rotten.

I didn't really blame Stahl. He had behaved just as I would have expected him to. There was no reason for me to believe that Bloomfield Weiss would be any more human than Dekker.

I dialled Luís. It took several attempts to get through Rio's overloaded exchange, but finally I heard the ringing tone. Luís picked up the phone immediately.

'Nick?' His voice was breathless, full of hope.

I shattered it. 'Stahl won't change his mind. Bloomfield Weiss are going ahead with the deal.'

Luís snapped. 'No!' His voice cracked. There was silence as he pulled himself together. 'Couldn't you persuade him? Does the man have no feelings? Perhaps I should talk to him.'

'There's no point, Luís. He's not going to change his mind.'

'I'll call him,' said Luís. 'I'll tell him.'

So I let him go and try his luck with Stahl, knowing there was no chance it would work.

I slept little that night. I got up at about two and called Luís. I wasn't surprised to hear that he had had no luck with Stahl. Our last hope would be if he could persuade the kidnappers that there was no point in killing Isabel; that they should accept money instead. Luís was optimistic, I wasn't. Eduardo didn't need money. Eduardo hated me. He probably hated Isabel too.

The next day, Thursday, was a long one. My room felt like a cell. I couldn't leave it, except to wash and eat as quickly as possible. I avoided Jamie and Kate as much as I could, gulping down my meals and disappearing back up there.

But at least now I knew Isabel was still alive, and while she was alive there was still hope. There was a chance the kidnappers would spare her. Maybe they would switch back to the ransom demand as Nelson had suggested.

I couldn't just stew in my room doing nothing, letting the minutes tick away, waiting for Luís to try to persuade Zico to let Isabel live. Anyway, it wasn't Zico who needed persuading, it was Eduardo.

That was it! I couldn't talk to Eduardo, but I might just get somewhere with Ricardo.

I rushed downstairs, picked up the phone and dialled his number.

'Dekker.'

It was strange to hear that voice again. Crisp and in control.

'It's Nick Elliot.'

Silence for a moment. Then, 'Yes, Nick, what can I do for you?' The voice was cold but polite.

'I want to talk to you.'

'I'm listening.'

'No, not on the phone. In person. I'll meet you on one of the benches outside Corney and Barrow.' I looked at my watch. It was a quarter to two. 'At three o'clock.'

A pause. 'OK,' said Ricardo, and the phone clicked.

I asked Kate to drive me to the station. We passed the brief journey in silence. Kate didn't ask what was on my mind, and I didn't tell her. A train journey and a taxi-ride later, and I was at Canary Wharf. It was ten past three when I reached the benches outside Corney and Barrow. Ricardo was there, waiting.

I sat next to him. It was a warm day. He was jacketless,

with his shirt cuffs rolled up. He was staring at the rusty old boat that was permanently moored in the dock. The odd burst of laughter came from the open doors of Corney and Barrow, where determined lunch-time drinkers lingered on into the afternoon. Above and behind us rose the Canary Wharf tower itself, proud and white in the afternoon sunlight.

'What do you want? I'm busy,' Ricardo said, without looking at me.

'Isabel's still alive.' I watched him closely as I said this. I thought I saw something flicker in him, a slight widening of his eyes, a stiffening of his posture, but then it was gone. He sat there impassively, staring ahead. 'But, then, you know that, don't you?'

'I didn't know that,' he answered. 'I'm glad to hear it.'

'And you also know that Bloomfield Weiss is in discussions with Lord Kerton about taking over Dekker Ward.'

This time Ricardo said nothing.

I continued, 'Isabel's father has received a message from the kidnappers that unless Bloomfield Weiss call off their bid by Friday, she will die.'

Still no response. I pressed on regardless.

'I want you, and Eduardo, to know that I've spoken to Sidney Stahl, to ask him to stop the takeover. He didn't listen to me.' I could feel the desperation welling up inside me. 'Ricardo, I can't stop this takeover! You have to believe me!'

He turned to face me. The cool blue eyes looked me up and down, judging me.

At last he spoke. 'Why are you telling me this?'

'Because you organized the kidnapping!' I said. 'Or if you didn't, Eduardo did, which amounts to the same

324

thing. And I don't want you to kill her.' I was pleading now, begging. But I didn't know what else to do.

Ricardo looked right through me, his face stone cold. 'You have betrayed me. You are trying to sell my company to my biggest rival. And now you come up with some cock-and-bull story about how I arranged the kidnap of one of my own people. I want Isabel to live as much as you do. More, probably. I know nothing about the kidnap, Nick. So I can't help you. Now, I must get back to work.'

He stood up and walked quickly back across the square towards the Tower.

'Well, at least talk to Eduardo about it,' I said, walking beside him. He ignored me. 'Eduardo's got to know what's going on. Talk to him!'

'Leave me alone, Nick,' Ricardo said, glancing at me coldly.

I stopped and watched him as he reached the varnished entrance to the tower complex.

'Ricardo!' I shouted. 'You can't let her die! You can't!'

My voice echoed off the squat blocks of offices around me, bouncing off Ricardo's back as he disappeared inside the huge building.

I made my slow way back to Dockenbush Farm. Tube, train, and then a walk from the station. It was six o'clock by the time I arrived back there.

All the way my mind wrestled with my meeting with Ricardo. He had been convincing about his ignorance of Isabel's kidnap. But then Ricardo was convincing. Always. There was a chance that Eduardo had arranged the kidnap without Ricardo's knowledge. Perhaps Ricardo would talk to him now. Persuade him not to have Isabel killed. Perhaps tell him to release her.

I was clutching at straws.

That evening, I spent ten minutes wolfing down my supper, and mumbled something about more problems with my thesis to Jamie. Then I went back upstairs to stare into space.

Both Luís and I were confident that Zico would call him at midnight Brazil time, which was four a.m. in England. There was no chance of sleep before then.

At about eleven, Kate knocked on my door. 'I just came to say goodnight. I'm off to bed now.'

'Goodnight.'

She sat on the bed. 'What is it, Nick? What's up?'

'Nothing.'

'Of course there is. It's not just about the takeover, is it? It's more than that.'

I blurted it out. 'Unless I can work out some way of stopping Bloomfield Weiss from taking over Dekker in the next five hours, Isabel will die.'

'But I thought – '

'That she was dead? Well, the good news is that she isn't. The bad news is that she soon will be,' I muttered bitterly.

'But why would the kidnappers care about whether Dekker gets taken over?'

I told her my theories about Ricardo and Eduardo.

She listened in shock. 'I can't believe it!'

'Can you think of any other explanation?'

Kate frowned, and shook her head. 'So what are you going to do?'

'Wait for the deadline.'

'Oh, God. I suppose you've spoken to Bloomfield Weiss?'

I nodded.

'And they took no notice?'

I sighed and nodded again.

'What about Ricardo?'

'That was where I went this afternoon. He was very tight-lipped. He denied any knowledge of the kidnap and walked off.'

'Do you believe him?'

I shook my head. 'You know how plausible Ricardo can be.'

'Oh.' She thought for a moment. 'What about Andrew Kerton?'

I stared at her.

'Well, presumably he has to agree to a sale?' she said. 'Have you spoken to him?'

'Christ! No, I hadn't thought of that.' Then I frowned. 'He'd be hardly likely to call off the deal for me, would he? I mean, this is his only chance to sell.'

'You won't know until you try.'

I looked at my watch. A quarter past eleven. Just under five hours to go till Zico's deadline.

'Do you know where he lives?' I asked Kate.

'No idea. But you can try Directory Enquiries.'

'I bet he's ex-directory.' I tried. He was.

'Jamie might know,' said Kate. 'I think he's been to his house before.'

'I want to keep Jamie out of this,' I said.

'I don't think you have a choice.'

Jamie was drying up dishes in the kitchen. 'Jamie, do you know where Lord Kerton lives?' I asked breathlessly.

He turned and frowned. 'Why do you want to know?'

'Oh, come on Jamie, just tell us,' Kate implored.

'Somewhere in Kensington Square, I think. I forget the number.'

'Come on, Nick. I'll drive you,' said Kate.

Jamie put down the glass he was wiping. 'What's going on?' he asked.

'Tell you later,' said Kate, and I followed her out of the front door.

26

It took us three-quarters of an hour. Kate drove fast and there wasn't much traffic. Kensington Square is a quiet gathering of large houses just to the south of Kensington High Street. We had no idea which one was Lord Kerton's.

An old envelope was lying in the back of Kate's car. I took it, stuffed the car manual into it, and picked a house at random. I rang the bell. After a couple of minutes, a grey-haired man in an old dressing gown answered. He didn't seem at all bothered about being disturbed at midnight.

'Can I speak to Lord Kerton?' I asked.

'I'm afraid you've got the wrong house. He doesn't live here.'

'Oh. I'm sorry, sir. I have an urgent message for him,' I said, brandishing the unopened end of the envelope. 'Can you tell me which is his house?'

'Four doors down,' said the man helpfully, pointing.

I thanked him, and headed for Kerton's house. Kate saw me and climbed out of the car.

'It's OK. I can do this myself,' I said.

'He'll be more likely to listen to the two of us.'

She was right.

I rang the doorbell. It was answered quickly. Kerton

was wearing old green trousers and a striped cotton shirt. No shoes, just socks.

He frowned as he saw me, his expression one of deep distaste. 'What the hell do you want?'

'Can we come in, sir?' I asked.

'No. Bugger off.'

He tried to shut the door. I leaned into it. 'Please. Just five minutes.'

'I said bugger off. Or I'll call the police.'

Kate squeezed between us. She was a lot shorter than both of us, but she looked determinedly up to Kerton's chin. 'If you throw us out, Isabel Pereira will die.'

This made him pause for a moment. 'So she's still alive?'

'Yes. For the time being.' said Kate.

He thought for a moment. He obviously looked on Kate more kindly than me. 'Well, I don't know what the hell you're talking about, but you'd better come in.'

He led us up some stairs to a large, comfortably furnished sitting room on the first floor.

'Sit down,' he said, gesturing to the sofa.

He swiftly picked an open novel off an armchair and placed it face down on a small table. I just caught a glimpse of the cover: it was one of Terry Pratchett's *Discworld* books. He saw I saw and reddened slightly.

'Now, explain what you want, and go.'

He looked tired. It wasn't just the hour: he looked worn down. Seeing his company fall apart around him must have taken its toll.

'Do you know Isabel?' I asked.

Kerton nodded. 'Yes, vaguely. She's quite, ah, noticeable.'

I wasn't surprised that Kerton appreciated Isabel's charms, most men would, but it was a good sign.

'Well, as you know, she was kidnapped last month. It looked like she'd been killed, but it turns out that her kidnappers were just hiding her. Yesterday her father received a threat that unless the Bloomfield Weiss take-over of Dekker Ward was called off, she would die. Luís Pereira and the kidnap specialist who advises him take this threat very seriously. So do I.'

Kerton was listening. 'What do these kidnappers care about the takeover?'

'I think it highly likely that Eduardo Ross was behind Isabel's kidnapping.'

'No! Do you have proof?'

'No firm evidence, no. But, as you say, why the interest in Dekker's future?'

'I don't believe Eduardo Ross would do something like that,' Kerton said, with a primness that sounded ridiculous.

Kerton knew Eduardo. Anyone who knew Eduardo knew he just might be capable of kidnapping.

I raised my eyebrows.

'OK,' said Kerton. 'But how did Eduardo find out about the takeover? I thought we'd kept Ricardo out of it.'

I shrugged. 'Leaks.'

'Hum. What do you expect me to do?'

'Call the deal off.'

Kerton frowned. 'I can't. You know that. Dekker Ward is insolvent. If I sell to Bloomfield Weiss, the firm might survive in some form, and I just might get some value out of it. If that deal goes away, I'll have to call in the receiver.'

'Well, can't you delay it? Manufacture some problem. Something to give us more time.'

'I don't have much time. If the market moves down

any further the deal will fall through. I can't afford to wait and risk that happening. Anyway, what would you do with a few more days?'

I had been thinking this through in the car on the way to Kerton's house.

'Find out who kidnapped Isabel, and get her released.'

'But if the Brazilian police haven't been able to find her kidnappers over the last couple of months, why should you be able to find her now?'

'Because now we know her kidnapping is linked to Dekker Ward. It's likely that Ricardo or Eduardo Ross is involved. It will make it easier to track her down.'

Kerton sighed. 'Look, I'm sorry about Isabel, but there's really nothing I can do. I have no choice.'

'Yes, you do!' said Kate. The forcefulness of her tone grabbed Kerton's attention. 'If you don't call the deal off and Isabel is murdered, you'll have her death on your conscience for the rest of your life. You'll never be able to forget it. Sure, when you look at your bank statement and see a few million more on it, you'll remember why you let her die. But that won't give you satisfaction. You'll feel as guilty as hell.'

That rattled him. 'Look. I'm not the one who's killing her,' he protested. 'It has nothing to do with me.'

Kate shook her head. 'It has everything to do with you.'

Kerton glared at me. 'Why should I do this for you? You were the one who got Bloomfield Weiss involved in the first place.'

'It isn't for him, it's for Isabel,' Kate said. 'Look, I know you don't know anything about all of this, but you *are* chairman of Dekker Ward. This *is* your responsibility.'

Kerton stood up. He strode across to the large

window overlooking the garden in the middle of the square. Kate and I watched him. We could see the tension in his back and shoulders.

He turned round, and ran his hands through his hair. 'I can't call the whole deal off. Bloomfield Weiss are giving me their offer tomorrow. But, if you like, I'll put off responding until Monday.'

'Wednesday.'

Kerton glanced at me in irritation. 'All right, Wednesday. But next Wednesday morning I will accept Bloomfield Weiss's offer, provided it's a reasonable one. And I hope you will have found Isabel by then.'

'Thank you,' I said. Kate smiled at him. She was right, he wasn't all bad. 'Can you give us your number here? In case we need to contact you.'

Kerton went over to the table by the phone, scribbled a number on a piece of paper and gave it to me.

'Oh, one other thing,' I said. Kerton frowned. It was clear he wanted to get rid of me. 'Can I use your phone?'

The frown deepened.

I checked my watch. One o'clock, or nine o'clock in the evening in Brazil. 'I need to let Isabel's father know so that he can tell the kidnappers there's been a delay.'

Kerton shrugged and nodded.

I moved over to the phone, and dialled Luís's number. I got through first time, and Luís picked up the phone straight away.

'Alô.'

'Luís, it's Nick. I've spoken to Lord Kerton, chairman of Dekker Ward. He says he will delay accepting Bloomfield Weiss's offer until next Wednesday.'

'Thank God,' he said, with relief. And then the worry returned. 'What do we do then?'

'I said we'd find Isabel.'

'And how do we do that, Nick?'

Kerton was watching me. 'Let's think about that tomorrow, shall we? But call me after the kidnappers have been in contact.'

'I will.'

I put the phone down.

'You don't have a clue where she is, do you?' said Kerton.

I smiled and shrugged.

For the first time, he smiled back. 'Well, good luck.'

Kate drove us straight back to Bodenham. 'Thank you,' I said. 'If it hadn't been for you, I don't think he would have gone along with it.'

'But he did.'

'Right.'

'So what are you going to do now?'

'Wait for Luís to call back. Go to bed. Sleep. Then think.'

It was after two by the time we arrived home. Jamie was still up waiting for us. The television was on, and a whisky glass and tumbler were by his chair.

He stood up, agitated. 'What's going on?'

'We needed to see Lord Kerton about something.'

'What? See him about what?'

I shrugged.

'Look, he's the chairman of my employer. You can't just go and "see him about something" without telling me what it is, Kate!'

Kate stood in anguish in the middle of the sitting-room floor. She glanced at me. I nodded. I couldn't expect her to hide it from Jamie any more.

She walked over to the sofa, and flopped into it. Jamie

sat down again next to his whisky glass. I remained standing.

'We were asking Andrew Kerton to delay selling Dekker Ward to Bloomfield Weiss until next Wednesday,' she said, in a quiet voice.

'Sell to Bloomfield Weiss! What are you on about? Bloomfield Weiss aren't about to buy Dekker.'

Kate nodded. 'Yes, they are. They've been in secret negotiations with Andrew for the last couple of weeks.'

'God.' Jamie slumped back into his chair. 'And what have you two got to do with it?'

I swallowed. 'It was my idea,' I said.

'Your idea?'

'Yes.'

'Why?'

'Ricardo deserved it.'

Jamie still looked shocked. 'I can't believe you did this!' He looked at Kate. 'And you knew all about it?'

'I only found out a couple of days ago.'

'And you didn't tell me?'

Kate avoided Jamie's eyes.

'This is incredible! How can you do this to me, both of you?' As the shock wore off, the anger grew.

'Look, Jamie,' I said, in as reasonable a tone of voice as I could muster, 'Dekker are in big trouble. They might well go bust. If Bloomfield Weiss take them over, you'll keep your job.'

'That's not the point!' Jamie stood up and began pacing up and down the room. 'We're a team! And, like it or not, Nick, we're Ricardo's team. You would be breaking us up.'

Now I got angry. 'You're sounding just like Ricardo! He's not some victim of the financial establishment, and neither are you. He's a very wealthy man, who's made

335

money from screwing all those around him. Including me!'

Jamie glared at me. I glared back. I tried to control myself. 'Isabel has been kidnapped by someone who wants Dekker to remain independent. That someone has threatened that if Dekker is taken over, she will die. Now don't tell me Ricardo isn't behind that somehow or other!'

Jamie was silent, thinking through what I had just said. In the end, he spoke. 'Nick. I know we've been friends, but I can't have you in my house while you're plotting with Bloomfield Weiss against Ricardo.'

'Jamie!' Kate protested.

'I'm sorry, Kate, but you shouldn't have helped him.'

'I was only trying to stop that poor girl from being killed!'

Jamie ignored Kate, and turned to me. 'I want you to leave,' he said.

'He can't. He hasn't got anywhere to go!' Kate cried.

'Well, I want you out next week, and the less I see of you in the meantime the better.' With that he left the room, and I could hear his heavy step clumping up the stairs.

Kate looked at me wide-eyed. She bit her lip. 'Nick, I'm sorry.'

'No, I'm sorry,' I said. 'Go up to him. It's important you go with him.'

She nodded and followed him up the stairs.

I sat alone in the dimly lit room. I fetched another glass, and poured myself some of Jamie's whisky.

I should have anticipated Jamie's reaction. He was a loyal Dekker man. I had always put this loyalty down to greed, or at least ambition – the ambition to make a fortune, which was almost the same thing. But it was more than that. Jamie was one of Ricardo's people. He was what I would have become if I had stayed there. Ricardo looked after his people well, and expected total loyalty. In Jamie's case he'd got it.

Jamie had always liked to follow the doctrine of whatever institution he was in. At seventeen, he had become the embodiment of the public-school virtues, and was rewarded by becoming head-boy. At Oxford, he had led a successful university career in social and sporting terms, if not quite academically. At Gurney Kroheim, he had been able to don the mantle of the stuffy merchant banker whenever it was required by his colleagues or his customers. And now at Dekker he was keen to follow Ricardo's rules and do well by them. So far he seemed to be succeeding.

But Jamie was my friend, dammit! How could Ricardo take away my friend from me? Surely our loyalty to each other stretched back further, ran deeper?

In which case, why had I gone behind Jamie's back to sell Dekker to Bloomfield Weiss? I was beginning to regret that. Now it looked as if that decision was going to lose me my best friend. And, barring a miracle, it might lose Isabel her life too.

But I had genuinely believed that Jamie would be just as well off if Bloomfield Weiss did take over Dekker.

And what about Kate? I shouldn't have dragged her into this. She and I were good friends, and I could feel her losing her respect for Jamie. The last thing I wanted to do was pull her away from him. But, unless I was careful, that's what would happen.

Of course, I still had the hardest problem of all waiting for me. How to find and release Isabel.

I sighed, drank down my whisky, and looked at my

watch. Three o'clock. The kidnappers' deadline was four, British time. One hour to go.

I nodded off in my chair, and was woken by the phone ringing. It was ten past four, and I could hear the scattered chirping of the first blackbirds outside the window.

'Nick? It's Luís.'

'What did Zico say?' I asked him.

'They'll keep her alive. I told him that the deal wasn't called off, but merely delayed. He said that as soon as they hear that the deal is closed, they'll kill her.'

'So we have until next Wednesday to find her.'

'Yes. But at least she's still alive.'

'At least she's still alive,' I repeated.

With the hope that Isabel would live glimmering like the dawn light seeping through the curtains, I dragged myself upstairs to bed.

I woke at nine. Five hours' sleep was enough for me to feel refreshed. Kate was taking Oliver to his nursery school, and Jamie had left hours before. I made myself a cup of coffee and some toast, and went back upstairs to think.

I put all thoughts of Jamie, Kate, where I was going to find a job and where I was going to live out of my mind. I had to work out how to find Isabel by next Wednesday. I pulled out some fresh clean white sheets of paper, and stared at their emptiness.

Whoever had organized Isabel's kidnap wanted Dekker to remain independent. Ricardo and Eduardo were the two people most likely to want Dekker to remain independent. Yet Ricardo refused to admit any knowledge of the kidnapping, and it would be impossible to tie them into it from here.

But what about the other end? What about Brazil? What about Rio? Now we were getting somewhere. I began to jot down some thoughts.

The kidnappers were a Rio gang. I had been attacked by a gang in Rio, even if it was only a gang of kids. Dave had guessed that this was linked to Martin Beldecos's death in Caracas, and money-laundering at Dekker. Money-laundering that was organized by Francisco Aragão, Ricardo's brother-in-law.

But why would Francisco Aragão want to kidnap Isabel?

I looked over my jottings. It was clear that if I was to work out who was holding Isabel, I would have to go to Brazil. But, in the meantime, there was one lead in England I should follow up.

I pulled out my list of Dekker home numbers and dialled one.

'*Aló*.'

'Can I speak to Luciana Ross?'

'Speaking.'

'Oh, hallo. This is Nick Elliot. We met at your party in April, I don't know if you remember?'

'Ah, Nick, of course I remember!' Her voice was husky, warm and friendly. 'How are you doing?'

'Um, not too bad. You talked about some of the Latin American designs you do, and since I'm planning to redecorate my flat, I wondered if I could come and see some?'

'Of course. Any time you like.'

'Today?'

'Sure. Come round here for some lunch.'

'OK.' I checked my watch, and thought about train times. 'I'll be there at about one.'

'See you then.'

*

The Rosses' apartment was in one of the grand squares of Belgravia. I chained my bike out of the way down some steps, and rang the bell. I was wearing the smartest casual clothes I could muster, but I knew I would look more in place in the School of Russian Studies common room than here.

A disembodied voice crackled through the entry-phone. 'Nick?'

'Yes.'

'Second floor. Take the lift.'

There was only one door on the second floor, and I rang the brass bell beside it. In a moment, it was opened, and Luciana appeared. She was wearing a simple white top, and jeans that clung to her hips and legs. Her full black hair shone round her shoulders. She gave me a broad smile, as though she had known me for years. 'Nick, come in!'

She proffered her cheek, and I kissed it, smelling a hint of expensive perfume. Then I followed her into the sitting room.

It assaulted my eyes. Dark polished wood, lush carpets, gold trim, and large, heavily patterned drapes clamoured for attention. But I was drawn to the walls, where three long paintings swirled in greens, blues and reds.

Luciana followed my gaze. 'These are by an up-and-coming artist from Bahia. Do you like them?'

'They remind me of my mother's.' And, in a strange kind of way, they did. Although the subject matter, Norfolk beaches and tropical forests, was entirely different, the whirling brush strokes evoked the same kind of dark despair. It was uncanny.

'Really?' said Luciana. 'She must be a good painter.'

'She is,' I said, thoughtfully.

Luciana watched me closely. She knew and liked these paintings. It was as though she knew my mother.

'Would you like a glass of wine?' she offered.

'That would be lovely.'

'Have a seat, I'll be back in a minute.'

I sat down on a sofa, and looked around at the carpets, vases, clocks, candlesticks, some old, some new, all expensive. Between the paintings hung a vast, gilded antique mirror. What sort of people would like to have their homes done up like this? I wondered. Rich people, I presumed.

I could see no trace of Ricardo anywhere. He probably had an office stuck away out of sight. This was Luciana's territory.

She returned with two glasses of white wine, and curled up in a large armchair next to me. I noticed she was barefoot. Red toenails.

It seemed to her perfectly natural that a junior ex-employee of her husband's firm should come to see her to talk about designs. Somehow, I had guessed it would.

'So, you're decorating your place?' she asked.

'Yes. Now I've earned some money I thought I ought to brighten the flat up a bit. And I liked some of the things I saw in Brazil, so I thought I would come and ask you for ideas. If you don't mind?'

'I don't mind at all,' said Luciana. Her dark eyes looked straight at me over her glass. 'But let's have a drink and some lunch first, shall we? It's just a salad.'

I gulped at the wine. I felt uncomfortable. In her own way, this woman was as powerful as Ricardo. She was used to getting what she wanted. Well, I needed something from her, and it seemed best to come to it straight away, before I lost control of the situation.

'Actually, there is something else I wanted to ask you about.'

'Oh, yes?'

'It's about your brother, Francisco.'

This surprised her. Her smile wavered, and those dark eyes hardened for a second. 'Why do you want to know about him?'

'You know Isabel Pereira was kidnapped, don't you?'

'Yes. That was awful. These things happen in Rio. It is terrible.'

'Well, it seems that Dekker Ward have been dealing with drug gangs. It may be that there's a connection between this money-laundering and Isabel's kidnappers.'

'And you think this connection might be Francisco?' Luciana looked shocked but not offended.

I took a deep breath. 'I have heard rumours that Francisco is connected with some drug gangs.'

'Are you saying my brother is a narco-trafficker?' Luciana still looked more amused than offended.

'No, Luciana. I'm saying your brother is a businessman. I'm sure he doesn't deal in drugs, but he deals in money, doesn't he?'

'I guess so.'

'Well, people invest money with him, he invests money with other people. Perhaps he invested some money with Ricardo? Money belonging to contacts of his? Contacts in the import–export business?'

I was guessing and Luciana could see it. She smiled. 'And why should I tell you anything about this, even if there is anything to tell?'

'What's the harm? I don't care where Francisco's money came from. I have no desire to get him into trouble. All I care about is tracing Isabel, and I need some sort of lead. If I don't find her in the next week, she will die.'

'She means a lot to you, doesn't she?' Once again, Luciana's gaze was direct.

I nodded.

'Your glass is empty. Let me get some more wine.' She disappeared again, to the kitchen presumably, and returned with the bottle. She filled her own glass and mine.

She sat down next to me on the sofa, and touched my arm. I didn't move. But it was very hard to remain detached with such a beautiful and intensely sexual woman next to me.

'Ricardo doesn't like you very much, does he?' she said.

'No. I don't think he does. Do you mind that?'

'No,' she said, running her finger along my sleeve. 'I rather like it.'

'Will you tell me about your brother?' I asked.

'Maybe,' she said, and smiled, looking up at me through blackened eyelashes.

I knew what I would have to do to get my question answered. And, looking at Luciana, just how bad could that be?

But in the same way that I didn't want to be manipulated by her husband, I didn't want to be manipulated by this woman. She moved even closer to me, I could feel one of her breasts touching my arm. 'Don't be shy,' she said.

'Do you do this often?'

'Sometimes. For fun. And it is fun, I can assure you.'

'That's what Jamie says,' I lied.

'Does he talk about me?' she said, in mock anger.

I nodded. 'We're old friends.'

'And I thought you English men were too uptight to talk about sex!'

'What does Ricardo think? Does he know how you amuse yourself at home?'

'We never talk about it. I think he must guess I have some outside interests. I don't think he realizes that some of them are his own people.'

'And doesn't that bother you?'

'I like it.'

'You like it?'

Luciana sat upright. 'When you're married to someone like Ricardo he tries to control you. Well, I don't like to be controlled. I want to decide what I want to do, and if he knows it, so what?'

'I think I can understand that.'

'Most people don't stand up to him. You did. You drive him crazy. Maybe that's why I like you.'

'And Jamie?'

'I think Jamie likes to think he can fuck the boss's wife. Well, that's fine with me. He likes living dangerously and so do I. And he is cute.'

'So where does that leave us?' I asked.

She leaned forward, and kissed me gently on the lips. 'Right here.'

Suddenly my confusion resolved itself. Either I could stay and be laid by this woman and then perhaps hear some lie about her brother, or I could leave now.

'Well, thank you for the wine, Luciana,' I said, pulling myself to my feet. 'I'm sorry I can't stay to lunch.'

I left her curled up on the sofa, coolly drinking her wine.

'*Tchau*,' she said.

27

For the third time in the last three months, I saw the brown dusty mess of Rio's northern suburbs through the window of an aeroplane. But it was different this time. Before, I had felt anticipation and excitement. Now I felt desperation and fear. Fear for Isabel, and fear for myself. I had nearly been killed on my first trip, and kidnapped on my second. What would happen this time, I wondered.

The ticket for the British Airways flight departing that evening had cost me half of what was left of the money Ricardo had lent me. I had had no choice but to pay it. I had to do all I could to find Isabel, and that involved flying to Brazil. If I didn't go, and the kidnappers carried out their threat, I would never be able to forgive myself.

Luís had been pleased to hear of my plans, and Kate had been understanding. Her willingness to help me save Isabel was touching, but no less than I would have expected of her. She asked me to keep her informed of events. Jamie was at work. He would, no doubt, be happy to find me gone when he returned.

My feelings towards Jamie were confused. I was angry with him. Angry that he had turned his back on me in favour of Ricardo. And angry that he had been so callously unfaithful to Kate with Luciana. I could imagine him justifying it now: 'It was just a bit of fun, a bit of adventure,' he'd say. 'I don't even really like Luciana, but I love Kate.' Yuk.

But I also felt guilty. About plotting against Dekker from his house, and about making his wife my accomplice. I bore my responsibility for the destruction of ten years of friendship.

Still, now I was down here, I had to put all that behind me, and focus on one thing: setting Isabel free. It would be hard to find her by next Wednesday, but I had an idea that just might extend the deadline further. We would see.

Luís met me at the airport with a smile and an embrace, and his chauffeur drove us back to his apartment in Ipanema. There, Nelson, Cordelia and her husband Fernando were waiting. Cordelia was noticeably larger; I was relieved that Isabel's disappearance hadn't disrupted her pregnancy.

They greeted me with handshakes and smiles, and I was pleased to be among them again. We sat in the living room, and despite the difficulty of our task, there was an almost palpable feeling of optimism among us. It was as though now we were together again our collective determination to find her would succeed, despite the odds.

'So, what do you think, Nick?' Luís asked.

'I'm pretty sure I can guess who's behind Isabel's kidnapping.'

'Who?' asked Cordelia, leaning forward.

'Francisco Aragão.'

'Francisco Aragão? Ricardo Ross's brother-in-law? I wouldn't be surprised,' muttered Luís.

'I think he's working together with Ricardo and Eduardo Ross. I don't know who's calling the shots, but my best guess is that between the three of them they had Martin Beldecos murdered, and Isabel kidnapped.'

'But why?' asked Luís.

'I think Dekker Ward is laundering drug money for Francisco. He approached Dekker through his sister Luciana, who is, of course, Ricardo's wife.'

'Have you spoken to Luciana?' Luís asked.

'Yes, I have.' I coughed. I didn't want to go into the details of that conversation. 'She didn't actually admit it, but the idea didn't seem to surprise her either.'

Luís nodded, and I continued. 'Francisco set up accounts at Dekker Trust in the Cayman Islands with the help of an American attorney in Miami named Tony Hempel. They're both under investigation by the American Drug Enforcement Agency. Martin Beldecos was on the point of uncovering this arrangement, so he was murdered in Caracas. I might have been attacked for the same reason.' I paused and looked out of the window towards Ipanema beach and the sea. The stretch of sand where I had been knifed was just out of view. 'Over there.'

The four of them were listening to my words closely.

'OK, but what has Isabel's kidnapping to do with this?' Luís asked.

'I can't be sure, exactly. At first it looked like a standard Rio kidnapping. For money. We all assumed that Isabel was kidnapped so that you would have to pay a ransom.'

Luís nodded.

'But now it looks as though that wasn't the real motive. The kidnappers seem more interested in protecting Dekker than in extorting money.'

'So why did they kidnap her in the first place?'

I had given this much thought on the plane journey down, and I believed I had an answer. 'Well, it wasn't just her that was snatched. They took me as well. Perhaps they thought that I had some knowledge about Martin or Francisco that would compromise them. They wanted me out of the way. Even when I escaped, they kept me distracted by launching into negotiations for Isabel's ransom, and, of course, I left Dekker soon after I returned to England.'

'So why didn't they just kill her, like they did Martin Beldecos?' asked Nelson.

'Good question. I don't know the answer.' Actually, I could guess at why Isabel hadn't been killed, especially if Ricardo was involved in the operation in some way. But I didn't want to tell Luís about his daughter's affair with Ricardo if I could help it. I knew she wouldn't want me to. 'For some reason they wanted us to believe she was dead. That's why they dropped the ransom so suddenly, and didn't respond to the proof-of-life question. But they obviously decided to keep her alive. Thank God.'

'Do you have proof of all this?' asked Nelson.

'No, I don't, but it all adds up. What do you think, Luís?'

Luís rubbed his chin. 'I think you might be right. What you say makes sense.'

'Do you know him?'

'Francisco? No. I mean, I've met him once or twice but we've never done business together.'

'What does he do? All I know is he's some kind of financier.'

'His father is a senator, and so was his grandfather. His elder brother runs a contracting company that makes good profits from government contracts. But in Brazil, that's normal.'

'And Francisco himself?'

'He made a lot of money in the eighties through offshore investment companies. It was easy, and very profitable. A lot of people did it. It involved currency speculation against the various government exchange-rate programmes. It had to be offshore to avoid exchange controls.'

'By offshore, do you mean Panama?' I asked. I remembered Tony Hempel and International Trading and Transport (Panama) Ltd.

'Panama, certainly. And the Cayman Islands, the Bahamas, even Miami. People made a lot of money. Then many of them lost it all.'

'How?'

'The *Real* Plan. It was introduced in nineteen ninety-four, and linked the new currency, the *real*, to the dollar. Interest rates were high, and for the first time inflation was under control. The easy money was over. Banks and finance companies went bankrupt all over the place.'

'But not Francisco?'

Luís shrugged. 'Not as far as I've heard. It looks as if he diversified into real estate and commodities trading. And he is supposed to deal with the narco-traffickers. If they bankrolled him, he would be OK.'

Luís paused. His mouth tightened. 'If that bastard has harmed my daughter, I'll kill him,' he whispered.

'So what do we do now?' asked Cordelia.

'Tell him to give my daughter back!' growled Luís. It was as though the anger he had felt at the loss of his daughter was emerging, now that he had someone to direct it against.

'What will you say to him?' asked Nelson.

'I'll tell him he's the son of a whore,' said Luís, reddening. 'I'll tell him that if he doesn't give my daughter back I will tear off his . . .' he searched for the English word ' . . . testicles and shove them down his throat.' Luís's chest was heaving as he said this. The control he had shown over the last few weeks was finally in danger of breaking down.

'I don't think that will work,' said Nelson, quietly.

'Why not?' Luís glared at him.

'Because Francisco will deny he has Isabel,' said Nelson. 'And we have no proof. So he won't let her go, and we won't know where she is. On the other hand, it will warn him that we have figured out what he's up to, and he and whoever are his accomplices will be able to cover their tracks.'

Luís stood up from his chair, and began pacing up and down. We all watched him in silence. He was breathing heavily, trying to regain control. Eventually he stopped and turned to Nelson. 'You're right. I'm sorry. This is not the time for anger. This is the time to be clear-headed. So what can we do?'

'Find out a bit more about Francisco,' I suggested. 'What he's up to now. Who he deals with. If he does deal with drug gangs, which ones.'

'I can check up on that,' said Luís.

'I'll ask my police contacts,' said Nelson. 'If he is close to these guys, they will know.'

'And what about the kid who stabbed me?' I asked. 'If that was organized by a drug gang, might there be rumours in the *favelas*?'

'Possibly,' said Nelson. 'I can ask about that as well.'

'So can I,' Cordelia said. 'My kids run all over the city. Normally I'd hate to ask them those kinds of questions, but in this case . . .'

Luís looked at us over his glasses, his face finely balanced between desperation and hope. 'Well, at least we can *do* something now.'

Luís and I sat out on the balcony overlooking the bay. I was drinking a beer, he was drinking water.

'I shouldn't have lost my temper this morning,' he said.

'It's understandable.'

He sighed. 'It's been a hard six weeks.' His deep voice was heavy with the fatigue of waiting and hoping. 'I always believed she was alive, but it was fantastic to hear from Zico again. I'm just worried that if we don't get her out by next Wednesday . . .'

'We'll find her.'

'That soon?'

I cleared my throat. Now was the time to try out my idea. 'There is a way that we might be able to buy ourselves more time.'

'Oh, yes?'

'You remember that you said Banco Horizonte was beginning to think about expanding overseas?'

'Did I say that?'

'Yes, I think so. Is it true?'

'Well, yes. We're thinking about setting up operations in the other Mercosul countries, perhaps Argentina or Uruguay.'

'What about Dekker?'

'Buying Dekker Ward, you mean?'

'Yes.'

Luís creased his forehead. 'It's an idea. But no Brazilian bank has bought a major European firm before.'

'You could probably afford it. Bloomfield Weiss are only offering Kerton ten million pounds.'

'Yes, we could afford it,' he said carefully. 'And it would be a great strategic fit. We'd become the premier investment bank in South America. But the problem is the bond portfolio. From what you've told me, it's huge and it's heavily underwater. You'd need to be a Bloomfield Weiss to trade your way out of that. We just don't have the capital.'

I was disappointed. 'So you couldn't make a bid just to delay things?'

Luís hesitated. 'We could, but I don't think Lord Kerton would listen. It wouldn't be credible. He'd know we couldn't take on the bond positions. He'd think we were just playing for time, and accept the Bloomfield Weiss bid instead.'

My heart sank. 'Well, anyway, let me get some of the information on Dekker, and see what you think.'

I disappeared inside, and returned with my copies of the Bloomfield Weiss documents on Dekker.

'I'm not sure you should be letting me see these,' Luís said.

'Why not? If there's any way they can help to save Isabel, I'll use them. And I'm not impressed by rules made up by one shark to help it swallow another.'

Luís grinned and studied the papers. I looked out over the bay. It was almost the middle of the Brazilian winter, and there was a soft, cool thickness to the air as it blew in from the sea. The temperature was cold by Rio standards, but pleasant by mine. So although it was a Saturday, the beach wasn't crowded, but there were still the games of volleyball, beach football, and that skilful hybrid of the two that so fascinated me. Towards the horizon the familiar cluster of half-domed islands lurked low in the sea, which shimmered in the weakening late-afternoon sunlight.

'You know, there is a way,' he said at last.

'What's that?'

'KBN, the big Dutch bank. They're the people who I introduced to Humberto Alves to resurrect the *favela* deal. They're one of the biggest players in the emerging bond markets. They could handle the Dekker bond portfolio.'

'So you'd suggest that they buy Dekker Ward.'

Luís smiled. 'Oh, no. I want to buy Dekker Ward. But they can take on the bond portfolio.'

'Would they do that?'

'We could structure it to make it worth their while.'

I smiled. 'Well, then?'

Luís stood up, tucking the papers I had given him under his arm. 'I have a few telephone calls to make.'

Luís spent Sunday on the phone, interrupting the weekends of his partners at Banco Horizonte and some senior people at KBN. Cordelia spent much of her weekend in the shelter in the *favela*. And Nelson called in favours with his former police colleagues. I stalked impatiently around Luís's apartment, occasionally providing him with information on Dekker Ward.

In one of the brief moments when Luís was off the phone, I decided to ring Kate, to let her know what progress, or lack of it, I had made. I dialled her number, praying that Jamie wouldn't answer. Kate was usually first to the phone in their house.

But not this time.

'Hallo,' Jamie said.

For a moment I considered simply hanging up. But that was silly. If I wanted to speak to Kate, I should just ask.

'Hallo?' Jamie sounded irritated.

'Jamie? It's Nick. I'm ringing from Brazil.'

'Oh.'

'Can I speak to Kate?'

Silence. Oh, come on, he couldn't forbid me from speaking to her.

'She's not here.' His voice sounded strained.

'When will she be back?'

'I wish I knew.'

'What's wrong? Is she all right?'

Another pause. 'She left me. Last night. She took Oliver. She's gone to her sister's.'

'Why did she leave?'

'Why don't you ask her yourself?' The venom sped down the phone line, and then the receiver went dead.

I stared at it a moment. Jesus, Kate had left. I should have seen it coming, I supposed, but I still couldn't believe it. Oh, God, was it my fault? I'd persuaded her to help me against Jamie. Except it wasn't Jamie I was conspiring against, it was Ricardo. And I was only trying to save Isabel. Without Kate's help she'd be dead by now. But, of course, Jamie wouldn't see it that way.

I remembered their wedding. It was of the traditional English variety, in the large fifteenth-century church in the Sussex village where her father was a doctor. It was a glorious June day. Jamie looked dashing in his morning suit, and Kate gorgeous in her wedding dress. Both sets of parents beamed. I can't remember the details too well. For most of it, I was worried about my best-man duties, but I held on to the ring, and my speech was short and even raised a couple of laughs. After that the champagne flowed, and with it a warm glow of pleasure that two people I liked so much had decided to live their lives together. At some weddings, the couple seem right for each other, and at others they don't. At this one they seemed perfect.

I still believed they had been then. But things had changed, or they had changed, or something.

I had Kate's sister Liz's number in my address book. I dug it out and dialled it. Liz answered. She put me through to Kate right away.

'Kate, it's Nick. What happened?'

She sighed. 'I've moved out.'

'So Jamie told me. Are you all right? You must feel awful.'

'I do,' she said flatly. 'But it's good to be out of the house. I need a few days to think it over.'

'It's not because of me, is it?'

'Oh, no, Nick. Not really. Although I didn't like the way he threw you out with nowhere to go. He's changed, Nick. And I don't like what he's changed into.' Kate's voice was quiet. 'Has he ever . . . you know, with other women?'

I realized it was a question she had wanted to ask me for a long time. I thought of Luciana. I thought of Jamie with the 'model' on his knee at Eduardo's party. 'I don't know for sure,' I said, feebly.

Kate sobbed. I heard her sniff as she tried to regain control. I felt badly: she'd wanted the truth and I hadn't given it to her. But how can you tell a woman that her husband has cheated on her?

Of course she knew.

'Have you spoken to him about it?' I asked.

'Not directly. But he knows my feelings. I don't like him selling his soul for some mythical million-dollar bonus. And I don't like him messing around with other women. He's not going to change, Nick. You know that.'

'But he loves you,' I said, and I really believed he did.

'I used to love him. I still do. The old Jamie. But in ten years' time he's going to be a fat, crooked banker with a collection of slinky mistresses dotted round the world. And I don't want to have anything to do with that.'

Her voice was heavy with sadness. Silence stretched across the thousands of miles between us.

Eventually she spoke.

'I'd have been much better off with you,' she said, and before I could reply, she had hung up.

Luís went into Banco Horizonte on Monday morning, and came back at lunch-time with a smile on his face. Nelson, Cordelia and I were sitting round the table on the balcony, waiting for him. We were all anxious.

'Well, they'll go for it. Banco Horizonte will be putting in a bid for Dekker Ward of twenty million pounds, subject to due diligence. KBN will support us.'

'Good,' I said.

'I'll phone Lord Kerton with our offer this afternoon.'

'But it won't bring Isabel back, will it, Papai?' Cordelia looked gaunt and irritated.

'It will buy us some more time, Cordelia,' said her father, more soberly. Her comment had destroyed his brief optimism, replacing it with guilt that he had succumbed to his natural enthusiasm for a deal when Isabel was still in danger.

'Did you find out anything about Francisco?' I asked.

Luís sighed. 'Not much. He is very secretive. But over the last couple of years he seems to have gained access to much bigger funds. He's rumoured to have been involved in some major real-estate deals both in Brazil and the United States.'

'Where's the money coming from?'

'Narco-traffickers, people say. And not just from Brazil. He's supposed to have developed contacts in Colombia and Venezuela as well.'

'That might explain why Martin Beldecos was murdered in Caracas,' I said.

'But no idea which particular drug gangs he deals with?' Nelson asked.

Luís shook his head. 'It's all vague rumour. Did you hear anything?'

'He's been seen with most of the big players in Rio at one time or other. Any one of them could be holding Isabel. I've found out where he lives and works, and I have a man watching him. But he hasn't gone anywhere interesting in the last two days.'

'Anything on the kids who attacked me?' I asked.

'Yes. I spoke to a detective who was involved with the case. He had a hunch that the attack was more than just a mugging, that it was planned. No one was talking in the *favela*, and my contact got the feeling that they were scared to talk, rather than that they just didn't know. The police were under pressure to keep it simple. A mugging gone wrong was bad enough. It would not look good if a foreign businessman had been injured in some drug-related stabbing on Ipanema beach.'

'So it looks as if Nick was right,' Luís said. 'There *is* a connection between the attacks on Martin and him, and Isabel's kidnapping.'

Nelson nodded, his round orange face grim. 'Francisco is behind this, there's no doubt in my mind at all.'

Luís slammed his hand on the table rattling the plates and glasses that had been set for lunch. 'OK, but now we know that, is there nothing we can do?'

'All we can do is try to find out where Isabel is being held,' said Nelson calmly.

Maria brought lunch out on to the balcony – steak and a salad. We munched through it in silence, each wrapped up in our own thoughts. I shared Luís's frustration. If we knew Francisco was responsible for Isabel's kidnapping, surely there must be something we could do. I could see there was no point in going to the police without proof. Talking to them had almost got Isabel killed. And I could see that confrontation was a waste of time, Nelson was right. But what about negotiation? Suddenly, I had an idea.

'We could talk to Francisco,' I said.

28

We drove up a steep, winding road, Luís's car shuddering over the cobbles. On either side, behind wrought-iron gates and walls dripping with flowers and greenery, stood colonial mansions, gleaming in the afternoon sunlight. Behind us stretched Guanabara Bay, above us hovered the statue of Christ, brushed by wisps of cloud.

'These houses must have cost a bit,' I said.

'You're right,' said Luís. 'Santa Teresa is one of the most expensive areas of Rio. It's where the ambassadors' residences used to be when Rio was the capital of Brazil. Francisco must have done well for himself.'

There were four of us, Luís, his driver, Nelson and me. Nelson's associate had told us Francisco was at home, so we had driven straight there. We passed a shabby Toyota parked at the corner of a side-road, and Nelson got out to join his friend. His anonymity was important to him professionally, so he didn't want to meet Francisco face to face.

Fifty yards further along the road, we pulled up outside some iron gates. Luís's driver spoke into an intercom in the wall. We were told to wait.

It took several minutes. An old yellow tram clattered down the road behind us, brown bodies spilling out from all sides.

Finally, the intercom crackled, a motor whirred and the gates swung open. We drove into a walled courtyard in front of a newly painted white colonial house with tall, elegant windows and ornate trimmings. As we emerged from the cool of the air-conditioned car into the warmth of the afternoon, I was almost overwhelmed by the scent of the blossom all around us, purple, blue, orange and white flowers draped over the walls and urns. Delicate blue and black butterflies skipped and danced beside our feet.

A butler opened the door and ushered us into a hallway, cool once again. As we followed him to a door at the far end, a boy of about seventeen scurried down the stairs, and rushed past us out of the house, giving us barely a glance. He was tall, gangly, and dressed designer-casual.

We entered a large, airy sitting room. In one half of the room was a big dark-wood desk, and some of the paraphernalia of modern office technology, and in the other was a suite of sofas and chairs. Behind them was a small garden and a stunning view over the city to the bay.

A moment after the butler disappeared with our coffee requests, Francisco entered. He and Luís spoke quickly in Portuguese. I was impressed by Luís. He had controlled his anger completely. He was relaxed and urbane, as though this were simply a social visit with an old friend. As they exchanged pleasantries I was unable to understand, I watched Francisco. He was about forty, a bit below average height, bald and heavy. I could see the family resemblance to Luciana. But the genes that had given her a voluptuous figure had made him merely fat. His eyes were almost black, like hers, and they were hard. He had her flashing white smile, but between his thin lips it looked more like a snarl.

I heard my name and the words 'Dekker Ward', as Luís nodded towards me.

'Delighted to meet you,' said Francisco in good English. 'Please, take a seat.'

Luís and I sat down next to each other on a low sofa. Francisco sat opposite. 'How can I help you?' he asked, opening his hands in a friendly gesture.

'Well, Francisco, my daughter has been kidnapped.' Luís managed to say this as casually as if he were telling him Isabel had caught a cold.

Francisco put on an expression of polite shock. 'Oh, no! That is terrible. One hears of these things in Rio, of course, but to have it happen to you is horrible. Have you heard from the kidnappers?'

Certainly, I had expected Francisco to feign astonishment, but it was all I could do to fight back the anger when I saw his response. He wasn't a good actor. I knew then for sure that he had organized Isabel's kidnap.

Luís kept his cool. 'Yes, we have, as a matter of fact. Indeed they made a rather unusual demand.'

'Oh, yes?'

'Yes. They wanted Nick here to try to prevent the takeover of Dekker Ward by an American investment bank. Nick had instigated the takeover, and I suppose the kidnappers thought he might be able to stop it.'

'How extraordinary.'

'Yes, it is strange, isn't it? But there's nothing Nick can do. The American investment bank won't listen to him. So we have another idea.'

'I don't see what all this has to do with me,' said Francisco. But he was listening.

Luís ignored his interruption and continued. 'As you know, I run Banco Horizonte. We intend to put in an offer today for Dekker Ward. You see, Dekker is about to go bankrupt. If my bank were to take it over, we would ensure that any investors or depositors were protected. I don't just mean that they would get their money back, but that their identity would remain confidential, should there be an investigation. That is, of course, as long as my daughter is released.'

Francisco wore a slight frown, as though he were puzzled at why Luís was telling him all this. But he let Luís continue.

'So, if Isabel is released, Banco Horizonte will take over Dekker Ward, and shy investors will be protected.' He stopped and fixed Francisco with a calm gaze.

Francisco shifted in his chair. 'That is an interesting idea, but I still don't see what it has to do with me.'

Luís stayed silent, never moving his gaze.

Francisco blundered into the uncomfortable silence, eager to maintain the fiction of a normal conversation. 'OK, Ricardo Ross is my brother-in-law, of course. But we don't do business together. I have nothing to do with Dekker Ward. We have different outlooks.' Francisco leaned forward, his tone conspiratorial. 'Dekker Ward is, you know, a little aggressive for me. I prefer more conservative institutions.'

I was taking a sip of coffee as Francisco said this, and almost choked on it. Francisco ignored me.

Luís stood up. 'Well, thank you for your time, Francisco. No doubt I will hear from the kidnappers soon as to whether this would be acceptable.'

Francisco stood up. He was clearly confused, not knowing what response was expected of him. In the end he settled for a concerned tone. 'I still don't quite understand why you wanted to tell me about this. But

I'm very sorry about your daughter, Luís. I hope she is released safely soon.'

'So do I, Francisco, so do I.' For the first time there was an edge to Luís's voice.

As Francisco led us out through the hallway, I paused to ask a question. 'Oh, by the way, Senhor Aragão, was that your son I saw earlier?'

'Yes. Francisco *filho*. He's in his last year at high school.'

'Ah.' I smiled, and Luís and I left Francisco a truly puzzled man.

'He's definitely got Isabel,' I said, as soon as the car was safely out of sight of Francisco's property, and we had picked up Nelson.

'Yes, he has,' growled Luís. 'It was all I could do not to strangle the man. Sitting there, smiling like that, when he has my daughter!'

'Do you think he'll go for it?'

'I hope so. He was certainly listening. But who knows if he is really the one calling the shots? Perhaps it's up to the Ross brothers. They wouldn't want Dekker taken over by Banco Horizonte, even with guarantees of anonymity for investors.'

'Although Francisco might act unilaterally if he thinks that's the best hope to protect himself,' Nelson said. 'I mean, release Isabel, let you take over Dekker, take his money and run.'

'That's what we have to hope,' said Luís. 'I'd love to turn him in to the authorities,' he muttered.

So would I. And I was beginning to realize that this was the true weakness of my plan, although I hadn't mentioned it to Luís. Francisco would have to rely essentially on Luís's good faith not to turn over Dekker account records to the authorities if Isabel was released. Perhaps he would judge he was better off forcing us to find a way to delay and then overturn the takeover. And if Dekker was taken over, and he didn't trust us, why keep Isabel alive? Francisco looked as if he wouldn't lose sleep over killing her.

Luís's driver dropped him off at the bank, and took Nelson and me back to the apartment. Luís returned after a couple of hours. We were all waiting for him.

'Well, I spoke to Lord Kerton,' he said. 'He says that he might entertain our bid. But he wants to see me in person, plus a senior representative from KBN, on Wednesday, so that he can decide whether to take us seriously.'

'So are you going?' asked Cordelia.

Luís sighed. 'I'll have to. I'd like to stay here, and wait for a response from Francisco. But I can do more in London. Our best hope now is to buy Dekker and persuade Francisco that we will lose the evidence of his investments.'

Luís packed hurriedly to catch the flight to London that night. Just before he was about to leave for the airport, the phone rang. Luís picked it up.

Zico.

Nelson listened in. I watched. Their faces became graver and graver. Luís protested. Then the conversation was over.

'What did he say?' I asked the second the phone was down.

'He said that there was to be absolutely no change in the kidnappers' terms. If *anyone* takes over Dekker, that's either Banco Horizonte or Bloomfield Weiss, then they'll kill her.'

My heart sank. 'Did they say when they would release her?'

He shook his head. 'They said they'll keep her as long as there's any danger of Dekker being taken over.'

'Did they mention Francisco?'

'No. I asked about him, but Zico said he had never heard of him.'

We stood looking at each other in silence. Cordelia bit her lip, trying not to cry.

'So he didn't go for it,' I said.

Luís gave me a thin smile. 'It was worth a try, Nick.'

I summoned a smile back. Yeah, but it didn't work, I thought.

Luís sighed. 'So, what now?' he asked Nelson.

Nelson shrugged. 'Well, you should still go to London. That, at least, will delay things for a few more days.'

'You're right.' Then his eyes passed from Nelson to Cordelia to me. 'For God's sake, find her,' he said.

None of us had the confidence to answer him.

Luís left us, and flew to London. More waiting, more tension. Tuesday passed, and still no news of Isabel. Cordelia and Nelson joined me on Wednesday morning. We knew Luís was meeting Lord Kerton for a working lunch.

The phone rang. I answered it. It was Luís.

'Well, we're in with a chance,' he said. 'I offered twenty million pounds, subject to due diligence. He was interested. But he said he wanted to give Bloomfield Weiss an opportunity to come up with a better offer. So he wants to hold an auction. Sealed bids from ourselves and Bloomfield Weiss.'

'How long have we got?'

'One week. He's holding the auction next Wednesday.'

'Only a week!' I exclaimed. Somehow I had hoped we might get a month. Although with the progress we were making in finding Isabel, a month or a week wouldn't make any difference.

Luís shrugged. 'He says he needs to have a deal in the bag before the end of the month. The thirtieth of June is a reporting date for the regulators. There will be no hiding from those losses then.'

'Can you mount a bid in a week?' I asked.

'I think so. The market seems to have stabilized, so KBN are more confident in taking on the bond portfolio. We've devised a structure for the transaction that will give them some nice profits if Dekker does well once we've bought it. And I've offered Lord Kerton a seat on the board.'

'I bet he liked that.'

'I think he did. We got on quite well. How are you doing?'

'Nothing yet.'

'Nothing!' Luís was disappointed, but his voice held a tinge of anger too.

'Sorry, Luís. We're trying. No one seems to know anything.'

'*Merda!*' he muttered.

'Something will turn up,' I said.

'I hope so, Nick. I really hope so.'

And it did. The next day. Cordelia called to say that one of her kids had discovered something. He would agree to talk to us, but it had to be in the shelter.

Nelson drove me to the *favela*. It was a grey day, and it had rained earlier. We crawled through the damp streets pushing along with the traffic. The tunnels through the mountains formed periodic bottlenecks, which added to the congestion.

At last we made it to the bottom of the hill below the *favela* where Cordelia worked. We set off up the same path that Isabel and I had climbed two months before. It had been a hot day then, it was damp and humid now. The air was heavy with the smell of wet garbage. There were fewer people outside, but kids and young men stared at Nelson and me as we made our slow way up the hill. I felt exposed on that hillside, my back unprotected and vulnerable, a perfect target. Any moment I expected to hear the crack of a gunshot.

Finally we made it to the plateau with the little church and the shelter. The *favela* brooded beneath us in the grey moist air. We knocked on the door, and Cordelia met us.

'Follow me,' she said, and led us to a small store room, packed high with boxes of school materials and dried food. Sitting on a box was a thin boy of about twelve. I recognized him immediately. Euclides.

'Hallo, meester,' he said, with a nervous smile.

'Hallo, Euclides.'

Cordelia and Nelson sat on the two chairs, and I squatted on the floor. Cordelia introduced Nelson to Euclides, who looked at him with extreme suspicion. He no doubt recognized an ex-policeman when he saw one.

Nelson's voice was firm but kind, as he asked Euclides some questions. The boy responded in tough monosyllables, only expanding on his answers when coaxed by Cordelia. Although I couldn't understand a word of what was said, I could see the relationship between the three people. Euclides distrusted Nelson but he thought the world of Cordelia, although he tried to hide it. The odd glances towards her for approval and the way he responded to her gentle encouragement gave his affection away. But the eyes were still hard. This kid understood violence.

'What's he say?' I asked, during a pause.

'He says that he knows one of the kids who was in the group that attacked you. It was all planned. There's a man by the name of O Borboleta who organized it. He runs a gang in one of the *favelas* near here.'

'Have you heard of him?'

'No. But O Borboleta means "The Butterfly".'

'Why's he called that?'

Nelson turned to Euclides and rattled off a question, which the boy answered.

'He was a footballer. Very skilful, apparently. No one could catch him.'

'That could be Zico,' I said.

Nelson thought. 'Could be. But the real Zico had a lot of admirers. Any soccer fan could have picked that name. And there are many soccer fans in this country.'

'Well, does Euclides know whether this Borboleta is holding Isabel?'

Nelson sighed. 'He says he doesn't know anything about Isabel.'

'Ask him to find out where she is.'

Nelson shrugged, and asked the question. Euclides grunted '*Não*.'

'Ask him why not.'

Nelson repeated my question in Portuguese, and Euclides mumbled something. 'He says his friend might be able to find out. But Euclides doesn't want to ask too many questions. It would be too dangerous.'

'Tell him it's Cordelia's sister. Her only sister. He has to help us find her.'

Euclides picked up the urgency in my voice and lifted his eyes towards me. Nelson asked the question. Euclides glanced guiltily at Cordelia and shrugged.

'Does he have a sister?'

'Yes,' Cordelia answered. 'She's here.'

'No, ask him,' I said.

She asked the question and Euclides nodded.

I asked a string of questions, which I insisted that Nelson translate. 'What's her name?'

'Marta.'

'How old is she?'

'Eight.'

'Do you love her?'

A pause. 'Yes.'

'Do you like Cordelia?'

Another pause. 'Yes.'

'Well, if you lost your sister, would you do anything you could to help her?'

The boy didn't answer. He looked closely at me. I held his brown eyes. They carried so much for a child of twelve. Bravado, fear, insecurity, but also, somewhere, warmth.

'Cordelia has saved many children's lives who have come here. Now you can save her sister.'

He still didn't answer. But I could see he was wavering.

Then Nelson bent down and took something out of a holster strapped to his ankle. It was a small revolver. The metal gleamed in the dim light of the store room. He handed it to Euclides. Cordelia and I looked on, shocked.

The twelve-year-old took the gun, and stuffed it into his trouser belt. 'OK,' he said. 'I'll find her for you.'

Friday disappeared, and the weekend dragged on. Luís remained in London, supported by reinforcements from Banco Horizonte. We didn't hear from Euclides.

We did, however, hear from Zico. I was alone in the apartment when he called.

'Hallo?' I said.

'Who is that?' The deep voice growled.

'Nick Elliot. Luís is in London.' Luís had warned Zico that I might answer the phone while he was away. Zico, it seemed, spoke some English.

'OK. Is the takeover stopped?' His English was slow and precise, as though he had rehearsed the sentence. His accent was strong. Stopped became *stop-ped*.

'Not yet,' I said. 'But Banco Horizonte is still making a bid. We hope to delay things so that Bloomfield Weiss will give up.'

'I see. Well, I hope you succeed. Because when someone take over Dekker, Isabel dies. *Anyone* you understand? Bloomfield Weiss or Banco Horizonte.'

'I understand,' I said.

The phone went dead.

I put my head in my hands. Next Wednesday only one of two things would occur. Either Lord Kerton would sell to Bloomfield Weiss or he would sell to Banco Horizonte. Neither would satisfy Zico.

I shuddered. What was Euclides doing?

Cordelia and her husband had arrived at the apartment on Friday night. They said they would spend much of the weekend with me to keep me company, and to stay near Luís's phone. Fernando brought a copy of *Dr Zhivago* in Russian with him, which he had acquired through a friend from the university. I accepted it thankfully. I had read it before but I could read it again, and I was able to lose myself in it for half an hour at a time, before worry about Isabel brought me back to the present.

'Do you think Euclides just took the gun and ran?' I asked Cordelia, during a subdued supper.

'I don't know,' she said. 'I don't think so. He's a brave boy, and he's proud of his courage. A lot of these kids are.'

'People don't seem to care so much about death here,' I said.

'You're right. Life is cheap. Do you know what train-surfing is?'

'No.'

'It's a big sport for the street children. They leap on trains as they are moving, and climb on to the roofs. The most dangerous part is when the trains go through tunnels. The kids compete with each other to see who is the last to jump off. Dozens die every year doing this. Euclides had quite a reputation as a train-surfer.'

'But will he find Isabel?'

'I think he'll try to look for her for me.'

'He's very attached to you.'

Cordelia's shoulders sagged. 'Yes. So he takes a gun and he risks his life with people who would kill him if they knew what he was doing. He'll use that gun one day, you know.'

Fernando put his hand on hers. 'You had to give him the gun, *minha querida*. It is not like the normal world. In the *favelas* you have to do things for your family that you would not do outside. You know that. You've seen that.'

'Yes, I've seen others resort to guns and violence,' Cordelia muttered. 'But I never believed I would.'

After supper, as we drank *caipirinhas* on the balcony, Cordelia watched me, smiling. It was a bit like her sister's smile, though stronger, more self-confident. But still a reminder of Isabel. It was nice.

'It's funny, finally, to meet one of Isabel's boyfriends,' she said.

'Does she keep them well hidden?'

'She claims there aren't any. Or none since Marcelo, anyway.'

'That's what she told me.' I decided not to mention Ricardo. 'What was this Marcelo like?'

'Good-looking. I mean, really good-looking. But he knew it.' Cordelia wrinkled her nose. 'Isabel was completely gone on him. And I think, when he was with her, he was in love with her. But then when she went to the US his attention wandered. I knew it would. Isabel took it badly. I think it's good they never got married.'

I agreed with that. 'Anyway, I don't know if I qualify,' I said.

'As a boyfriend?' Cordelia's eyes twinkled. 'I'm sure you do, if she's got any sense. And Isabel has got sense.'

'We'll see.'

We talked a lot, that weekend, Fernando, Cordelia and me. I was really beginning to feel part of the Pereira family. Yet Cordelia's words had both encouraged and disquieted me. I sometimes felt I hardly knew Isabel herself. She had already spent more time in captivity than I had known her outside it. If we did get her out alive, would our relationship ever come to anything? Logically I couldn't be sure. But from what I had seen of her, and the way we were together, I had to believe it would amount to something. She had to live, so that I could find out.

By Sunday there was still no news from Euclides. We only had three more days.

Cordelia went to the shelter early on Monday morning. She phoned me at the apartment soon after she arrived. Euclides was there, waiting for her. He had found Isabel.

Once more Nelson and I made our way up to the shelter. We met Euclides in the same room we had seen him in before. This time he was much more talkative, his eyes shining from his adventure. His friend had not known where Isabel was held, but he did know a couple of her captors, and had shown Euclides where they parked their pick-up truck, which was always full of junk. On Sunday, Euclides had hidden in the back, and had been driven up to the hills behind Rio. The truck had eventually passed through a village and up a dirt track, to a deserted farmhouse. Euclides had taken note of the name of the village. Fortunately, he hadn't been discovered, although if he had been, he said he had a story ready about how he was trying to hitch a lift out of town. It seemed to me he had taken an absurd risk, but I was very glad he had.

The name of the village was São Jose.

Euclides agreed to show us the place. We went in Nelson's car, and he stopped on the way to buy a baseball cap for me so that my pale English features would be partly obscured in the car. We drove for an hour and a half northwards, through a range of steep green hills of pasture and forest, before coming to the village of São Jose.

It was a collection of white-painted houses with orange rooftops and bright blue doors, nestling at the head of a valley. Sheep grazed meadows on either side. Euclides led us out of the village and over a bridge and then told us to stop. A poorly metalled road branched off to the right, and wound up the hillside, through the sheep pasture. It passed two small farms, and seemed to peter out near the top of the hill, at a single small white building.

He pointed to it. '*La*,' he said.

We drove back to Rio in heated discussion.

'We have to go to the police,' said Nelson. 'We have no choice. It's Monday today. The final bid for Dekker Ward will be decided on Wednesday. We must free her before then.'

'But you know what happened last time,' I protested. 'The kidnappers were tipped off. Isabel was almost killed. They will definitely kill her this time.'

'There's a risk. I know there's a risk. But the Rio police have a lot of experience.'

'Oh, come on. I bet they'll burst in, guns blazing, shoot all the kidnappers, and hope that Isabel is the only one left alive.'

'I tell you, Nick, it can work. If they have surprise.'

'But they won't have surprise, will they? Some little policeman will tip the kidnappers off.'

'I'll talk to Da Silva. We won't tell the police who it is we're freeing until the last moment. There are a dozen kidnap hostages hidden somewhere in Rio today. If there is a policeman passing on information, he won't know which one we are targeting until it's too late.'

We drove on in silence, Euclides in the back, listening closely to the argument even though he didn't understand it.

'Look,' said Nelson. 'I know how you feel. But if we leave Isabel where she is she'll probably be killed. If the police go in to get her she has a better chance of survival. It's as simple as that. We'll talk to Luís when we get back, and then I'll phone Da Silva.'

I didn't reply. I knew he was right. Either way there

was a good chance that Isabel would die. I couldn't avoid that. All I could do was watch while Luís made the most logical decision: send in the police.

Of course, this had been implicit the whole time we had been looking for Isabel. The unspoken assumption was that we would get her out once we found her. But then the idea of finding her had given us a glimmer of hope. Now that we knew where she was, and a rescue attempt seemed inevitable, all the risks that that involved suddenly became much more apparent.

I thought of Ricardo and Eduardo and felt a surge of anger. They were responsible for this. Together with Francisco. He was a father. How would he feel if it were his son in that farmhouse, with only a day or two to live?

Of course!

'Nelson, I have an idea.'

He sighed. 'Another one. We're running out of time for ideas.'

'No, listen. This one will work.'

29

We were a ramshackle gang. Cordelia was at Luís's apartment by the phone. Nelson, his associate Ronaldo, Euclides and I were in the car, one of two Nelson had bought the evening before from a car thief he knew. And Luís himself was in London at the Savoy Hotel, praying for our success. Nelson, Ronaldo and I had guns. We had let Euclides come with us as long as he left his treasured gun behind. He might turn out to be useful.

I had never carried a handgun before. It was stuffed in the belt of my jeans, under a loose sweatshirt. It was heavy. The metal, at first cold, had been warmed by my body. Nelson had quickly shown me how to fire it, but the idea was that I should only use it in an emergency.

I was scared. Now I was truly risking my own life as well as Isabel's. But I also felt elated. For the first time, I felt I was doing something positive that might actually get her released. Nelson was cool, deliberate, tense. Ronaldo stared stolidly ahead, watching the traffic drive by. Slight, with an unremarkable crumpled black face and a wispy moustache, he was a former colleague of Nelson's in the Rio police force.

The car was parked down the road from Francisco's house. This wasn't going to be a well-planned snatch.

It didn't have to be. Speed was of the essence, here. We had no need to keep our identity secret, or escape detection. There was little chance of police involvement. But we did need to achieve a resolution quickly.

It was Tuesday morning. The sun was still low enough in the winter morning sky to throw shadows across the road. At six thirty as usual, the gates to Francisco's house opened and a little grey Renault edged out. There was occasional traffic on this road. Someone would see us, but Nelson was sure that the most likely response of the average Brazilian motorist would be to drive on.

As the Renault turned left down the hill, Nelson started his engine. He accelerated across the road, smashing into the other car with a jolt, driving it into the wall. The seat-belt bit into my chest and shoulders on impact. I quickly released it and leaped out of the car. Nelson had already pulled open the door of the Renault. Francisco *filho* hadn't been wearing a seat-belt, and had hit his face on the steering wheel. There was blood on his mouth and he was dazed. Ronaldo and Nelson dragged him out of the Renault, and I ran to the other car we had parked a few yards down the road. Euclides had the boot open, and we bundled the kid in before he knew what was happening. Then we were in the car and off.

I had noticed several vehicles drive past during all this, but as Nelson had expected, none of them had stopped. Neither had I seen anyone run out of Francisco's house just up the road.

Ronaldo drove fast and accurately, a typical Ayrton Senna in Rio's morning traffic. Nelson pulled out his mobile phone and told Cordelia we had the boy.

The car banged and rocked, especially when we stopped at traffic lights. Sitting in the back, I could hear muffled shouts. But the commuting *cariocas* around didn't seem to hear, or if they did, they took no notice.

It seemed to take us for ever to get out of Rio. Although we were generally going in the opposite direction to Rio's rush hour, we had planned on a slow journey. But it added to the tension. I sat stiff in the back seat, my hands clasped tightly together, the gun biting into my thigh. Nelson and Ronaldo seemed perfectly calm in the front. Euclides sat next to me with shining eyes and a big smile. None of us said a word.

An hour later, as we were finally beginning to break free of Rio, Nelson's phone chirped. He answered it, spoke for a few seconds and put it down.

'Cordelia has contacted Francisco.'

'What did he say?'

'He said he needed time to think. He said it might be a set-up. Cordelia said if we wanted to kill him, there would be many easier ways. She gave him ten minutes.'

Oh, God. We needed Francisco to respond immediately. A prolonged stand-off would be much harder to deal with. The families of kidnap victims were advised to be cautious about accepting kidnappers' first demands as Francisco would well know. But we weren't asking him for money. We merely wanted him to go somewhere to pick up a message.

The ten minutes ticked slowly past. It was fifteen before Cordelia called back.

Nelson listened quickly and grinned. 'He's agreed,' he said. 'He's taking a mobile phone so Cordelia can stay in touch with him.'

We were out of the city now, and heading up into the hills. After half an hour, we reached an empty stretch of road about twenty kilometres from São Jose. We stopped in a lane just off the road, with a clear view down a hill to a petrol station, bearing the by now familiar orange and green insignia of Petrobrás. Cordelia would instruct Francisco to park on the forecourt, and wait for a further message. The two men working the pumps had been paid to see nothing.

We hauled the junior Francisco out of the boot of the car, gave him some water, gagged him, bound his hands, and then stuffed him back in.

His cheek was swollen where he had bumped it on the steering wheel of the Renault when we had snatched him, but his mouth had long ago stopped bleeding. His eyes were wide with fear, and he babbled pleas in Portuguese. I felt sorry for the kid. It wasn't really his fault that Francisco was his father. But, if all went well, he would be released soon.

We waited. Ronaldo smoked endless cigarettes, and Nelson borrowed a couple from him.

'I didn't realize you smoked,' I said.

'I don't,' he replied.

Cordelia called to say that Francisco was two kilometres away. She had delayed saying exactly where he was to stop until she knew he was almost there.

Nelson pulled out his binoculars and trained them on the petrol station.

Within five minutes a blue car pulled up. It parked on the forecourt, and sent the petrol pump attendant away. No one got out, but I could see there was only one occupant. We waited another ten minutes to make sure Francisco was unaccompanied, and then Nelson started the engine, and drove the car down the hill.

As we neared the petrol station we could see Francisco in the front seat of his car, looking at his watch and then at us. Nelson swung into the forecourt, and we parked right next to him.

Nelson and I got out of the car, as did Francisco. He was hot: beads of sweat oiled his bald brow, giving it a grimy shine. He had never seen Nelson before, but he recognized me. He was about to say something, but then thought better of it. He still didn't know how much we knew.

'Thank you for coming,' I said. 'Do you mind if we search you and your car?'

'Yes, I do!' protested Francisco, but Nelson flung the heavier man against the car and frisked him. Francisco struggled briefly, and then held still. I bent down and quickly searched the car. There was a gun in the glove compartment, which I handed to Ronaldo.

When Nelson finished his search, Francisco turned and glowered at us. 'Where's my son?' he demanded.

Nelson beckoned to him to follow him round to the back of our car, and unlocked the boot. Francisco junior was writhing and grunting, but when he saw his father he stopped, his eyes full of alarm.

'You can't keep him there! Let him out!' growled Francisco.

'We will,' I said. 'In good time. But first come with us. We'll take your car.'

I sat in the back with Francisco, and waited while Nelson quickly handed the petrol pump attendant some banknotes to add to those he had given him earlier. Then he climbed into the driver's seat and drove off. Behind us were Ronaldo and Euclides, with Francisco junior still in the boot.

We drove back the way we and Francisco had come, and after a few kilometres took a turning to the left towards São Jose. Francisco watched the road ahead grimly, his thin lips pursed, his brow and shirt damp. He didn't say anything.

As we made our way further into the hills, the sky became greyer and the sun disappeared. We were driving up a broad valley, with a river rushing down its centre. There was farmland on either side, and every few kilometres we came across a village. Further up the hillsides were dense trees. I was reminded of my night blundering through the Tijuca forest.

We soon reached São Jose, and turned left up the narrow road Euclides had shown us the day before. We drove past the second farm and stopped. Above us, about a quarter of a mile away at the end of the road, was the farmhouse where Isabel was being kept. Above that, pasture turned into trees and rock-face, as the valley melted into the mountainside.

I opened the door of the car and motioned for Francisco to get out.

It was cooler up here. The grass and poorly tarmacked road were glistening with moisture. A stream tumbled down under a small bridge a few feet in front of us, carrying the recent rain on its steep journey down to the Atlantic. There was little sound, the straining of a truck's engine from the road up to São Jose below us, the urgent rushing of the water, and the occasional bleating from a group of bedraggled sheep further up the hill. The farmhouse behind us was quiet, and we couldn't see any signs of life in the building above. Two large black raven-like birds circled over it, almost as though they were reconnoitring it for us.

'Isabel Pereira is being held in that farmhouse up there,' I said. 'We want you to release her.'

Francisco, who had been silent since we had set off from the petrol station, chose this moment to protest.

'I told you, I know nothing about her kidnapping! I can't release her. Just give me my son back. Now!'

'No, Francisco,' I said, trying hard to keep my patience. 'I want you to walk up to the house, and explain to those men that they should let Isabel free. We will have your son down here. As soon as she begins to walk down the hill to us, we'll send him up. We give you our word that we won't inform the police about any of this. You and whoever is up there with Isabel can go unharmed.'

'You don't listen to me!' cried Francisco. 'I don't know anything about this!'

I interrupted him. 'I'm sure you'll think of something to persuade them to let her go. We'll be waiting. Oh, and by the way, if Isabel isn't making her way down that hill in ten minutes, we leave. With your son.'

'What will you do with him then?'

'We'll leave that to Isabel's father to decide when he returns. I don't think he likes you very much. I doubt he'll be sympathetic. Now, go!'

I pushed Francisco along the road towards the farmhouse.

He walked quickly up the hill, his arms swinging on either side of his ample backside. As he reached the house the door opened, and he disappeared inside.

That was a good sign. It meant that whoever was in there knew him. Although I hadn't really believed Francisco's protests, at the back of my mind I had been worried that perhaps he really had had nothing to do with Isabel's kidnapping, and we had made some horrible mistake.

Nelson pulled Francisco *filho* out of the boot, and stood him upright in the middle of the road facing up towards the farmhouse.

We waited, Ronaldo, Nelson, me and the scared boy.

The two big black birds were joined by a couple more. A tractor drove up the road towards us from the village, but turned off into the first farm below. We were exposed here, exposed to local curiosity, and also to the kidnappers calling up reinforcements.

My eyes never left the door of the farmhouse. Although farmhouse was probably too grand a word for it. Peasant hovel was closer. It cannot have held more than two or three small rooms on each of its two floors. The walls were partially covered in white paint, which was peeling to reveal concrete underneath. I wondered what it would be like to be cooped up in there for two months. A red pick-up truck was parked next to it, presumably the one Euclides had hitched a ride in.

My nerves jangled. It wasn't just the obvious fear that Isabel wouldn't make it, though that was bad enough. After all this time, now that there was a good chance I would see her, I was nervous. What would she be like after so long in captivity? Would she be all right physically? Would she have suffered psychological damage? And what about me? How would she feel about seeing me again? Would she care? It was a selfish thought, but I realized that part of what scared me was the fear that, after all my efforts to set her free, I would discover that I meant nothing to her.

Where was she? I checked my watch. The ten minutes was up. It had taken Francisco a few of them to puff his way up the hill but, even so, he should have sent her out by now.

I glanced at Nelson next to me.

'What do you think?'

He looked at his watch. 'We can give him a bit more time. Maybe they're having some kind of discussion.

But we can't risk staying here too long. We don't want to meet the rest of the gang on the way down.'

I glanced anxiously down towards the road to São Jose. The traffic was infrequent, but the odd car did pass up or down. We had no way of knowing if it was the kidnappers' friends. But if they were coming all the way from Rio, and it was a good guess that they were, it would take them a while.

A quarter of an hour. Still no sign of her. Why hadn't we told Francisco to take his mobile phone with him so we could talk to him and find out what was going on? Stupid!

I began to think about what we would do if we were forced to leave without Isabel. All would not be lost. We'd still have Francisco *filho*, and while we held him Isabel should be safe. But a long stand-off would be difficult to sustain, and not just emotionally. Francisco and his men knew who we were. They'd be looking for us and looking for the boy, and they would be willing to use more ruthless methods than we to get him back. No, we had to avoid that if at all possible.

I glanced again at Nelson. He shrugged. Francisco *filho* was biting his lip. He was just as anxious as us. Poor sod.

Then his eyes widened. I looked up the hill to see the door of the farmhouse open. A figure was pushed out. Slight, long hair blown over her face. Isabel.

She straightened up, and began to walk slowly down the hill.

I looked across to Nelson, who gave Francisco *filho* a rough shove. He stumbled up the hill towards her.

I would guess it was about four hundred yards between us and the farmhouse. Although he was going uphill, Francisco *filho* was covering more distance, so that he was soon further away from us than she was from them.

Suddenly a figure broke out of the farmhouse and began to run down the hill. He was tall, lithe, fit. Francisco followed, shouting.

'Run, Isabel!' I screamed.

She paused, looked up, turned to see the man bearing down on her, and only then began to hurry. Francisco *filho* was quicker off the mark. He broke into a run straight away.

Damn! I couldn't shoot the boy, but if I let him go, we'd lose our chance to free Isabel. I'd have to catch him before he reached the kidnapper, who was hurtling down the hill towards him.

I sprinted.

I heard two shots behind me, as Nelson fired at the kid, and saw dirt leaping up away to his left. Nelson was firing to miss, and was only scaring the kid into running faster.

But not as fast as me. I had some distance to make up, but I was closing on him, the gun in the waistband of my trousers biting into my groin with every stride. He had no power in his long legs, and he was finding the gradient difficult. His hands were still bound and his gag must have made it difficult to breathe. Above me, the man had caught up with Isabel, throwing her to the ground. As they struggled to their feet only a few yards ahead, I dived and grabbed at the boy's ankle. He tripped, and I was on him, gun out, and to his temple. I flicked the safety-catch off.

He lay still, scared, his chest heaving. With the gun pressed to his head, I looked up at Isabel. She was on her feet now. A man was holding her round her neck with his left arm, pointing a gun at her head with his right. He was breathing heavily. Her brown eyes stared at me, wide with fear. I caught them for a second, trying to give her reassurance, tell her she could still be free, and then she was yanked backwards up the hill by the man. He was in his thirties, wiry and capable looking.

'Stop!' I shouted. 'We can still make the exchange.'

'No! I take her!' and he pulled Isabel up the hill with him.

The voice was deep and authoritative, and I would have recognized it anywhere. Zico.

I pulled Francisco *filho* to his feet. 'Let her go!' I shouted. 'We'll let you escape.'

'How do I know that? Perhaps the police wait for us. No, Isabel goes with me!'

He dragged her up the hill. I followed with the boy. At the top I could see Francisco and another man, who looked little more than a kid. A fellow kidnapper, presumably.

We were nearing the farmhouse and a red pick-up truck.

'Stop!' I said. 'Or I'll shoot him!'

'No!' cried Francisco.

Zico laughed. 'Go ahead. Shoot him. I don't care. He's not my son.'

He looked into my eyes, mocking me. Of course I wasn't going to shoot the boy. I released my grip on the kid, and let my gun fall to my side. He ran up the hill to meet his father.

Zico dragged Isabel towards the pick-up truck. She looked back at me, her eyes helpless, pleading with me to do something.

Damn! There she was, just a few feet away. The elation that I had felt seeing her walk out of the farmhouse had turned to almost unbearable anxiety. I was so close to freeing her and now Zico was simply going to drive her away from me, right under my nose. I couldn't try to shoot him. He'd kill her first, and probably me too. The only experience I'd had with a handgun was the five minutes Nelson had taken to show me how it fired. Now it felt heavy and useless in my hand.

If Zico got away with her, what then? He might kill her. Or he might let her go when he had no more need for her. Or he might ransom her for cash. She still had a chance. Stay calm, then, and let him go. She'd be OK as long as I stayed calm.

I saw movement some distance behind the pick-up. Thin black limbs scurried across the ground to a water drum. A moment later a head and a short grey barrel peeked out from behind it. Euclides! And he had the gun Nelson had given him. Where the hell did he get that? He must have hidden it on him somehow. Oh, shit! The last thing I wanted was some cock-eyed heroics from a twelve-year-old. Someone would get killed, and it would most likely be Isabel.

Zico glanced at me as he neared the truck, and I quickly switched my eyes back to him, not wanting him to realize I had seen something. I moved slowly closer.

'Keep away!' he shouted.

I stopped.

Behind him, Euclides ran from the drum towards the pick-up truck. I still don't know what he was trying to do. Hide in there, probably, and surprise Zico later on. But he trod on some old corrugated iron that gave out a sharp clatter. Zico spun round. Euclides stopped in his tracks, caught in the open. He began to move his gun towards Zico, and hesitated, presumably afraid of hitting Isabel. Zico whipped his weapon away from

Isabel's temple and pointed it at Euclides. Two shots rang out, and Euclides uttered a sharp cry.

I had no time to think. Instinct made me raise my arm, and point it towards Zico. I looked down the short barrel straight into Isabel's terrified eyes. I jerked my arm to the left and pulled the trigger in one motion as Zico turned back towards me. I hit him in the right shoulder, throwing his arm back. His gun went spinning to the ground.

He let go of Isabel and bent down to pick it up. I ran towards him. There was another shot, Zico's head jerked sharply to one side, and he fell.

Euclides lay on the ground, gun pointing towards the crumpled figure of Zico, a broad smile on his face. There was a dark patch on the grass around his chest.

I ran to Isabel, who was squatting on the ground, sobbing.

'Are you OK?'

She looked up and a smile broke across her tear-stained face, the smile I had played through my mind so many times over the last few weeks. She nodded.

I turned and ran over to where Euclides had fallen. He was lying in a pool of blood, which grew in front of my eyes. It was pumping out from somewhere underneath him. I hesitated, unsure what to do. Euclides was struggling to keep his eyes open. His lips moved. I bent down to listen.

'I hit him, meester,' he whispered.

'Yes, you did,' I said.

I turned his small body over and tried to use his flimsy shirt to staunch the flow of blood from the hole in his chest. It was hopeless. Within a minute, life had drained away from him, into the damp grass.

30

Isabel was slumped in the other corner of the back seat of the car, watching the road ahead absently. Ronaldo was driving us back to Rio, leaving Nelson to clear up the mess we had left behind.

And there was quite a mess. Nelson and I had decided to let Francisco and his son go. We had, after all, promised as much to him when we had set up the exchange for Isabel, and he had kept his part of the bargain. It was Zico who had run after Isabel at the last minute. And implicating Francisco with the kidnapping would involve prolonged wrangling with the authorities. We thought it was better to wrap things up as quietly as possible. Nelson had, however, promised to bring back Euclides's body for a proper burial.

Isabel didn't look too bad after her ordeal. She was thin, but then she'd always been thin. Her skin was paler than it had been, after so many weeks away from the sun, I supposed. And there was a sort of fragility to her. But basically she looked unharmed.

'Are you OK?' I asked.

She looked at me and smiled, reaching out her hand for mine.

'I'm OK,' she said. 'I'm just so glad to be free.'

There was so much to say, so much to ask her, but I wanted to do it at her pace so I kept silent.

'Where's my father?' she asked.

'In London.'

'In London?' She raised her eyebrows.

'Yes, it's a long story. But Cordelia's waiting at his apartment.'

'How is she? I mean . . .'

I smiled. 'Don't worry, she's fine. She's growing bigger every day.'

Isabel smiled. 'Good.' Then, after a moment, 'Did he pay a ransom?'

'That's a long story too.'

'Tell me.'

'I can tell you later, when you've had some rest.'

'No, tell me now. That's all I've been thinking about over the last two months. What's been happening at home? Tell me.'

So I told her everything. About the initial ransom demands, about the long silence after the failed police raid, and then about the renewed demands once I had suggested Bloomfield Weiss take over Dekker. I told her how Ricardo and Eduardo must have been in league with Francisco first of all to have Martin Beldecos murdered, and then to have her and me kidnapped to prevent the discovery of Francisco's money-laundering operations. And finally I described how we had snatched Francisco's son to force an exchange.

She listened in amazement. 'So Ricardo was behind it all?' she said quietly.

I nodded. 'I'm afraid so.'

She looked out of the window at the Rio suburbs drifting slowly by. 'Bastard,' she whispered. She turned to me. 'It looks like you were right about him, after all.'

'Right now I don't care who's right or wrong,' I said. 'I'm just glad you're alive.'

She squeezed my hand. 'Thank you. Thank you for all you did for me.'

There were loud squeals when we reached Luís's apartment. Cordelia hugged her sister hard and long, and Maria danced around. Fernando was there as well. The excitement roused Isabel out of the daze she had been in since her release, and she became more animated. Within a minute she was on the phone with Luís at the Savoy in London. Tears flowed. Portuguese words were spoken at a hundred miles an hour. I watched with a huge grin on my face.

The one sour note was Euclides. Cordelia was shaken by news of his death. It had affected me too. But it wouldn't have surprised the boy himself: I doubt he had expected to reach adulthood. Cordelia had been right, he was brave. He had been stupid to take Nelson's gun with him, and to try to sneak up on Zico. But he was only twelve, how could you blame him? He had been trying to save Cordelia's sister and impress us. In fact, he had died with a gun in his hand, having just shot a bad guy; by Euclides's reckoning that probably was a good way to go. But it was a waste. And a waste for which we were all responsible: the Brazilian government and middle class who allowed such poverty and violence in their midst and, more particularly, Nelson, Cordelia and me, who had armed him and encouraged him on his last adventure. I wouldn't forget Euclides.

Isabel had a long bath, and then told us about her ordeal. She had been looked after well. For the first couple of weeks she had been kept in a tent inside a basement. Then she had been hurriedly moved up to the farm, and had been imprisoned in a barn with only one window that was fixed shut. She had had heat, light, adequate food and drink. She was allowed to wash once a day, and had been given a radio, books and newspapers. She had only seen her captors wearing masks, until that last day when she had finally seen Zico, but of course she had soon grown to recognize their voices. There seemed to have been five of them, who guarded her in shifts.

Right from the beginning she had decided that her best chance for survival was to co-operate with them. She had frequently asked about the progress of negotiations but they had told her nothing. The only indications she had had that there had been any communication with her father were the two proof-of-life questions she had received. The first, asking the name of her teddy-bear, had made her smile. It was typical of the sentimentality of her father, and it reminded her of the security of her childhood.

But, through it all, she kept calm. She knew that kidnappings could take months, but she also knew that her father would find a way to pay her ransom. It was clear that she had been a lot less worried about her safety than we.

She told us all of this in a mixture of English, for my benefit, and Portuguese for Maria's. But when her story had finished, and the conversation had broken up into rushed questions and answers, I left them to it. Despite all the time I had spent with them, I wasn't really part of their family. I grabbed a bottle of beer, and went out on to the balcony to watch the sunset, glad that Isabel was finally free.

I felt a hand on my shoulder, and looked up.

'Hallo,' said Isabel.

'Hi.'

She bent down and kissed me, her hair falling on my face. Then she stood up and looked out to sea. 'You can't believe what it's like to see the sea again,' she said. 'This view. These people.' A pause. 'You.'

A warm glow of happiness ran through me. It was just what I had hoped to hear. I reached up and pulled her lips down to mine again.

Eventually she broke away. 'What will you do now?' she asked.

'I don't know. I haven't thought about it.' And, in truth, I hadn't. My plans had gone no further than Isabel's release.

'Is Papai really going to take over Dekker?' she asked.

'We'll soon find out. The auction is tomorrow afternoon. It's between him and Bloomfield Weiss.'

'So Ricardo has finally lost? I still can't believe he did that to me. Had me kidnapped. I know our relationship was over, but I thought I meant more to him than that.'

'You know what he's like,' I said. 'With the survival of Dekker Ward at stake, he'd do anything. And at least you're still alive.'

Isabel frowned. 'I guess you're right.'

It was getting dark quickly. The floodlights were on, picking out the white spume of the waves on the beach. I had stared out at this view often, worrying about Isabel in captivity. And now she was here, next to me.

My thoughts turned to Luís in London, and the auction tomorrow. I prayed he would be successful. I badly wanted Ricardo to see that he wasn't invincible. That he couldn't mess up so many people's lives, especially mine and Isabel's, and get away with it.

Isabel was obviously thinking the same thing. 'Let's go and help Papai,' she said.

'What do you mean?'

'Let's go to London. Tonight. To help him with his bid tomorrow.'

'It's too late, isn't it? And shouldn't you rest?'

'I've been resting for weeks. I want to see my father. This is an important time for him. There's a flight that leaves at about ten o'clock, I think. We've plenty of time.'

I grinned. 'OK. Let's go.'

The plane arrived at Heathrow airport early the following afternoon, and Luís said he'd meet us. Isabel had bought first-class tickets on the Varig flight and I hadn't complained. Despite what she'd said about too much rest, she was tired. The excitement of her release had worn her out after her weeks of inactivity. So she slept for the entire flight, while I stayed awake mulling over the last few weeks, and letting my hopes play with the idea of a future with Isabel.

I spotted him first, his domed head rising above the press of people waiting outside customs at Terminal Three. His face lit up with pleasure when he saw Isabel. She ran to him and they embraced. He stroked her hair, and a tear appeared in his eye. Eventually he broke free and shook my hand. Or pumped it, more like. The man I had spent so much time with over the last few weeks, bowing but not broken by the pressure of his daughter's kidnap, was transformed. It was a pleasure to see.

Luís and Isabel talked excitedly in Portuguese as they made their way to his chauffeur-driven car. But as we sped down the M4 into London, Luís switched to English.

'I've booked you both rooms at the Savoy, where I'm

staying. I'll drop you off there, but then I'll have to go into the City to put the final touches to our bid.'

'How's it going?' I asked.

'Pretty well. We've hired Gurney Kroheim to act for us. Do you know them?'

They were Jamie's old firm. They were also one of the foremost British merchant banks, who had built a reputation for advising on international takeovers. Not only would they provide good advice but they should add weight to Banco Horizonte's bid.

'They have a good reputation,' I said.

'They deserve it. And KBN are tied in. We've put together quite a complicated structure with offshore companies and convertible preference shares. It gives KBN economic control of the bond portfolio, without recognizing a loss at Dekker that would wipe out its capital. KBN will end up with twenty per cent of Dekker, and we get the remaining eighty. With KBN behind it, the new Dekker should have better credibility with the markets. And also with the SFA and the Bank of England.'

'What do KBN think about Dekker's bond position?'

'They're enthusiastic, thank God. The market has been strengthening the last few days. It looks like Congress will abandon the Pinnock Bill.'

'That's good news,' I said.

'Good and bad. It's good in that it makes the whole bid less risky. It's bad in that it makes Dekker Ward more expensive. And Bloomfield Weiss can afford to pay up more than we can.'

'Oh, I see.' Bloomfield Weiss's capital was many times that of Banco Horizonte so they could pay more if they wanted to. But Sidney Stahl did not look the kind of man who would overpay for anything. We were still in with a chance. 'Have you heard anything from Ricardo?'

'Nothing. Kerton thinks he's keeping him in the dark, but we know he knows there's something going on. I guess he's just trying to cope with the bond position and hoping that with Isabel's life under threat we would stop the takeover somehow.'

'Except that Isabel is free. He'll know that by now.'

'Yes,' said Luís, thoughtfully. 'I expect he will.'

We were silent for a moment, each one of us thinking what Ricardo would do next. 'Did you ask Francisco about him?' Luís inquired eventually.

'No, I didn't. Francisco was pretty clever, really. He never admitted any involvement with the kidnapping himself, let alone the involvement of anyone else.'

'And you just let him go?'

'Yes,' I said. 'I had promised him I would. And, besides, Nelson said it would get very messy with the authorities if we tried to get them to prosecute him.'

Luís sighed. 'A shame, but I understand. One day I'll make him pay.'

'You'll make Ricardo pay today,' I said.

Luís chuckled. 'Ah, yes.'

'Have you decided how much to bid, Papai?' Isabel asked.

'Not yet,' said Luís. 'It depends on the strength of the market. We'll decide just before the auction.'

'When's that?'

'Five o'clock. At Dekker Ward's office in the City.'

'Can we come?' Isabel asked. 'We'll keep out of the way.'

'Of course,' said Luís. 'I want you to see this, whether it works or not. Come and meet us at Gurney Kroheim, when you are ready.'

Luís dropped us off at the Savoy. He had booked us into separate rooms, of course.

'What time shall we meet?' I asked Isabel. 'Would you like a rest?'

Isabel smiled that wicked little smile that made my heart melt. She shook her head. 'Say, two minutes?'

'I'll be there,' I said.

It was an hour and a half before we left the Savoy for the City. We could have stayed there all day, but we didn't want to miss Luís's bid deliberations.

Gurney Kroheim's offices were a hundred yards away from Dekker Ward's, in the heart of the City. Their meeting room was more like Dekker's than Bloomfield Weiss's. A couple of baronets in top hats watched over the route to the room, but once there, the pictures were Victorian landscapes, originals subtly illuminated. The room gleamed with polished wood. But there was no chance of ever mistaking Gurney Kroheim's offices for a country house. Most of the great and good of British industry had certainly visited here, but to do battle with each other, to eat and be eaten.

The room was crowded. Luís was sitting next to one of his partners, Sergio Prenzman, who had borne the brunt of the work of putting the bid together while Luís was distracted by Isabel's kidnap. Next to him were two earnest associates who had spent night after night feeding numbers into computers. Also round the table were two Dutch bankers from KBN, a couple of lawyers, and a team of three from Gurney Kroheim, led by a director, Charles Scott-Liddell.

Luís introduced his daughter with pride, and me with thanks as the man who had secured her release. There were broad smiles all round. As well as working for

Luís, it was clear that these City professionals liked him.

'You've arrived at a good time,' Luís said. 'We're just about to discuss the price.'

We sat at two empty chairs at the other end of the long board table. All eyes were turned to Luís.

'So, Charles, what have we got?'

Scott-Liddell, every inch the smooth merchant banker, examined the sheets of figures in front of him.

'Well, we've plugged today's market prices for the bond portfolio into the model. As we suspected, it makes quite a difference. Using method one we get a valuation of sixty-three million pounds, and using method two . . .' he paused as he flipped through the papers in front of him ' . . . seventy-two million.'

Things had moved on from the twenty million that had been talked about the previous week. The market must have improved, I thought.

Sergio butted in. 'I'm much happier with method one than method two. I don't trust these discounted cash-flow valuations for a stockbroker. They make no sense to me.'

Luís smiled. 'I know, Sergio. But an opportunity like this will only come once. If we can get Dekker Ward, Banco Horizonte will become the first truly inter-national investment bank in Latin America. That has to be worth something. What did we say was the maximum we could afford?'

'Seventy-five would be the limit,' said Sergio. 'Beyond that, our capital ratios would be stretched. You know how we've always kept a conservative balance sheet. But seventy-five million would be too much to pay for Dekker anyway.'

Luís stared at the numbers. Then he stood up and

walked over to the window, looking down on the lunch-time London traffic.

With his back to the room he said, 'We'll bid eighty million pounds.'

31

The first person I saw as I followed Luís into the Dekker Ward boardroom was Sidney Stahl, perched on a chair, a cigar in his mouth. 'Hi, guys!' he croaked, with a grin. A gloating grin. He thinks he'll beat us, I thought instantly. Behind him was Dwight Godfrey, who avoided my eyes.

We walked further into the room. Kerton rose from behind the table to greet us, some envelopes in front of him. I ignored him. My attention was grabbed by the man sitting next to him, legs crossed, calmly smoking a cigarette.

Ricardo.

Kerton was making introductions, and fussing over Isabel, but I wasn't listening. What the hell was Ricardo doing here? Then I glanced quickly at the envelopes in front of Lord Kerton. There were three.

Ricardo was speaking to me. 'Good afternoon, Nick, Luís,' he said. And then, when he saw Isabel, 'I'm so pleased to see you. I didn't know you'd been released.'

I didn't say anything. I just collapsed into a seat next to Luís.

There were a number of other people there: lawyers, advisers, that sort of thing. We'd brought a lot of them with us. But I didn't really take them in. The only person in the room for me was Ricardo. Even though he was an interloper, he had the air of someone in complete control, not just of himself but of all of us in the room.

'Thank you for coming in person,' Lord Kerton said. 'It seemed the best way to do this. Then you would at least know that you were both being treated fairly,' he addressed this to Stahl and Luís. 'This morning I received a call from Ricardo, asking if he could put a bid in for the firm. I couldn't really refuse, so I invited him along.'

Of course I wasn't surprised that Ricardo had found out about the auction. And it was just like him to take the initiative, and not sit idly by while his firm was sold underneath him. But it was still a shock to see him there, competing with us for Dekker.

'I object!' said Stahl. 'I admit I was kinda surprised to see Ricardo here. But I thought he was just here to watch, not to bid.'

'Well, Sid, he's put together a bid of his own,' Kerton said. 'A sort of management buy-out, you could call it. Or I think you would term it a leveraged buy-out.'

Kerton pronounced leveraged the British way, lee-vraged, to irritate Stahl. He succeeded.

'Well, I don't like it. You change the ground rules on me and I'm outa here!'

'I don't think I mentioned how many participants there would be when I invited you to bid. You just assumed that there would be two. Well, there are three. If you wish to withdraw your bid or change it, you are free to do so.'

Damn! If Stahl changed his bid because he knew Ricardo was there, then it would only be upwards, and leave us with even less chance of victory. Lord Kerton was being quite canny.

Stahl thought for a moment. He pulled on his cigar, and coughed. 'No,' he said. 'Our bid stays as it is right there in that envelope. I'm not gonna let you ambush me into paying you more than I have to for this shit-heap.'

Kerton smiled politely. He turned to Luís. 'It's only fair to make you the same offer. Would you like to change your bid?'

Luís shook his head. He was paying as much as he could afford anyway. More.

'OK. Well, without further ado, I shall open the bids.'

He picked up an envelope. I recognized the Banco Horizonte logo. 'Taking them at random,' he said, slitting it with an elegant brass paperknife. 'I have the bid here from Banco Horizonte . . . Eighty million pounds.' He spoke quietly and calmly, and handed it to the lawyer next to him to verify.

Ricardo took a drag of his cigarette. Stahl puffed his cigar. I chewed a pencil.

The next envelope was Bloomfield Weiss's. I couldn't read the words printed on it, but I recognized the distinctive typeface. Kerton attacked it with his fancy paperknife.

'Bloomfield Weiss's bid is . . .' he scanned the letter quickly ' . . . seventy-six million pounds.'

Yes! Stahl had cut it too fine. He had done the same calculations as Scott-Liddell, come up with the same numbers, and added a bit. Well, Luís had added a bit more.

I glanced across at Stahl. He was still chewing his cigar, not looking at anyone in particular. He was trying to put on a brave face, to let us know he'd get over it. But his face was reddening, and his jaws were clenched so tight on the cigar that I was surprised he hadn't snapped the end off. Sidney Stahl was not happy.

But all eyes were now on the third envelope. As Kerton picked it up, I glanced at Ricardo. He was sitting in exactly the same posture of studied relaxation. His wedding ring was gliding gently over his fingers. The announcement of the two bids hadn't prompted the slightest reaction. But just then I knew he'd won. In a sealed-bid auction involving Ricardo there could only ever be one winner. I suddenly knew why we hadn't heard from him during this whole process. It was so that he could time his entrance into the struggle perfectly, so that he could snatch Dekker for himself before we or Bloomfield Weiss had time to respond to the threat.

'And Ricardo Ross's bid is eighty-eight million pounds.' Kerton put down the final plain white envelope. Ricardo allowed himself a faint smile. 'Congratulations,' Kerton said to him. 'I accept your bid.'

They shook hands.

'Wait a minute!' exclaimed Stahl. 'How d'you know this guy has the money?'

Kerton raised an eyebrow to Ricardo. It was a fair question, but anyone who knew Ricardo knew that if he said he would pay a certain sum for something he would always be able to get hold of the money. The employee trusts would be an obvious place to start.

'I'll have the cash in an escrow account tomorrow morning, Andrew. If it's not there, then you can ignore my bid.'

'Fair enough,' said Kerton. 'And that, gentlemen, is all.'

Stahl was angry. He muttered furiously to Godfrey, while throwing dark glances towards Kerton and

Ricardo. He glowered as he stalked out, not even pausing to say goodbye to anyone.

I had problems controlling my own temper. I had difficulty in believing what I had just witnessed. After all the trouble I'd gone to to engineer the sale of Dekker Ward, only to see Ricardo steal it from under our noses! Now he would have complete control of Dekker. I had hoped that by this afternoon he would have lost his job. More than hoped, I was confident that one way or another someone would soon be firing Ricardo Ross. But he had outwitted me. He had outwitted us all.

Luís caught my eye, shrugged and said, 'Let's just say goodbye to Kerton and go.'

Lord Kerton stood very upright as he held out his hand. The three of us shook it. Then Luís spoke to him quietly. 'Why did you do it? You know Ricardo almost ruined you. Why did you sell to him?'

Kerton looked uncomfortable, but he answered Luís honestly. 'A week ago this firm was worth ten million pounds. It's now worth eighty-eight. There comes a time when one should just take one's money and run. And I think this is the time.'

And so we left, ignoring the new owner of Dekker Ward.

Sergio joined us for a subdued dinner that evening. Luís was disappointed by the defeat. But I couldn't help noticing the way he kept glancing at Isabel. She was alive, and that was all that really mattered.

I still had nowhere to go, and Luís insisted on putting me up in the Savoy for another couple of nights, to give me time to find somewhere. I didn't complain. I knew I had a lot to worry about and plan, but with Isabel beside me I just wanted to think about the present.

When we arrived back at our rooms there was a message that someone was waiting to see Isabel and me in the American Bar downstairs.

It was Ricardo. He was sitting in the furthest corner of the bar, nursing a glass of fizzy water. He fitted in well with these surroundings, immaculate in his suit, monogrammed shirt, silk tie, wealthy Latin appearance.

Isabel and I both stopped dead when we saw him. 'What does he want?' she said.

'I don't know. Let's find out.'

Ricardo rose to his feet when we approached but didn't extend his hand. I hardly felt welcoming, and Isabel's look was as cold as ice.

'Nick, Isabel, thank you for seeing me,' he began.

'We didn't know it was you,' said Isabel.

'No. You didn't, did you?' he said, as though it was an unfortunate omission on someone else's part. 'But I'd be grateful if you could give me a few minutes. I'd like to continue the conversation Nick and I had a couple of weeks ago.'

It was a good way of winning my attention. 'OK,' I said, and sat down. Isabel followed my lead. Ricardo beckoned to a waiter and ordered a beer for me and a glass of white wine for Isabel. We waited for him to talk.

'I'm so pleased you were released unharmed, Isabel,' he began. 'You must have been through a terrible ordeal. And I'd like you to know that I had no part in your kidnapping.'

He paused and looked at us both with his clear blue eyes. Leaning slightly forward, his hands towards us, his handsome face open and steady, he looked as though he was telling the truth. But Isabel and I just stared back at him. He would need to do better than that.

Ricardo let the pause go on for an uncomfortably long time before continuing. 'I know you don't believe me, and I suppose I'm not surprised. But listen to me. I think we can help each other.'

Still no response from us.

'You told me a lot I didn't know that day, Nick. That Isabel was still alive, and that her kidnappers were demanding that the takeover be pulled.'

'You didn't seem surprised to hear it,' I said.

'I didn't know how to react.' He looked up, grabbing my eye again. 'I didn't know whether you were telling me the truth. You have to admit you were quite a devious opponent. You could have been putting pressure on me to give in to Bloomfield Weiss. But then when you mentioned Eduardo's name, it occurred to me that you might have something. Maybe Eduardo was doing things without my knowledge. It wouldn't have been the first time.'

'And was he?'

'No. I spoke to him, and he denied it.'

'Of course he did.'

'Nick, I can tell with my brother. I know when he's hiding something, even if I can't always tell what it is. And I can tell when he hasn't got a clue. Believe me, he didn't have a clue.'

'But he did get some heavies to beat me up and wreck my flat, didn't he?'

Ricardo shrugged. 'I'm sorry about that. He gets over-enthusiastic sometimes.'

'And you nobbled Russell Church to make sure I wouldn't work at the School of Russian Studies again.'

Ricardo nodded. 'That's true. I've always been tough on people who walk out on the team. As you know, I was disappointed in you. I felt you'd let me down.'

I could feel the anger boiling up inside me. 'I'd let you down!' I almost shouted. 'And what about Martin Beldecos? Was his death a result of over-enthusiasm? Or was it just disappointment?'

'No, no, it wasn't. I thought he was the victim of a hotel burglary gone wrong. And when you were stabbed on Ipanema beach, I thought that was just a mugging.'

'I *know* it wasn't just a mugging,' I said.

'Well, now I suspect it wasn't too,' said Ricardo. 'In fact, I suspect you know quite a lot about what's going on that I don't. That's why I'm here. Tell me what happened in Brazil.'

'Do you know Francisco Aragão?'

'Ah.' Ricardo raised his eyebrows. 'Of course I do. He's Luciana's brother. Does he have something to do with this?'

'He certainly does.' I wasn't sure whether Ricardo really had no idea of Francisco's involvement, but I saw no harm in telling Ricardo all I knew. Isabel joined in when she described what had happened to her after she had been kidnapped.

Ricardo listened to every word, weighing each new piece of information, putting it in its proper place. When I had finally finished, he didn't say anything, he just looked up and stared unfocused towards the door. Thinking.

'Well?' I said, hoping to provoke a response.

'Hm?'

'Well? Does Francisco invest drug money with Dekker Ward?'

Ricardo's eyes focused. 'Not that we know of. We have no record of him investing with us. Every investor is known personally by one of us, and we don't deal with anyone who has known links to drugs. In my book,

Francisco definitely has drugs links, and I've spent most of my career trying to avoid dealing with him. I thought I'd succeeded.'

'But someone at Dekker must have dealt with him.'

Ricardo shrugged. 'You may be right. I don't know. It's all very mysterious, isn't it?' He paused for a moment. 'Of course, if I did discover that Francisco had somehow been laundering drug money through Dekker Ward without my knowledge, I'd be quite concerned. I'd certainly let the proper authorities know.'

Suddenly, he gulped his fizzy water, stood up and reached into his wallet for a ten-pound note for the drinks. 'I've got to go back to the office now. Whether you believe me or not, Isabel, I'm very glad to see you alive. And, of course, you still work for Dekker Ward. You're welcome back in the office any time.'

Isabel shook her head, but allowed herself a small smile. 'No, thank you. I think you'll be receiving my resignation letter soon.'

'That, too, I can understand.' He leant over and kissed her on both cheeks. 'Good luck,' he said. 'And, Nick, I'm sorry it didn't work out at Dekker. You've been a difficult opponent. I would have liked to have kept you on my side.'

I couldn't help smiling as I shook his hand.

'Now, I really have to be going. We've got a little crisis on. One of our clients has started to sell all his bonds. You probably remember him, Nick. Alejo? One of Jamie's. Jamie, I'm afraid has gone home in disgust. Sometimes things get to you in this business. Oh, well. Goodbye.'

I watched him walk out of the bar, stunned. Suddenly, I knew Ricardo had been telling the truth.

'Nick? Nick?' I heard Isabel next to me.

'Oh, um, Isabel. I'm sorry. I've got to go somewhere.'

'Nick, what do you mean? It's late.'

'I'll try to get back tonight, if I can. If not, I'll see you tomorrow morning.' I kissed her quickly, and I was off.

32

The taxi fare to Dockenbush Farm was huge. I paid off the driver and steadied myself before walking up to the door. It was a warm summer night, with stars and moon illuminating the farmhouse in front of me. Pools of light spilled out of two downstairs windows on to the gravel driveway. An owl called from somewhere above and behind me.

Ricardo had known it was Jamie, I thought. As soon as I had told him about Francisco, he had worked it out. Alejo was Jamie's account, ostensibly acting for a secretive Mexican family. But, in reality, Alejo worked for Francisco. Luciana had indeed been Francisco's intermediary, but with Jamie, not Ricardo. She had known Ricardo wouldn't do business with her brother. Now Francisco was scared and, through Alejo, was selling everything he had with Dekker Trust.

And Ricardo had let me know this, to give me a chance to get to Jamie first. I was sure I could rely on Ricardo to deal with Francisco.

I rang the bell.

It took a while before he answered. He had changed out of his suit into jeans and an old denim shirt. He leaned against the door.

'Oh, it's you. I thought someone would come, but I didn't think it would be you.'

He reeked of whisky. His eyes were shining, but not quite focused. I had seen Jamie the worse for wear many times before. This looked like another one.

'Can I come in?'

'Sure.' He led the way through the hallway, and into the sitting room. Music was playing: I recognized a Leonard Cohen album that I hadn't heard since we were at university. It had been a favourite with Jamie for about a term, and then he had forgotten it.

He slumped into an armchair. A crystal tumbler of whisky three-quarters full perched on a small table next to him.

'Have a drink,' he said.

I fetched the bottle, and went into the kitchen for some ice. Several days' dishes were piled in the sink, and used Marks and Spencer's packets cluttered the work surfaces. Kate had been gone for ten days. The house missed her.

Jamie was staring at me as I returned. I sat opposite him. Leonard droned in the background.

'Isabel's free,' I said.

'Is she OK?'

'Yes. Considering she spent two months locked up in a tiny space.'

'Good,' said Jamie. He looked up at me. 'You know, don't you?'

I nodded.

He sighed, and swilled his whisky around, before sipping some. 'I'm glad they looked after her. They told me they would.'

'By "they", you mean Francisco?'

Jamie nodded. 'How much do you know?'

'I know that Francisco opened an account with Dekker Trust through you to launder money. The account was managed by Alejo in Miami, who you claimed worked for some rich Mexican family you'd known since you were at Gurney Kroheim. He did huge business with you. Then, I suppose, Martin Beldecos began to get suspicious.'

Jamie snorted. 'He was a jerk. So officious! If he'd been like any normal compliance guy, we wouldn't have had a problem. But he always checked on everything. And if he'd found proof, he would have gone straight to the authorities. There would have been no chance of getting Ricardo or Eduardo to cover anything up.'

'Did he find anything?'

'He was getting there. He wanted to visit Alejo in Miami after he'd been to Caracas.'

'So you had him killed.'

Jamie bit his lip. 'I didn't want him killed. But Francisco insisted. I didn't want him to do it.'

'And me? What about me? You wanted me killed as well?'

'No,' said Jamie. 'No.' He shook his head, staring straight at me. He sighed. 'Francisco wanted you dead. I'd told him how close you were to figuring out what was happening. When you mentioned you wanted to talk to me about a fax for Martin Beldecos, I looked for it in your desk and took it. But I knew you'd work it all out in the end.'

He gulped his whisky. 'I told Francisco it had been stupid to kill Martin. It raised the stakes. Suddenly it wasn't just a white-collar crime we were on the line for, it was murder. Two murders would be obvious. But he went ahead with it anyway. When I found out what had happened to you in Brazil, I was furious with him. But there wasn't much I could do by then.'

I believed him. 'So why did you kidnap Isabel?'

Jamie glanced up at me. 'It wasn't Isabel we were trying to kidnap. It was you.'

'Me?'

'Yes. It was the only way I could think of of taking you out of the picture and keeping you alive. I told Francisco it would give us time to cover our tracks and allow the trail to go cold. And if we hadn't kidnapped you, Francisco would have had you killed by now. I knew you'd told Isabel a lot about what you'd found out, so it seemed a good idea to take her as well.'

I remembered telling Jamie I had discussed Francisco Aragão with her. And to think he'd told me I couldn't trust her!

'Besides, Isabel was the perfect cover,' he went on. 'It made it seem like this was a standard Rio kidnapping. And it worked, too. Even after you escaped, you were so taken up with the negotiations that you forgot about all the other stuff.'

'Why didn't you release her?'

'I wanted to. But after the police raided the kidnappers' hideout, Francisco wanted her killed. And the kidnappers themselves wanted a ransom first. It was a real mess.' He looked up from his glass, willing me to understand. His face was pale and lined as he recalled the strain of the last few weeks. It was amazing I hadn't noticed it before; he had hidden it well.

'So that's why the ransom demand dropped so fast at the end?'

'Yes. But we reached a compromise. We'd keep her alive, but in captivity, and we'd let her family and Dekker think she was dead.'

'All the time I was staying in this house, asking you what you thought was going on, you knew where she was?'

Jamie nodded. 'At least I could keep an eye on you here. And when I saw you were getting nowhere with the authorities, I was relieved. Until I read the Bloomfield Weiss documents on Dekker you left lying around. I couldn't let that go ahead. If Dekker had been taken over our little scheme would have been found out in no time.'

'And you used Isabel to force me to get the takeover called off?'

Jamie stared at his glass. 'It was worth a try. We had to do something.'

I sat back in the chair, drinking my whisky. Here, alone with Jamie, having a quiet drink in his house as I'd done so many times before, it seemed absurd that we were discussing money-laundering, kidnap, murder. Three months ago this part of Jamie's life, what he did in the City between seven in the morning and eight at night, had meant nothing to me. Now I knew.

'Why?' I asked.

'What do you mean, why?'

'Why did you do all this?'

Jamie sighed. He stood up and refilled his glass, leaving just a small amount in the bottom of the bottle, which he tipped into mine.

'One thing led to another. I mean, when Luciana told me Francisco wanted to open an account without Ricardo knowing about it, it seemed like a good idea. Of course I could guess where the money came from, but what did I care? It was new business, business that Ricardo couldn't get for himself. And it turned out to be huge. You saw how much turnover Alejo did. We were so successful that Francisco kept on coming up with more and more funds. Of course I didn't ask where he was getting them.'

Probably the Colombian and Venezuelan contacts Luís had heard about, I thought.

'And I didn't understand why Ricardo wouldn't deal with Francisco. I mean, Ricardo wins business by breaking the rules. It seemed to me that not dealing with someone just because he had a bad reputation was a mistake. You can't afford to be picky in this business.'

'Can't you?' It seemed to me that, as in all things, Ricardo knew just when to be picky.

Jamie shrugged. 'Well, you're right. I made a mistake. It seemed easy at the time. Dekker is set up to confuse auditors and investigators. If bloody Beldecos hadn't come along, we would have been fine.'

Jamie ran his hands through his hair. His face was gaunt and his eyes were staring. 'And then it all went wrong. Especially when I let Francisco . . . deal with Martin. Then it went really wrong.'

He looked at me, staring. 'It was weird, you know. It was like leading two completely different lives. Most of the time I was working normally, talking to you, being with Kate and Oliver, behaving like any other investment banker. And then I had all this other stuff going on that looked all the time as if it was going to blow up, but somehow I kept it all together. Until now.'

'Until now.'

'So what are you going to do, Nick?'

He looked at me, eyes pleading, what for, he didn't seem to know. A way out, probably, a way out where he had been able to find none.

'I don't know.' And I didn't. It was too much to take in.

We sat in silence, his eyes fixed on mine. They showed a cocktail of emotions bubbling inside him: guilt, remorse, anger, fear, loneliness, self-pity. They were all there, agitated by the alcohol.

'I need a slash,' he said, and staggered to his feet.

I waited for him. The house was quiet, save for the owl hooting outside, and the scarcely audible tick of a clock on the mantelpiece. Leonard had ground to a halt. I sat immobile trying to sort it all out in my mind. How could Jamie, who had been such a good friend over all these years, have done this? To me. To himself. It was absurd. Incredible.

A thought drifted through my mind, like a cold gust of air, that made me physically shiver. It wasn't absurd. It had happened. And, knowing Jamie as I did, I could see how. Jamie was ambitious, and he liked to take risks. And up till now they'd always worked. He was charming, intelligent, hard-working, the probabilities fell his way. He was lucky. If he could land Francisco's account, and others like it, he'd build up his own business, get that million-dollar bonus, who knows, maybe even become another Ricardo one day. To him, money was money. The lives ruined and ended by the international drugs trade were an abstraction about which fuzzy intellectuals like me might worry, but not Jamie. He wouldn't get caught. Not Jamie.

The same with Luciana. He could seduce Ricardo's wife and get away with it. No one would catch him. Not Jamie.

But he had been caught. By me. And what was I going to do about it?

I heard Jamie come back into the room. I turned. The